Finn

The Cosantóir (Protectors) MC– Book 1

By Michael Geraghty

Michael Geraghty
AUTHOR

Published by Scarlet Lantern Publishing

Copyright © 2021 by
Michael Geraghty & Scarlet Lantern Publishing

All rights reserved.

This is a work of fiction. Names, characters, businesses, places, events and incidents are either the products of the author's imagination or used in a fictitious manner. Any resemblance to actual persons, living or dead, or actual events is purely coincidental.

This book contains sexually explicit scenes and adult language.

1

The Egyptian cotton top sheet lay barely covering the torso of Finn O'Farrell as he stared up at the ceiling. A quick glance to his left revealed 3 AM, and he was awake - once again. Finn turned his head slightly and could see the blond curls cascading on the pillow next to him. Soft snores escaped her mouth as she lay on her back, and the rhythm of her breathing started to fray Finn's nerves. Her breasts moved the down comforter that covered her in time with the noise emanating from her mouth. The light cough that escaped her lips startled Finn and was aggressive enough to shake the comforter loose and expose her left breast. Her nipple perked immediately as the coldness coming from the central air reached her. Still, she made no move to do anything and slept peacefully.

Finn shook his head, climbed out of bed, and grabbed the pair of black boxer briefs he had shed earlier in the evening. As he pulled the shorts on, he wracked his brain, trying to remember the name of the girl who occupied more than half of his bed now.

It's something with a K, he thought. *Kyla? Kyrie? Krystal?*

The name escaped him, much like the names of the many others he had brought up to his penthouse condo in Saratoga Springs over the years. Whether it was out at one of the bars in the city or at a party thrown by his law firm or one of their clients, there always seemed to be a Brittany, Ashleigh, or Kyra that wanted to go home with him. He rarely turned down the opportunity, but he knew this situation would end up like all the others.

Finn paced into the kitchen, took one of the many water bottles from the fridge, and made his way to the second of the three bedrooms in his penthouse. This bedroom, unlike the other two, contained no bed at all. Finn had set it up as a pseudo gym to work out in. Even though the complex at 38 High Rock had its own facilities, Finn disliked working out there. People looked at it more like a social station or pick-up joint and did little working out and more talking or gawking. Instead, he placed mats across the extra bedroom, lined the room with some equipment, and kept his heavy bag in the center.

Finn pulled on his black gloves for bag work and began his workout. He swung heavy left hooks, striking the bag forcefully right away that sent the bag rocking. Ten reps later, Finn used his right before mixing in solid jabs. He glided to the north side of the room and repeated his steps, working up a fast sweat that rolled down his chest and abs. Finn's grunts got gradually louder the more he went at the bag with ferocity. His concentration was at a peak when he felt the gentle tap on his shoulder. Finn's eyes widened as he twisted around, ready to throw another punch. The squeal from the naked woman in front of him was the only thing that kept him from landing a blow.

"What the fuck, Finn?" the woman yelled at him.

"Sorry," Finn panted. He stared at her, still unable to recall her name, as she stood in front of him. "What are you doing?"

"What am I doing?" she answered exasperatedly. "It's three in the morning, and you're in here throwing punches. I was sound asleep until I heard grunting and got up to look for you. Why don't you come back to bed?"

The woman sidled behind him and draped her arms over Finn's back, pressing her bare breasts firmly against him. Her hands worked down over Finn's chest and crept lower before reaching his waist. Finn then spun around, grasped her hands, and looked her right in the eyes.

"Nah, I'm up now. I'm going to finish my workout, take a shower, and do some work before going to the office. Can I call you a ride or something?"

"Wow, they weren't kidding about you, huh?" the woman said with her hands on her hips.

"What are you talking about?" Finn replied. He reached for a towel hanging on the back of the door to wipe some sweat off his body.

"My friends at the party. They all warned me about you and what a shallow prick you could be. I guess they were right."

The woman turned and marched out of the room and down the hall toward Finn's bedroom. Finn watched as her hips swayed as she moved before he slowly followed her. By the time he got to the bedroom, she had already pulled her dress over her head and was looking for her shoes.

"What did you expect?" Finn said as he filled the doorframe to the bedroom.

"A little bit more than 'come back to my condo and fuck me and then go home,'" she barked.

She scanned the room once more, still looking for her footwear.

"Where are my damn shoes?" she yelled.

Finn sighed and walked out to the living room, spotting the shoes next to the couch where the couple had begun their session. An empty rocks glass sat on the coffee table, leaving telltale rings underneath that aggravated Finn. He reached down and plucked the black sequin high heels in his left hand and grabbed his cell phone off the side table where it was charging. He quickly arranged for an Uber to arrive in ten minutes, too long in

Finn's mind to wait, and walked back to the bedroom, dangling the shoes in his hand.

"Here they are," he announced. The woman's head popped up over the far side of the bed. She had been kneeling, looking under the bed for her shoes.

"Your ride will be here in ten minutes," Finn offered. "You want a coffee or water?"

She rushed over and pulled the shoes from Finn's hand.

"How generous of you," she replied. "You mean I don't have to wait outside?"

"You can if you want to," Finn sighed, rubbing his chin, hoping she might go for the third option.

"Why did you even ask me up, Finn?" she asked, stepping into her heels and storming to the kitchen. Finn winced as he thought about the scuff marks she was leaving on the elegant wood floor.

"I thought we might have a good time," he answered. "And we did. If you knew how I was, how did you think the evening would play out?"

Finn knew this made him look even more like a bastard, but at this point, he cared little. He just wanted her to leave.

"I guess I didn't expect you to be a complete dick," she shot back. She tossed an entire bottle of water toward Finn's head that he grasped before it reached him.

"Look, I'm sorry…" Finn wanted to continue that thought but was still fumbling for her name.

"You don't even remember my name, do you?"

"Sure, I do… Kayla," he said, taking a shot.

"It's Karen, you jackass," she hissed as she stormed to the front door and walked out of the condo towards the elevators.

Finn locked the door as she left and then recalled that she was Karen, one of the new admin assistants the firm had just hired in the past week. No doubt, he would now get all kinds of dirty looks when he arrived at the office.

Without an afterthought, Finn went back to working out. He put in an hour with weights, cardio, and the heavy bag before heading to the shower. Finn pressed his hands against the shower wall as the hot water cascaded down his body, washing the sweat away. He spent longer than usual there and found his mind drifting between thoughts of the cases he was working on, his hopes to finally get the coveted partner slot that was open, and how hard he had toiled to get where he was now.

With nothing more than a towel wrapped around his waist, Finn went through his morning routine before making himself a cup of coffee. He had specially ordered a bag of custom roasted Jamaican Blue Mountain, paying a premium for it. The aroma alone made him feel that it was worth the price. Finn had no problem indulging himself in the finer things in life that he wanted now. He resolved that he worked hard to get far and earned every penny, so if he wished to own a luxury watch, custom suit, or expensive car or bike, he deserved it. The youngest of the top associates in the firm, his defense of clients had brought in millions of dollars in a short time. He made his mark so well that some clients requested that only he handle their cases.

Finn glanced at the clock on the microwave to see it was still only 5:30. There was just a sliver of potential sunrise peeking out the window, and Finn went out to his patio and sat, still draped in just a towel, so he could enjoy his coffee and the morning air. Early August weather always meant heat, even in Saratoga. The mornings were often the best time because it would usually be in the fifties. He enjoyed feeling the fresh air as he relaxed.

Finn propped his feet up on the ottoman before him and sipped his coffee. He considered going to get his laptop to go over emails and check today's calendar for meetings before deciding against it. There was plenty of time in the day to accomplish everything that needed to get done. Maybe he could even try to finagle a lunch with old man Peterson himself, the head of Peterson, Morris, and Associates. While Bob Morris was still a chief partner, Finn had a much better relationship with David Peterson, the one who had hired him right out of law school and gave him the best chance at making a partner.

Finn closed his eyes and imagined what it would be like to have his name on the firm's header. Everything would be going his way at that point with work, monetary success, and women, right? Hell, he was even listed as one of the top twenty-five most eligible bachelors in one of those silly city articles recently. It was no wonder that Karen – *that was her name, right?* Finn thought – had practically thrown herself at him at the party last night, and Finn was more than happy to oblige.

It was the sound of breaking glass that jolted Finn's eyes open. He was unsure how long he had dozed off for, but the sun was shining brightly down on him, and he felt the heat right away. He also noticed that he had dropped his favorite coffee mug, shattering the ceramic to pieces and spilling out the precious liquid inside.

"Shit!" Finn thundered. He jumped up from his cushioned seat, being careful not to step on any shards. His movements caused his towel to drop from his waist. As Finn bent to pick up the broken mug, he heard a catcall from across the street.

"Nice ass," the female voice yelled. Finn spun around to see two women sitting on their porch across the street, enjoying their morning coffees, looking up at Finn from just below.

"Even better front," the brunette wearing a red sports bra shouted at him.

Far from embarrassed about his physique, Finn smiled and waved at the women. He filed their location in the back of his mind, noting where they were, so he hoped he might run into one or both sometime soon.

After gathering up the shards and throwing them away, Finn walked to his bedroom to choose his suit for the office. He slid into gray boxer briefs before examining his selection in his walk-in closet. It was then he heard the faint ringtone from his cell phone.

Finn looked around the bedroom and saw no sign of the phone. The ring continued before he realized he had left it on the counter in the kitchen. He hustled over to it, hoping it wasn't his assistant Susannah, letting him know about a meeting he was missing or about the office gossip regarding how he treated yet another admin assistant.

He picked up the phone and saw that it was from his aunt. It had been months since he had spoken to Maureen, and he considered just letting it go to voicemail. She probably just wanted to invite him to another family get-together that he really wanted no part of. This time, however, something told him he should answer.

"Aunt Maureen?" Finn spoke. "I'm sorry I haven't called recently. Things have been busy at the office. I'm just on my way in, so do you think I can call you later…"

"Finn," Maureen insisted. The sternness in her Irish brogue was something Finn had not heard in years, causing him to snap to attention like he had when he was younger. "Listen to me, won't you?"

"What's up?" Finn uttered.

"It's your father," Maureen said softly. "There's been an accident."

2

Finn made all the necessary arrangements as quickly as he could. He contacted Susannah to let her know that she should cancel his appointments and tell Bob Morris he would be out today. Finn didn't give the reason for his absence to Susannah. He never talked about his family at work or really to anyone at all, and he wanted to keep it that way. Finn packed a bag with clothing for a few days, grabbed his laptop and phone, and was on his way, leaving whatever mess in his home there was to the housekeeping due to visit.

Aunt Maureen provided few details of what had exactly happened to his father. She noted she had a brief conversation with Liam, Finn's older brother, and he was tight-lipped about the event himself. Instead of stopping off at his aunt's home in Albany, Finn decided to just stay on the New York State Thruway and make his way down toward Harriman. It was in this small town where his brother and father still lived. The ride would take about two hours, too much time in Finn's mind to think about his family.

It had been just about ten years since he was in Harriman, and Finn hadn't even given the place a second thought since then. He left at eighteen to go to college and never looked back. Finn lived with Maureen and her husband, Oscar, while he went to SUNY Albany for his undergraduate degree. He then went to Cornell Law School but still saw them often since they had become his de facto parents at that point. However, once Finn joined Peterson & Morris, he visited and called less and less, making excuses not to take the easy one-hour drive to the point where he phoned just a few times a year and nothing more.

As he sped his white Lexus down the Thruway and approached New Paltz, Finn felt a knot form in his stomach. His relationship with his father and brother had been nonexistent since he left for Albany, and even before that, it was strained at best. Conor O'Farrell was not an easy man to deal with. After Finn's mother had passed when Finn was sixteen, Conor became mostly unbearable toward his youngest son. When the opportunity came for Finn to leave, he jumped at the chance. Now he had no idea how he would deal with his father or his brother.

It wasn't until Finn had reached the Harriman exit on the Thruway that he realized he was unsure of just where he was going. The house he had lived in with his father and brother was sold shortly after Finn left school. That left him guessing about where to start the search. Everything around Finn from the time he got off the highway was unfamiliar now. The area had grown exponentially since he left it ten years ago, with more traffic, strip malls, towering houses, and fast-food places than had existed in the past. The surroundings were more unrecognizable than Finn had imagined.

After making a few wrong turns to locate places and marks that he remembered, Finn gave up and pulled into one of the several Dunkin' Donuts that now dotted the town. He went in and grabbed a black coffee and knew as soon as the liquid touched his lips that it was a far cry from the custom origin stuff he was accustomed to. The coffee was bitter and slightly burnt, and Finn regretted buying it immediately. He returned to the counter and purchased a plain bottle of water instead and sat himself down at a corner table to use the Wi-Fi. Finn opened his laptop and quickly scanned through his email to see if there was anything important that Susannah may have passed along to him. With nothing pressing visible, he switched to Google. He accessed a map of the area so he could familiarize himself with what was nearby. Scanning over streets and businesses finally triggered a thought to Finn – Darren Hughes.

Darren was the one person Finn knew was still in the area. Best friends through high school and beyond, Finn had kept in touch with Darren over the years, though it had become more sporadic lately, just like all Finn's relationships. They had exchanged emails more than anything, and Darren had come up to Albany and Cornell while Finn was in both places. It had been a couple of years since they met in person, but Finn knew it was the one relationship he had always been able to count on.

Finn gathered up his things and walked up to the counter just as a tall young man with glasses left with a tray filled with iced coffee and iced tea. Finn smiled at the clerk, who, while smiling back, looked at Finn with wonder and worry about why he was coming to the counter three times in about ten minutes.

"Do you know if Millie Malone's is still open?" Finn asked.

"What is that?" the clerk said confusedly. Finn realized the guy was probably no more than seventeen and didn't look like the type to get out much.

"Millie Malone's," Finn insisted. "It's a bar in Harriman, or at least it was back in my day."

"I don't know, bro," the young man replied, shaking his head.

"He's talking about that old place on River Road, Steve," a female voice shouted. Finn watched as the girl clad in her customary corporate polo shirt and visor walked over to the counter.

"The Irish place on River Road, right?" she said with a smile as Finn felt her gaze looking him over. The girl, whose nametag read "Annie," reached down to switch off the microphone to the headset she wore.

"Steve, go cover the drive-thru for a second. I got this," she said, shooing Steve away.

"You know the place?" Finn asked with surprise.

"Sure," she answered. "My girlfriends and I go there sometimes on the weekends. It's usually a little quieter than some of the other places around here. I don't think I've ever seen you there, though. I'd remember that." Annie grinned widely.

"You're old enough to get in there?" Finn asked with doubt in his voice.

"I'm twenty-two," Annie said, leaning over the counter and bringing her face closer to Finn. She bade Finn come closer to her with her finger. "Old enough for a lot of things," she whispered.

"I bet you are," Finn said, smiling back at her. "But I'm only in town to see an old friend for a day or two."

"That's too bad," Annie replied with disappointment. "It's still in the same place, though it's cleaner than it was years ago. The guy who runs it has fixed it up a bit."

"That's my friend," Finn admitted as he pulled out his phone to glance at the message that had just come in.

"You're friends with Darren?" Annie said with a jump. "My girls and I go there just to see him. He's so nice, and that Irish way of talking he has…"

"He still has his brogue?" Finn laughed. Finn had always been glad he had shed his in college.

"Oh yeah," Annie replied, practically melting onto the counter. "It's so sexy. We go in there sometimes just to listen to him talk. Did you talk like that?" Annie rested her head in the palms of her hands and batted her eyes up at Finn.

Finn felt a bit of a blush come across his face. "A long time ago, I did," Finn told her. Finn saw there were now a few people lining up behind him, getting more than annoyed at having to wait for their mid-morning caffeine fix.

"Thanks for the info Annie, I appreciate it," Finn offered and placed a twenty-dollar bill in the tip jar.

"You could just buy me a drink there tonight instead, if you want. I get off work at 4. I can be there around eight or so."

"Maybe," Finn told her as he smiled and walked out the door.

Finn climbed into his car, turned the ignition, and glanced at the clock. It was only 10:30, and Finn had no idea what time Darren opened the pub. Other than some brief listings in a Google search, Finn found no information on the bar at all. He'd have to take a ride over and see it for himself. He looked at the message that had come in from his aunt while he was chatting/flirting with Annie. Aunt Maureen had asked if Finn had information on his father yet. Finn tapped out a quick *Nothing yet* and sent it along. He hadn't even come close to finding out anything and wasn't sure just how eager he really was in the first place.

****

Siobhan McCarthy leaned back in her desk chair, rubbing some of the heaviness from her eyes. It was partly from the little sleep she had been getting lately, which was more from the stress she had of trying to protect the woman and her children central to her latest case. Her caseload had grown, thanks to the budget cuts that had cost them two of the social workers on staff that had caused her as director to take on cases herself. Three more cases had just come in, and Siobhan had no idea who she would assign them to.

Her desk chair groaned as she leaned back and stared at the ceiling, noticing the telltale water stain marks on several of the drop ceiling panels. With every heavy rainstorm, the old building's roof leaked a bit more. The grant money Siobhan had applied for was still out there in government red tape and limbo, with little to no signs of ever turning up. It was a matter of time before something gave and caused significant water damage that might force them out of the building, perhaps permanently, giving Siobhan one more thing to add to her list of worries.

A Safe Place was one of the few not-for-profit agencies in the county dedicated to assisting survivors of domestic violence, teen violence, and human trafficking. Siobhan had taken over as director two years ago after the previous director moved on to a higher paying government position. Siobhan had received her master's in social work from Fordham University, taking classes at night, online, on weekends, and whenever she could find the time. Her hard work paid off, not necessarily in a huge salary. Still, she found meaning and fulfillment with the work that had gotten her respect in her field at a young age.

Siobhan kicked off the black heels she hated to wear and slipped into the sneakers that she loved. She re-tied the hair tie in her red hair to tighten up her ponytail, brushing a few stray strands off her face before she got up to walk out of her office. She passed the small cubicles the office had that the social workers handled cases in, and all were occupied. Siobhan stopped at one where a young woman sat, holding an infant on her lap with a toddler at her feet on the floor, discussing her current situation quietly. She peeked her head in and smiled before squatting down next to the toddler.

"Hey there," she said softly, running her hand through the long dark hair of the girl. The toddler looked up and smiled at Siobhan. "What's her name?" Siobhan asked the mother. The woman smiled slightly and whispered, "Felicity."

"Hi, Felicity. Your daughter is beautiful," Siobhan commented as she tickled under Felicity's chin to elicit a giggle.

"Thank you," the woman stated.

"Don't worry," Siobhan reassured the mother. "We'll help you out however you need. Donna will see to that." Siobhan smiled over at Donna, the more senior social worker sitting across from the mother.

Siobhan stood up and left the room and went down the hall and through what they called their phone center, which was not much more than a couple of old six-foot banquet tables donated from a catering company going out of business with phone stations and old laptops arranged on them. During the day, volunteers were manning all four, with just two phones used overnight so that there was around-the-clock coverage. Siobhan had even set it up so that overflow calls would go right to her cellphone so that she could assist from home if needed.

She crossed into the kitchen and dining area they had set up to provide meals for anyone who needed them. There were a few people scattered at the various tables. Volunteers worked in the small kitchen. The agency relied heavily on donations from local restaurants and the community to get meals and keep a pantry available to cook and give food to those in need. Siobhan poured herself a cup of coffee from one of the urns set up. She smiled at a couple of people seated and having bagels before moving to the outer office near the entrance.

Tracy Watson, Siobhan's admin and one of the front door guardians, was hard at work at her desk, organizing appointments and trying to arrange things like transportation to safe houses for individuals and families. Tracy gave a light wave to Siobhan as she nodded and kept talking. Siobhan worked her way over to Benny Sargent, one of the security guards that the agency used.

Because of budget constraints, the agency could only afford to have two security guards at any given time. Benny took the day shift while his twin brother J.J. took the night shift. As much as Siobhan wished they didn't need the added protection, there had been too many incidents early on of angry ex-husbands, boyfriends, fathers, and others showing up at all hours threatening violence and more. A Safe Place added outdoor and indoor cameras and security doors at the front and back to ensure there was some protection level for victims, employees, volunteers, and anyone else. Siobhan had even enrolled all the volunteers and employees in self-defense classes. While she hadn't let anyone know yet, she had recently acquired her gun permit and license to carry, even though she did not have a gun on her person while at the office. At least not yet.

"How's everything going today, Benny?" she asked as she stood in front of the security desk where consoles revealed all the current camera angles.

"Pretty quiet so far today, Ms. McCarthy," Benny replied politely as he adjusted his navy-blue tie.

"Benny, we've known each other for years. You can call me Siobhan. I keep telling you that."

"I know, Ms. McCarthy," Benny said humbly. "But I'm working for you while I'm here. You're the boss; you've earned respect."

Siobhan just sighed and shook her head. Tracy had hung up her phone and was signaling to Siobhan to come over to her desk.

"Whatever you are comfortable with, Benny," Siobhan laughed as she paced over to Tracy's desk.

"What's up?" Siobhan asked as Tracy arranged paperwork.

"We've got some volunteers heading out this afternoon for food pick up. We should have two families here to spend the night tonight, so I'll make sure the rooms back there are in good shape. I know we were having a problem with a couple of fans. I want to make sure they are working since the AC conked out."

"It's still out?" Siobhan hollered before quickly lowering her voice. "I thought Ernie was coming to fix that yesterday after I left?"

"He never showed," Tracy replied. "Ready for some more bad news?"

"What else?" Siobhan said, feeling her temples start to pound.

"Gavin Elliott called to cancel his lunch meeting with you today."

"Again?" Siobhan exploded. "The SOB has done that three times in the last 3 weeks. I need to meet with him to talk about funding for renovations to this place and maybe get some of our staff back. What is his excuse this time?"

"He had a property meeting with the county today that they were expecting to run long. He said you can call his assistant to reschedule. I'm sorry, Siobhan."

"Not as sorry as I am," Siobhan lamented. "He's pretty much our last shot. All the other businesses and donors have turned me down. I don't know how long we can keep operating like this, Tracy. I'll have to call his office again. And get Ernie on the phone, so I can yell at him, please. Thanks."

Siobhan slowly made her way back toward her office. Her cell phone buzzed before she got halfway there. She looked with the hope that it would be Gavin's office. It turned out to be Cara Murphy, her best friend.

"Hey, Cara," Siobhan said as she shuffled along the hallway. "I hope your day is going better than mine. How're things at the hospital?"

"Siobhan, listen to me," Cara interrupted. "I can only talk for a minute. I'm working in the ER today. Conor O'Farrell was brought in this morning."

Siobhan stopped dead in her tracks.

"Are you sure it's him?" she asked shakily.

"I went to check when I saw the name. It's him for sure. Siobhan, it's bad."

"Jesus," Siobhan said softly. She instinctively reached up and grabbed the gold cross that hung around her neck.

"What happened to him? Has... has anyone come to see him yet?"

"I'm not sure if it was an accident, a fight, or what," Cara explained. "I saw Liam here, and a few of the Cosantóir were out in the ER waiting room. I thought you should know."

Siobhan stood quietly for a moment. The Cosantóir – Gaelic for 'Protectors,' were the motorcycle club that Conor had led for thirty years.

"Vonnie? You okay?" Cara said.

"Yeah... I'm alright. Can you keep me posted, Cara? Let me know... let me know if I need to get there."

"Sure thing. Talk to you later. Love you, Vonnie," Cara said quickly before hanging up.

Siobhan walked to her office and closed the door, sitting down in her leather desk chair to help get her bearings. Hearing about Conor was the last thing she had expected. All she could think about was her grandmother reminding her in her inimitable Irish way that bad things are grouped in threes. Gavin canceling was one. Conor was two.

"What's coming down the road?" Siobhan said to herself.

3

Finn drove slowly over the gravel of the parking area next to Millie Malone's. He silently cursed Darren for never having the parking lot paved as he could hear pebbles dinging the sides of his Lexus. Finn spotted Darren's wreck of a green Audi, a car Darren had purchased used while Finn was still in law school, nearest to the pub, indicating Darren was at least inside even if the place wasn't open yet. Finn stepped out of his car and caught a hint of odor from the water treatment plant not far down the road, a quick reminder that he was back in familiar haunts. Living in the area made most people accustomed to the rank smells that occasionally came from the plant when the weather was humid. Finn's senses were overwhelmed right away as he wrinkled his nose and hustled to the front door of the pub.

Finn pried open the well-worn oak door and entered the pub. The space was mostly dark, with a few lights over the bar barely lit. A quick look around let Finn know that Annie was right – the bar had been updated a bit from when Finn and Darren were younger and would come to the place when Darren's parents ran it. The old booths with the torn black vinyl seats were gone and updated with more contemporary stalls and green vinyl colors. There was a small wooden stage tucked in the corner that never existed before, and Darren had put up some flat-screen TVs around the space for people to watch while they drank. The floor looked better, with the old wood apparently polished and restored to look new again. All the stickiness that Finn remembered so well from the past (Darren's father always said it was part of the charm) was long gone.

Finn made his way from the bar entrance and saw a shadow towards the end of the bar with its back to him.

"Sorry, fella," the familiar brogue stated without turning around. "We're not open for another hour or so."

"Don't be a tool, barkeep," Finn yelled back, trying to turn his brogue back on after many years. "Just pour me a pint, and I'll be on my way."

Darren snapped around and peered through the dim lighting.

"Jesus, has a ghost just walked in?" Darren said as he smiled and hopped over the bar to move towards Finn.

The two men embraced, and Darren slapped Finn's back heartily.

"I can't believe it's really you," Darren said with awe. "Look at you with your blond hair all nice and straight and your chin clean. It's a long way from your teens, Finnbar."

Finn cringed when he heard 'Finnbar.' Darren knew full well that it wasn't Finn's given name, but he had always made fun of Finn that way since they were kids.

"I see it still gets under your skin," Darren laughed as he led Finn over to a barstool. "Sit, and I'll pour us a couple."

Finn glanced at his silver Rolex and saw it wasn't even quite eleven.

"A little early for me," Finn said as he watched Darren deftly begin to pour a Guinness.

"Have you gone soft up there in Saratoga?" Darren asked as he let the Guinness settle before beginning a pour again. "We used to drink this for breakfast when we helped my Dad clean up in the mornings." Darren reached over and grabbed Finn's wrist to get a better look at his watch. "Christ, man, how many people did you keep out of jail to afford that? It probably costs more than my car."

"That doesn't mean much, Darren," Finn said as he pulled his wrist back. "You're driving the same piece of shite you had years ago."

Finn didn't realize how easy it was to slip back into old habits. He hadn't used 'shite' in so long, but it flowed out without a hitch now.

"Hey now," Darren retorted as he finished pouring the first Guinness and started the second one. "I only have to drive four miles a day most days round trip. This car will get passed down to my grandkids."

Darren slid the pint glass in front of Finn and returned to pouring the second. Finn glanced down and saw the shape of a four-leaf clover in the foam in front of him.

"Fancy," Finn mocked. "Your Dad would have a stroke if he saw that, you know."

"Yeah, well, the younger crowd gets a kick out of it," Darren told him as he completed his own pour. "Gotta do something to keep the customers happy. Dad was never too concerned about that. He was more of a drink what's in front of ya or get out kind of guy."

"Slàinte Mhath," Darren said as the two men clinked glasses and drank. Finn gulped down a portion of the Guinness after saluting his old friend.

"How are your parents?" Finn asked as he wiped the foam from his lips.

"Good, good," Darren said as he went over to turn the lights up a bit. "Ma loves being in the warm weather in South Carolina, and Dad hates it because no one knows how to pour down there, but his health is a bit better."

"And your sister?" Finn took another sip.

"Rose? Ahh, she's okay. Shacking up with some guy down in Jersey. I keep trying to get her to come up here and work for me while she finishes school, but she won't have it. She's like you – first chance to get away from here, she jumped at it."

"Different circumstances. You know that," Finn said seriously.

"Yeah, I know, brother, I know."

Finn watched as Darren reached over towards the corner of the bar and grabbed his wallet.

"Come on, man, you still have that worn piece of crap wallet after all these years?"

"Of course, I do," Darren replied proudly, holding up the faded and cracked pieces of leather that barely held together. "You know who gave me this."

Darren reached into the wallet and pulled out a worn picture and slapped it in front of Finn. It was a picture of Millie Malone herself, Darren's grandmother on his mother's side. She was sitting in a folding beach chair in Darren's parents' backyard wearing her sunglasses and flowered housecoat, not quite smiling but not quite scowling, as was her way, at the camera.

"Ah, good old Millie," Finn said with a laugh. "I remember she gave you that wallet when we graduated high school."

"That's right," Darren offered. "It had a fiver in it and this picture, and she told me to always keep both to remember her. I've still got the fiver in there too."

"God bless her," Finn said. "She used to run us out of here all the time."

"If you go down the hall there," Darren said, pointing towards the back of the bar, "you'll see pictures of her and my Granddad from when they got married and then opened this place. A nice memory of the family, you know."

Darren reached behind the bar and grabbed a bottle of Jameson's off the counter with two shot glasses. He poured into both and handed one to Finn.

"To Millie," Darren toasted as both held their shots up to her picture on the bar before drinking the whiskey. The shot blasted a burn down Finn's throat, who spent more time drinking fine Scotch now than Irish whiskey.

"Now for the $10,000 question," Darren said as he refilled the shot glasses. "What the hell are you doing here?"

"Maureen called me this morning and said Dad had an accident but didn't have any details. I drove down here but realized I have no idea where to find him... or Liam. I don't suppose you know anything?"

"Shite, Finn, I don't," Darren said solemnly. "I mean, I don't know exactly where your Da lives, but that won't help you too much finding out where he is now. I'm sorry, man."

"Have you seen Liam at all?" Finn asked, drawing on his Guinness.

"The Cosantóir don't come in here, Finn. You know that," Darren replied. "I see him around town now and then, but we haven't talked in a long time. If you are looking for him, you know where to find him."

"I do, but I really don't want to have to go there. Is the Hog House still in the same place?"

"Yep. Just out past the train station and before you get to the state park. They have a big house out in the woods there. Probably not a good idea to just walk in there, though. You're considered a stranger now, and you know how they feel about outsiders coming to the house uninvited."

"I don't see how I have many choices," Finn said as he polished off the rest of his Guinness and rose from the barstool.

"You're going now? You just got here," Darren said to him. "If you wait a bit, I can at least go with you when I have some staff here."

"No, no. This is all on me, Darren," Finn admitted. "Don't worry. I'll be back later, and we can talk more."

"If you're still able to walk by then," Darren cautioned.

"I'll be fine," Finn assured his friend. An older gentleman walked through the door as Finn neared it. The gentleman shuffled up to Finn and craned his neck to stare at Finn through his thick glasses.

"Customers already, Darren?" the old man shouted.

"Easy, Paddy," Darren told him. "Paddy is usually the first pour of the day," Darren said to Finn. "Paddy, that's Finn O'Farrell. Finn, you remember Paddy Walsh, don't you?"

"How are you, Mr. Walsh?" Finn said, offering his hand. Paddy looked down at Finn's hand and then back up at his face.

"Conor's boy, right?" Paddy said with some disdain.

"That's right," Finn resigned. He would always be 'Conor's boy' around here.

"Your grandfather was a much nicer man," Paddy added, avoiding Finn's hand. "And your mother… Aoife… now she was a saint." Paddy shuffled over to what was his usual perch at the corner of the bar.

"You're right on both counts, Mr. Walsh," Finn replied. "That shot there is for you, on me, sir," Finn added, pointing to the shot he didn't touch and nodding to Darren. Darren slid the whiskey over in front of Paddy.

"Thank you, son," Paddy said with a slight grin as he picked up the glass.

Finn walked out the front door and headed back into the now oppressive heat and humidity of the day. He climbed into his car and turned the AC up as much as he could before pulling out of the parking lot.

Going to the Hog House was something he did not relish doing, but it was the only way he would find Liam and learn more about his father. The problem would be the reaction of anyone who might be there right now and what they might do to him when he arrived.

4

Siobhan had a hard time keeping her mind on Conor O'Farrell for the rest of the morning. She spent time going through the motions with tasks, including yelling at Ernie to get the AC fixed like he had promised so that anyone staying in their shelter for the night had a comfortable place to rest. The shelter had three bedrooms that allowed some privacy for individuals or families and then a larger room with cots and bunk beds so that they could house up to about thirty people at a time if they had to. It was rare the place was ever full, but they came close on a few occasions or acted as an overflow area to help the homeless during the winter.

Siobhan thought about calling Gavin Elliott's office to reschedule time with him, but she decided to go one step further. She had Gavin's cellphone number, something she had shared with no one, not even Cara. Gavin had tried on several occasions to get Siobhan to go out with him, and she had consistently rebuffed his advances. She wanted to keep things professional, and Siobhan honestly had little interest in seeing Gavin socially. Gavin was attractive and successful, and many women showed interest in him. Still, Siobhan always felt something wasn't quite right with him. She didn't like how he seemed to approach business and people, often talking down to others he saw as beneath him while trying to keep his façade of a nice guy. Many bought into it; Siobhan didn't. She saw doing business with him as a necessary evil since he had political and commercial influence and had directed many donors and much assistance to her organization when they needed it.

Siobhan shut her office door and took a deep breath before typing a text message to Gavin.

Are you around?

She hit send before she could change her mind, and within ten seconds, her cell phone was ringing.

"Hello?" she answered cordially.

"What a pleasant surprise that was," Gavin said smugly. "How are you today?"

"I'm fine, Gavin," Siobhan answered. "And I would be doing better today if you hadn't canceled our lunch meeting. You keep putting me off to talk about funding for the center."

"Siobhan, I'm sorry," Gavin replied. "These county meetings are taking up a lot of my time. We're trying to get permits for the new water lines and a tunnel so that we can get my project underway, and I must get everything going. I can make it up to you, I promise. Let's get together tonight for dinner, and we can talk about it. We can go to RP Prime if you like. I have a regular table there. Or we can just go back to my place, and I can have Cassandra whip something up for us. Whatever you prefer."

"Gavin, I just want to talk about the funding. If you take some time to look at my proposal and what the money will go towards, you will see how much it can help us. I only need about 15 minutes of your time."

"Great," Gavin answered. "That leaves us plenty of time for drinks and dinner then. Come on. It will beat whatever you were planning to heat in the microwave in your apartment tonight."

Siobhan rankled every time Gavin slighted her or what she did. He had become a piece in her life over the last year or so, and the longer she worked with him, the more persistent he grew in his pursuit of her. Siobhan also realized that at some point, with all her rebuffs, Gavin was bound to just get the hint and cut himself off from her completely, which meant losing funds and connections.

"Fine," Siobhan sighed. "I'll meet you at the restaurant."

"Wonderful!" Gavin exclaimed. "I'll have my driver come by the office and pick you up at seven."

"I can drive myself..." Siobhan tried to interject.

"Nonsense," Gavin insisted. "You deserve to ride in comfort and style, not that jalopy you have. You are dressed appropriately, aren't you?"

"Excuse me?" More than a hint of annoyance at the question ran through Siobhan's voice.

"I have no doubt you look beautiful in anything, Siobhan," Gavin backtracked. "But the RP Prime... well, they do have some standards. It's not Chili's."

"If it's a problem, Gavin, we can just forget about it," Siobhan told him sternly.

"No, no!" Gavin rushed. "Whatever you're wearing is fine. The car will be there at seven. See you later."

Gavin hung up as Siobhan slumped back into her chair.

A gentle knock on the door snapped Siobhan's head up, and Tracy entered the office.

"Ernie is here to work on the AC," Tracy added as she clutched papers for Siobhan to sign. "I just need you to sign the work order."

Siobhan took the paper from Tracy and sighed loudly as she scribbled her signature.

"Everything okay?" Tracy asked.

"I suppose," Siobhan told her. "I think I just sold my soul to the devil."

"What happened?"

"I called Gavin Elliott," Siobhan told Tracy as she handed the papers back. "The only way he would talk to me is if I agreed to have dinner with him tonight."

"I'm sorry," Tracy said. "Honestly, he kind of gives me the creeps. It seems like he's always staring at the women around him, especially when he comes in here."

"I think he's harmless," Siobhan responded.

"He's just..."

"A horny dog?" Tracy said with a smile.

Siobhan tried to stifle a laugh. "Well, he does seem to be that, but it's nothing I can't handle. I grew up with four older Irish brothers, remember? I was going to say he's just the last gasp chance we have for the money we need. I have to at least have dinner with him and try to win him over."

"You're a more dedicated person than I am, Siobhan," Tracy added.

"I can't bear the thought of what would happen if we weren't here," Siobhan rose from her desk and tightened her ponytail. She walked over and unzipped the garment bag she kept behind her office door and pulled out the contents. She had a red floral sleeveless dress she kept in there, along with a black suit that she had on hand for last-minute meetings.

"Which one?" she said as she held them up for Tracy to look at.

"if you want Gavin's full attention, you already know the answer to that question," Tracy said as she nodded toward the dress.

"I guess I was hoping you'd say something else," Siobhan said as she hung the suit back up and draped the dress over one of the chairs.

"Let me go make sure Ernie gets this right this time," Siobhan stated as she left her office. The entire way down the hall to the back rooms, all she could think to tell herself was that she was doing the right thing.

****

Finn drove past the train station on his left and then slowed down a bit so he could find the turn-off to go towards Hog House. He spotted the unmarked dirt road on the right just before he went beyond it, slammed on his brakes, and made an awkward turn to start up the hilly road. All Finn could think about was more damage that rocks, gravel, and debris were doing to the finish of his Lexus.

Dread started to creep over Finn the further up the hill he went and the narrower the road became. It felt like the trees were closing in on him to the point where he could see the beams from his headlights even though it was the afternoon and sunny out. It had been many years since Finn made the trek to Hog House, the home of the Cosantóir motorcycle club that his father had founded. Conor O'Farrell had chosen this location for several reasons. The land was cheap at the time. It bordered Harriman State Park, so no one would ever be able to build around them. The location afforded him the privacy he wanted for the club.

Finn reached the apex of the hill, and the area flattened out so that he could see the large house standing before him. The house was quite different from the rundown place he knew as a teenager. The rickety porch had been wholly replaced, newer siding, and what looked to be a new roof shone in the sunshine that beamed down on the clearing. There was even a satellite dish proudly aimed into the sky. If it weren't for the row of motorcycles parked out front, a person might pull up and think it was a respectable bed and breakfast in the woods.

Finn parked his car away from the motorcycles and sat staring at the house. Now that he was here, he wasn't sure exactly what his next move would be. Conor wasn't here, and he was unsure how Liam would react if he saw him come through the door. That was assuming Finn could even make it that far. If the Cosantóir members that didn't recognize him saw him enter the house, they were likely to wonder why a stranger walked in and physically remove him without asking any questions.

Now or never, Finn thought, and he climbed out of his car and locked the doors. He kept his keys close by in the front pocket of his jeans. He knew he could probably get a few punches off before he got jumped by several. If he positioned a key between his knuckles, he could cause some more damage to buy some time. He glanced up at the sign hanging off the eaves of the front porch that spelled out Hog House etched into the wood. The sign had the Sandhogs logo on one side and the Cosantóir logo, a Dara's knot with the words 'Cosantóir,' 'Meas,' and 'Bua' surrounding it.

Before entering, Finn recalled how funny his Dad always thought it was to call the place Hog House. It had a dual meaning – representing the Sandhogs, the tunnel workers that made up the club and who called their worksite shack a hog house – and representing a motorcycle club of men riding their hogs. Finn gave his father credit for being creative, something he never thought the old man was.

Finn tugged on the door, surprised to find that it was not only unlocked but that no one was guarding it. In his younger days, Finn always remembered a member perched on a stool at the entrance, Guinness in hand, checking to make sure only those welcome entered. If you were unexpected, you better have had a damn good reason for being there. Finn's senses were overloaded as he crossed the doorway. The aroma of beer, whiskey, cigars, cigarettes, and weed all combined together into some sort of oddball potpourri you would only find in a place like this.

Finn looked at the steep staircase right in front of him and then glanced to the right in the short hallway. He stepped left where the sound of music and murmurs seemed to come from. A few quick paces later, Finn was standing in the doorway of what could best be called the entertainment area. A large bar wrapped the room's back wall while couches lined each of the far walls with tables in the middle. They were all directed toward the small stage that sat behind where Finn stood now, and above the stage were three large televisions. Now, all three were playing Blue Velvet.

Two bikers immediately rose off the couch they were seated at and strode to where Finn stood. Finn glanced to his right and saw that the biker sitting there with an arm around a woman stared at Finn but did not move. He looked as if he were just waiting for a nod from one of the two approaching Finn before he would react. Finn readied his fists but kept them at his side and shifted his feet so he was in his boxing stance.

Both men now loomed over Finn, which was no simple feat considering Finn himself was almost 6'3". The man on the left had a green bandana wrapped around his bald head. His dark beard was close-cropped, and a quick survey of his form let Finn know that he had something in his front jeans pocket that could be a weapon. The biker on the right wasn't nearly as cryptic, and a black baton could be seen swaying from his belt.

"You look like you're lost, friend," the biker on the left said, smiling. Finn saw the telltale tobacco stains on his teeth as he grinned. "This is private property and a private social club." The biker looked Finn over once again, catching a glimpse of the Rolex on Finn's wrist.

"If you're looking for Woodbury Commons, this ain't it," the biker laughed, causing the others in the room to laugh along. "Go back down the hill, follow the road, and you'll find your way to Armani or whatever it is the fuck you're looking for."

The biker went to put his arm around Finn, and Finn jerked away from him, causing the behemoth on the right to move in to grab Finn. As he moved to take hold of Finn's wrist, Finn hit him with a left cross that dropped him in a heap. The other biker on the couch moved now, faster than Finn had expected. Finn struck the man nearest to him with a gut punch to the solar plexus to take the wind right out of him and sent him to his knees. The third biker from the couch was shorter than Finn but was built like a tank. He barreled into Finn and tackled him, gliding both men across the polished wood floor and up against the stage. Finn tried to escape the grip he was in, and it squeezed on his ribcage. Finn felt the air rushing out of his body, and his face burned red.

The first biker that Finn had dropped now stood above him with a swollen jaw, hurt pride and his baton clutched in his hand.

"Drag him up and outside, Ronan," the biker barked as he spat some blood out onto the floor. "I'll teach you some manners, you Langer."

Finn struggled to his feet as he stayed in the grip of Ronan, who had locked his hands together like a vise in front of Finn's chest. Finn gasped for air and noticed the other biker still down on one knee, trying to catch his breath. It was then that Finn saw two others walking towards him. Before he got a good look at the duo, Ronan was wrangling Finn out the front door and onto the porch.

"C'mon Danny," Ronan puffed. "I can't hold this eejit forever. Do somethin'."

Danny smiled and raised his baton as Finn shut his eyes and braced for the blow that he expected on his skull. When nothing happened, Finn opened his eyes. He saw that a woman dressed in a white t-shirt and jeans had grasped the baton before Danny could bring it down.

"Maeve? What the fuck?" Danny said as he held onto the baton. Maeve shot her right hand up and slapped Danny in the face, shocking him and sending him stumbling back as he released the weapon.

"Talk to me like that again, and I'll crack this across your thick head," Maeve warned Danny. She turned and looked at Finn, still in Ronan's grip. "Let him go, Ronan," Maeve ordered. Ronan moved his hands, and Finn slumped to the porch, gulping air as it came back to his burning lungs.

Maeve squatted down in front of Finn and took his chin in her hand so she could turn his face up to her. "I thought it was you," she said softly as she smiled. "You move just like the two of them. And you've got your Da's temper in you too, I see."

"Do I know you?" Finn said as he tried to focus and breathe normally.

"Ah, you might not remember me too well, but yes Finn, we know each other. I've been a part of your family's life for many years now, especially after your mother passed. I'm guessing you're here about your father."

"Yeah," Finn said, still fuzzy and befuddled.

"Come in, have a drink, and we'll talk," Maeve said, giving her hand to Finn to help him up.

5

Finn followed Maeve back inside as she made her way towards the bar. She took a sharp left once she was there and nodded to the older gentleman behind the bar as she went past towards a back hallway. The bartender watched Finn like a hawk, along with the biker that Finn had taken the air out of just minutes earlier.

Maeve entered a large room towards the back of the house and invited Finn to follow her. She shut the door as he came in and pointed towards a couple of chairs positioned near the far window. Finn looked around the room and saw it was sparsely decorated but held some pictures on the mantel and the walls of his father and Liam, his father and Maeve, and even a couple of his father and mother. As soon as Finn spied the picture of his mother, he walked over to it. It was a photo from when his father had just bought the Hog House, something his mother was initially against. The two stood on the front porch, the house looking somewhat dilapidated at that time, but both were smiling as they held each other.

Maeve gave Finn a moment to examine the picture before she walked over to stand next to him.

"Your mother was an amazing woman, Finn," Maeve admitted. "We all had so much fun together here in the house, as much as she may not have wanted your Dad to be here."

"I don't ever remember her coming here to hang out," Finn insisted.

"You wouldn't," Maeve answered. "She always made sure if she was coming that you were at home with a sitter. Once you were older, she slowed down when she came, and then she got sick, and well…" Maeve's words trailed off.

"But you weren't at the funeral or anything," Finn stated as he walked over to one of the leather chairs to sit. "I was old enough to remember that. The Cosantóir were there."

"No, I wasn't there," Maeve lamented. "And it's something I'll regret for the rest of my life. Aoife and I were awfully close, Finn… best friends for a long time. When she got sick, your father didn't know how to handle it well. He avoided the truth, worked more, drank more, and… well, he did a lot of things he shouldn't have done."

Finn recoiled at just the memory of what those times were like for him.

"I spent a lot of time helping your mother while you were in school and while she was in the hospital. You and I saw each other some, but not much. Towards the end, when your Ma decided she didn't want any more treatment or care, she asked me not to come around. I ignored her at first. I didn't want to lose my friend. It was too painful for both of us, though, with me just sitting here and watching her die. I said goodbye to her three days before she passed. It hurt like hell, Finn, and it still does for me as I'm sure it does for you. I visit her grave once a month just to leave her flowers and talk to her."

Finn began to soften toward Maeve the more she spoke about his mother. They were painful memories for Finn since he and his mother were close. He did recall his mother insisting he keep up with school and not let it slide no matter how things were with her.

"So how long was it before you shacked up with my father?" Finn said maliciously. "Or did it happen before Ma died?"

"I wouldn't do that to your Mom, Finn," Maeve responded strongly. "It was months after she died. You remember how your Dad was, dontcha? He was falling apart, getting involved in things he shouldn't have done, neglecting you. I stepped in and begged him to get help, but he refused. Tough old Irishman, Conor was and still is. He said he could handle it, but I knew he couldn't do it alone. So, I started taking care of things around Hog House first, and then, more and more at home. When you left to go to college, Conor raged. He said he wouldn't let you leave. He said that you should be working in the tunnels because that's what O'Farrell's did. I told him he had to let you go for your own good and for Aoife. So, he did, begrudgingly. After that, we started to get closer. I made him get cleaned up if he wanted to be with me, and he did. Has he slipped now and again? He has, for sure. He's not perfect, Finn, but he's a damn sight better than what you remember, and I love him for it."

"Sure doesn't sound like the Conor O'Farrell I grew up with," Finn admitted. "If this is the way it is, then why aren't you down at the hospital? Are you two married? And what happened to him?"

"We're not married," Maeve told Finn. "Your father, for all his faults, said he would never marry anyone else. I didn't fight him on it. I know he's committed to me now. I don't need a ring or piece of paper to prove it. As for what happened, I'm not sure. They found him early in the morning over at one of the work sites. It looked like some machinery had slipped into the shaft and knocked him off the platform he was on. He was only there to do a site inspection. Liam insisted I stay here while he and the crew went down to see how he was. Liam's supposed to call me when he has more information. All I know for sure is that they are keeping your father in a coma while they hope the swelling around his brain goes down."

Maeve was visibly shaken and exhausted after explaining the past and present to Finn. It was a lot for Finn to take in all at once but still provided him with little information about how Conor was at the moment. Maeve sat in the chair opposite him and stared out the window. Finn took notice of the tattoo on Maeve's triceps. It was the Celtic Sisters Knot with the initials A.O. in it, and underneath it read 'deirfiúracha i gcónaí,' Gaelic for 'Always Sisters.'

"Ah, I got that after your mother passed," Maeve said, her eyes clouding. "We always talked about getting it together, but your Ma, she was old-school Catholic, you know. She always said marking the body was immoral, and she wouldn't do it. I never felt the same way, obviously," she chuckled. Maeve rolled up the short sleeve of her t-shirt to reveal the Cosantóir logo tattoo that was customary for all members to have.

"I should probably get going," Finn said. He stood up and groaned a little, his ribs still sore from the tussle out front. "I guess I should head down to the hospital and find a place to stay for the night."

"Here," Maeve said, tossing a set of keys to Finn. "Those are the keys to your Dad's house... well, our house. I spend a lot of nights here anyway. You can use the guest room. It's all made up and ready for someone. There's some food in the fridge, too. If you feel like coming back here, just stop by. I don't think anyone will give ya any trouble now that they'll know who you are. I will say, though, it took some balls for you to come walkin' through the door like that. You held your own with them. Danny and the boys will never live that down, being you look like such a pretty boy."

"Thanks... I guess," Finn replied to the backhanded compliment. "I can just stay at a hotel, really."

"Nonsense," Maeve remarked. "Family sticks together, even those we haven't seen in a long time. Now go see your father and brother. I'm sure they need you right now."

"Thank you, Maeve," Finn said sincerely.

"You're welcome, Finn. Take my cell phone number," she said, grabbing Finn's phone from his hand. "You can let me know how your father is. Liam isn't so prompt about getting back to people. I have a feeling you're a bit more responsible when it comes to that."

"I'll call or text you, I promise," Finn noted as Maeve walked him back out to the main room. Finn got stares from the bartender again and angry glares from Danny and Ronan as he walked by.

"Keep your glares to yourself, you saps," Maeve chastised. "This is Conor's boy, and he deserves some respect even if he isn't Cosantóir."

Maeve hooked her arm around Finn's and guided him to the porch.

"That your car?" Maeve noted.

"Yes, it is," Finn replied as he stepped down the porch, proudly smiling at his vehicle.

"You might want to check the tires and look at the finish to make sure there aren't any gouges in it. The boys are kind of sore losers."

Finn did a quick tour around his Lexus and didn't notice any problems. Still, he made sure to get away from the Hog House as quickly as he could before anyone changed their mind about him. He raced back down the hill and got onto Route 17M to head towards Good Samaritan Hospital.

****

By the time Finn had pulled into the visitor's parking lot at the hospital, he had spent the fifteen-minute drive trying to come up with just what he would say when he had met up with his brother. He and Liam rarely got along, even under the best of circumstances when they were younger. Finn was always the little brother who was getting in the way or tried to tag along with his older sibling. The two were nothing like each other than they came from the same bloodline. While Finn was light-haired with blue eyes and shorter but fit like his father, Liam was a stark contrast. Liam was dark hair and eyes and got his mammoth size from his mother's side of the family. At 6'7," Liam towered over his brother. When the two were younger, Liam used his size as much to his advantage as he could when giving Finn a hard time. Finn imagined that seeing his brother now could be even worse with the animosity that was between them.

Finn walked into the hospital and immediately moved to the ER to track down where his father was. The ER was typically filled on a late Friday afternoon. Finn waited patiently in line before he got to the desk where people signed in.

"I'm looking for my father," Finn said politely as injured and sick people moved about. "Conor O'Farrell. I know he came in here this morning."

"Let me take a look," the young nurse behind the computer screen told him as she typed rapidly.

Finn saw that the woman behind him, holding an infant, was getting restless as he waited for an answer.

"He's not here," the nurse told Finn. She looked past him and towards the woman with the infant.

Finn shook his head.

"What do you mean by he's not here?" Finn asked. "Was he discharged? Did he die? Did they move him someplace?"

"I can see that he was here, but now he isn't," the nurse insisted. "If you can give me a few minutes, sir, I can try to find out for you. I need to get to the next person so we can get them on our list. Can you please take a seat and wait?"

Finn clenched his left hand as he felt the anger rise in his throat. He held back from saying what he wanted to say so he wouldn't cause a scene. Instead, he moved over to the side and found an empty seat where he could sit and wait. A quick glance up at the TV showed an episode of Growing Pains, and Finn groaned at the sight of it on the screen.

Finn pulled out his phone and checked to see if there were messages or emails he needed to attend to. Susannah, his assistant, had ably taken care of everything for him, wiping a lot off his plate for today and early next week if he had an extended stay. He could afford to miss a day or two but missing several days or more might become a problem for Finn and the firm. Finn answered a few emails he had lingering in his inbox and sent some notes to Susannah. Mike Seaver was deep in discussion with his father on the TV screen, something Finn never could relate to. The only in-depth conversation he ever had with Conor was when he told him he was leaving Sandhog's work and was going to school. That talk was more of a yelling match that led to Finn leaving the house as soon as his father left for work that night to drive to Albany and start living with his aunt. The two hadn't spoken a word to each other since then.

His eyes shut, and his head leaning against the wall behind him, Finn ran through scenarios in his head about what meeting up with his father and Liam could be like. Nothing he thought of ended well. He had seen Liam twice since the blow-up. Once Liam drove to Albany on his bike just days after Finn had left for a confrontation on his Aunt Maureen's front lawn. Liam threatened his younger brother several times during the shouting match. The two then ran into each other about three years ago in Saratoga. Finn and a few friends from the firm were out having drinks when Liam and a couple of the other Cosantóir walked in and claimed a booth. Finn had spotted his brother right away and did his best to avoid him, but as Finn and his friends were leaving, Liam spied his wayward brother. Another round of arguing ensued before Finn ushered his friends out before the Cosantóir stepped in and did damage to his buddies and the bar.

"Finn?" a familiar voice startled Finn out of his half-sleep, half-daydreaming state. Finn blinked his eyes open and saw a nurse in blue scrubs standing before him. The woman looked familiar, but he could not immediately place her face.

"Yes?" he answered confusedly.

"It's Cara, Cara Murphy," she said as she pointed at herself. Recognition finally clicked in Finn's brain. Cara was part of the close-knit group of friends he and Darren hung out with while in school. It was then that Finn remembered that she was also always best friends with Siobhan McCarthy. Images and feelings came flooding back to Finn like a tidal wave.

"Cara, how are you?" Finn said. He stood up and hugged Cara briefly. "I didn't know you worked here."

"Well, how could you?" Cara said. "I haven't seen you since you were eighteen. Look at you. You've grown up."

"Yeah, you have too," Finn said awkwardly.

"You're here about your Da," Cara said solemnly.

"Do… do you know something? Where is he?"

"He was down here this morning, but they moved him up to ICU a while ago." Cara looked down at the tablet she was carrying.

"Do you know how he is? What happened? If you have anything you can tell me, Cara, it will help."

Cara brushed the blond hair from in front of her face. She sat down next to Finn.

"I didn't work on his case, but I saw him when he came in. He had head trauma. There was a lot of blood on him, and I think he had some broken bones as well. All I know for sure is that it was life-threatening, and many people were working on him, Finn. I'm sorry. I wish I could tell you more. I can take you up to the ICU if you want."

Finn nodded and whispered, "Thanks," as he followed Cara towards a bank of elevators. The two climbed on and began the ride up in silence.

"How long have you been a nurse?" Finn said, trying to come up with small talk.

"I went to RCC after high school and got my nursing degree, and then my Bachelor's. I've been working here for a few years now. I hear you're a big-shot lawyer now," she said with a bit of a smile.

"Hardly a big-shot." Finn played down his work, something he never did, especially with a woman. "Who told you that?"

"Oh, I go over to Darren's every now and then on the weekends when I'm off. He likes to brag about you when he can. There are still a few of us around from high school."

Finn considered asking about Siobhan, but the elevator came to a stop, and the doors slid open before he could get the words out. Cara slipped out first and waved for Finn to follow her down the hall to the left. A few steps later, they had reached the desk for the ICU ward. Cara smiled at one of the nurses behind the desk.

"Ellen, I have one of Mr. O'Farrell's sons here with me," she began. "Do you know what room he is in?"

"He's in 614," Ellen indicated, "but I think there is someone in there with him right now. You'll have to wait in the waiting room until you can go in. You aren't going to give me the same trouble your brother and the others have, will you?"

"No ma'am," Finn answered as he put on his manners. "I'm just here to check on my father."

"Thank you," she sighed. "Maybe you can talk some sense into the rest of them. I keep having to go down there to control things. The next time I'll have security come up to get rid of the group. The waiting room is just down the hall on the right. Your father's room is right across from it. You'll have to gown up before you can go in there. It's precautionary, so you don't bring anything in that might give him an infection."

"Do you know what happened?" Finn asked Ellen.

"You might want to wait to speak to one of the doctors," Ellen replied. "Dr. Wright should be around in a little bit. I'll let her know you are down there."

"Thank you," Finn nodded. Finn turned to Cara. "Thanks for your help, Cara."

"No problem at all," Cara answered. "How long will you be in town for?"

"I'm not sure just yet," Finn told her. "At least through the weekend. We'll see how things progress."

"Well, take my cell number," Cara said as she grabbed a pad of sticky notes from the desk and jotted down her number. "If you need anything, or want to get together, just let me know."

"Thanks, I might do that."

Finn stuffed the note into his back pocket and walked down the hall towards the waiting room. He already heard the ruckus coming from the area, letting him know that the Cosantóir had taken up residence. Finn stepped into the doorway and looked in. As soon as he was there, the loud talking came to an end. The two men sitting on the couch along the far wall stared at Finn, causing the man with his back to the doorway to stop speaking and turn around. Chills ran through Finn as he recognized Liam. Even though Finn was an adult now, he felt Liam looked more immense than ever. Liam's black hair had flecks of gray in it, and it was down near his shoulders. His beard showed some gray as well, and his blue eyes were just as piercing as Finn recalled. If anything, Liam was more muscular than Finn remembered. Upon first look, Finn saw that Liam didn't recognize him. It wasn't long before Liam put it together, however.

"Well, the prodigal son has returned," Liam spat out, fashioning his brogue for extra emphasis. Liam spun around and began to walk towards the door where Finn had frozen. All the feelings of getting pushed around as a young boy and teenager flooded back to Finn. It wasn't until Liam was in front of Finn that he reacted.

"How are you, Liam?" Finn asked. He attempted with great difficulty to look Liam in the eye. Liam towered over his brother and was even taller with his riding boots on.

"What the feck are you doing here?" Liam huffed.

"Liam, I didn't come here to start trouble," Finn began. "Aunt Maureen called me and said something happened to Dad, so I came down as fast…"

"Oh, how big of ya," Liam scoffed. "You haven't given a rat's ass about the old man for ten years now. Feelin' guilty for the way you took off on him? Well, you can go on back to your rich friends and snooty life upstate, boyo. We don't need ya here."

"Liam, I just want to see him and find out how he is," Finn replied as he looked Liam in the eyes.

"Enough of this shite," Liam barked. "Even if he knew what was going on, he wouldn't want to see ya. He wrote you off the day you walked out the door. Drag yer ass back to Saratoga and good riddance to you."

Liam turned and strode back towards the men on the couch.

"Liam!" Finn yelled. "I'm not leaving. We're not kids anymore. I want to know how he is."

Liam pivoted and grinned at Finn.

"Oh, so you've got a backbone now, do ya? I guess you've forgotten the beatings I would throw ya when you were just a scrawny kid who would run to Ma cryin'. You're not too old that I can't do the same to you right here, right now."

Liam stormed over and was back in front of Finn in just a couple of long strides. He had shed his black leather coat along the way. Finn saw not only the muscular arms and shoulders throughout his youth but also more tattoos than he ever saw before on Liam's body. Finn immediately shifted his weight to prepare to throw a punch, hoping if he got a good one in first, it would be enough to stun Liam and give Finn the advantage.

Liam growled as he readied his right fist and reared back, only to be intercepted. An older man stepped in front of Finn, grabbed Liam's right forearm, and twisted it so it was behind Liam's back in no time at all. He pinned Liam up against the doorframe and held him there.

"Do you want to get us all busted now, you eejit?" the old man said as he pushed Liam.

"Give me a break, Preacher," Liam said as he struggled. "It's not like the kid doesn't have it coming."

"Your Da's across the hall fightin' for his life, and you're doing this nonsense. You're supposed to be a leader, Liam. Time to step up and act like one."

The old man shoved Liam back into the waiting room towards the other two of the Cosantóir who had risen from the couch and were ready to intervene. The elder gent turned to Finn and smiled.

Recognition flashed across Finn's mind as he looked at the man called Preacher.

"Cillian?" Finn said quietly.

"Nice to see you, Finn," Cillian stated. Even though Cillian was Finn's father's age, he looked in fantastic shape. Finn recalled Cillian Meehan from his childhood. He was Conor's best friend through thick and thin and worked with Conor as a Sandhog. The story always was that Cillian had been a Catholic priest in his younger days but gave it up. Conor called Cillian Preacher, and Cillian was the one man Conor trusted most and listened to.

Cillian rubbed his right hand over his shaved head before he turned back to Liam.

"Your brother has every right to be here," Cillian offered. "Let him go see his father in peace."

"What the hell for, Preacher?" Liam yelled. "So he can ease his guilty conscience? We've lived fine for ten years without him being around."

"It's fine, Cillian," Finn added. "I knew this was a bad idea."

"You're damn right it was," Liam told his brother.

"Shut your mouth, or I'll shut it for you," Cillian yelled to Liam.

A security guard appeared in the doorway.

"That's enough, now," the guard said. He scanned the room and saw all the large men around him and spoke into the radio on his shoulder.

"I need some guards up to ICU, now," he radioed.

"We've had lots of complaints. You guys are going to have to go. All of you," the guard ordered. Finn could see the guard was nervous and was slowly moving his hand down to his belt where his weapons were. Finn prayed the guard wouldn't make the mistake of trying to go for one.

"We're just on our way out, sir," Cillian said calmly. "But this young man is on his way over to see his father." Cillian moved Finn along out the doorway and over towards his father's room. He left Finn standing there while he herded Liam and the other club members out of the waiting room.

"Let's go, boys," Cillian remarked. The two bikers in the room left as soon as Cillian told them to, while Liam cast his glare from the security guard to Cillian to Finn before he moved at all. Finn knew his brother was trying to figure out how he could inflict some harm on someone before he left the room.

Liam slid out of the waiting room past the guard, who stood nearly a foot shorter than Liam. Liam laughed heartily as he stared down at the man before he went over and placed himself in front of Finn.

"Make your visit quick, little brother," Liam said through his gritted teeth. "Do you want me to wait downstairs for ya? I can hold your hand and walk you to your car."

"Do what you want, Liam," Finn told his brother. "You want to meet me outside later, that's fine. I'll meet you anywhere you want."

"Ha!" Liam laughed. "Don't waste your energy, Finn. Unless you want an adjoining room to Da's. He wouldn't want that anyway. Better you just leave before you wind up in a ditch somewhere."

"Move!" Cillian insisted, grabbing Liam by the arm and pushing him towards the others down the hallway.

"Go see your father, Finn," Cillian insisted. "It might not seem like it, but he'll know you're there."

Cillian marched Liam down the hall, leaving the security guard to release a loud exhale as they went. Two

other guards appeared out of the elevator. They moved
quickly aside as the Cosantóir members filled the now-
empty elevator car.

"I'm not going to have trouble with you, am I?"
the guard said shakily to Finn.

"No, I'm just here to see my father. I promise, no
trouble."

"You know those guys?" The guard asked as the
other guards joined.

"Sort of," Finn replied. "One of them is my
brother."

"That big dude?" the guard said with shock. "He
sure doesn't look like you."

"We aren't much alike," Finn agreed.

Finn walked into the room, marked 614, and saw
an outer space that led to where his father was. There was
a list of protocols to follow before entering the room,
including putting on a gown, gloves, mask, hat, and shoe
covers and then disposing of everything in the bin when
leaving. Visits were not to be more than 20 minutes at a
time, and the room was watched with cameras.

Finn quickly slipped into the blue gown, covered
his sneakers, and put the cap and gloves on before putting
on the mask. He took a deep breath before entering his
father's ICU room. As soon as he went in, he was
inundated by sounds and smells. Even with all the
machines beeping and whirring and the sterile smell that
seemed to permeate the air, Finn could only focus on the
figure of his father in the bed. Finn knew it was Conor
but seeing him in that state made him believe it had to be
someone else. Conor looked frail and vulnerable, nothing
like the man Finn had grown up with. Tubes and wires
connected all over Conor's body, monitoring everything
about him. As Finn drew closer to the bed, he saw that
Conor's face was severely bruised, with his right eye
swollen shut. Bandages covered much of Conor's scalp,

and a splint supported his left arm. The tubes down Conor's throat helped him breathe, and Finn could hear every time the automated machines came on to check blood pressure and oxygen levels or when they moved to dispense medicine.

Finn dragged one of the two chairs in the room over to sit next to his father. He struggled to think of what to do or say. Mixed emotions raged inside Finn. He was angry not just for how Conor had treated him most of his life but indignant that Finn had to come back home under these circumstances and not better ones. Deep inside, Finn was scared as well.

He leaned close to his father and whispered, "Da?" as he slipped back to what he was like as a child.

The door to the room swooshed open and startled Finn. The gowned-up figure stood at the end of the bed, holding a tablet.

"You can keep talking," the figure assured. "He likely can hear everything that is going on."

"No, it's okay... I just wanted to see him for a minute," Finn explained.

"Are you the other son?" the figure asked. "The nurses told me you just arrived. I'm Dr. Wright. I'm part of the team working on your father."

"I'm Finn... Finn O'Farrell," Finn told the doctor. "Can you tell me anything about what happened or his condition?"

"We don't know all the details about what happened," the doctor explained. "Apparently, there was an accident at the worksite over in Sloatsburg. They are putting in some new water tunnels, and I guess your father is part of the project. He was down below when some machinery slipped out of place and struck him. It knocked him off the platform he was on and dragged him to the bottom. Honestly, I don't know how he survived the fall. It had to be almost 30 feet. He fractured his arm, his ribs, dislocated a knee, and suffered severe head trauma. The swelling around his brain is dangerous, and one of his lungs collapsed, so we put him in the coma and on the ventilator."

The facts of the situation overwhelmed Finn.

"Do you know what the prognosis is?" Finn inquired. Part of him had no desire to hear the answer.

"It's too early to tell right now. There are a lot of factors in play, with so many things going on. You need to know that once we placed him in the coma and on the ventilator, there's no guarantee that he's ever coming back. I tried to explain that to your brother earlier, but he was… well, let's say he was adamant about his feelings regarding the situation. I wish I could tell you something more. We may know more in a day or two."

Finn just nodded while he stared at his father.

"Is there anything else I can answer for you or do for you?" Dr. Wright asked.

"No, thanks, doctor," Finn said without looking over at her. "Can I just stay with him for a bit longer?"

"Sure," Dr. Wright noted. "Take your time. We'll monitor him and watch him all night. I'll leave my card on the table outside if you need to get in touch about anything. If you leave me your number, I can contact you if anything…" Dr. Wright caught herself before she could say what Finn assumed was "happens."

"If anything changes," she completed.

"Thank you," Finn replied. "I'll leave my card out there. I'm staying in the area at least for the weekend."

Dr. Wright departed, leaving Finn alone with his father again.

Finn sat back in the creaky chair. He tried to think of something, anything to say to his father, but no words came. He sat silently, the beeps echoing off the walls around the two of them.

6

Siobhan looked at her watch quickly and saw it was nearly 6:45. The afternoon had been a frenzy of activity, with Ernie working and finally getting the air conditioning operating so that everyone could be comfortable for the night. Siobhan made sure there were meals available and pushed one of the old TVs they had on carts to the back so that children could watch one of the movies available if they wanted. She then rushed back to her office to throw her dress on before the car would get there to take her to meet Gavin.

Siobhan had just finished slipping the dress over her head and zipped up the back when Tracy walked in, giving her a wolf whistle.

"Wow, you have legs!" Tracy commented sarcastically. "Who knew?"

"Thanks," Siobhan answered. "I do wear dresses now and then."

"Not in the office you don't," Tracy noted.

"I just want to look decent, is all," Siobhan told Tracy as she stepped into a pair of white heels she kept in the office. "What do you think?" Siobhan turned around slowly so Tracy could see her from all angles.

"Gavin will pay attention to you for sure," Tracy said, nodding towards the cleavage Siobhan was showing.

"Ugh," Siobhan groaned as she tried to pull the dress up a bit for more modesty. "I don't want him staring at my chest while I'm talking financials."

"I don't think you have much of a choice with him," Tracy added snarkily.

Siobhan heard the intercom on her desk phone beep.

"Ms. McCarthy?" Benny's voice crackled. "You have a ride here waiting for you?"

"Yes, Benny," Siobhan said. "I'll be right out."

Siobhan locked her office door, and Tracy followed alongside her as the two walked towards the entrance.

"Why are you still here?" Siobhan asked Tracy as she placed her cellphone in her purse.

"I'm just waiting for the last family to arrive before I turn everything over to the night shift," Tracy answered. "I'll be on my way out after that. Doug and I are taking the kids to the movies later."

"Okay, have a good time," Siobhan smiled. "I'll let you know how things go. Call me if we need anything. Any excuse I can have to get out of dinner after I make my pitch will work."

"I'll text you at 8:15 before we head into the movie, so you have your excuse," Tracy laughed.

"Perfect!"

Siobhan nodded at Benny so he would open the door. He undid the locks and pulled the heavy door open.

"Want me to walk you out?" Benny asked as he looked over towards the gray limo idling in the parking lot with a gentleman standing by the driver-side door.

"I think I'm okay, Benny," Siobhan reassured. "Thanks."

Siobhan paced over to the waiting car where Perry, Gavin's longtime driver, stood.

"Hi, Perry," Siobhan said with a smile.

"Good evening, Ms. McCarthy," Perry added politely as he pulled the passenger door open.

Siobhan settled into the luxury back seat and saw a bar choice available laid out for her.

"Help yourself to a drink if you would like, Miss," Perry said as he sat at the wheel. "Mr. Elliott said to make sure you have whatever you want."

"That's kind of you, Perry, but a bottle of water is all I need," Siobhan answered as she grabbed a bottle and twisted it open.

The ride to RP Prime was short and uneventful, and the sight of a limo pulling up in front of the entrance turned more than a few heads of the patrons walking in and out. Even the valets noticed that Perry leaped out to open Siobhan's door before one of the young valets came over to do it.

"Enjoy your meal, Miss," Perry said with a smile and a nod.

"Thank you," she answered politely as she made her way up the stone steps.

The RP Prime was a restaurant that Siobhan never went to. It was well beyond the budget she had for meals, but Gavin Elliott frequented this kind of place and liked to let people know he did so. Siobhan walked up to the greeter's podium and was met by an impeccably dressed young woman. Siobhan felt like she was under great scrutiny suddenly as her hands nervously smoothed out her floral dress.

"Can I help you?" the woman asked. Siobhan detected a hint of disdain in her voice.

"Yes, I'm meeting someone here at seven," Siobhan said nervously as she craned her neck to look around.

"Well, do you have a reservation?" the woman asked.

"Yes... I mean, I think he does... I'm meeting Gavin Elliott..."

"Oh, you're Mr. Elliott's guest!" the woman exclaimed. Her demeanor changed dramatically. "Please, follow me. Mr. Elliott has a regular table. He's been expecting you."

Siobhan followed the woman through a maze of tables and rooms and up a staircase until they walked through a curtained area and into one of the small catering rooms that existed. There, next to the bay window, sat Gavin at an elegant table. As soon as he spied Siobhan enter the room, he stood up and smiled.

Siobhan heard her heels nervously click across the wood floor until they reached the table.

"Siobhan," Gavin beamed. "I'm so glad you made it. Thank you, Monica," Gavin noted to the hostess. Monica smiled and nodded.

"Enjoy your meal," Monica replied before departing the room.

Siobhan heard soft classical music playing over the sound system as she went to sit down. Before she could even pull out the chair, a member of the wait staff was there to get it for her, surprising her. As soon as she sat, her water glass was filled for her, and a menu appeared as if from nowhere into her hands.

"Good evening, Miss," the waiter said with charm. "My name is Carl. I'll be waiting on you this evening. Is there anything I can get you from the bar?"

"Oh, no, water is just fine for me, thank you," Siobhan answered.

"Are you sure?" Gavin added. "They make some fantastic cocktails here. Perhaps a Cosmo?"

"No, really, I'm fine," Siobhan insisted.

"I'll take another Manhattan, Carl," Gavin ordered, lifting his empty glass.

"Right away, sir," Carl said with a bow before he scurried out of the room.

Siobhan gazed around the room at the décor. It was the fanciest restaurant she had been to in many years.

"This is your regular table?" Siobhan asked, sipping her water.

"Well, no, not quite," Gavin answered. "My regular table is downstairs in the main dining room. When you agreed to meet me, I asked for something a bit more private. They had this catering room open, so I took all the tables so we could be alone."

Nerves fluttered through Siobhan's stomach at Gavin's reply.

"That seems a bit excessive, don't you think?" Siobhan said, gulping more water. "I mean, it's just a business meeting, Gavin."

"Well, it doesn't have to all be about business, Siobhan. We can relax, have a fine meal, and get to know each other a bit better."

"I guess..." Siobhan added with hesitation. "But I really want to talk more about the funding we need..."

Carl reappeared to interrupt, placing a Manhattan in front of Gavin.

"Can I answer any questions you may have about the menu?" Carl said. "Perhaps you would like an appetizer to start? We have an excellent selection of East or West Coast oysters this evening."

"Oh, I haven't really had a chance to look at anything yet," Siobhan said in a rush. She picked up the menu to look it over.

"There's no hurry," Gavin said, pushing Siobhan's menu down so he could look at her. "Carl, can you bring the steak tartare and a selection of oysters? Whatever the chef thinks are the best tonight."

Siobhan tried to refrain from frowning at the idea of watching Gavin eat raw steak and then suck down oysters, neither of which she was a big fan of.

"And bring a bottle of the Beringer Private Reserve Cabernet as well. 2013."

"Right away, sir," Carl exclaimed before rushing off again.

"You will love the Beringer," Gavin insisted. "It's exceptional."

"I'm not much of a wine drinker," Siobhan insisted. "Gavin, can we talk about the funding now?"

Gavin swirled his Manhattan in his right hand while looking at Siobhan. He had started looking at her cascading red hair and green eyes, but, as Siobhan observed and expected, his leer came to rest as soon as it reached her cleavage.

"Of course, Siobhan," Gavin said with a calm, casual grin.

"Great," she said, putting down her water glass only to have it immediately refilled by one of the busboys who appeared and disappeared like a ninja.

"I didn't bring the numbers with me or anything, but I have emailed them to you several times. I hope you have had a chance to look at them. You see, we're going to have a shortfall this year with the state cutting back on funding, and we really need some repair work and renovations done, along with funding for more staff. I know it seems like a lot to ask, but I know you have come through for us in the past, and I'm sure you saw in my charts…"

Siobhan had rushed everything out of her mouth before looking over at Gavin to see he was casually sipping his cocktail and looking out the bay window at the impending sunset.

"Gavin? Did you hear me?"

"Yes, yes… I heard. You need money," Gavin replied.

"Well, my research and work support our need. The charts indicate…"

"I'm sure they do, Siobhan."

"You're sure?" Siobhan asked indignantly. "Have you ever looked at them? I sent them three times, starting months ago."

"Honestly… no, I haven't looked at them," Gavin admitted. "I'm sure my staff has at some point, though."

Siobhan inhaled deeply to calm herself.

"Then why are we even having this conversation? If you have no idea what I'm talking about, how can you decide anything?"

"Siobhan, I will look at the numbers, I promise. And I'll consider them closely and what my advisers add to it. Lots of organizations are looking for handouts right now with the Governor slashing things again. I must think about my projects and investors as well. We have so many things in the fire right now that have potential…"

"I'm not looking for a handout, Gavin," Siobhan said, raising her voice. "Our group does essential work in the county, helping women and families who need it most. Your donation, not a handout, makes a difference to thousands of people. If you had no knowledge of what I wanted to talk about or any intention of having an honest discussion, then what am I doing here?"

"You messaged me and insisted we get together," Gavin told her. "I never promised anything. I did, however, look forward to seeing you and spending time with you. So, now that business is done, let's get down to choosing dinner and enjoying each other's company."

"I think I've lost my appetite," Siobhan said with disgust. She tossed the napkin that had been in her lap onto the table.

Carl appeared with a silver platter holding the plate of steak tartare on crostini along with a plate of a dozen assorted oysters just as Siobhan rose from the table.

"Enjoy your meal," Siobhan said as she stormed across the room and out the curtain to go down the stairs. She hurried her way out, trying to find her way through the maze to get back to the entrance. Siobhan shoved open the front door, nearly knocking over an older couple in the process.

"I'm so sorry," Siobhan said as she went down the steps. She checked left and right and spotted the limo parked just to the right of the entrance. She marched her way over towards the car, where Perry was seated in the driver's seat, listening to Phil Collins.

"Perry," Siobhan said as she caught her breath, "can you take me back to my office, please?"

"Of course, Miss," Perry said as he jumped out of the car to open the passenger door. Before he could get the door open, Gavin appeared, running down to catch Siobhan.

"Siobhan, wait," Gavin pleaded. "I'm sorry. Please, come back inside and have dinner."

"I thought this would be a legitimate meeting, Gavin, not a dinner date."

"I'm sorry if I misled you, but getting you to agree to come out socially seemed impossible. Can't we do a little of both? Let's forget dinner and just go back to my home and relax, and we can talk there."

"I don't think so," Siobhan offered. "Now, can Perry take me back to my office, or should I call for a ride?" Siobhan began scrolling through her phone to contact a ride service.

Gavin nodded to Perry, and Perry opened the door for Siobhan to slide into the car. Perry closed the door, and Siobhan stared ahead, not even looking at the tinted window where she could hear a muffled Gavin asking her to roll down the window. Perry climbed into the driver's seat while Gavin was still talking.

"Should I leave, Miss?" Perry asked.

"Please do," Siobhan answered as the car pulled away, leaving Gavin standing there.

****

The limo arrived back at A Safe Place, and Siobhan went straight to her car. She plopped herself in the driver's seat and looked at her phone before starting

the engine. She saw several text message pleas from
Gavin asking to reply to him or reconsider. Siobhan
ignored those and the two phone messages he left
without even listening to them. The evening disastrously
capped off the whole day. Siobhan knew that without the
money, the organization was perilously close to losing
everything. There was little available for her to fall back
on, and if A Safe Place closed its doors, it would be a
tremendous loss for the community.

After Siobhan finished deleting all the messages
from Gavin, she heard one from Cara.

"Vonnie, I'm not sure where you are or what you
are doing tonight. My shift ends at 8. Meet me over at
Millie's if you can. We need to talk!"

At first, Siobhan thought about just skipping the
whole thing. Going to a crowded bar on a Friday night
after the day she had was not high on her to-do list.
However, Cara sounded excited, and Siobhan
remembered Conor O'Farrell. Cara might have some
more information regarding what happened and what his
condition was. Siobhan did want to know how he was,
and meeting her best friend for a drink right now might
be just what she needed to help lift her spirits.

****

Finn left the hospital after spending time with his
father. Finn really didn't know what to do or say, and he
spent more time just listening to all the noises in the room
than anything else. Part of him thought some miracle
might occur and that Conor's eyes would fly open
because he sensed his son in the room. The rational side
of Finn's brain knew better. After about ten minutes,
Finn exited, shed all his PPE equipment, and picked up
Dr. Wright's business card to keep in his pocket. He
made sure to leave his card there for her as well before
he departed.

The evening had settled in, and the muggy air quickly enveloped Finn when he walked out of the hospital. He scanned the area to see if Liam or any of the Cosantóir were still hanging around waiting for him. There were no signs of any bikes in the visitor's lot, and Finn made his way to his car to head out.

Figuring out where he was going was another issue. He could swing over to Suffern and get a room at the hotel. He also remembered that Maeve had given him the keys to his father's place if he wanted to go there instead. Finn, however, didn't want to be alone. Most of the time, being by himself was something he thrived on. Tonight was a different story.

Finn drove up 17M north through Sloatsburg. He drove by Rhodes Tavern, one of the few local places that bikers did frequent. As his car idled at the stoplight, Finn looked over to the smaller parking lot where many of the bikers parked. He could see the row of five Harleys, all with emerald green colors on them, letting him know the Cosantóir was there living it up before they made their way back to the Hog House. Finn didn't want to tempt fate any further and instead drove on, staying on 17M. There were many signs all through Sloatsburg and Tuxedo that things were changing. Construction was underway on many projects all along the roadway and right up to Harriman. The area was a far cry from what it was when Finn was younger, and his parents moved up from Brooklyn to be part of the Irish enclave that Harriman and Monroe had become. Sandhogs fit right in with the firemen and police officers that dominated the neighborhoods at that time, all striving to give their families a different life from what they knew in New York City.

The one place Finn knew he could find a friendly face was at Millie Malone's. He drove to River Road and saw that the parking lot was quite full. Darren had a packed house tonight, with music blaring from the building as Finn walked up to the front door. Finn was surprised to see Darren had a couple of bouncers positioned at the entrance, and he paid his five-dollar cover charge to get in and tried to make his way to the bar.

Finn spotted Darren at the far end of the bar and worked his way through the crowd to get there. He waved and got Darren's attention, who pointed to an empty stool at the corner. The seat had a small white cocktail napkin draped over it that read "Reserved." Finn laughed as he picked up the napkin and sat down.

"How did you know I was coming?" Finn asked loudly to get through the din of the music.

"Where else are you going around here?" Darren laughed as he began to pour a Guinness.

"Damn, Darren, you're crowded!" Finn said with disbelief.

"Hey, this isn't the old codger bar my Dad ran anymore," Darren said proudly.

"If Millie heard you with a Southern Rock band in here, she might have a few choice words for you," Finn laughed.

"True enough," Darren replied. "But the only time I get a crowd for Irish music is around St. Paddy's. I'd like to think she'd understand the business end of it, you know."

Finn took a swig of his Guinness and swiveled his chair, so he was facing the band. They were doing a cover of "Statesboro Blues," and Finn was impressed at how much like Gregg Allman the lead singer sounded and looked. Suddenly, a body popped up right in front of Finn.

"You made it!" the girl exclaimed. Finn took a moment to recognize the girl before realizing it was Annie from Dunkin' Donuts. She was dressed a far cry from the uniform she wore at work. She was wearing a black spaghetti strap crop top that showed off the belly ring she had, which led down to the short skirt she was wearing. No longer wearing the obligatory corporate visor, Finn got a good look at her long, curly black hair as it bounced on her shoulder blades. Her skin was a beautiful caramel color, and she wore just a hint of perfume that got the attention of any male near her.

"I made it," Finn added, not knowing what else to say.

"Do you think you could get your buddy's attention for me?" Annie said, leaning close to Finn so that her hair brushed lightly against him.

Finn dutifully waved to grab Darren's attention, and he smiled widely as he arrived.

"What can I get ya?" Darren asked, turning up his brogue just a bit for his audience.

"Can I get a couple of mojitos?" Annie asked, swaying to the music playing.

"You got it, darlin'," Darren answered as he moved off to make the cocktails.

"Uhhh, are you sure you don't talk like that anymore?" Annie said, looking at Finn.

"Sorry," Finn replied with a shrug of his shoulders.

Darren came back down, holding two glasses, and handed them to Annie.

"That's $16," Darren told her.

"I got it," Finn interrupted, handing Darren a twenty.

"Well, thank you, kindly," Annie added, batting her eyes at Finn. "Why don't you come over and sit with my friends and me? We're in that booth over there," Annie indicated by pointing her elbow. There were two other girls in the booth, both of whom looked as young as Annie.

"I just might do that," Finn said. "Let me just catch up with my friend here for a bit, okay?"

"Don't wait too long," Annie said with a wink. Finn watched as Annie made her way through the crowd, weaving in and out, holding her drinks and swaying her hips.

"Looks like you made a friend," Darren laughed.

"I guess so," Finn answered, sipping his beer.

"Don't sit here too long, Finn," Darren advised. "She's a wily one who can change her mind fast. If you want company tonight, get over there."

"I'm not so sure I want company tonight," Finn told him.

"How'd it go with your Da?"

"He looks pretty bad. And then I ran into Liam at the hospital, and that didn't help much either," Finn added as he finished his Guinness.

Darren grabbed the empty glass and turned to start another one for Finn.

"I'm sorry, brother," Darren told him. "If you want, I can take a ride down with you tomorrow morning."

"Thanks. I'd appreciate that."

Darren slid the freshly poured Guinness in front of Finn. Finn turned and saw Annie waving him to the table.

"Ah, the siren is calling you to sea," Darren said.

"I see that. God, Darren, she makes me feel like an old man, though."

"Cripes, Finn, you're only twenty-eight! Get over yourself and go have some laughs. I'll come to check on you later."

Finn rose from his barstool, and Darren placed the "Reserved" sign back down on the chair. Finn made it to the booth and smiled at the ladies there.

"Good evening, ladies," Finn said, trying to recall his brogue a bit. All three girls lit up with smiles.

"This is Becky and Tamara," Annie said, pointing at the other two girls at the table. "This is Finn," Annie gaped.

Annie patted the vinyl cushion next to her, and Fin slid into the booth. No sooner was he sitting there when Annie was draping her arm on his shoulder.

"Slainte," Finn said as he raised his glass. The girls all laughed and clinked glasses with Finn.

****

Siobhan parked her car at the far end of the lot, where there were a few empty spaces. She strolled to the entrance of Millie Malone's, watching as a couple of college kids enjoying their last weekend before going back to school stumbled past. One halted and promptly ran for the dumpster and went behind it while his friend struggled along. It wasn't long before Siobhan heard retching sounds and then the words "Dude, gross!"

The bar was crowded even more than usual on a Friday night, and Siobhan had to wend her way through the high-top tables to the bar where she caught a glimpse of Cara. She moved next to her friend and tapped her on the shoulder, getting Cara's attention while she sipped her drink.

"Hey, you!" Cara yelled, giving Siobhan a hug. "Where have you been? I wasn't sure you were even coming."

"It's been a shitty day, Cara, from start to finish," Siobhan said. Luckily, the person next to Cara relinquished their seat so Siobhan could sit. Siobhan got the attention of the female bartender nearest to them so she could order a drink.

"Guinness, please," Siobhan ordered.

"I can't believe you drink that stuff," Cara remarked.

"We both grew up with it, Cara. I can't believe you don't."

"I'll take my rum and Coke every time. Besides, the guys see you drinking a Guinness, and…" Cara cut herself off.

"And what?" Siobhan asked.

"Well, honestly, Vonnie, they think you're not girly… there, I said it." Cara went back to sipping her drink.

"Any guy who's gonna worry about me drinking a Guinness instead of some frou-frou drink isn't worth the time of day anyway. If they want a girly girl, I'm not it, and proud of it!"

"I don't know; you look girly girl right now," Cara commented. "Look at you wearin' a dress and all. What's the occasion?"

"Ugh, don't remind me about that," Siobhan lamented. "I had a meeting with Gavin Elliott that I thought would be about funds for A Safe Place. Instead, I think he was hoping that I would just go with him."

"You should know better when dealing with that one," Cara remarked as she drained her drink. "He's been a tool since high school and was always trying to get in your pants."

"He's mostly harmless," Siobhan told her friend. "Honestly, I don't know where else I can go for the money we need. I've tried everything."

"Let's not worry about that now," Cara said. "I have other things to talk to you about."

"That's right," Siobhan answered. "How's Conor?"

"Not good, I'm afraid. The doctors put him in a coma. He has a severe head injury, fractured ribs, a broken arm, and other broken bones. They are worried about internal bleeding and brain swelling. I didn't get up to see him. He's in the ICU."

Cara got another rum and Coke and lightly sipped and then coughed a bit.

"That's not all, though," Cara told her friend.

"There's something worse than that?" Siobhan asked.

"No, not worse, but something you should know. Finn is back in town."

Siobhan sat stunned for a moment.

"Finn? Finn O'Farrell?" Siobhan said, aghast. "How do you know? Did you see him?"

"He came to the hospital to see Conor. I only talked to him for a minute before I brought him upstairs. I heard there was a problem with Liam up there too. They had to call security."

"I'm sure there was if the two of them were together. I can't believe Finn came back." Siobhan's words drifted off, and she sat silently for a moment.

"You know you want to ask," Cara pointed out.

"Ask what?"

"How he looked," Cara said with a smile.

"Don't be ridiculous," Siobhan remarked. "That was a long time ago, Cara. Ten years at least. I'm sure he's long moved on, just as I have."

"Have you now?" Cara asked. "Well, even though you didn't ask, I can tell you he looks fantastic - Blond hair, blue eyes, all grown up. When I hugged him, you could tell he works out every day. Lots of muscle."

"You hugged him?" Siobhan said with a hint of envy.

"I think you're turning as green as your eyes, Vonnie," Cara laughed. "Of course, I hugged him. He's an old friend of mine I haven't seen in ten years. We were all as thick as thieves, you know."

Cara lifted her drink and stopped when it came to her lips.

"Shite," she said with a hushed tone.

"What? Did you swallow an ice cube, or are you fawning over the Gregg Allman singer again? He's probably old enough to be your Da," Siobhan laughed.

"No, Vonnie," Cara whispered, leaning into Siobhan. "He's here. Right now. Finn is over in the far corner."

Siobhan placed her pint glass on the bar and tried to take a subtle look through the crowd. There he was, plain as day. Finn O'Farrell was sitting in a booth, a girl draped all over him. Siobhan sat utterly still for what seemed like an eternity before it happened.

They locked eyes on each other.

7

To Siobhan, it felt like Finn looked right through her. There wasn't a hint of recognition on his face that she could detect, and with the young girl practically sitting in his lap, she didn't feel surprised. Disappointment, hurt, and anger all overcame her at once. She not only grew up with Finn, but they had been closer than she had ever been to anyone else all through high school and right up until the day Finn left. *That's right. Finn left me,* Siobhan thought to herself. *Then why am I feeling so jealous that this girl is all over him?*

Finn and Siobhan hadn't been a couple in ten years. Siobhan had her share of boyfriends since then and more than a few men who would love to be with her now, and she knew it. But there was that nagging feeling in the pit of her stomach that she just could not shake. She had spent a long time getting over Finn when she was eighteen, and knowing he had family and friends still in town didn't make things easier at first. She learned to deal with it better once she realized Finn had no intention of returning to Harriman. And yet here he was, across a crowded bar. Surely he had seen her just as she saw him.

Siobhan tried not to watch as the girl ran her fingers over Finn's chest, giggling like a schoolgirl, but it became impossible for her to look away. An eerie silence crept over Siobhan, and she blocked out everything in the room. Part of her just wanted to look away, while another part secretly wished for him to stand up and walk over to her.

Then it happened – Finn got up from the corner booth. The knot in Siobhan's stomach got tighter as his gaze came her way once again, and he took steps in her direction. Siobhan sat straighter on the barstool, and her mind worked as to what she would say when Finn came over. She looked down at her beer, concentrating on the bits of foam floating in her glass as she prepared to look up at him when he arrived in front of her. The problem was he hadn't come. Siobhan glanced over at Cara and could see she was staring out at the dance floor.

When Siobhan looked up, she saw Finn dancing with the girl he was with. The girl had to put her arms around Finn's waist since she wasn't tall enough to get around his shoulders. Siobhan caught a glimpse as they turned, seeing the bare midriff of the girl as she stretched up to whisper something into Finn's ear and laugh.

Siobhan grasped her pint glass and downed what was left of her Guinness before forcefully putting the empty glass on the bar. The noise was louder than expected, even with the crowd and music, and it certainly got Darren's attention. Darren spun on his heels and strode over to Cara and Siobhan.

"Refills, ladies?" he asked.

"I think I'm done, Darren," Siobhan muttered.

"Really? It's still early, Vonnie," Cara added. "Come on. Don't let this bother you."

"Don't let what bother you? Someone giving you a hard time?" Darren asked as he leaned in.

Cara used her head to direct Darren's gaze towards the dance floor.

"Oh," Darren said, recognizing the issue. "Yeah, Finn's home. He came in earlier."

"Jesus, Darren, you could have given us a heads up," Cara scolded.

"I didn't think it would be a big deal. I'm a little busy back here, Cara," Darren said as he waved his hand over the crowd at the bar.

"He didn't come in with her," Darren noted to Siobhan, who was still watching the couple dance.

"I don't think that makes things better, Darren," Cara added.

Siobhan took a ten out of her purse and placed it on the bar.

"That should cover me," Siobhan told Darren. "Stay if you want, Cara. Enjoy the band. I'm tired."

"You know I'm not takin' your money, Vonnie," Darren insisted as he pushed the money back towards Siobhan.

"Then give it to Maggie," Siobhan said. "I'm sure she's earned it tonight."

Siobhan stood up from her stool and gave Cara a hug.

"I'll talk to you tomorrow," she said in her friend's ear.

Siobhan worked her way to the door without looking back.

****

Finn sat in the corner booth with Annie and her friends, sipping his Guinness and trying to make polite conversation with the girls – he thought of them that way since they seemed much younger than him – that he had nothing in common with. Annie made sure to continually wrap her hands around Finn in some way, whether it was putting a hand on his bicep or his shoulder. Under the table, she repeatedly rubbed her bare legs up against him. Annie even slipped a hand delicately onto his lap once or twice to hold his interest. Each time she did it, she gave him a sly smile.

"So, what do you do, Finn?" Tamara asked as she sucked on the straw in her drink.

"I'm a lawyer," Finn replied with a nod.

"Ooh, a lawyer," Becky added. "A young, good-looking lawyer with an accent like that. How is a guy like you unattached?"

"Don't get any ideas, Becky," Annie said defensively. Annie wrapped her arm around Finn and pulled him close.

The band kicked into a cover of "Wonderful Tonight," and Annie's eyes lit up.

"Come dance with me," Annie said as she climbed over Finn, straddling his lap to get out of the booth. Annie then grabbed Finn's hand and tugged, not taking his pleas against the idea seriously. Before Finn knew it, he was out on the dance floor, trapped among the dozen other couples moving slowly to the song.

Finn dutifully put his hands on Annie's hips as he tried to keep some space between the two of them as they danced. Annie had other ideas and enveloped Finn, pressing her body against him. Her head rested against Finn's chest as they moved.

"I'm not much of a dancer," Finn admitted,

"It's okay," Annie replied. "This is just fine."

After a couple of moves through the crowd, Finn began to get antsy and hoped the song would end soon. Annie saw he was distracted and stood up on her tiptoes to whisper into Finn's ear.

"If I'm boring you, we can leave and go do something more to your tastes," she said with a laugh.

"I think that might be…" Finn caught himself as he spied Darren at the other end of the bar talking to Cara. It took him a second before he noticed the red hair of the woman next to Cara. Finn came to a stop.

"It might be what?" Annie asked, hopefully.

Finn watched as he tried to get a better look with people moving in front of him, blocking his view. When it was clear, he saw the red hair had turned to go toward the door.

"I'm sorry, Annie," Finn offered. "I need to go. I'll see you later."

"Really?" Annie said firmly. "You're gonna leave me in the middle of the dance floor?"

Finn looked back at her and shrugged as he moved toward Cara and Darren.

"Cara," Finn said as he worked through the crowd to her spot at the bar.

"What's up, Finn?" as Cara casually sipped her rum and Coke.

"Was that Siobhan here with you?"

"Yep," she nodded. "She had to go. You can go back over to your groupies."

Finn pulled two twenties from his wallet and left them on the bar for Darren.

"That's for Annie's drinks and Cara's," he told Darren. "I'll call you in the morning."

"Hey, I drink for free here," Cara said, insulted. She picked up one of the twenties and stuffed it into her back pocket.

"Finn, just let her…" Darren said, but by then, Finn was already headed to the exit.

Finn waded through the crowd that tried to get into Millie Malone's before he finally got outside. He scanned the dark parking lot, hoping to catch a glimpse of Siobhan so he could go to her, but the lighting was dim and offered little help. Finn did see several cars leave the lot, but he had no clue which might be hers. He resignedly trudged to his Lexus instead of going back inside and face the wrath of his angry dance partner. He sat in the front seat for a few moments, pondering what to do next.

He thought about asking Cara where Siobhan lived now so he could go to her and see her. Finn knew there was a lot of ground to cover over the last ten years, including why he had left her the way he had without ever looking back. Priming himself for that conversation might take more than Finn had in him after a draining day. As Finn reached into his pocket for his keys, he felt the shamrock fob that Maeve had given him with the key to his father's house. He recalled his promise to her and sent her a quick text to update Maeve on Conor's condition. Maeve replied immediately with thanks and let Finn know that the house was at 33 Shadowmere Road.

Finn had to look at her text reply a couple of times to make sure he had the address correct. He had a general idea of where the house was located and was surprised that his father would live there. Finn slowly made his way up Harriman Heights Road towards Shadowmere. He then drove carefully so he wouldn't miss the turnoff at Sapphire to Shadowmere. He recalled the days when he and Darren would ride their bikes down this way to head out towards the local lakes.

Once on Shadowmere, he crept the car along until he spotted the reflector on the mailbox for 33. He went down the driveway in the darkness until motion lights flooded the area in front of the house, illuminating a large white house with a garage just as oversized. All Finn kept thinking to himself is that Maeve gave him the wrong address, and the police would be behind him at any moment to question him for trespassing.

Finn grasped the fob in his hand and walked warily toward the front door. He slid the key into the lock and turned, and the door opened quickly. He felt for a light switch on the near wall and flipped it on when his hand discovered it, blasting light into the living room.

Finn was awed by what he saw. The house was nicely decorated and in order, not what he was expecting at all. When Maeve first made the offer to Finn, his concern was staying in a dilapidated, unkept home that he would have trouble sleeping in, not a stately place like this. Finn tossed the key on the end table and looked around, going from the living room to the dining room with a large table and chairs set and into the kitchen. He opened the fridge to see that it was well-stocked with healthy choices for food and beverages. It was nothing like what Finn thought Conor would have, and it was far from Finn's experience of what a home was like after his mother passed. It was often cheese sandwiches, PB and J, or ramen for dinner if he was lucky, and the fridge always had more beer in it than anything else.

Finn continued to explore the house, noting the master bedroom downstairs with its private bath. Down the hall from there were double doors that, when Finn tried them, were locked. He slowly moved upstairs and saw three other bedrooms, all made up like they were ready for visitors at any moment. After a look, Finn moved back downstairs and out the kitchen's back door to the patio.

Again, motion lights went on immediately, and the surrounding trees held the glow in so that Finn could walk in the grass down towards the small dock that led out to Shadowmere Lake. A small boat was tied to the pier, awaiting someone to take it out for a ride. A short walk up from the dock area was an in-ground pool and spa, followed by a fenced area housing a tennis court and basketball court.

"Who the hell is this guy?" Finn wondered aloud.

Finn understood that his father likely made a good living now. While pitted with dangers, the work could be a lucrative career—men doing the job as long as his father had easily earned six figures. However, Finn had no recall of his father ever showing any signs of wealth when he was younger, both before and after his mother passed. A hint of resentment crossed his mind when he considered how hard Conor had been on him throughout his life.

Finn crossed back to the house and into the kitchen. He reached into the fridge to grab a bottle of water and then opened the door to the left of the kitchen that led into the garage. Finn turned on the lights, and the overhead fluorescent lights flickered on. The garage space was immense, but it was also well filled with gadgets and toys, namely Conor's motorcycles and car. Three bikes took up space in the garage, all Harleys, with all three of them having the Kelly-green colors of the Cosantóir. One motorcycle was clearly Maeve's since it bore her name on the license plate. There was also a bike covered by a tarp. Finn pulled the canvas off to reveal a 1951 Indian Blackhawk Chief 80 with a sidecar.

Finn was stunned to see the bike, a classic, in pristine condition. The bike looked brand new for something nearly seventy years old, and it was evident that Conor, or someone, had put love, care, and sweat into keeping it at its best. Finn couldn't resist the opportunity to sit on the bike to see what it felt like. The leather had just the slightest give to it, and a glance at the odometer showed the motorcycle barely had over 3,000 miles on it. Finn figured this bike alone cost Conor more than the house the family grew up in.

Finn left the bike uncovered and went back to the house, weariness finally catching up to him. It had been a single whirlwind day, and exhaustion settled in. Finn sat in the recliner in the living room, kicked off his sneakers, and closed his eyes. Thoughts raced through his head as he considered where he was and who he had seen. Finn tried to concentrate on getting some rest and struggled to put images of work, the law firm, Annie, Darren, his brother, and his father out of his head. The only thing he let linger there was the vision of Siobhan.

8

Finn groggily rolled over, and his face turned toward the sunshine streaming through the window. The sunlight elicited a groan from Finn. He immediately turned in the opposite direction so that he faced the doorway instead of the window. A glance in that direction revealed a dog sitting and staring at him. The vision was startling enough, but this was not a tiny chihuahua before him. Instead, it was a stocky, brindle Pit Bull looking Finn in the eyes. Finn jumped back a bit, recoiling so that his head smacked loudly on the wooden headboard.

Finn winced and yelled, "Shit!" causing the dog to move from the doorway closer to the bed. Unsure of what to do, Finn sat up and looked around to see if there was anything nearby he could use to protect himself. The dog inched nearer, panting a bit now before it placed its two front paws up on the bed.

"Easy there," Finn said softly. Finn slid out from beneath the blanket and off the opposite side of the bed nearest the window. Clad in only his boxer briefs, he watched the dog closely to see what its next move might be and what he could do to get out of the room. The dog hopped up on the bed and inched closer to Finn.

"Jameson!" a voice yelled, causing the dog to turn its head. Cillian appeared in the doorway, holding a cup of coffee. "You know you're not supposed to be on the beds. Down!"

Jameson obediently jumped off and stood next to Cillian.

"Sorry about that, Finn," Cillian said as he handed the hot mug to Finn. "He knew someone was here the minute we walked in and set about finding you."

"Is he... friendly?" Finn said tentatively.

"Jameson?" Cillian scoffed. "He's a mush. He looks meaner than hell, and if you made a move on Conor or Maeve, he'd take your arm off, but he's mostly harmless. I'm surprised he didn't jump on you since you look so much like your Da."

"He's not yours?" Finn replied, pulling on a t-shirt from his bag.

"Me? No. He's your father's. They rescued him a couple of years ago. He was a fighting dog, in bad shape, but your Dad worked hard to get him to trust him and nurse him back. I took him yesterday when I heard what happened to Conor. Maeve told me last night that you were staying here, so I thought I would leave him with you."

"I don't think so, Cillian," Finn replied. "I don't know anything about taking care of a dog, and I might only be here for a day or two. I can't believe Dad has a dog. He refused for years to let me have one growing up. He said it was too much trouble, and I wasn't responsible enough, and that he had no time or inclination to have a dog."

"Your Dad isn't the same person you remember, Finn," Cillian spoke. "If you had bothered to come around at all the last few years, you would know that."

Cillian walked out of the room with Jameson dutifully following behind. Finn pulled on a pair of jeans and went after him.

"It's not like he tried to come to see me either, Cillian," Finn shot back.

"Oh, I know it," Cillian agreed as he sat at the kitchen table. "Many times, I told him he should pick up the phone and call you or drive to Saratoga. He knew you were there. Your aunt kept him up to date on you. But he's as stubborn as you are. 'He can come to me,' he would shout. Your father can be a tool when he wants to be."

Cillian pushed a brown paper bag in Finn's direction.

"Sausage and egg sandwich," Cillian remarked. "No cheese."

"Thanks," Finn said hungrily as he snatched the bag. "I can't believe you remember that."

"Ay, I don't forget a hell of a lot of things, you know," Cillian laughed. "I'm on my way down to see your Da with Maeve this morning. Are you coming down?"

"Is Liam going to be there?" Finn asked in between bites of sandwich.

"Most of the club goes for a ride Saturday morning, so he probably won't get there until early in the afternoon or so. It would buy you some time. You two may not have a choice and will have to be civil to each other for a bit, you know. There's no telling how long your father will be in the hospital."

"There's a lot of baggage there. You know that, Cillian," Finn added as he polished off what was left of his sandwich.

"I know it," Cillian nodded. "The three of you have been carrying all this around for way too long. They were both hard on you, Finn, and there's no excusing any of it. 'Let all bitterness and wrath and anger and clamor and slander be put away from you, along with all malice. Be kind to one another, tenderhearted, forgiving one another, as God in Christ forgave you.' Ephesians."

"Don't quote me scripture, Cillian. They made life hell for me," Finn spat back.

"Shouldering all that for the rest of your life serves no good for anyone, Finn. You know better than that. Your mother taught you that."

"Don't…" Finn said as he stood up. He caught himself before his temper got the better of him with Cillian. "Don't bring her into this." Finn worked to slow his breathing now.

"Let's leave it for now and just get down to see your father," Cillian said calmly. "I'm going to pick up Maeve and ride down with her."

Cillian reached into the pocket of his leather jacket and pulled out two sets of keys. "In case you want these."

"What are these?" Finn asked.

"One set are keys to the extra Cosantóir bike in the garage. The other keys are a spare set for the house. You should have them anyway, and I'll give Maeve her keys back."

Finn reached for Maeve's keys on the table and tossed them to Cillian.

"I have my car here," Finn said. "I don't need the bike keys."

"You might decide you want to ride," Cillian offered. "or you might decide you want to come to Hog House, and if they see your car there again, I can't guarantee something won't happen to it. The bike is safer."

"Fine," Finn huffed. He already felt like he was being pushed into the life he worked hard to get away from.

"I'll meet you down there," Cillian said. "You know, it does matter that you're here, Finn."

Cillian walked out the front door, leaving Finn alone in the kitchen with Jameson staring at him. Jameson casually walked over to the spot next to the refrigerator where his empty food dish was and sat there, returning his stare to Finn.

"I get it," Finn sighed. He scouted the lower cabinet, found the bag of dog food, and dutifully filled the bowl for Jameson. Jameson licked his lips and sat obediently, staring at the dish and then back at Finn, waiting for the okay to eat.

"Go ahead," Finn pointed with aggravation, but the dog didn't move.

"Eat!" Finn yelled. Jameson recognized the command and dove into the morsels.

Finn brushed some stray crumbs from his bare chest before going upstairs to finish dressing to go to the hospital.

This day must get better, he thought.

****

Siobhan sat at her small kitchen table, sipping her coffee and staring out the window. She had already texted Cara at the hospital to see if there was any news about Conor's condition, and she anxiously waited for a reply from her friend. Siobhan made sure not to include anything about Finn in her text. However, she was dying to know whether he had asked about her at all or even mentioned to Darren or Cara that they had seen each other.

He had seen me, right? Siobhan thought. *He looked right at me. I didn't imagine that.*

The ringtone of her cell phone startled Siobhan, and she rattled her mug onto the table. She saw a call was coming in from Cara.

"Hey," Siobhan said, trying to be as casual as she could.

"I don't have long to talk, Vonnie," Cara replied. "Conor's condition hasn't changed. No better, no worse. I'll head up there a bit later to check in and see if I can find out anything."

"I... I was thinking about coming down," Siobhan admitted. "I feel like I should stop in and at least see him. Is anyone there yet?"

"I can't say, either way, Vonnie," Cara answered. "There's always a chance you'll run into somebody. Are you okay with that?"

"I'm just going to go in and out. I'll be there a few minutes, tops. Can you… just give me a heads up if you see anybody? I can always delay my visit."

"Siobhan," Cara told her, "I'll text you if I see anyone, but I'm working. I don't know what will happen. I'm sure you can handle it if the Cosantóir is there… or Finn. You know, Vonnie, it's a small town. If Finn is here for even a few days, you are going to run into him at some point."

"Did he say anything about me after I left?" Siobhan asked quietly.

"Come on, Vonnie," Cara sighed. "We're not in the gym locker room anymore where you ask me if he talked about you in study hall. We're all grown-ups now."

Siobhan held the phone silently.

"Yes, he knew you were there," Cara stated. "Does that change anything? I've got to go, Vonnie. Let me know when you get here. If I have a break, I'll meet you. Love you."

"Love you," Siobhan replied as she heard Cara hang up.

Siobhan sat back in her chair and lifted her coffee mug. She took a quick sip before she reached for her keys. She held the keys in her hand before deciding to stand up and leave the apartment to go to the hospital.

Siobhan couldn't decide whether she should speed to get down to the hospital as quickly as possible or go slowly so that whoever might be there would be gone when she got there. After just a few minutes in the car, she put all misgivings aside and just went forward with determination.

"What's going to happen will happen," she resolved as she drove through Sloatsburg. Even this early in the morning, a quick look at Rhodes showed bikes in their bike lot. Still, Siobhan couldn't make out if any had the telltale colors or insignia of the Cosantóir. Everyone in town knew they typically rode on the weekends. Still, Siobhan wondered if they might put that aside with their leader hospitalized and show up en masse at the hospital instead.

Siobhan pulled into the visitor lot and saw no signs of motorcycles anywhere in the near-full lot. She breathed a sigh of relief as she shut off the car and then tapped out a text to Cara to let her know she had arrived. Siobhan paced over to the entrance and got her visitor ID so she could go to the ICU. She listened to the sound of her foot rapidly pat the tile of the elevator as it climbed to the correct floor. Siobhan approached the desk to locate Conor's room and received permission to go see him.

"Is anyone in there right now? I can wait if they are," Siobhan asked the desk nurse.

"No, no one has come up to see him yet today. You're all clear," the nurse smiled.

"Thank you," Siobhan breathed. She walked quickly to Conor's room and looked to get in and out without anyone seeing her there. After gowning up before entering, she slid into the room and gasped when she saw Conor lying there. Siobhan hadn't expected him to look as bad as he did, and she choked up immediately. Siobhan pulled one of the chairs over to Conor's bedside. She gently took his hand, which was battered and bruised from a combination of the fall and the regular injections and needles poked into him.

"Oh, Conor, I am so sorry," she whispered. "If you can hear me, know that I am praying for you."

Siobhan bowed her head and offered up an internal prayer before opening her eyes again.

"Finn came home to see you," Siobhan's voiced wavered. "I… I know he's worried about you. We all just want you to get better so you can come back to us."

Siobhan reached into the front pocket of her jeans and pulled out a silver necklace. The necklace bore the Celtic Shield knot, designed to protect those ill or warriors injured in battle. She placed the chain in Conor's hand and attempted to close his hand around it.

"Let this knot protect you," Siobhan offered.

Conor's hand instinctively closed round the chain and Siobhan's fingers. Tears formed in her eyes as she felt Conor's response to her.

Just then, the door to the ICU room swung open, and a nurse entered, frightening Siobhan and causing her to pull her hand away from Conor's.

"I didn't mean to startle you, honey," the nurse offered. "You could certainly hold his hand. I'm just checking on him." The nurse noticed the hint of the chain dangling from Conor's hand.

"He can't have anything like that in here on his person," the nurse chided. She pried open Conor's fingers to take the necklace away.

"No, wait," Siobhan shouted. "He responded when I put it in his hand. He took hold of it and held my fingers. He knows it's for his protection."

"He was probably just reacting to you touching him, which is good news," the nurse replied. She held the shield knot in her hand and looked at it. "However, he can't have any jewelry. It's just for safety reasons. We gave his other items to his son when he came in."

"Can you just leave it on the table there, at least?" Siobhan implored. "It won't be in the way or anything."

"Fine," the nurse sighed, placing the necklace down on the side table.

"Thank you," Siobhan answered as she rose to go. Siobhan left the room, taking one last look at Conor through the window as she removed the PPE she wore.

Siobhan pushed open the door to the ICU room and stopped dead in her tracks once outside. There in the

waiting room across the hall, looking right at her, was
Finn.

9

After he dressed in jeans and a black t-shirt, Finn resigned himself to having Jameson with him while he occupied his father's house. Jameson had already made it known he didn't plan on going anywhere when he cozied himself on his dog bed that lay in the August sun streaming through the living room window. Finn glanced at the snoring dog and whipped out a text message to Darren to let him know he was going down to the hospital. Finn picked up his keys and the set of keys Cillian had left for him. He briefly considered going out to the garage and taking one of the Harleys out there, but Darren replied that he would like a ride, putting an end to bike thoughts for now.

"Watch the place, Jameson," Finn said sarcastically as the dog continued snoring, though he did peek one eye open as Finn went out the front door.

Finn hurried his Lexus over to Darren's place, the same house Darren's parents owned all through the time they lived in Harriman. Darren was out waiting in the driveway when Finn pulled in.

"Nice ride," Darren offered as he climbed into the passenger seat. "You really have moved up in the world. If your teen self saw you now, he would call you a preppy asshole."

"No one used preppy when we were growing up," Finn retorted. He backed out of the driveway and made his way towards 17M so they could head down to the hospital.

"Can we swing by and get some coffee?" Darren asked. "I could use another cup today."

"I'm not going to Dunkin' for coffee," Finn answered. "I don't want to take any chances that Annie might be there. I'm sure she's pissed at me."

"Probably, but since when did that bother you? I thought you were 'Mr. Love 'Em and Leave 'Em' up there in Saratoga."

"I was... I mean, I am, I guess," Finn admitted, "but I've got enough going on down here right now. I don't need another headache."

"She's gotten in your head already," Darren sighed.

"Annie? No way. We barely know each other."

"Not Annie... Siobhan," Darren replied. "As soon as you knew she was there last night, you started. Did you catch up to her?"

"I didn't start anything," Finn shot back. "And no, I didn't see her. She was gone by the time I got outside."

"If you really want to see her, we can just go over to her apartment or her office. She works right in Harriman. She's the director at A Safe Place. It's on 17 near where Nepera used to be," Darren provided.

Finn considered the option for a moment before he accelerated faster down 17.

"Maybe later," Finn said. "We need to get down to the hospital before Liam and the Cosantóir get there. They might not be quite as kind to me as they were yesterday."

Finn drove speedily to the hospital, bypassing the coffee options Darren pointed out all along the route there. They pulled into the visitor lot and made their way up to the ICU unit without any incident. Finn went directly to the nurses' station to let them know he was here to visit his father.

"There's someone in there with him right now, Mr. O'Farrell, but as soon as they are done, you can gown up and go in. Only one person at a time, though," the young nurse stated as she looked at Darren.

"Oh, don't worry, darlin'," Darren said with a smile. "I'm not planning to go in. Just moral support."

The nurse blushed slightly at Darren's response with his brogue while Finn rolled his eyes.

"I'm going down to the waiting room," Finn told Darren.

"I'll meet you there," Darren replied. "Perhaps Maryann here can point me in the way of a cup of coffee." Darren turned back to the nurse and gave a quick wink.

Finn paced to the waiting room and grabbed the chair that had the best view of his father's room, right across from the doorway. If someone was there that might cause an issue, Finn wanted to see them first, mainly if it was Liam. There weren't any other club members lingering in the waiting room, so Finn thought perhaps Maeve got here already with Cillian and was in the room.

Finn stretched his legs out in front of him, clasped his hands behind his head, and sighed. Too many thoughts raced in his head that caused feelings of uneasiness in ways he hadn't felt in many years. All the reasons he left the area in the first place were bombarding him now. After spending years trying to push all that way, it was now confronting him head-on.

The door across the hall had creaked open. Finn peeked to see who was walking out, and he was taken aback when he saw Siobhan standing there. Finn was unsure how to react. The image of her was more than he remembered. Finn had always been swept up by her long red hair, and her emerald green eyes routinely melted him. Hence, she inevitably got her way with him, no matter what.

Finn rose from his chair and walked out into the hallway where Siobhan stood. She had averted her gaze from him when she saw Finn stand, and Finn saw her fidget for a second until he was right before her.

"Hi, Siobhan," Finn said, keeping his composure. "It's been a long time."

Siobhan continued to look down before lifting her head to look Finn in the eyes.

"Hello, Finn," she said quietly. "Yes, it has been a long time. Ten years, if I remember right. That is when you up and left without so much as a goodbye, isn't it?" she asked coolly.

Finn hadn't expected a barb right away, but he should have if he had any memory of Siobhan at all.

"Still as strong-willed and stubborn as ever, I see." Finn gave a nervous chuckle at first and then realized he probably shouldn't have egged her on.

"Really? That's what you want to lead with, Finn?" Siobhan barked. Finn could see her cheeks were getting red, but he focused more on the freckles she had across them and her nose, another feature of hers he always adored.

"I'm the one that has a right to be angry, don't you think?" Siobhan snapped to gain Finn's focus.

"Siobhan, I had so much going on with me then. I had to get away from it all."

"I get that, Finn, but the way you handled it was shite."

The angry Irish lass he knew back then was out in full force now as Sibohan's temper flared.

"I don't know what I can say to make things better," Finn shrugged. It seemed no matter what he said, he came across as a selfish prick, and he moved to go into his father's room.

"What a shock," Siobhan huffed. "Nothing's changed in ten years, I see. You still have nothing to say and are going to run away."

Finn slammed the ICU door closed.

"Look, I could say I'm sorry a hundred times to you, and it's not going to change what I did. I left without a word because I thought it was the best thing to do then. It was a clean break. It hurt me too, you know," Finn shouted.

Siobhan stepped closer to Finn and glared at him. Even though he was a good half a foot taller than her, she didn't back down.

"A clean break, is that what you think it was? You really are a callous ass, Finn. You disappeared, never told me you were leaving and didn't tell me where you were going or went. No one knew where to look for you. For all I knew, you drove off on your bike somewhere and went off a cliff or got buried in one of those tunnels you were working on with the Sand Hogs. You never even tried to contact me. You never came back."

Finn lost the staring contest this time as he turned away from Siobhan and looked at his boots.

"Just like I thought," Siobhan said as she shook her head. "Speechless again. Go see your Da, Finn."

Siobhan turned away from Finn and went to move. Finn's left hand shot out and grabbed hold of her by the elbow.

"That's not fair, and you know it," Finn seethed.

"Let go of me, Finn," Siobhan said as she attempted to pull from him. "You know better than to put a hand on me."

Darren and Cara both dashed over to intervene between the two before things escalated more.

"Well, I see the reunion is going swimmingly," Darren said as he moved Finn away, so he released

Siobhan's arm. "Finn, why don't you go in by your father."

"Vonnie, come with me," Cara insisted. "We'll go down to the cafeteria."

"I'm not finished saying my piece to him," Siobhan said as she moved back towards Finn as Cara tried to restrain her. "He doesn't have the backbone to say what he's thinking anyway."

"Hey, I didn't want to hurt you," Finn roared. "That's why I left like I did!"

"You think it didn't hurt just to have you disappear like that? How the feck did you get through law school with that brain of yours?"

"How did you know about law school?" Finn said confusedly.

"We both know people, Finn. It wasn't hard to learn about," Siobhan said as she looked at Darren.

"What did you expect?" Darren offered. "It was years after you left, and she asked me if I knew what happened to you. Did you think no one would ever ask about you again?"

"I knew it was a mistake coming back here," Finn said as he pulled from Darren.

"That's right… run back home upstate, Finn," Siobhan shouted. "God forbid you should be around when people need you."

Cara and Darren did their best to keep the two apart, but when the two suddenly stopped holding onto their friends was when all the shouting stopped, and heads turned. Liam and several members of the Cosantóir were just steps away from all of them.

"I see the gang is all here," Liam laughed. He stood next to Siobhan and looked down at her.

"Hey there, Ginger," Liam said to her with a guffaw. "What brings the wallflower out of the woodwork?"

"I came here to see your father," Siobhan spat. "Nothing more."

"We don't want any trouble, Liam," Darren interjected. Darren, a large man himself, was dwarfed by Liam's size.

"You won't get any if the lot of you get out of here now," Liam responded. He looked over Darren's shoulder at his brother.

"I'm going in to see Dad," Finn told Liam.

"You saw him yesterday," Liam said as he moved closer. "Once in ten years should be enough for you, brother. It's our time to see him now."

"Do we really have to go through this again?" Finn answered. "I'm not afraid of fighting you, Liam."

"You really should be," Liam smiled. Liam tossed Darren to his right so that Darren slammed into the wall. Liam reached over and grabbed Finn's t-shirt in his fist before pinning him to the wall.

"I'd hate to mess up that pretty lil' face of yours with your girlfriend watchin'," Liam growled. "But it might be good for her to see what a real man is like and how thankful she should be that you left her."

Finn braced himself for wherever the first punch was going to land, but unlike when he was a kid, he refused to close his eyes and stared back at his brother, ready to take it. Before Liam could throw the punch, Siobhan popped in at Finn's side.

"Liam!" Siobhan shouted. "You made your point. Come on, Finn, let's just go."

Siobhan grasped Finn's hand and slowly guided him from Liam's grip.

"Smart decision, Ginger," Liam said as he straightened his leather jacket. "Let the Ginger protect you, brother. She knows what's best. Ya never should've let that one go, but she's better off for it."

Siobhan kept a firm hold on Finn's hand and pulled him towards where Cara was checking on Darren.

"What are you doing?" Finn said quietly. "I'm not scared of him."

"I'm saving you," Siobhan whispered. "Even if you thought for a minute you could take him, the rest of the club would make sure you didn't walk out of here. You would be grateful we're at a hospital. Walk away, Finn."

Darren was up on his feet and had caught his breath as Cara helped him.

"You alright?" Finn asked his friend.

"I'm fine," Darren replied. "I forgot how big your brother is."

"Can we go now?" Cara asked. "If you tough guys are finished with your pissing contest, that is. We're all impressed, alright? My shift is over. Can we all go and get breakfast?"

"I don't know if that's such a good idea," Finn replied. "You guys can go. I can do something else."

Cara raised her eyebrows at Siobhan.

"Finn," Siobhan sighed. "Come to breakfast. We'll all go to Dottie Audrey's."

Cara and Darren nodded in agreement and began to walk down the hall.

"Where's that?" Finn asked.

"It's where the Duck Cedar Inn used to be," Darren told his friend as he pressed the elevator button. "Good food, good coffee. I'm sure I pointed it out to you when I was begging you to stop."

The four friends rode the elevator down in awkward silence. Finn gave constant side glances Siobhan's way from the elevator out the hospital doors and into the parking lot.

"I'm over there," Siobhan pointed. "Where are you two?"

"Finn's car is right there," Darren said as he pointed to the white Lexus glistening in the warming sun.

"Fancy," Cara mocked. "My car is over in the staff lot. I'll meet you three there."

"I guess we'll meet you at breakfast," Finn said to Siobhan.

Siobhan brushed a few red strands from her face as she looked at Finn.

"See you there," she nodded as she walked to her vehicle.

Finn and Darren got into his Lexus and were on their way to the restaurant in no time.

"That was fun," Darren said sarcastically.

"This is going to be incredibly awkward," Finn told Darren. "All she did was read me the riot act the whole time. Why am I going to breakfast?"

"Because even if she's mad as a hornet at you, you want to be around her. I could see the spark between the two of you. It's just like how it was when the two of you would argue when we were teens."

"Yeah, those aren't the times I wanted to remember, Darren," Finn admitted.

"Did you think you were just going to show up and see her, and she would fall for you? Christ man, she's not one of the chippies you bang in Saratoga; this is Siobhan we're talking about. She's tougher than half of the Cosantóir. If you want back in her good graces, you're going to have to work for it."

No doubt about it, Finn thought as he pulled into Dottie Audrey's parking lot.

10

Siobhan's ride to the restaurant for breakfast had barely started when her cell phone rang. Before she even picked up with her Bluetooth, she knew it would be Cara. "Yes?" Siobhan asked as she drove.

"That's not how I expected things to go," Cara started. "From the way you spoke to me last night, I thought you wanted to see Finn, not tear him a new one."

"All that just came out," Siobhan told her friend. "He walked over to me, and I couldn't help it. I have a lot of anger built up still over the whole thing, Cara. It's not going to just go away overnight. Seeing him again... well, it's a double-edged sword. I don't want him to think he can just waltz right back into my life and then up and leave again in three days without a word. If he wants to be my friend again, he will have to prove to me he's serious about it."

"Friend, huh?" Cara snorted. "That's all you're hoping for out of this? C'mon, Vonnie, we both know that's not true. Remember who you're talking to here."

"I'm not that girl who was pining over Finn O'Farrell for years anymore, Cara," Siobhan insisted. "It took me too long to get past that the first time. I've grown up. Seeing him today made me realize that. Besides, what am I supposed to do? Follow him around for a few days, have some fun, and just let him go?"

"Why not?" Cara offered. "You don't think he would do that? From what Darren says, that's pretty much how he lives his life in Saratoga. Why aren't you entitled? God knows you could use it, Vonnie."

"What the hell is that supposed to mean?" Siobhan asked, taking offense.

"Siobhan, I love you dearly," Cara said honestly. "You're the sister I never had. Let's be honest, though. It's been a while since you've even had a boyfriend, let alone someone who could make you..."

"Let's just leave it there," Siobhan interrupted. "My priorities are different now, Cara. I'm not going to just jump into bed with someone for the sake of it."

"Why not? It can be a lot of fun," Cara laughed.

"Ugh, if your mother heard you..." Siobhan said as she pulled into Dottie Audrey's lot.

"If she did, she would agree with me," Cara replied. Cara parked her car right next to Siobhan's and looked over at her with a big grin.

"Can we cool the sex talk a bit before we meet up with the fellas?" Siobhan asked as she got out of her car.

"Oh, the good Irish Catholic girl is coming out now," Cara poked.

Siobhan and Cara walked together onto the front porch and met Darren and Finn, who waited by the front door. As reluctant as Finn seemed to look, Siobhan spied him, watching her the entire way up the steps to meet them.

"Ladies first," Darren said gallantly as he opened the door so the girls could enter.

"How chivalrous of you, Darren," Cara told him with a nod and a smile.

"A first time for everything," Finn mumbled under his breath at Darren.

The four waited in line as tantalizing aromas of fresh bread, pastries, and breakfast items wafted through the restaurant. Siobhan positioned herself directly in front of Finn, and she knew his gaze was on her. The electricity she had not experienced in a long time coursed through her body and brought a smile to her lips and a light blush to her cheeks.

After ordering, the friends sat at a table outside to enjoy the warmer weather. As soon as the beverages arrived at their table, Darren dove into his coffee, and a serene look came over his face.

"Ohhh, that's so good," Darren moaned.

"Jesus, Darren," Cara said as she sipped her chai latte, "Do you want some alone time with your coffee?"

"Hey, I worked until 3 AM. I need this." He insisted.

"Don't give me that," Cara interjected. "I put in hours at the hospital after being out last night. I'm working on about 3 hours of sleep. You can deal with pouring beer and wiping down tables!"

"Are they always like this?" Finn asked, turning to Siobhan.

"Pretty much," she said with a smirk.

"I just can't stand to hear his whining," Cara added. "Before he starts up again, let's hear something from you, Finn. What's life in Saratoga like?"

Siobhan watched as Finn's eyes scanned the table, and everyone was staring at him.

"There's not much to tell, really," Finn began. "It's a great city with lots to do indoors and outdoors. I have a nice place there, go to restaurants and clubs, outdoor events, the track is great in the summer. You should come up and see it."

"I guess if we were ever invited, we could," Siobhan said quietly as she added another jab at Finn.

"Can we get through breakfast before you start tearing him down again?" Darren asked as the food arrived at the table.

Siobhan did her best to concentrate on her meal and friendly conversation with Cara and Darren to avoid getting into it again with Finn. The friends reminisced over times they had in high school, and beyond and after about twenty minutes of talking, they were all laughing loudly as if they had never been apart. Siobhan watched as Finn relaxed more and glimpses of how he was years ago with her and his friends broke through. When Darren recalled a story of the four of them off-roading in Cara's father's Jeep with all of them getting jostled around as Cara drove, Finn reached over and grabbed Siobhan's hand instinctively and held it. It was only when they both noticed what he did that Siobhan and Finn looked at each other, and each pulled their hand away.

With the morning meal complete, all rose from the table and walked out to the parking lot towards their respective cars.

"So," Darren said as the four stood behind Finn's Lexus, "Everyone coming by Millie's tonight? I've got another band playing. They're new for me – Captain Carraway and the Seeded Ryes. They sound good. There'll be a food truck outside tonight too."

"When are you just going to open the kitchen back up again?" Cara complained.

"When I can afford a cook and staff to do it," Darren insisted.

"What do you say, Vonnie? Drinks, dancing, and empanadas tonight?" Cara asked.

"I don't know," Siobhan said. "I'm pretty worn out from this week with work. I think I need a night of Netflix and chill. Sorry, Darren."

"No trouble," Darren replied. "If you change your mind, there's always a stool for you. What about you, Finn?"

Siobhan saw Finn look at her before he gave a response.

"I think I'm going to drop you off at the pub and head back down to the hospital to see my Dad. After that, I'm going back to his house and relax for a bit. Did you know he's got that big house over there on Shadowmere?

It's a hell of a place. A far cry from what I grew up in for sure."

"I had no idea," Darren replied.

"I knew he was there," Siobhan offered.

All eyes turned to Siobhan to hear more.

"I mean, I had heard that's where he was living now a couple of years ago. I run into him now and then around town," Siobhan said hurriedly as she started to fish for her car keys in her purse.

Siobhan grabbed her keys and looked up as the group stared at her.

"Okay, then. I'm off," Siobhan smiled. She gave Cara a hug.

"Talk to you later, sweets," Cara told her as they hugged. "Love you."

"Love you too," Siobhan replied. Siobhan then hugged Darren and turned and stood before Finn.

Siobhan hesitated, unsure of what she should do for a moment. Before she had a chance to decide, Finn leaned over and gave her a hug. Siobhan felt her heart pounding as she drew close to Finn, first with nervousness and then with a warm familiarity that overtook her. She found herself closing her eyes and squeezing his muscular body.

"Maybe I'll see you later," Finn said into Siobhan's ear as he held her.

"Maybe," she whispered back to him before breaking their hug.

Siobhan hurried to her car at the far end of the lot. She could hear Cara moving quickly behind her to catch up. Just as Siobhan went to put her key in the driver's side door of her car, Cara stepped in front of her to block her.

"What the hell was that?" Cara said, grinning.

"What are you talking about?" Siobhan said defensively.

"That extended hug you just gave to Finn. An hour or so ago, you were ripping him a new one, and now you are pawing him in the parking lot."

"I think you're reading way too much into this, Cara," Siobhan said as she moved Cara aside so she could open the car door. Siobhan sat in the driver's seat, but Cara prevented her from closing the door.

"Don't give me that, Vonnie," Cara said. "One minute you are asking about him, then you're tearing his head off, and then you're holding hands at the table."

"We were not holding hands," Siobhan insisted.

"Okay, call it whatever you want. You're a big girl, Vonnie. You can do what you want. Just don't set yourself up for disappointment with Finn O'Farrell."

"Trust me, Cara, that isn't going to happen. He'll be gone in a few days, and I'm sure everything will be back to the way it was. You heard me at the hospital. It took me too long to get over him the first time. I'm sure I won't put myself through that again. You were right from the start. It's just seeing an old friend at this point, and nothing more."

"If you say so," Cara said warily. "Call me or text me if you decide to go out tonight. I'm going home to crash."

Cara walked over to her vehicle, and Siobhan shut the door. She glanced over at Cara and gave her a wave as she started the engine and backed out. Siobhan pulled out onto 17M and saw that she wasn't far behind Finn's Lexus.

Siobhan thought about her hands touching Finn's at the table and the hug he gave to her — *he hugged me,* Siobhan reassured herself — but no matter how hard she tried to convince herself that it was Finn who had initiated the physical contact both times, she couldn't get beyond how that contact made her feel inside.

****

Finn spent the better part of the ride to Millie Malone's downplaying his interaction with Siobhan to Darren.

"Finn, there's nothing wrong with you feeling something for her," Darren said. "You guys were together a long time. That has to have an impact on you."

"We were kids, Darren," Finn replied. "Yes, I cared for Siobhan a lot back then. Am I sad things had to play out like they did? Of course. But that was the only way I could change something in my life at that moment. I'm not that kid anymore. Besides, you saw the way she yelled at the hospital. She's got a lot of bitterness about it all."

"I'm not buying into any of this," Darren told him. "You can play the rich bachelor, the carefree living guy with your pals in Saratoga, but this is me you're talking to. I knew you before all that when you were just a pale-faced kid who couldn't grow facial hair. I know you, mate. Siobhan is not someone you ever just forgot about."

"Well, I guess you don't know me as well as you think," Finn said with a tinge of anger. "If any of that were true, do you think I would have left her the way I did without ever talking to her or seeing her? I've moved on, Darren, and so has she. Let's drop this, okay?"

Finn slammed on the brakes as he arrived at Millie Malone's parking lot.

"You aren't at least gonna take me to my house to get my car?" Darren said with surprise.

"You live two miles from here," Finn told Darren. "I'm sure you can make it if you need the car that badly."

"Bad form," Darren said as he got out of the car. "Hey, seriously – be careful if you go back down to the hospital. It's a matter of time before Liam does more than talk about pounding you."

"I can handle Liam," Finn said, unsure how much he believed the statement himself.

"No, you can't," Darren said solemnly. "Finn, Liam's reputation is well-earned. When he doesn't like someone, they don't stick around these parts too long, usually not by choice. Watch yourself. Come by here tonight, so I know you're okay."

"Thanks, Darren. I'll talk to you later."

Finn rolled his car out of the parking lot. He went back towards Good Samaritan Hospital, taking care to watch the roads for any signs of the Cosantóir along the way. He wouldn't be shocked if, at this point, Liam had him followed or spied on to see what he was doing. A smattering of bikes was in the Rhodes parking lot as Finn drove by, but there was no telling on a weekend how many of the Cosantóir were in different places. They could be riding, at the Hog House, at a bar, the hospital, or any of a dozen other places. Finn was unsure just how big the club was now compared to what he remembered as a teenager and would occasionally ride with the club.

Finn reached the hospital and audibly groaned when he saw several Harleys still in the visitors' lot. He considered waiting in his car until some of them left, perhaps evening the odds for him a bit more if he had to deal with Liam or any of the others. Finally, after sitting for about ten minutes, there was no point in hanging out there longer. He got out of the Lexus and strode into the hospital, getting his visitor's badge and heading right up to the ICU floor without hesitation.

Finn clenched and unclenched his fists several times as he rode the elevator up. He bounced on his feet much in the way he would do before he sparred with anyone when he would drop in at one of the boxing gyms in the Saratoga area. The older woman in the elevator with Finn stepped a bit away from him as he moved. She hustled out onto her floor as soon as the elevator doors opened for her.

He arrived at the ICU and went straight to the desk so he could sign in. He marched to the waiting room, where a couple of Cosantóir that he did not recognize sat. Finn let out a small breath of relief and sat in one of the chairs facing the doorway to watch his father's room and see if Liam or anyone else came out and charged him.

Finn quickly learned he didn't have to worry about getting set on in the waiting room when he saw Cillian turn the corner and enter.

"You're here," Cillian said as he popped open a bottle of iced tea. "Liam had said you came and went already."

"I did, I guess," Finn admitted. "Liam kind of insisted on it. Is he in there now?"

"Liam? No, he and some of the others left a bit ago. Maeve is back in there with him now. She might be awhile. I hope you don't mind waiting."

"No, no, it's fine," Finn answered. "She should be with him as much as she can be. How's he doing today?"

"No change, from what the doctors said," Cillian admitted as he shook his head sadly. "There's still swelling around his brain, and they are worried about internal injuries and potential lung collapse. The staff is watching him closely. Nurses and docs are in and out of there all the time. This could be a long haul, Finn. I know you must have to get back to Saratoga next week, so if you need to go after the weekend, I can keep you posted on things. Your Dad would understand."

"I don't know that he would understand any of this in the first place," Finn answered. "I'll be here for another few days at least. I can move my calendar around if I need to."

Cillian nodded and smiled at Finn.

"I'm glad to hear it," Cillian replied. "Do you want to say a quick prayer for your Da?"

"What?" Finn said confusedly. "I'm not really… I thought you gave all that stuff up?"

"Just because I'm not a priest anymore doesn't mean I don't have a relationship with God, Finn. We talk all the time. There's nothing wrong with that, you know. I'd be glad to pray with you."

Finn looked around the room as Cillian closed his eyes and brought his hands together as he began to recite the Lord's Prayer. Finn saw that one of the bikers across the room removed his bandana, closed his eyes, and began to pray along while the other bowed his head. Finn closed his eyes and fell into the routine, joining right in with the prayer as if he had never stopped saying it years ago.

When Cillian completed the prayer, he added another of his own, one Finn was not familiar with.

"Dear Lord, You are the one I turn to for help in moments of weakness and need. I ask you to turn this weakness into strength, this suffering into compassion, sorrow into joy, and pain into comfort for others. May your servant trust in your goodness and hope in your faithfulness, even in the middle of this suffering. Let him be filled with patience and joy in your presence as he waits for your healing touch. Please restore your servant to full health, dear Father. Remove all fear and doubt from his heart by the power of your Holy Spirit, and may you, Lord, be glorified through his life, Amen."

The bikers across the room both said "Amen" loudly while Finn made sure to quietly add his own.

"Your mother would be glad that you are not only here but that you did that, Finn," Cillian said proudly.

"I have to admit, Cillian, that it's been a long time since I've done that. It felt…"

"Peaceful?" Cillian smiled.

"Well, I was going for awkward at first," Finn admitted, "but yes… peaceful. Thank you."

"My pleasure," Cillian laughed, slapping Finn's knee. Finn watched as the door to his father's room opened and Maeve walked out. She was visibly shaken, and her make-up was smudged from obvious crying.

Cillian and Finn both rose from their seats, and the other bikers walked over to be near Maeve.

"Everything okay?" Finn asked worriedly.

Maeve hugged Finn and began to cry.

"It just hurts to see him like that… not moving, needing machines to do everything for him. I can't even tell if he knew if I was there or not," Maeve wept.

Finn held Maeve, a stranger to him just one day ago, and tried to provide her with comfort. The two members of the Cosantóir eyed Finn closely, and Finn took notice.

"Is there a problem?" Finn said, feeling his temper rising.

"Easy, Finn," Cillian said as he stepped in.

"He's fine," Maeve insisted to the two men as she put her hands up to ask them to halt. "I'm sorry, Finn. Liam insisted I have a couple of the guys with me for protection."

"Protection from what? From me?" Finn said with disgust. "He has no right…"

"No, not from you," Maeve answered. "He's convinced what happened to your father wasn't an accident. He thinks it was purposeful to send a message, and he doesn't want anything to happen to me."

"Why would he think that?" Finn questioned. "I haven't seen or heard that the police think it was more than an accident. If there's something you need to tell me, Maeve, let me know. I might be able to help."

"I don't know any more than you do, Finn," Maeve told him. "I just know Liam is very secretive about it all and has been closing ranks of the Cosantóir and the Sand Hogs since yesterday. Lots of behind closed doors meetings and phone calls."

"Cillian?" Finn asked, turning to his father's closest friend.

"I don't really have anything I can add to it, son," Cillian replied. "I wasn't there when it happened. All I know is what Liam told me... told us."

"Go in and see your father, Finn," Maeve insisted. "He should have someone with him as much as he can."

Finn went to his father's room and sat with him for much longer than the usual twenty minutes. For a while, he sat silently, watching his father, seeing his chest rise and fall in rhythm with the ventilator, wondering what, if anything, his father might see, feel, or hear right now. Conor lay in what looked like a peaceful sleep to Finn, bringing back memories of what Conor looked like when he might sleep on the couch when he had a weekend off during good days, or when he was sleeping one off on the floor or in a chair on the bad ones.

When Finn realized no one was coming in to ask him to leave, and the silence was getting more than he could bear, he found himself having a one-sided conversation with his father. He began to tell Conor about what his life was like in Saratoga, the good and the bad, his successes and failures, and years' worth of things he wanted to talk about.

Feeling spent, Finn finally blurted out, "How come you were never this easy to talk to when I was a kid? Life would have been much better for both of us if you were. I never understood it, Dad. Is it because you thought I was more like Ma than you? She spent more time with me than you ever did. Once she was gone, it felt like I had nothing left. Even when I did Sand Hog work with you for that time, you still rode me tough. I don't know. It all could have been much different, you know. You made me not want to be here anymore... well, you and Liam anyway. Now we may never get the chance to hash things out. I have a lot I wanted to say to you, you know. And it's not all good, but you need to hear it. You made life hell for me, Dad, whether you knew it or not. Nothing I did was ever good enough, and you made sure to let me know with your words and your fists. After a while, I just stopped trying and did stuff I knew would piss you off to see how you would react. When Mom wasn't around to intervene anymore, I put up with it because I had no choice until I finally saw a way out. I knew you would never understand it or me, but I made something of myself despite your best efforts. I've hated you for a long time now, and I want you to know that. You created that. I just wish you could hear me and respond so that I knew you understand it."

Finn had raised his voice and found that he was gripping the hospital bed's steel rails tightly. He pushed himself back in his chair to move away from Conor. Finn had the urge to reach over, grab his father, and shake him in the hopes he would wake up so he could acknowledge what Finn had told him. Instead, all Finn could hear was himself breathing loudly and the various machines' constant beeps keeping his father alive.

Finn looked over at the table next to his father's bed and noticed a necklace there. He picked it up and gazed at the medallion, recognizing it as a Celtic Shield Knot. He recalled how his mother and grandmother always regaled him with tales of Ireland's superstitions and myths. In particular, his grandmother took the stories to heart. She believed wholeheartedly in what protections, curses, and magic the different symbols held in folklore. Finn always thought they made fun stories when he was younger but never took much stock in them, but he wondered just who might have left the charm with Conor.

He knew for sure there was no way Liam would do it, and he doubted Maeve thought it would offer any help. Cillian? Not likely either as a man of religion more than a myth. Siobhan then crossed Finn's mind once more. He remembered how Siobhan's family was when he was younger, more wrapped up in heritage and stories than even his own family was. Siobhan was not always a better Catholic than Finn was. Still, she held more belief in good luck, protection, jinxes, curses, and the like, even if she was the most rational person he knew.

Finn held the medallion in his hands, turning it over and feeling the cold metal in his fingers. He touched the raised parts of the knot to handle them as he thought back on what the Shield Knot was believed to provide to warriors on the battlefield. The shield would keep the evil spirits away so that the gods could offer to heal the ill or wounded.

"Who's trying to protect you, Da?" Finn asked quietly as he held the medallion.

****

It wasn't until a nurse and doctor walked in that Finn was startled out of his chair. He had clearly dozed off for some time, and when Finn jumped out of the chair, the nurse and doctor both took a step back from him.

"We didn't realize anyone was in here right now," the nurse said as she went about her business to check Conor's vitals.

"I'm sorry," Finn admitted. "I guess I dozed off in here for a bit."

"It's fine," the doctor answered. "It's good that he has someone in here with him."

"Is he improving at all?" Finn questioned.

The doctor looked over the information on his tablet and what the nurse provided to him. Finn watched as the doctor adjusted his glasses with his gloved hands.

"Not much, unfortunately," the doctor said as he turned to Finn. "He hasn't worsened, which is a good thing. Tests this morning show the swelling has eased a bit, but he struggles with internal injuries. We're just trying to keep him stable for now. It's only been a day. These things can take some time."

"How much time?" Finn said, exasperated.

"I can't give you a definitive answer," the doctor told him. "It could be days, weeks, or longer. I'm sorry. We're doing everything we can't right now to make him comfortable and give him a chance to fight."

"Well, he was always good at fighting," Finn added, looking down at his father. "Thanks, doctor."

Finn left the ICU room and shed his PPE, stretching and yawning before walking out to the hall. He was shocked when he saw outside the window in the waiting room that it was getting dark out. He saw Maeve sitting by herself, knitting, and moved toward her. Just as Finn reached to stand in front of Maeve, someone came racing across the room to push him out of the way.

Finn tumbled face-first to the floor before rolling over and getting ready to stand up to defend himself, but a large boot on his chest prevented him from getting up at all. Before him stood one of the Cosantóir, clad in his leathers. The man was immense, perhaps even larger than Liam, Finn thought. Finn saw the fluorescent light in the room bounce of the biker's bald brown head, and the sneer the man had on his face was enough to make sure Finn didn't try to move at all.

"Demon!" Maeve yelled. "It's okay! He's Conor's son."

Maeve placed her hands on the man's chest to guide him off Finn, who gasped for breath once the boot was removed from pressing on him.

"Seriously?" Finn yelled. "Do I have to watch my back with every one of you fucking guys?"

"Finn," Maeve said calmly. "He's just protecting me. He didn't mean anything. It's his job."

"Sorry, man," Demon answered. "I can't be too careful about this shit. Now I know who you are. We're good."

Demon offered his hand to shake Finn's, and Finn cautiously took it. Demon's hand enveloped Finn's quickly, and even if he didn't mean to offer a tight grip, Finn assumed Demon couldn't control it. A scan of the man shaking his hand let Finn know that this biker had to be almost seven-foot-tall, well over 300 pounds, and built like an armored truck.

"I'm Finn," Finn told him as he worked to get air back in his lungs. "Demon, huh? Quite the opposite of Preacher, I guess." Finn tried to laugh it off until he noticed Demon wasn't laughing.

"One might say it is a bit of a dichotomy," Demon offered as he brushed some of the dirt from the hospital floor off Finn's back. "It's just my name with the club and with the Sand Hogs. My real name is Darryl."

"Demon was a professional wrestler," Maeve said as she patted Demon's back. "That was his name back in the day."

"Fought for the title a couple of times," Demon said proudly. "You probably don't recognize me. I always wore a mask. I didn't want to mess up my pretty face," he said with a smile, showing off his bright, white teeth. "Still got all my original teeth, too."

"You work in the tunnels?" Finn said with surprise. "How do you fit down there?"

"Obviously, I don't take on the closed space jobs. I can outlift or out-dig anyone on the site, though, and I'm damn proud of it. And it's a hell of a lot safer and better paying than wrestling."

Finn turned back to Maeve.

"How come you left me in there so long? Someone else could have gone in."

"Finn, out of you, me, and Preacher, you're the one that needs the most time with your Dad. I didn't want to interrupt whatever you had to say to him or do in there. Even if it meant you falling asleep in the room with him. At least it brings you together again."

Maeve sat back down and picked up her knitting.

"Was it helpful for you?" she asked as she went back to her project.

"I guess so," Finn agreed. "Though it would have been better if he could have given me some answers about what happened to him, and... well... other stuff."

Maeve just nodded as she knit.

"I know. I want the same thing. Soon, God willing."

"I guess I should get going," Finn said as he looked at his watch to see the time. "You should go in..." Finn said before Maeve interrupted him.

"Yes, go back to the house and rest. It's all been stressful. I'll pop in and sit with him for a bit after I finish this next row."

"I would never have pegged you as a knitter," Finn stated.

"Why? Because I ride a bike and have tattoos? Lots of tough women and men knit, Finn. Russell Crowe, Ryan Gosling, Meryl Streep, Eleanor Roosevelt, even Charles Manson was a knitter," Maeve answered with a smile. "It's very relaxing. You should try it."

"She's working on a hat and scarf for me for the winter," Demon grinned.

"My plate's a little full right now," Finn replied. "I'll check in with you later," Finn told her. "Nice to meet you, Darryl."

"Same here, man," Demon told him as he slapped Finn on the back.

Finn found his way to his car, unsure of what to think of his experience in the hospital with his father. It had been cathartic in a way for Finn, but Finn was uncertain if it helped him at all without any recognition from his father. He was also glad he had not had a run-in with Liam and avoided more trouble.

Finn was able to take in the fresh air with the car windows rolled down for the ride home to help revive him after being inundated with hospital smells. He couldn't wait to get back to his father's house to take a shower and wash off whatever it is that seemed to cut through his clothes down to his skin. The ride home also gave Finn time to reflect on what Maeve had said about his father's events not being an accident. Finn always suspected his father of being involved in shady dealings from the time he was young. His mother never wanted to talk about what Conor did on the job or at Hog House. When Finn got older, he saw with his own eyes that it was not always moral, ethical, or legal. He wouldn't be shocked if Conor had involved himself in something wrong enough that someone would want him out of the way permanently.

Finn pulled into the long driveway for his father's home and got up close to the house. The first thing to get his attention was that the motion lights did not light the area in front of the house. Finn turned off the car and got out, making sure to close the car door quietly. He stealthily moved up the front porch and to the front door when he noticed the door was ajar. Finn's mind raced as to what to do. He could call the police and hope they would get there. He could get back in his car and leave. Or he could enter the house and see what was going on. Finn resolved to push forward and opened the door more to slip inside.

Once inside, he saw all the lights were off. He glanced to the right where he knew Jameson's bed was and saw in the moonlight through the bay window that the dog bed was empty. Either Jameson had slipped out, knew the intruders, or something terrible had happened to him. Finn stepped lightly down the hall towards the kitchen before hearing some noise near his father's bedroom.

Finn peered around the corner and could see a shadow hunched over the doorknobs to the locked room across from the bedroom.

"I can't get this fuckin' thing open," the voice said hoarsely. Footsteps from the kitchen came closer to the door, but Finn only saw another shadow lurking over the other man.

"Can't I just kick the thing in?" The man trying to open the door said.

"No," a deep voice commanded. "It's supposed to be like no one was ever here. The kid must have the key. Keep picking at it."

Finn thought about the keys he had in his pocket and wondered if one did open that door. He did his best to keep quiet as he felt for the keys. It was then Finn felt something sidle up next to him. Finn turned, holding in a gasp as he saw Jameson take a seat next to him. The dog let out a light, happy bark, causing the man at the door to turn around and spot Finn and the dog.

"Shit!" the man exclaimed and jumped to his feet. Finn watched as he saw him reach into a bag on the floor and pick up what looked like a crowbar. Finn scrambled back down the hall and toward the front door, trying to get himself into a lighter area so he could see what was coming. Footsteps were now coming down the staircase as well.

"The kid's only got a computer and some clothes. Nothing to help us," the voice that bounded down the stairs said. Finn ran right into that body and fell back to the floor. He looked up into the dark and saw that whoever it was wearing some type of mask.

"Look who's home?" the voice said with a laugh. A sizeable, gloved hand reached down and pulled Finn to his feet. Finn saw the man ready to throw a punch with his right fist. In an instant, Finn heard a deep growl and saw Jameson lunge toward the man, latching on to the free arm. A scream filled the air as Finn was released from the grip. He looked down and saw Jameson clenching the arm tightly as the man cried and tried to wriggle free.

It was then that Finn felt someone bump into his back. The man with the crowbar stood there, and Finn hit him with a right hook to the ribs and a stiff jab that hit right on the chin, causing the thief to drop to the floor. Finn still heard the other man pleading with the dog to let him go as he grabbed the dark sweatshirt the man on the floor was wearing and pulled him up so Finn could get a better look.

Finn went to throw another punch to the wheezing man when a sharp sting rattled his own chest from behind. Finn winced in pain and dropped the thief. Before he could spin around to defend himself, there was a thud on the back of his skull and then blackness.

11

"What happened, darlin'?"

The voice echoed in Finn's head before he could even open his eyes. He blinked several times in the hopes of seeing things clearly, but there was just a blur. The only thing he knew for sure is that there was a shadowy figure, a female form, looking down at him. Finn tried to shake out the cobwebs, moving his head from side to side, but it caused the splitting headache he had to worsen.

"Lay still, honey," the voice told him. He felt a soothing hand rest on his cheek. The familiarity of the touch caused him to sigh and relax. After closing his eyes once more, Finn took a deep breath, hoping it might help him feel better. It was then he was hit by a scent he knew all too well. That mix of lily of the valley, roses, and jasmine was unmistakable. It was the perfume his mother wore for her special occasions. Finn opened his eyes immediately and saw the familiar smile looking down on him.

"I know it was quite a fall you took, Finn," his mother said.

"Ma?" Finn said confusedly. "How... what's going on?"

"Take it easy, Finn," his mother insisted. "You know he didn't mean to push you like that. Once he starts drinking..." she said softly. His mother looked around to make sure no one was listening.

Finn tried with all his might to focus on his mother and his whereabouts so he could see where he was and what was happening. He noticed that he was at the bottom of the stairs in the house he grew up in. Chills ran down his spine as he recalled the scene that had him end up there.

"I'm sorry, Ma," Finn said. Finn choked up. "I was trying to help…"

"I know you were," his mother hushed. "It's all going to be okay, Finn. I promise you that."

Finn watched as his mother stood up, straightening the yellow floral skirt she loved to wear. She smiled back at her son once more as she began to walk towards their old home's kitchen.

"Ma, wait! Don't leave! I want to talk to you!"

Finn struggled but could not get to his feet as he watched his mother pass through the kitchen doorway. His attention then turned to the top of the staircase, where a shadowy image stood, looking down at him.

"Wait!"

Finn bolted up to a sitting position, and pain shot down his neck.

"Ahhh," he groaned. Finn turned to his right and saw Siobhan sitting on the floor next to him. Siobhan reached over, grabbed his right hand, and gently guided him back down to where a pillow from the couch lay.

"Finn? What happened? Are you okay?" she asked worriedly.

"What's going on? What are you doing here? Where's Ma?"

Siobhan stared at Finn with a puzzled look on her face.

"Finn, I stopped by to see you, and the door was open, and you were here on the floor. You're in Conor's house."

Siobhan waved over to one of the EMTs on the scene, and he sat next to Finn.

"Mr. O'Farrell, can you look at me for a minute?" the EMT asked.

Finn turned to stare at the young man while he checked his eyes and his head.

"Do you remember what happened? Did you fall down the stairs?" Siobhan asked.

Finn was unsure of just what was real or imagined. It was only when Jameson bounded over to him, sending the EMT scrambling across the floor and away from Finn, did he recall any of what occurred.

"There was someone in the house when I got here," Finn said softly. One hand instinctively went to the back of his head, where he felt the sensitive knot that had grown there from the blow he received. Simultaneously, the other hand began to mindlessly pet Jameson on the top of his head.

"Did you see who it was?" a male voice said from across the room. Finn turned his head gingerly to the right and saw someone walking towards where he sat. The man was dressed in a suit, unlike the police officers and others on the scene.

"You are?" Finn asked.

"Detective Fremont," the gentleman said. He extended a hand toward Finn, eliciting a low growl from Jameson that made the detective recoil.

"I didn't think they assigned detectives to a breaking and entering case," Finn replied.

"No, the state troopers can handle that end of it, for sure," Fremont indicated. "I'm investigating other matters, including what happened to Conor O'Farrell. When I heard there was a break-in here, I came over."

"I thought my father's injuries were an accident on the job site," Finn responded.

"There may be more to it than that." Detective Fremont pulled his cellphone from his pocket and began to look at notes.

"New-fangled things," Fremont said with a laugh. "I liked it when we just used a notepad. When was the last time you talked to your father?"

"When I was at the hospital earlier today," Finn answered. Finn went to try and get to his feet, but he needed Siobhan's help to do it. He placed an arm around her shoulder as she assisted in lifting him. Finn kept his arm there as much for comfort as it was for support.

"He spoke to you?" Detective Fremont said anxiously.

"Of course not. My father is in a coma. I did speak with him, though."

"I'm not really in the mood to play a game of semantics with you, Mr. O'Farrell," Fremont chided. "When was the last time you and your father had an actual conversation?"

"About ten years ago, when I called him an asshole and left," Finn spat back.

"You haven't spoken to him at all since then? No phone calls or emails?"

"Detective, my father was never the warm and fuzzy kind of guy to call and see how I was."

Finn sat back on the couch with Siobhan's help, so he could be comfortable. He noticed there was some faint blood spatters on the floor leading to the front door.

I'm glad Jameson got his pound of flesh, Finn thought.

"He seems to have a fine relationship with your brother," Fremont noted as he stood in front of Finn.

"Good for the two of them," Finn added.

"If you don't have a relationship with either of them, Mr. O'Farrell, what are you doing here? You're staying in your father's house."

"I was invited to stay," he told Fremont. Finn's head was pounding, but the lawyer in him cried out not to reveal too much.

"By whom?"

"A friend of my father's." He looked at Siobhan, hoping her face would give him some support. She reached over and took Finn's left hand and squeezed it.

"Ah, you must mean Maeve Walsh," Fremont said as he glanced at his notes. "Interesting woman. I didn't realize you knew her."

"I didn't, until yesterday," Finn responded. "Detective, unless you have something important to tell me or get at, do we need to continue this conversation right now? I don't know that I'm really up for interrogation right now."

"I'm not interrogating you, Mr. O'Farrell," Fremont said with a grin. Finn noted the yellow-stained teeth that peeked through Fremont's smile. "If I were, you would already be at the station. I'm just trying to put some pieces together, like why someone would attack you in your father's home."

"Maybe because they know he has a nice house out in the woods that no one would see them break into and weren't expecting me to come walking through the door."

"You didn't see any cars... or bikes in the driveway when you pulled up?" Fremont inquired.

"Not a thing. The motion lights didn't come on."

"That didn't seem strange to you?" Fremont pumped.

"For all I know, my father forgot to pay his O&R bill, and they shut it off. I've been here for a day, detective. You probably know more about all this than I do. Are we done now?"

"Sure," Detective Fremont nodded. He pulled a business card from his pocket and handed it to Finn. "If you think of anything important or want to talk, just give me a call. Thanks for your help. You should get that looked at," Fremont said, pointing to Finn's head.

"Yeah, thanks," Finn answered warily as he took the card and watched the Detective walk to the front door.

"We should go to the hospital," Siobhan insisted.

"No, I'm fine," Finn said as he rubbed the back of his neck.

"Finn, don't be a hero," Siobhan said. "You got knocked out cold. You might have a concussion."

"I've been hit worse," Finn recalled. "Really, Bon, I'm alright."

Finn caught himself saying 'Bon.' No one called Siobhan that except for him back when they were kids. He looked down immediately after he said it but caught a small smile creep across Siobhan's face.

The EMT walked over to where Finn and Siobhan sat on the couch. He had a state trooper along with him.

"Mr. O'Farrell, we have an ambulance outside to take you down to the hospital," the EMT indicated.

"Thanks, but I don't need it," Finn said as he stood up.

"I would strongly recommend that you go and get checked out," the EMT told him.

"I appreciate your concern, but I'm not going to the hospital," Finn said forcefully.

"Finn, stop…" Siobhan said as she grabbed his arm.

"Siobhan, I don't need the hospital, and they can't force me to go. I appreciate all you guys have done, but I'm okay. I just want to go upstairs, take some aspirin, and lay down."

"You can refuse to go, Mr. O'Farrell," the state trooper added. "However, staying in this house tonight may not be an option for you. We still have the scene to look at, and we'll leave a car here tonight to keep an eye on things, but it's probably best if you go somewhere else for tonight. There's a hotel over by Kohl's that I'm sure has rooms."

"You'd be better off at the hospital with someone to keep an eye on you to make sure you are okay," the EMT added.

Finn began to argue back and forth with the EMT and the trooper before Siobhan intervened.

"Enough, already!" Siobhan shouted. "The night's been stressful enough. Do you three really need to stand here and argue about it? Mr. O'Farrell can come and stay at my place. I'll keep an eye on him, and then we can come back in the morning. I promise if I see any problems, I will personally drag him to the hospital. Is that good enough for everyone, for feck's sake?"

The EMT and trooper both stared at Siobhan while Finn cracked a smile. He always loved it when Siobhan got mad or frustrated enough to start swearing.

"What did she just say?" the trooper asked.

"Don't mind her, officer," Finn explained. "When her Irish gets up, she can be difficult to understand."

"Let's go," Siobhan grabbed Finn's hand and tugged him from the room and out of the house. Finn took the front steps of the porch carefully and found himself led toward Siobhan's car. Just as they reached the passenger side of Siobhan's auto, Siobhan opened the door of her faded gray Corolla. She tried to get Finn to slide in, but he resisted.

"Now what?" Siobhan sighed in frustration.

"I can't leave him here," Finn said, pointing to the porch. Siobhan looked over her shoulder and saw Jameson sitting obediently, staring at the couple.

"Finn, I don't know; my place is pretty small. I don't even know if the landlord lets me have a dog there."

"He may have saved my life, Bon," Finn said solemnly. Finn saw Siobhan give him a nod, and Finn cried out, "Jameson, come!" Jameson dashed off the porch and climbed into the back seat, resting his head on

Finn's shoulder. Finn reached up and gave Jameson a scratch behind the ear, causing Jameson to let out a happy sigh as he closed his eyes.

"Not exactly how I planned my evening to go," Siobhan grumbled as she climbed behind the steering wheel.

"Me either," Finn replied. "Wait a minute... how did you plan the evening to go? Why did you come to the house?"

Finn saw Siobhan blush and fumble for words as she drove.

"I... well... I don't know, Finn," she blurted out. "When you said 'maybe I'll see you later,' I thought you were inviting me over to talk. I wasn't going to come. I figured you might be tired from everything that had gone on so far, but... well, I just had a feeling..."

"Oh, no. I know you and your feelings," Finn said sarcastically.

"Shut up, Finn O'Farrell!" Siobhan said, half yelling and half laughing. "My gut feelings kept us out of trouble more than once, you know. Remember when you and Darren were talking about going swimming in the Gentry's pool at 2 AM? I told you I had a bad feeling about it, and what happened?"

"Darren and Sadie McDowell went skinny-dipping in the pool anyway, and Mrs. Gentry came out on her patio for a smoke and saw them and nearly keeled over, and Mr. Gentry came running out with his service revolver. I never saw Darren run so fast. Poor Sadie was left scrambling for her clothes."

Finn laughed heartily, so much so that his head began to ache. He watched Siobhan as she turned and headed up 17M towards Monroe.

"I also recall when you and I were in your room, and your parents were away, and you put a halt to everything because you had a bad feeling about it."

Finn glanced at Siobhan and could swear he saw a blush on her cheeks as they drove past a streetlight.

"I was right about that, too," Siobhan said softly. "My Aunt Colleen walked through the door, not ten minutes later."

"I remember," Finn smiled. "We barely made it to the living room couch to turn a movie on before she opened the front door. As I recall, you put your shirt on inside out."

"Lucky for you, she never noticed," Siobhan answered. "She stayed and watched all of 'Halloween' with us, too."

The two sat in silence as Siobhan turned the car to go down the small hill between the tire shop and the local mechanic's paint shop until she reached the large house. She pulled the car to a stop near a door on the bottom floor.

"You live here?" Finn asked. "We always wondered what the apartments were like."

"Well," Siobhan replied, "I can tell you they're nothing special. Can you make it on your own?"

"I think so."

Finn grabbed the car door jamb and pulled himself out and up. A bit of a head rush occurred as blood rushed to his skull, and he wavered. Siobhan rushed to his side to grab hold of him.

"Now it feels like old times," Siobhan said as she shuffled along with Finn. "Nights when I had to sneak you back into your parents' place after you had too much at Millie's when we were too young to be drinking there."

Siobhan propped Finn up against the side of the house as she unlocked her front door. Before she could enter with Finn, Jameson had made himself at home, rushing through the doorway to check everything out.

Siobhan led Finn over to her worn sofa, and Finn plopped down on the cushions. Immediately, Jameson jumped up next to him and started wagging his tail and licking Finn's face. Finn was hit with slobber and dog breath all at once, making his stomach turn. Jameson let out a few happy barks before Siobhan tried to shush him.

"Quiet!" If Mrs. Morrison hears you, she'll have my head. Finn, please," Siobhan begged.

"I don't know how to make him stop," Finn stated. "I only met him this morning."

"Well, he acts like he's known you for years. Just do something."

Finn looked around and noticed a small brown teddy bear seated on top of the couch. He grabbed the bear and tossed it, and Jameson tore after it before putting it in his mouth and quietly chomping on it.

"That's your solution? To let him destroy my things?" Siobhan said, shaking her head.

"I can try to take it from him if you want," Finn offered. "But at least he's quiet."

"That bear was sentimental. I got it at the Orange County Fair at one of those game booths. I remember he had to play six times..." Siobhan cut herself before finishing that thought.

"Gift from a boyfriend, eh?" Finn said with a nod.

Siobhan busied herself, trying to straighten up the piles of paperwork on the small table she used for her meals.

"I suppose he was, for a while," Siobhan said lightly. "Finn, you were long gone by then, and I..."

"Bon, you don't have to explain anything to me," Finn told her. "It's your life. You do what you want. I was living mine too."

"That's what I heard, anyway," Siobhan remarked.

"Do you really want to get into this tonight?" Finn asked as he rubbed his temples.

"That's what I thought we were getting together about tonight, Finn. I need some answers. I'm entitled to that much, don't you think?"

"I know," Finn relented, "but I didn't plan on someone trying to bash my head in tonight either."

"Fine," Siobhan huffed. She walked over to the hall closet and grabbed a blanket and pillow, and tossed them on the couch next to Finn.

"Get up," Siobhan ordered.

"For what?"

"You can sleep in my bed. I'll take the couch," Siobhan commanded.

"There's no way I am taking your bed from you," Finn told her. "I'll be okay out here."

"Stop being a pompous ass and take the bed," Siobhan insisted. "You need to be comfortable. I'll grab you some aspirins from the medicine cabinet. Now either get up and go to bed, or I can call you an Uber, and you can go to the hotel or wherever else you want. Your choice."

"Time certainly hasn't taken the feistiness out of you," Finn said as he got to his feet and walked towards the bedroom.

"You're damn right it hasn't," Siobhan said proudly.

Finn lay down on the soft bed and his body melted into the mattress. He sighed and closed his eyes before he felt a thud on the bed next to him. He opened his left eye and saw Jameson making himself comfortable on the pillow.

"Uh uh, no way," Siobhan shouted. "There's no way he's sleeping on the bed."

"Sorry, buddy," Finn said as he looked into Jameson's eyes. Finn pointed to the floor next to the bed, and Jameson obediently jumped down and curled himself into a ball.

"Here's your aspirin and some water," Siobhan said as she handed over the two white pills and a bottle of water.

Finn popped the aspirins into his mouth and chased them down with a slug of cold water.

"Need anything else?" Siobhan asked as she rummaged through the top drawer of her dresser.

"I think I'm good," Finn replied. "Thank you... for everything."

Siobhan nodded and smiled at Finn.

"You're welcome. Now get some rest."

Siobhan hit the light switch and closed the door, darkening the room so that only slivers of moonlight came through the curtains. Finn looked down and saw Jameson already peacefully snoring. He turned to look at the ceiling, noticing some cracks in the paint that spidered out towards the ceiling fan in the center. The fan gently moved the warmth around, but the room was still too hot for Finn's comfort. He stripped off his shirt and pants, leaving him in his boxer briefs. Pulling the shirt over his head had caused him to wince in pain. Even his hair hurt right now, and Finn silently hoped for the aspirins to kick in soon as he closed his eyes.

****

"No! Stop!"

The yell caused Siobhan to jump up from her spot on the couch and sit up straight. She felt as though she had just fallen asleep before getting startled. The old couch proved to be anything but comfortable, and Siobhan resolved to get a new one as soon as she could afford it.

"Don't!"

The scream came from the bedroom, and Siobhan darted down the short hall and opened the door. She saw Jameson sitting worriedly next to the side of the bed where Finn was. Finn was tossing and turning, wrapped tightly in the down comforter in one moment before his body kicked it free. He continued thrashing about and speaking in a frightened voice.

Without thought, Siobhan climbed on the bed next to Finn and grabbed him, holding him close. She ran her hand over his forehead and through his hair, stroking gently.

"It's okay, Finn. It's just a dream," she said softly.

Finn attempted to roll to his side, still struggling and crying out. Siobhan let him move before she draped her arm around him to hold him. With her body pressed tightly to Finn's, he started to relax and calm down.

Siobhan felt Finn's heart pounding through his bare chest as she held him. She whispered into his ear, "It's okay, I'm here," over and over to him and then kissed his bare shoulder. Finn deeply sighed and pushed himself closer to Siobhan.

Siobhan lay there, not daring to move but not wanting to either.

****

Finn groaned as the smell of brewing coffee permeated the room. He sat up in bed, rubbing the last bit of sleep from his eyes before the dull ache returned to his body. His head was clear, but his neck, shoulders, and back felt like they had been thrown against a brick wall. Sunlight illuminated the bedroom, giving him a better view of the room itself than he had last night. There were clothes strewn about everywhere, including some piled in a clothes basket on a chair in the room. The sliding closet door was open, displaying the disarray that existed there.

The door to the bedroom was cracked open, but as soon as Finn moved to put his feet on the floor, the door sprung wide, and Jameson bounded in, leaping onto the bed to sit next to him. Jameson gave Finn a broad smile that frightened Finn until the dog leaned in and gave Finn a long lick on his cheek.

"Jameson!" Siobhan yelled from the doorway. "Get down."

Jameson leaped from the bed and sat on the floor next to Siobhan.

"Glad to see you're awake," Siobhan beamed as she handed a mug of coffee to Finn.

"You still take it black, right?" she asked before letting go of the mug. Finn had placed his fingers just over Siobhan's on the cup and held them there before answering her.

"Yes, thanks," Finn coughed as he took the coffee and gave it a sip.

"I'm sure it's not the ritzy stuff you're used to drinking, but it's good. It comes from a small roaster in Brooklyn I stumbled upon at a conference last year."

The warmth of the coffee and its satisfying flavor brought a smile to Finn's lips.

"Very nice," Finn answered. "I'm impressed. Good coffee, you have the dog trained, and you're dressed nicely, too."

Finn gazed up and down at the green dress Siobhan wore. His vision came to rest on her face as she smiled at him, her green eyes and red hair on her shoulders captivating him just as it had years ago.

"I see your bedroom hasn't changed much, though," Finn offered as he waved his hand around at the mess he perceived.

"Yeah, I was never too much for organization at home. I'll get it all put away eventually. I know where everything is, though. And I keep my office immaculate. As for the dog, he just needed a strong woman's touch to bring him in line. We have an agreement now."

Siobhan glanced down at Jameson and then patted his head.

"And the dress?" Finn asked.

"It's Sunday, Finn," Siobhan said as she turned toward the mirror over her dresser. "I'm going to church. You're welcome to join me."

"I'm pretty sure I'll get struck by lightning if I walk through that door," Finn replied.

"I think you give yourself too much credit. You might find it helpful with everything going on."

Siobhan turned to look at Finn as he sat on the bed.

"I'll pass, thanks." Finn looked around the room. "Where are my clothes?" Finn asked. He was never shy about the way his body looked. He stood up in his boxer briefs and walked around the room. Siobhan followed Finn's every step with her eyes.

"Oh, I tossed them in my washing machine," Siobhan said. "I figured you didn't have anything to wear and, well, there was some blood on them. You can put them in the dryer, and they should be done in a bit. You do know how to do that, don't you? Or do you have maids and dry cleaners take care of all that stuff for you?"

"Hilarious," Finn remarked. "I only send my suits to the dry cleaners, and the cleaning service comes twice a week and cleans my apartment. I take care of the laundry."

"Wow, I'm impressed," Siobhan mocked. "Finn O'Farrell, all grown up."

Siobhan looked down at her watch.

"I've got to run. I'll be back in an hour or so. There's more coffee in the pot, and if you want to take a shower, I'm sure you can find your way around. When I get back, I can take you back to your Dad's place if you want or down to the hospital."

"A shower sounds good," Finn offered as he walked past Siobhan and stood at the bathroom doorway.

"Oh, Finn!" Siobhan gasped.

"What?"

"Your back... the bruises and... and well, the scars..." Siobhan felt a loss of words.

Finn spun around to face Siobhan.

"Yeah, the bruises must be from last night," as Finn touched his shoulder blade lightly. "The scars... that's from a long time ago. Don't worry about those. Go. You'll be late for Mass, and that will be another strike against me with God," Finn joked.

Finn slipped into the bathroom and quickly closed the door. He turned slightly so he could look in the mirror. He saw the dark purple marks that spread across his shoulder blades and top of his back.

Whatever I got hit with sure left a mark, Finn thought.

He also caught a glimpse of the scars on his back. Many had faded over the years, but some still stuck out more than others. Most of the time, when someone noticed them, Finn would create a story about a car accident, a skiing mishap, or some outdoor adventure that went wrong. He had a feeling Siobhan, of all people, wouldn't buy any of those.

The shower allowed Finn the chance to let the hot water do its magic on his sore body for a bit. Siobhan's shower was a far cry from his own with the spacious stall and custom showerhead and faucet, but it did the job for him. He felt pain when he turned and let the water hit his back where the bruises were, but the steam and heat helped him clear his head. When he got out, Finn cleared the fog from the mirror with his forearm and saw that he had more stubble on his face than he was accustomed to. Just a couple of days' growth was immediately noticeable for someone that gave himself a close shave every morning, so he looked his best for work. With none of his own toiletries to use, Finn resigned to remain scruffy for the moment.

Finn paced the apartment with nothing but a towel wrapped around his waist, looking for something to do while his clothes dried. He saw the sparse furnishings and decorations around the apartment. A few cheesy wall decorations and souvenirs from trips that Siobhan had taken dotted the living room walls and shelves of her bookcase. Siobhan did have some old pictures of herself and her brothers, her parents, and even Cara and Darren around the place. It would have surprised him to see any hint of a reminder of himself anywhere.

Finn returned to the bedroom and lay back down on the bed, staring at the ceiling again. Jameson looked up at him, passing an annoyed look along that Finn would not just settle down in one space for a while. He noticed his phone, wallet, and keys on the side table and picked up his phone to see several missed phone calls from Darren. He pressed return to call Darren back, and Darren picked up immediately.

"What the hell, mate?" Darren began before saying anything else. "You didn't come by, and you didn't call me or anything like you said you would. Cara came to Millie's and said she hadn't seen or heard from you. I thought you were in a hospital bed or a ditch somewhere off 17, thanks to Liam and the boys."

"I almost was, I think," Finn added in. He regaled Darren with the tale of his visit to his father in the hospital and what occurred at his father's house later.

"So, where are you now?" Darren asked.

"I'm at Siobhan's," Finn added.

"Really?" Darren said with surprise. "I never would have expected that. How was it?"

"Don't be a dog," Finn chided. "I didn't want to go to the hospital, the cops wouldn't let me stay at the house, so Siobhan invited me here. She slept on the couch while I was in the bed… mostly."

"Mostly? What does that mean?"

"I'm pretty sure at some point she was in bed with me," Finn admitted. "Nothing happened. We just slept, and then she got up this morning and went to church."

"I can't believe she even came to your Da's house to see you, never mind brought you back to her place for the night."

"I'm a bit surprised too," Finn said honestly.

"So, do you need me to come to get you?" Darren asked. "I can bring you down to the hospital, or you can hang out at Millie's before you go back to your Dad's place. Your choice."

"Nah," Finn answered. "I just got out of the shower, and I'm waiting for my clothes to dry. I'll catch up with you later."

"So, you're sitting around Siobhan's apartment, freshly showered and naked, waiting for her to get back. Sounds perfectly reasonable to me, Finn."

"Go to work, Darren," Finn ordered and hung up the phone.

Finn walked from the bedroom to the washer and dryer and pulled his wet clothing out before tossing it into the small, stacked dryer above the washing machine. He poured himself a fresh cup of coffee and wandered back toward the bedroom, and sat on the chair tucked in the corner. His thoughts turned around to the day before and what occurred at his father's home. Finn was unsure who he had stumbled upon and what they might be seeking, and why the police were involved in any investigation at all. He had no facts to go on to piece things together, other than the sensitive egg on the back of his head. And what had happened last night with Siobhan? Why had she come to Conor's house? Why did she step in to help? And was she in bed with him?

Jameson strolled over and sat in front of Finn, pushing his head into Finn's hands to let him know he wanted to be pet. Finn mindlessly placed his hand on Jameson's scalp and started rubbing, much to the dog's delight.

"I wish you could help me with all this, buddy," Finn said to the dog. At the same time, he scratched behind Jameson's ear, prompting a thumping of the dog's hind leg rapidly on the floor.

"You're the one who has probably seen everything going on."

****

Siobhan left the church, making sure to exchange pleasantries with the other parishioners as she always did each Sunday. She thanked Father Mike for a beautiful sermon. Instead of lingering in the parking lot with some of the other ladies as she often did, Siobhan made a beeline to her car to get back to her apartment.

Rationally, there was no reason for Siobhan to rush home. Her house was less than a three-minute drive from the church, and she had nothing pressing that she had to do today. There were no phone calls or texts from anyone from the organization that she needed to tend to. Still, Siobhan sped back to her apartment with a sense of anticipation she rarely felt about going home.

Siobhan strode through the front door, smiling, and noticed that Finn had straightened up the kitchen a bit, putting things away and washing out the coffee pot.

"You just couldn't help but try to organize my place, could you," Siobhan shouted as she placed her purse on the clean, polished table.

She paced down the hallway and walked to her bedroom without thought.

"I would have done…" Siobhan stopped dead in her tracks as she had walked in just as Finn was pulling on his black boxer briefs. She got the full view of his well-toned legs right up to his bare behind before he tugged the underwear into place.

"I'm sorry," Siobhan gushed, turning around quickly. "I didn't even think that you would be getting dressed."

"Take it easy, Bon," Finn laughed as he turned. "It's not like you haven't seen me naked before."

"Well, that was before... I mean, it was a long behind ago... I meant time ago..." Siobhan could feel herself getting more and more flustered.

Siobhan felt Finn's hand on her shoulder as he guided her to turn toward him.

"It was a long time ago," Finn told her softly. "But that doesn't mean I have forgotten about it... or about you."

Finn placed his thumb and index finger just under Siobhan's chin and gently stroked. Siobhan closed her eyes and turned her chin up instinctively as if to go in for a kiss before she stopped herself. Her eyes flew open as Finn brought his lips close, just in time for her to pull herself away.

"You should have come to Mass with me," Siobhan said as she hurried out of the bedroom down the hall to let Finn finish getting dressed. "Father Mike gave a lovely sermon."

"I'm sure he did," Finn echoed from the bedroom.

Siobhan took a few deep breaths to compose herself and watched as Finn walked down the hall in his t-shirt and jeans.

"Thanks for letting me stay last night," Finn said as he put on his watch and stuffed his wallet into his jeans pocket.

"You needed somewhere to go, Finn, and you weren't supposed to be alone. I did what anyone would do."

"No," Finn said assuredly. "Not everyone would. Was... was everything okay last night?"

"What do you mean?" Siobhan asked.

"I thought I remembered… well, I remember you putting your arms around me last night… in bed. Did that happen?"

"I did come in to check on you like the EMT said I should," Siobhan shared. She hesitated to go any further with what happened.

"Okay," Finn nodded. "So, what are we doing today?"

"Today?" Siobhan was taken aback. "Oh, I thought you would want me to just take you back to Conor's place."

"Well, I do want that," Finn admitted, "but I also don't feel quite 100% yet for driving. I thought maybe we could go around town a bit to see some of the areas again. Liam and the Cosantóir will be at the hospital after their morning ride – I'm sure of that. Going down there now isn't the best idea for me. Unless you had other plans today for yourself… or with someone else?"

Siobhan looked at Finn and smiled.

"No… I didn't have anything planned—just a lazy Sunday. Let me just throw a few things to bring along in a bag, and we can go."

"Great," Finn said with a nod.

Siobhan went into the bedroom and stuffed some items into a tote bag. She then glanced over at Jameson, who had been sleeping soundly on the floor.

"What about Jameson?" Siobhan shouted to Finn. Jameson's ears perked up as soon as he heard his name.

"We'll bring him," Finn answered.

"Guess you're chaperoning today," Siobhan said with an eye roll as Jameson bounded out of the room to Finn.

12

Finn settled into Siobhan's car and rested his head back on the vinyl headrest. At the same time, Jameson made himself comfortable in the backseat. Once Siobhan was ready, she turned to Finn for some guidance.

"Where to?" She asked.

"I don't know," Finn answered. "What's new and exciting in the area?"

"New? There's plenty, Finn. You haven't been here in a long time. Exciting? Well, that might be a different story."

"Well, let's just drive, and we'll see what we come across," Finn resolved. "We don't have to limit ourselves just to Harriman and Monroe."

"Good," Siobhan replied. "Otherwise, this might be about a five-minute excursion."

Siobhan pulled out of her parking space and made her way into the scattered traffic of a Sunday morning. It didn't take long for Finn to turn his attention out the window to look at what was and wasn't around anymore.

"What happened to Mr. Cone?" Finn said with shock as they drove by where a large bank now stood.

"Oh, he's been gone for a few years now," Siobhan lamented.

"I can't believe it. That place was an institution around here. We would go there all the time for ice cream."

"Some of us would get ice cream," Siobhan reminded him. "You only ever wanted a shake."

"That's not true," Finn said as he defended himself. "Sometimes, I got ice cream."

"Whatever you say," Siobhan laughed. She drove a bit further as they passed the Captain's Table, a long-time stalwart in the area.

"Some things don't change," Finn noted as they crept past the already packed parking lot of the bar and restaurant.

"No, they don't," Siobhan noted.

"Do you go there much?"

"Not really," Siobhan said. "Cara and I mostly go to Millie's when we do go out. We hit the Captain's Table if Cara wants to go and see old high school folk so she can snidely mock them from afar."

Finn laughed heartily until they started to pass the cemetery on the right. He quieted down as Siobhan went by, and Siobhan noted a seriousness across Finn's face as they drove. Finn's mother was buried there, and Siobhan was unsure just when the last time Finn had visited her gravesite. She began to speak up but held back and made it as if she was clearing her throat.

"I have an idea," she said as she turned at the next light and headed over toward the Lake Street area and parked the car at one of the spots on the street.

"Let's go," she commanded as she stepped out of the car and went to the sidewalk. Finn climbed out and took Jameson's leash. The dog was more than happy about the outing.

"Where are we going?" Finn asked.

"It's Sunday," Siobhan remarked. "The Farmer's Market is open."

"Ooh, fun," Finn added sarcastically.

"Come on," Siobhan insisted and took Finn by the hand. She thought about letting go once she had pulled Finn to be next to her, but she felt Finn interlace his fingers with hers. The duo strolled through the crowd at the marketplace. Families were all about, stopping for fresh local produce, flowers, snacks, honey, and other items from local vendors. Siobhan greeted many people with smiles and hellos as they moved among the crowd.

"I didn't know I was out with the mayor," Finn told her as they stopped to look at some local vegetables.

"Not quite," Siobhan said as she picked up a bundle of basil and took in the aroma. "I do work around here and deal with the public, local businesses, and organizations all the time. I know a lot of people. I'm sure it's the same for you in Saratoga."

"Yeah, I'm not known for the same good reasons you are, Bon," Finn admitted. "People either recognize me because I defended them or went against them in court, or they saw me at some party somewhere."

"Or as one the most eligible bachelors in the area," Siobhan added as she added some fresh carrots to her basket.

"What? How did you know about that?"

"Did you really think Darren would keep that from us? He swore he was going to frame it and put it up at Millie's," Siobhan laughed.

Siobhan noticed it was Finn who seemed to blush now through the stubble on his cheeks.

"I didn't have anything to do with all that," Finn defended. "It's just some silly thing they do in the city, and the law firm thought it would be good publicity."

"You didn't say no, though," Siobhan added. "So," she continued as she plucked a head of lettuce from a bin, "Is it true?"

"Is what true?"

"That you're this grand bachelor royalty who goes out with a different woman every week?"

Siobhan peered over at Finn to gauge his reaction. She wanted to see if the question made him uncomfortable, and it had hit its mark.

"There's no point in me denying it," Finn admitted. "Yes, I do go out often with different women. It's my one social vice."

Siobhan strolled up to the vendor who was ringing up purchases and laid her produce out for him.

"Do you sleep with all of them?" Siobhan asked bluntly. Her question caught Finn off guard. Not only Finn heard it, and now several people were looking at the two of them, including the man placing the bunch of carrots in a bag.

"Jesus, Bon," Finn said as he handed the vendor a twenty and snatched the bag from his hand.

Siobhan watched as Finn stormed off, leading Jameson away as well. Siobhan turned and smiled coyly at the people around her.

"I'll let you know what he says," she told her audience before scrambling after Finn.

Siobhan caught up with Finn as he was reaching the car.

"What's the problem?" she asked.

"You had to ask me that in a crowd of people?" Finn chided.

"Why? You don't know any of them. Heck, you don't really know me anymore, Finn. You have nothing to be embarrassed about. I thought you would be proud to crow about your conquests."

A couple sitting outside the local deli sipping coffee at a table paid attention to the discussion. Finn acknowledged them with a nod and tugged on the locked passenger side door.

"Can you unlock the door, please?" Finn said through gritted teeth.

"Are you going to answer me?"

"Can we do this later?" Finn pleaded.

"You keep saying we're going to do this later, Finn," Siobhan said sternly. "How long do you want me to put it off for? For a few more days so you can leave again and not worry about it? I'm not letting you off that easy this time. I'm not that wide-eyed teenager that was madly in love with you at eighteen anymore. I deserve some respect."

Siobhan crossed her arms and raised an eyebrow to Finn as she waited for an answer. She did all she could to maintain her composure, though Siobhan rapidly tapped her left foot on the pavement as she waited.

"Okay," Finn growled. "Yes, I sleep with a lot of them. Not all, but many. Is that what you wanted to hear?"

"It's a start," Siobhan shot back as she clicked the remote on her car to unlock the doors. She watched as Finn led Jameson into the back seat before Finn sat down and slammed the door shut, causing the couple to jostle their coffee cups from the noise.

Siobhan got behind the wheel and started up the car before she squealed the tires and pulled out. She sped past the lakes to the stop sign, barely coming to a stop at all before she merged into traffic and continued through town.

The two sat silently for a minute or two before Finn spoke up.

"Maybe I should just go back to my Dad's place," Finn huffed.

"No way, we're here to see the sights and reminisce," Siobhan said as she gripped the steering wheel tightly. She sped her car along the winding portions of 17M that led out of Monroe toward Chester. Siobhan led Finn down the older section of Chester and out before taking a quick right to Main Street. Siobhan slowed down as they approached the rail station and came across bicyclists getting to the Heritage Trail for a ride before bearing right again.

"Where are we going?" Finn finally asked.

"I want a beer that isn't a Guinness," Siobhan told him as she pulled into the gravel parking lot and stopped the car. "Take Jameson around the side to one of the picnic tables and wait for me there. I'll get us something to drink."

Finn headed off to the outdoor area with an excited Jameson. At the same time, Siobhan went inside Rushing Duck to order the beer. She took a few deep breaths to compose herself before ordering a couple of sours. Siobhan carefully carried the glasses out onto the patio. She spotted Finn sitting glumly at a table with Jameson perched at his feet.

Siobhan placed a glass in front of Finn and sat across from him at the table.

"Slainte," she toasted before taking a healthy gulp of the beer.

"What is it?" Finn questioned, staring at the pinkish color in the glass.

"It's a sour," Siobhan told him. "It has some raspberry and mango in it."

"Really?" Finn said, holding up the pint.

"Don't they have local breweries up there in your city?" Siobhan added. "Just try it."

Siobhan took another draw on her beverage as Finn took a small sip of his. She watched as his lips puckered slightly from the initial sour taste before he smacked his lips.

"Tastes good," Finn admitted.

"Told ya," Siobhan said. "Now, don't tell Darren we came here. He takes it personally when I go somewhere else for beer."

Siobhan closed her eyes and let the sun warm her cheeks. When she opened her eyes, she saw Finn staring at her.

"What?"

"I'm sorry, Bon," Finn offered. "I didn't mean to yell at you like that. You just… caught me off guard, I guess. I wasn't expecting you to ask me stuff like that."

"Finn, I'm willing to listen to what you have to say, but you have to say something. You owe me that much. You lead your life how you want, just like I do mine. But you can't just waltz back here, put yourself in front of me and expect everything to be okay. It's not right, and I won't let it happen."

"Fair enough," Finn added before he took another sip.

Siobhan felt a bit of weight lifted from her after somewhat saying her piece and relaxed some as they each finished their beer before Finn went in to get the next round. Siobhan looked at the growing crowd at the other tables outside. She then turned her attention to the nearby farmland to take in the lushness before her. She relished the smells, sounds, and views outdoors and felt calmer than she had in days.

"Siobhan?" a voice said from behind her. She spun around and saw Gavin Elliott standing there holding a beer.

"Gavin," she stuttered. "I didn't know you came out here."

"I don't usually, but I was meeting some of the county officials here to talk about potential projects. There are some great spaces out here we can make use of to build up," he said proudly.

"Not everything needs to be built up and overrun, Gavin," Siobhan said. She looked past Gavin to see where Finn was and hoped Gavin would be gone before Finn returned to the table.

"Well, not everything, of course," Gavin conceded. "But we're a burgeoning area, Siobhan. More people from the city and Westchester are looking to come here. We need more businesses, more housing, more infrastructure. Growth is progress."

"Not always," she said softly.

"I'm glad I ran into you," Gavin said. "Is it okay if I sit?" Gavin asked as he went to sit next to Siobhan on her side of the picnic table. Jameson sat up, squinted at Gavin, and let out a low growl. Gavin immediately backed off a few paces.

"I didn't know you had a dog," Gavin said hesitantly.

"I'm watching him for a friend. He's very protective," Siobhan remarked.

"I see that," Gavin said with a nervous laugh.

"I wanted to see if maybe we could try again and get together next week to talk things over. We got off on the wrong foot the other day, and I apologize. I promise I'll look over your proposal before we have dinner again," Gavin uttered.

"Business, right?" Siobhan insisted. She looked over at Jameson and elicited another low growl from him.

"Absolutely," Gavin told her, crossing his heart with his fingers.

"Fine," Siobhan assented.

"Fantastic!" Gavin replied. "Call my office tomorrow and let me know what works best for you."

Finn arrived back at the table and placed the beer in front of Siobhan before standing in front of Gavin. Siobhan saw that Finn was looking Gavin over and sizing him up.

"Sorry, it took so long," Finn told Siobhan. "They're pretty busy in there."

"Thanks," Siobhan said as she gripped her glass. "Finn, this is Gavin Elliott. Gavin, this is Finn O'Farrell."

"O'Farrell, huh?" Gavin questioned. "Are you related to Conor and Liam?"

"I am," Finn replied cautiously. "Do you know my Dad and brother?"

"I've come across them a few times locally, and on some jobs my company has done. I think they are working on one of the tunnel projects I have going right now. Do you work with the Sand Hogs too?" Gavin asked smugly.

"Finn's a lawyer in Saratoga," Siobhan interrupted, hoping to speed the conversation along.

"Is that right," Gavin said. "What firm?"

"Peterson and Morris," Finn told him.

"Ah, good group," Gavin nodded. "I know Bob Morris. A good guy."

"I'll be sure to tell him you said hello," Finn added. He sat down at the picnic table next to Siobhan so that she was shoulder to shoulder with Finn.

"You do that," Gavin said with a smile. "I've got to get back to my group. Nice to meet you, Finn. Siobhan, I look forward to dinner this week." Gavin leaned in as if to give Siobhan a hug, but Jameson rose immediately and stopped him.

"Nice dog," Gavin noted before he waved and moved off.

Siobhan watched as Gavin disappeared back inside the bar and then turned her attention back to her beer.

"So, who's Gavin?" Finn asked.

"Local business magnate," Siobhan said casually. "He's helped my organization a lot, rounding up donors and getting grants."

"I see," Finn added. "Do you guys have dinner together often?"

"Not if I can help it," Siobhan admitted.

"It's just that you seemed a bit chummy is all, and he's clearly into you."

"We're not chummy. It's just business. And why do you care, anyway?" Siobhan challenged.

"It's hard to believe that a guy who fawned over you when we were in high school would just give that up if he saw you all the time," Finn said authoritatively.

"You remember him from high school?"

"Of course I do," Finn replied. "He was a year behind us. A rich kid who thought he was better than all of us who had parents that worked for a living. He used to give me the same dirty looks he gave me today when we were together."

"So then all of that just now was some pissing contest to show Gavin that you still have some claim on me?" Siobhan said strongly.

"No... Bon, that's not what I meant. Jesus, you're twisting everything I say around today." Finn shook his head while Siobhan chugged down the rest of her beer.

"I'm getting another," Siobhan said as she stormed away from the table and into the bar. She saw Gavin seated at a far table in the corner with his business cronies and turned away before he noticed her. Instead of her usual sour, Siobhan ordered a high alcohol stout and brought it back to the table. She made sure to sit down on the opposite side of the table from Finn when she arrived.

"What's that one?" Finn asked. "It smells boozy from here."

"Don't you worry about it," Siobhan said emphatically as she downed four of the eight ounces right away. She regretted her decision and began to feel light-headed but did her best not to let it show to Finn.

"Take it easy there, killer," Finn warned. "You still need to make it through the rest of the day."

"I'll be fine, Mr. O'Farrell," Siobhan told him, her voice slurred slightly. She picked up her glass and drank what remained in it. Siobhan closed her eyes and didn't feel like opening them again right away. She gazed at the stream of colors with her eyes shut tight and recognized that Finn said something to her, but she couldn't make it out.

When she opened her eyes, the bright sunlight caused her to recoil a bit and, she missed when she went to put her elbows down on the table and nearly hit her head. Finn had reached over just in time to prevent her from smacking the table.

"Okay, it's time to go," Finn ordered. Siobhan watched as he got up from the table and helped her to her feet.

"I'm fine, Finn," Siobhan insisted. Her voice seemed to echo inside her head as she felt Finn slide a hand around her waist.

"Yes, you are, but I think I'm finished," Finn added.

Siobhan tried to focus as Finn moved her from the table onto the grass and back out toward the parking lot. She recognized when they reached her car and went into her purse to grab her keys. As soon as she had them out, Finn grabbed the keys from her hands.

"Hey!" Siobhan shouted. "I'm fine to drive."

"I know, but I really want to see if I remember the roads around here. Just humor me," Finn told her.

Siobhan was guided over to the passenger side as Finn placed her in the passenger seat. He grabbed the seat belt and pulled it across her body, adjusting the strap to fit her properly.

"Trying for second base there, Mr. O'Farrell?" Siobhan said with a giggle.

"Not quite," Finn smiled. "Safety first."

Siobhan watched as Finn started up the car and began to drive. She kept her eyes closed, trying with all her might to fight what she felt going on in her stomach.

Her right hand struggled to find the automatic switch to open the window.

"What's the matter?" Finn asked as he drove.

"Take the lock off the windows so I don't puke in my car," Siobhan insisted.

"Yes, Ma'am," Finn said, and he opened the window for her. The gush of fresh air hit Siobhan's face, and she put her head back and kept her eyes closed.

"Thank you," she said to Finn. "There might be hope for you yet."

****

Finn drove along slowly, trying to keep one eye on the road while watching Siobhan to make sure she didn't get sick. He turned on the radio, hoping the music might help keep her mind off anything else. Bryan Adams's "Cuts Like a Knife" played, and Finn saw a smile creep across Siobhan's mouth as she began to sing along with the music. It brought Finn back to the way it was when the two of them would drive around anywhere, and she would sing with the radio, whether she knew the words or not.

As they reached Monroe, Finn took note of all the development going on and the high amount of traffic that seemed everywhere. It was a far cry from what he recalled growing up when kids could stay out late playing basketball, swimming in someone's pool, or just hanging out with friends without worrying about what was going on in the world around them. Now there were immense medical arts buildings, strip malls where none existed before, endless casual fast-food restaurants, and more traffic lights than he was used to even in Saratoga.

Finn went around the slight bend in the road and spotted the cemetery on the left. He tensed up slightly but then slowed down and made the left to go on the dirt road that led through the center. The car hit a divot in the pathway, and Siobhan jumped in her seat, forcing her eyes open.

"Where are we?" she asked as she peered through her barely open eyes.

"The cemetery," Finn said solemnly as he slowed down. "I wish I could remember where she is," he said softly.

"I know where she is," Siobhan told him. Finn followed her directions down the path until she brought him to a stop. Finn turned the car off and opened the windows all the way. He went over to the passenger side and opened the door for Siobhan, steadying her as she got out. Jameson looked to climb out to join them.

"Stay," Finn commanded, and Jameson slumped back down on the seat, bellyaching with a whimper.

"Wait," Siobhan told Finn. She reached into the back seat and grabbed the bouquet of cut flowers she had purchased at the Farmer's Market earlier.

Finn allowed Siobhan to lead him through a maze of headstones, many much older than his mother's. Much of the area was quite dry because of a lack of recent rain, but Siobhan pointed to a shaded area with a large oak tree looming over a headstone.

"She's there," Siobhan indicated.

Siobhan hooked her arm around Finn's, and the two walked together until they were under the tree. A polished granite bench sat just to the left of the headstone. Finn guided Siobhan to the bench so she could sit before he turned his attention to the grave marker. Finn wiped away some of the debris and branches that had fallen on the headstone so that it looked cleaner. There were some decaying flowers that he moved aside at the base of the headstone.

"It looks nicer than I thought it would," Finn said quietly. He turned and looked at Siobhan. She looked up at him and smiled.

"Your Da made sure she had a good spot," Siobhan admitted. "I'm pretty sure he used whatever influence he might have to ensure it."

"Do you think he comes out here? Or Liam? Or anyone? It's bad enough I haven't done it. I hate the thought that she's... well, that she's alone all the time."

"I can't speak for your father or brother," Siobhan said as she rose and stood next to Finn. "I can tell you she's not alone. Her friends come out here to pay respects, and I come out once a month to make sure she has some flowers."

Siobhan picked up the bouquet and placed it neatly by the marker.

"Fad is a mhairfimid beidh tusa beo freisin," Siobhan said as she touched the headstone.

"My Gaelic is more than a little rusty," Finn said quietly. "What did you say?"

"As long as we live, you too will live," Siobhan told him.

Finn nodded, unsure of what, if anything, he should say.

"If you want to be alone, Finn, I can walk back to the car. I'm fairly sure I can make it on my own," she said with a smile.

"No, it's okay. We can both go. I just wanted... to see her."

The two walked side by side back toward Siobhan's vehicle. At one point, she stumbled slightly on some loose stones, but Finn reached over quickly and took hold of her. After that, Finn made sure to hold onto Siobhan's hand until they got back to the car.

Jameson greeted them happily, with his face leaning out the window. Finn got behind the wheel, led them back out of the cemetery, and headed back through Monroe to Harriman. When he drove past Siobhan's apartment, she looked over to him.

"Where are we going?" Siobhan inquired.

"We should go to my Dad's house," Finn said as he turned to go up the road that led to his father's home.

He pulled Siobhan's car next to his and parked. There were no signs of any police cars or markings anywhere that he could find. Siobhan had already gotten out of the passenger seat and stood at the front of her car. Finn let Jameson out, and the dog proceeded to bound up the front steps to the porch he knew well.

"Okay," Siobhan sighed. "I can leave you to whatever you have to do," she said as she reached for the car keys in Finn's hand. Finn snatched them away before she could grab them.

"You probably shouldn't be driving just yet. You still look a little green," Finn told her.

"I'm fine, Finn, really," Siobhan said. She stepped closer to Finn and opened her eyes wide. "See?"

Finn gazed into her emerald eyes and paid little attention to anything else.

"I'm still not convinced," he offered.

"I have to get my groceries home anyway," Siobhan insisted.

"No, you don't," Finn replied. "We can have dinner here."

"What, you expect me to cook dinner for you?" Siobhan said, putting her hands on her hips.

"I never said that," Finn insisted. "I'll cook dinner."

Siobhan stifled a laugh.

"You're going to cook? The Finn O'Farrell I know could barely make a peanut butter sandwich without tearing the bread. I figured you just ate out at a fancy restaurant each night or had one of your concubines cook for you."

"You must think you're hysterical," Finn said. He went into the car and grabbed the bags of groceries from the back seat.

"I cook when I have time, and I'm good at it. You'll see," Finn said as he marched toward the front door.

"Oh, I have to see this," Siobhan scoffed and followed Finn to the house.

Finn halted briefly when they entered the house. He scanned around to make sure he didn't hear anything. Jameson had rushed in ahead of him and didn't bark, so Finn assumed all was well. He stepped over the area where some of the bloodstains from the attack still lingered.

After placing the bags down on the kitchen table, Finn went to the fridge and grabbed two water bottles. He handed both to Siobhan.

"Go sit out on the patio and hydrate. I'll take care of things here," Finn said authoritatively.

"I can't stay and watch?" Siobhan asked. "How do I know you aren't going to order delivery?"

"Out!" Finn pointed to the back door. "You're not the only one who can be bossy."

Siobhan slipped out onto the back patio, with Jameson following her, while Finn set to work in the kitchen. He scoured the fridge to see what his father had stocked and found a couple of excellent ribeye steaks. He seasoned the steaks generously and let them sit at room temperature. At the same time, he went to work on the vegetables that Siobhan had purchased. Finn had crafted a fine meal in no time at all, using what was in front of him. A few times, he caught Siobhan peeking through the kitchen window to see what he was up to before he chased her away.

It was just about an hour when Finn was satisfied with everything and called Siobhan inside. He watched as

Siobhan's face lit up with surprise as she saw the table set finely with a candle in the center. Finn pulled out Siobhan's chair so she could sit down, and he then delicately placed a white linen napkin in her lap. Finn then dutifully poured some red wine into a glass for Siobhan, poured one for himself, and sat across from her.

"Wow, I'm impressed," Siobhan noted as she examined the table and all its dressings.

"Me too, actually," Finn admitted. "Who knew my father had linen napkins and a selection of wines. We lived on pancakes, takeout, and frozen dinners with paper towels for napkins after Mom…" Finn stopped himself from going further.

"Anyway," he interrupted, "Ith gu leòir!"

Siobhan opened her eyes wide. "You do remember some Gaelic!"

"Nah, I cheated," Finn admitted. "I Googled bon appetit in Gaelic."

Siobhan let out a big laugh. "A for effort," she said as she raised her glass.

The two ate well on ribeye steaks, honey-glazed carrots, and twice-baked potatoes with a salad. Finn found himself relaxing more and more as he talked with Siobhan, and they went over old times and new. He told her about what law school was like and his aims for his law career while she impressed him with her directorship at A Safe Place and all she has done for the community. Soon, their plates were empty, the wine glasses had been refilled, and the conversation died down to a comfortable silence.

"You should be proud of yourself, Finn," Siobhan said.

"I told you I could cook," Finn stated proudly as he cleared their plates away.

"Not just with that," Siobhan said, "though I never thought I could eat an entire ribeye like that. What

I meant is you should be proud of all you have accomplished. I'm sure your family is proud of you."

"Aunt Maureen… sure she is. She came to my graduation from law school. I couldn't have done it without support from her and Uncle Oscar."

"I was talking about your Da," Siobhan replied.

Finn looked over and then went back to filling the dishwasher.

"Yeah, well, I have my doubts about that. If I didn't work getting callouses on my hands, I wasn't really working in Conor O'Farrell's eyes. The only other job he would have approved of for me is priest, and that wasn't going to happen," he laughed. "If he knew I was a lawyer, he'd have more than a few choice words for me."

"I don't think that's true," Siobhan added as she got up from the table and went into the kitchen. "I think Conor would be impressed at what you've become."

"I wish I had something to offer you for dessert," Finn said, changing the subject abruptly. "I hadn't planned on entertaining. Maybe there's something in the freezer." Finn closed the dishwasher and moved toward the fridge, but Siobhan stepped in front of him.

"It's okay. I hadn't planned on staying for dinner."

Finn stared down into Siobhan's eyes and found himself getting lost in them. Instinct had him placing his hands on her hips and pulling her closer to him. As he bent down to kiss her, Siobhan pulled away.

"No, Finn," Siobhan told him.

Finn opened the refrigerator door, grabbed a water bottle, and then slammed the door closed, rattling the appliance.

"What the hell, Bon?" Finn shouted.

"You still haven't told me," she insisted.

"Told you what?"

"Told me why you left me ten years ago!" she yelled with all her might. "You were just gone. No note, no phone call, no visits – nothing. We made plans together, Finn, and you tossed them out the window without any explanation at all. If that didn't hurt enough, you never called. You never came back. It took me weeks to find out from Darren that you went to live with your aunt, and even then, you still didn't contact me. You know how many times I just wanted to get in the car, drive to Albany and find you, and slap you? Even if you just said to me you were ending it, it would have devastated me, but at least it would have been something. I would have had closure. You left me with nothing, and it tore me apart."

Finn saw Siobhan breathing heavily after getting it all out of her system.

"Do you really want to know why I left, Bon? You want to hear all the details about how fucked up life was in the O'Farrell house before and after my mother died? All the stuff I could never tell you about when Da would come home drunk or high or whatever and beat the shit out of me because of something like I left an empty Coke bottle on the kitchen counter or didn't get all the laundry done, so he and Liam had clothes for work? Maybe I could have let you know about how he would throw me down the stairs if I forgot to turn off the light in the bathroom, and my Ma would patch me up on the floor. Or that last night when I told him I didn't want to work in the tunnels anymore and wanted to go to college, and we finally had it out."

Finn pulled his t-shirt over his head and turned his back toward Siobhan.

"See those scars? That's what happens when you get hit with an electrical cord over and over because you said you didn't want to shovel mud and shit for the rest of your life. I wasn't going to let him win that one. When he was done, I smiled at him, spat blood on the floor in front of him, and marched to my room. I packed, called my aunt, and drove off. Am I sorry I left you like that? Yes, I'm sorry. But I had to leave, dammit, or I was going to die in that house."

Finn stared at Siobhan and could see the redness in her eyes. His voice was hoarse from yelling, and he felt spent.

"You could have told me, Finn," Siobhan said. "I might have been able to help…"

"Help with what? There was nothing you or anyone could have done for me. I had to do it myself."

"You didn't even give me the chance to do anything! I loved you. I could have done something."

Finn rushed towards Siobhan, picking her up at the elbows, and pinned her against the far wall.

"What Bon? What would you have done?" Finn screamed.

Tears were flowing down Siobhan's face as she peered at Finn.

"Something, anything…" she whispered.

Finn was overcome and leaned against Siobhan, kissing her hard. Siobhan struggled in Finn's grasp at first, even biting his lower lip as he kissed her so that he pulled away. Finn could taste the trickle of blood on his tongue.

Siobhan stared back into Finn's eyes. He looked for any type of sign from her but saw nothing. Finn moved to back away from her, and Siobhan reached for his face with both hands, pulling him to her lips as she kissed him hungrily. All that pent-up anger and feelings Finn had came out as he pressed his body against Siobhan's tightly. His lips moved from hers, and he began to kiss her neck passionately. Siobhan gasped at the first contact of Finn's lips on her neck as Finn went further to the nape of her neck.

His left hand shot up to take hold of her red hair. He held Siobhan's hair firmly, tilting her head to the left so he could place kisses on her neck, up and down, slowly. Finn knew Siobhan was melting as she panted with each kiss. He felt her hands stretch down to his waist and then up to his bare back, her fingernails digging into him as his kisses worked on her. Finn moved back to her lips with a firm yet delicate action before returning to her sensitive neck again, causing Siobhan to moan. She leaned in close to him, her head on his shoulder before she turned and kissed and then nibbled on his ear, eliciting a growl from him.

Finn pulled back and hoisted Siobhan into his arms. She wrapped her legs around his waist, the skirt of her dress bunching up at her own midsection as he carried her over to the couch and tossed her down on it. Finn stared down at Siobhan as she looked at him with desire, merely nodding rapidly to give Finn the invitation he was waiting for. He wasted no time tearing at the buttons on the front of her dress, flinging it open and then pulling her up off the couch, so her torso was pressed against his once more. Finn peeled the top of her dress down and ran his fingertips lightly down her spine, sending shivers and chills through Siobhan's body. He teased his hand back and forth over her as his kisses returned to her body.

Every motion along Siobhan's spine caused her to arch her back and press closer to Finn so that he could feel the lace of her bra brush against him, exciting his own body more. On a pass of his fingers over the middle of her back, he deftly undid the hook of her bra so he could pull it from her shoulders and toss it aside.

Siobhan lay back on the couch, took Finn's head in her hands, and guided his mouth to her breasts. Finn obliged, placing his mouth on her left breast and kissing repeatedly. His tongue circled her areola over and over, causing Siobhan's waist and hips to push up against Finn's. Finn was doing his best to control himself, to hold out, to make the moment last. Still, Siobhan's movements and moans were making it more difficult by the second.

Finn felt Siobhan's hands wandering down his body further until she found the button for his jeans. Her left hand held the front of his jeans firmly as she rubbed roughly over the denim to feel him in her hands. She worked frantically to unbutton and unzip the jeans for him enough so she could slide her hand inside his pants and stroke his length through his briefs. Finn growled deeply at Siobhan's touch, and his mouth moved from just kissing her breast to enveloping her nipple in his mouth. Finn drew the nipple to him, swirling his tongue around it in his mouth, causing Siobhan to moan once again.

Finn's left hand moved over Siobhan's hip and down to the hem of her dress. He tugged at it to roll it up, and then his fingertips went to work on her thigh, caressing it slowly at first before gliding to the front of her white lace panties. The heat radiating from her body was intense as Finn placed the palm of his hand over the front of Siobhan's panties. Siobhan instinctively raised her hips to meet his hand, and Finn obliged by rubbing against her.

Finn's senses were overwhelmed. A familiarity was coming back to him with Siobhan, one that he missed and kept locked deep inside for so long but was anxious to emerge now. Finn pulled back from Siobhan's body as he rose from the couch. Siobhan looked at him with bewilderment, panting.

"What?" she gasped. "What's wrong?"

"Nothing at all," Finn grinned. He pulled his jeans off and reached into the back pocket to take out his wallet. He pulled a foil packet and held it in his fingertips.

"Always prepared, I see," Siobhan smiled.

Finn went to open the condom packet until
Siobhan sat up and stopped him.

"Let me do the unwrapping," she wickedly
smirked.

Finn stood still as Siobhan tugged on Finn's
boxer briefs, pushing them down his legs so he could kick
them aside. Finn watched as Siobhan slowly opened the
condom packet, pulled the condom out, and positioned
it right over the tip of his erection. He felt Siobhan's
index finger toy with the underside of his cock, gliding
back and forth and hitting its most sensitive spots.

"Dear God, Bon," Finn rumbled as he felt his
knees weaken at her touch.

Siobhan giggled before relenting and placing the
condom on Finn. She then lay back down on the couch
seductively, pulling her skirt around her waist as she
invited Finn with a motion of her finger.

Finn didn't need to be asked twice. He positioned
himself between Siobhan's legs, removed her lace panties,
and let a finger slide over her damp lips to cause Siobhan
to close her eyes and shudder. Finn couldn't wait any
longer, sliding inside her slowly. Siobhan drew him to her
body as Finn rocked in rhythm against her, taking his
time, varying thrusts, and speed that had Siobhan
breathless.

"Finn... please..." Siobhan moaned, wanting
more of him.

Finn leaned down and kissed her neck again as
the slow thrusting continued.

"Do you like that?" He whispered into Siobhan's
ear before he bit on her ear lobe.

"God, yes," Siobhan groaned. "I want..."

"What do you want?"

"More," she thundered as she wrapped her legs
around Finn and pulled him deep inside her body.

Their bodies now tightly entwined, Finn moved with Siobhan, the heels of her feet pushing to keep him close to her. Finn watched as he saw Siobhan close her eyes tightly, and her right hand gripped the top of the couch cushion. She cried out, keeping Finn deep inside her as Finn felt her tighten around him. It was more than he could take himself and Finn groaned as he felt himself come and collapse against Siobhan's body.

Finn lay still inside Siobhan before gently pulling out of her so he could dispose of the condom safely. He then slid next to Siobhan on the couch, taking her in his arms. He felt her heart steadily pounding like his own until the rapid rate began to subside. Finn lightly brushed aside the hair at Siobhan's shoulder so he could kiss her, sending chills and goosebumps through Siobhan's body that made her laugh. Finn noticed a throw blanket draped over the back of the couch, and he pulled it down to cover their bodies.

Siobhan's back curve seemed to fit perfectly against Finn as he held her tightly and worked to get comfortable on the couch.

"We don't have to stay like this if you don't want to," Siobhan sighed contentedly.

"I wouldn't want it any other way," Finn insisted.

13

Siobhan tried to stealthily move about the living room, gathering up her things so she could dress quickly and sneak out without disturbing a slumbering Finn. She slipped back into her dress, deciding it was the easiest thing to do before she would get out to the car.

"Where are you going?" Finn asked groggily.

"I'm sorry," Siobhan apologized. "I didn't mean to wake you. I was just going to head back home."

"Stay," Finn stated. "We can go up to the bedroom where there's more space to… sleep," Finn added with a grin as he sat up on the couch.

"I should go," Siobhan said as Finn reached over and took her hands, knocking her shoes from her grip. Finn pulled her close to him again.

"You should stay," Finn rose quickly from the couch and kissed her deeply before kissing the nape of her neck.

Siobhan closed her eyes, enticed by the idea of spending more time in bed before she pulled away.

"Finn, I have to be at work by 7," she added. "I need to go home, shower, and change. I've got stuff to do today. As much as I would love to stay with you, I can't."

Finn glanced at his watch and saw it was just past five in the morning.

"You don't have to rush out."

Finn grabbed his briefs and slid them on before taking Siobhan by the hand and leading her through the house and out the back door. They walked across the dewy grass barefoot, guided only by the outdoor lights on the patio and the one Finn had turned on that was closer to the wooden dock near the lake.

"Finn, what are you doing?" Siobhan asked as she hurried along to keep up.

"Just come on."

Finn stopped when they reached the end of the dock and sat down, patting the wood next to him, so Siobhan knew where to go.

Siobhan dangled her feet over the edge of the dock. She could feel some light spray from the lapping water beneath her, nipping at her toes.

Finn put his arm around Siobhan and pulled her close. She felt a chill run through her that caused her to shiver a bit.

"Are you cold?" he asked.

"it's chillier than I expected," she admitted.

"Hold on," Finn said and stood immediately, scampering away before Siobhan had a chance to protest.

Siobhan gazed out over the water, listening to the chirps of frogs and crickets starting to fade. There was barely a hint of the impending sunrise. The light breeze that went through the surrounding trees caused a sweet rustling sound in the otherwise quiet predawn. She inhaled deeply, taking in the pleasant smells around her.

Siobhan reflected on what had just transpired between herself and Finn. It was amazing for her, but she noticed herself lightly chewing on her thumbnail as she considered her actions.. Her hard feelings had melted away quicker than she had expected them to, and the last thing she wanted was to build up expectations in her head that Finn would not live up to. She had been down that road before when she was less mature, but now she could not put herself through that again.

The back door closed and cut through the silence around her, and Siobhan spun around to see Finn walking carefully toward her. He reached the dock and gingerly moved barefoot to where Siobhan sat. He handed her a mug and carefully poured out coffee from the carafe he held in his left hand. Finn placed the carafe down and then draped a blanket over Siobhan to warm her before he sat down and poured his own coffee.

"Now we'll both be warmer," Finn said with a smile. He cuddled up next to Siobhan as she cradled the warm cup between her hands.

"Finn, this is too much," Siobhan stated.

"It's just coffee," Finn said. "Dad has one of the real fancy brewers that make a pot in two minutes. Who knew he was so bourgeois?"

"I'm... I'm not just talking about the coffee," Siobhan told him as she turned to look at him. "What happened tonight... maybe it wasn't such a good idea. I think we just got caught up in emotions. I..."

Finn cut her off.

"You didn't enjoy yourself?" Finn asked pointedly. "I know I did, and it felt like you did too. Yes, Bon, I got caught up in emotions, but what happened between us was more than that."

"Was it?" Siobhan asked seriously. "Because if it wasn't, I want you to be honest with me, Finn. I'm not disposable like that, not anymore. If you were just looking to see if you could make that happen and go back to Saratoga in a few days without a second thought, tell me. I'm a big girl; I can take it. I'll be pissed as all hell, but I won't get my expectations up about you."

"Bon, I know I don't have the best track record with you or... well, with anyone, really. I can promise you that I'll be truthful to you. Will I go back to Saratoga in a few days? Most likely. But that doesn't mean I want to leave you behind me again."

"I don't see how that's possible," Siobhan admitted.

"Let me have these few days to prove it to you, to try and work it out. Give me a chance, Bon. I know I might not deserve it based on what happened in the past.

There's a lot that went on then, and that is happening now to work through. All I'm asking for is a little time."

Siobhan sat quietly for a moment and looked out over the water.

"You have a short leash, Mr. O'Farrell," Siobhan told him. "Don't feck it up."

Finn let out a belly laugh and spit out the coffee he was sipping.

"Yes, Ma'am," he replied as he put his arm around her.

Finn looked out over the lake. Through the darkness, he couldn't see to the other side beyond a couple of dim lights that blinked.

"That's how they did it," Finn whispered.

"What was that?" Siobhan asked.

"I've been trying to figure out why I didn't see any cars here when I got home during the break-in," Finn answered. "The front door was open, but no vehicles at all were in the driveway. That's because they came from here. They boated over from somewhere and were able to get inside. Do you know what's on the other side of the lake?"

"I haven't a clue," Siobhan admitted.

"I know what I'll be doing later today," Finn said.

****

After keeping Siobhan as long as he could before relenting and letting her go home to change for work, Finn spent time walking outside, determined to figure out how the intruders got into his father's home. Even though Shadowmere Lake wasn't large, it was big enough where Finn couldn't see clearly to the other side even when it was bright out. He realized there was something beyond the trees on the other side but was unsure if it was anything.

Finn returned inside, patting Jameson on the head as the dog followed him over to the table where he had set up his computer. Finn barely glanced at his work emails from Susannah and others at the law firm and focused more on doing a Google search of the area. He pinpointed his father's home on the maps and used Google Earth to get a bird's eye view of the immediate location. The map didn't reveal anything on the opposite side of the lake, but that didn't mean there was nothing there either. Finn could see a marked road that ran adjacent to the lake, making it worth checking out at least.

After getting dressed in his jeans, t-shirt, and black boots, Finn went downstairs and grabbed his keys. His first thought was to go to his Lexus and drive over, but he stopped himself. Instead, he turned towards the garage and headed to the motorcycles. He looked at his father's bike and decided against taking it if he was noticed by someone on it. The wrath for driving the leader's bike might be swift if he did that. Instead, he opted for the spare Harley in the green colors without any of the markings of his father's bike. He found the key for the motorcycle among those that Maeve had given him, grabbed the helmet, and sat down.

Before he started the bike and opened the garage door, Jameson had come and sat down next to the motorcycle. The dog looked up at Finn with pleading eyes.

"Sorry, buddy," Finn apologized. "You can't come with me this time. Maybe another ride."

Jameson appeared crestfallen, sat down, and watched as Finn used the remote to open the garage door. Finn started up the bike and listened to the roar of the engine. The familiar Harley sound whirred through his ears, bringing him back to the days when he would ride with his father. It was always one of the few times where the two of them got along and had something in common. Finn eased the bike out of the garage and up the drive, coming to a stop at the edge that led to the street.

He had given up riding for years while he went to college but found himself purchasing a used bike in law school to use to get around. Once he was practicing and making good money, he invested in nicer motorcycles, ending up with the Ducati that he kept in the garage up in Saratoga. He would tool around the region when he wanted time alone, riding up as far as Lake Placid on some trips.

Finn took some effort to get the muscle memory back that he needed for handling a bigger bike like this, but once he had it on the road, it all came back to him quickly. The trip to the other side of the lake would take just a few minutes, and he came off Sapphire Road to the more secluded Brower Road.

Homes in this area were few and scattered wide apart. Finn drove slowly while trying to avoid attracting any unwanted attention in the area. When he reached the point that he calculated was opposite his father's home, he stopped. A chain-link fence crossed the dirt and gravel road there with signs indicating it was a construction site, and there was no trespassing. The fence looked to be about eight feet high, with barbed wire all around the top of it.

Finn stopped the bike and dismounted. He walked over to the fence to see it was locked with not one but two different padlocks. Fishing the keys out of his jacket, he checked to see if any on his father's keyring matched the locks, but none did. He looked up and scanned the trees to see if any cameras were pointed in his direction. When he saw none, Finn removed the helmet and tugged on the chains to see that they were tight.

Seems a bit excessive for a remote construction site, he thought to himself.

Finn peered through the gate but could only see that the path rose a bit, obscuring whatever was at the end from view.

Finn turned back toward the road as a tan minivan pulled up to him and stopped. The window rolled down and revealed a woman looking at him inquisitively.

"Do you need help with something?" The woman asked cautiously.

"No, thank you," Finn said politely as he approached the car. He kicked into his lawyer charm, hoping to disarm the woman in case she was suspicious and would let someone know he was snooping around.

"I'm at the other side of Shadowmere and was out on the patio last night and saw some lights out here. I didn't think there were any homes on this side of the lake, so I wanted to check it out."

"You live on Shadowmere?"

"No, I'm just visiting some family and staying with them. It's such a lovely area, though; I was interested if there might be homes available on the lake. Have you lived here long?"

"Oh, we've had a house down the road for a bit," she said excitedly. "There aren't many neighbors around here, so it might be nice to have a new family here. Are you married?"

"No, it's just me right now," Finn smiled.

"Well, I know most of the homes they have been working on around here are quite large," she admitted. "It might be too much house for just one person. That development they are planning for here," she pointed at the fence, "I think the houses are monstrous."

"Is that what is down here?" Finn said, getting closer to the van.

"I don't think there's much of anything down there, to be honest," she said, almost trying to whisper.

"One day, they came in with a bunch of trucks and trailers, put the fence up, and that's been about it for the last six months. No one seems to know anything about it beyond that. Occasionally, I do see some other people on bikes around here. I thought maybe you were one of them."

"Why would you think that?"

"You have a bike that looks like theirs," she offered. "I see them around town a lot. You know, they have that big clubhouse out by the train station."

"The Cosantóir?" Finn asked.

"I guess that's what they're called," the woman said. She leaned a bit out of the car window, feeling more comfortable with Finn. "I can never pronounce it like that. A lot of them have that cute accent. Anyway, I wouldn't worry about that property since it's already taken. I know there are some lots available further around the lake near where our home is. I can give you the name of the realtor if you're interested. She helped us out quite a bit."

"That would be great if you have that information," Finn replied.

The woman reached over and began to look through her purse. A small voice from the backseat cried out, "Mom, when are we getting to the diner? I want pancakes!"

"Just a minute!" the woman scolded. She turned back to Finn with a gracious smile and handed him a business card.

"Patty Wells," she said. "She'll be a big help to you. Tell her Candice Howard talked to you about spots here."

"Thank you very much, Candice," Finn grinned. "I'll be sure to call her. You've been such a big help."

"No problem," Candice remarked, blushing slightly as Finn took her hand and gently shook it. "Maybe we'll be neighbors soon."

"Maybe," Finn answered. He gave Candice a casual wave as he tucked the business card in the inside pocket of his leather jacket.

Finn returned to his bike and started it up quickly as Candice honked and drove off. He made his way back out towards the route to the hospital, thinking all the while that he would give the realtor a call to see if he could find out more about what may or may not be going on. He took a quick look at the Hog House entrance as he drove past, wondering what their involvement was with the property and what it might have to do with his father.

****

Siobhan had dashed home to change out of her dress and into a more casual blouse and pants for the office. She had arrived back at her apartment early enough to shower and change and be on time at A Safe Place. She noticed her bed was still messy from Finn having spent the night at her place on Saturday, causing her to think back on what had transpired over the weekend. She didn't give herself much time to linger over the thoughts and feelings that came to her.

Siobhan arrived at the center at just past eight. She waved casually into the camera at the front door so Benny would let her in. As soon as she entered, Tracy's eyes turned to her. Siobhan smiled and walked quickly down the hall toward her office.

"How come you're so late this morning?" Tracy asked as she shuffled down the hall to catch up to Siobhan.

"What are you talking about?" Siobhan asked. "It's just after eight. I'm only a few minutes late."

Siobhan unlocked her office door, tossed her handbag on a chair, and turned her computer on.

"Sure, for the rest of us, it's just barely late," Tracy admitted. "But for you... you're usually here by seven or earlier."

"So I'm a little behind on a Monday," Siobhan said defensively. "It's not a big deal."

She sat down at her computer and nervously tapped her fingers as she waited for it to finish booting.

"Something is up with you today," Tracy said as she closed the office door. "I never heard from you on Friday. How did things go with Gavin? Any progress?"

"Friday was a dud, I'm afraid," Siobhan said dejectedly. "He didn't know anything about my reports or findings. He just wanted to have a date, so I left him at the restaurant."

"What are we going to do now?" Tracy asked with concern.

"It's okay," Siobhan said as she typed on her computer. "I'm going to call his office today. He said I could set up an actual meeting with him today when I ran into him while I was out with..." Siobhan caught herself as she spoke.

"Out with who?" Tracy questioned. When Siobhan didn't respond immediately, Tracy broke out in a grin.

"You went out on a date, didn't you?" Tracy said anxiously. She jumped into the chair in front of Siobhan's desk. "Spill it. Who was it?"

"It wasn't a date... really... I don't think... it's not that important," Siobhan rushed.

"Who was this 'not a real date' with, Vonnie?"

"It was nothing. Just an old friend who came to town," Siobhan answered, hoping to deflect the topic.

"Does this old friend have a name?" Tracy pestered.

"Finn O'Farrell," Siobhan rushed, looking to gloss over her answer.

Tracy sat back in her chair and stared at Siobhan.

"Is that the 'Finn' from all those years ago? I thought he was long gone."

"It is him," Siobhan replied. "He's in town because his father is in the hospital. We spent some time together over the weekend."

Tracy beamed at Siobhan.

"What?" Siobhan said, peering over her computer screen.

"He's the reason you were late today, isn't he?"

"I was not late," Siobhan insisted.

"I can tell by the blush on your cheeks, Vonnie. You can't just pass it off as nothing. You got some this weekend. Good for you! Don't try to hide it."

"Tracy, please," Siobhan pleaded. "Let's not make a big deal about it."

"It is a big deal! You hardly ever accept any dates, and to have one end up like this… well, it's something to crow about. Unless it was just a one night of passion thing. I never pegged you for a one-night stand gal, though."

"I'm not a one-night-stand gal!" Siobhan said in her defense.

"So, you'll be seeing him again then?" Tracy asked.

"Yes… I mean, maybe… I don't really know the answer to that yet. Don't you have work to do?" Siobhan was utterly flustered at this point. "I know I have phone calls to make." Siobhan picked up her phone, intent on beginning dialing.

"To Finn? Or to Gavin? They are just lining up for you," Tracy teased.

"Ugh, I should have kept my mouth closed," Siobhan groaned.

"Okay, I'm going," Tracy stated as she rose. "I'll let you know if I need you for anything."

Tracy left the office and closed Siobhan's door, giving Siobhan a chance to exhale. She was suddenly juggling even more than usual with Finn in the mix. It was a complication she hadn't expected but was glad to have in her life. Just the thoughts of how she spent the weekend with Finn and the passion she experienced with him made her body warm and yearn for him again.

Siobhan found herself gazing at her cellphone to see if there were any messages from Finn. She noticed a few from Cara asking where she was and what she was up to, along with one from Gavin letting her know that he could do lunch this week. It was almost like Gavin felt he had competition for her attention now. In Siobhan's mind, there was no contest.

It was just then that a text message came in and startled Siobhan. It was from a number she didn't recognize with a 518-area code.

You have my number followed by a winking emoji was all the message said. Siobhan knew it was Finn right away, and she giggled and just how many meanings the message could have.

****

Finn arrived at the hospital and took note of the lack of motorcycles in the visitor's lot. Members of the Cosantóir were all likely doing tunnel work at this time of the morning on a Monday. This gave Finn a bit of a reprieve from the confrontations that had become commonplace for him since he arrived in town. Going through the hospital steps had become routine, and in no time, Finn was up on the ICU floor, heading to his father's room. He glanced into the waiting room and caught sight of Cillian sitting in a chair, reading a Bible.

"A little light reading?" Finn remarked as he strode closer to the older man.

"There's always a good place in here to find some inspiration," Cillian answered as he held up the Good Book. "It wouldn't hurt you to pick it up now and then to find that out."

"I'll keep that in mind," Finn replied. "Is Maeve in there with Da?"

"She is, but I'm sure she would switch places with you. It's been a good couple of days."

"Is he awake?" Finn said excitedly.

"Not exactly," Cillian confided. "But he did open his eyes briefly and wiggle some toes and fingers. He responds better, and the docs say the swelling around his brain has gone down a bit. They are hoping today will be even better. I'd say we had a good weekend."

"I'm glad someone did," Finn grumbled, rubbing the back of his sore head.

"Why? Not so good for you? I know we didn't see you yesterday."

"I had kind of a rude greeting at Dad's house Saturday night," Finn said. He guided Cillian back to his chair so the two could sit and speak more quietly. "When I got to the house, someone was already there. At least three of them were wearing masks and trying to get into Da's office, from what I remember. They put a good knot in my head before they left, and the police showed up. I'm surprised they didn't come down here to talk to you about it."

"Cops have been in and out of here for days asking questions, but not about that," Cillian spoke. "Are you okay?"

"Yeah, just the bump. If Jameson hadn't been there, it might have been worse. I think he took a good chunk out of one of them. Cillian, what is Da mixed up in? You're his best friend. You must know something. If he's dealing again, he might be messing with the wrong people..." Finn said with concern.

Cillian interrupted the young man and looked him straight in the eye. "Finn, your father isn't dealing. He swore that shit off years ago. The Cosantóir, we don't get involved with stuff like that anymore. Back in the day when you were younger, yeah, we made a lot of mistakes. We thought we were tough and saw ways to make quick cash, but that's all in the past. I always tried to convince your Da to stay away from it. After your Ma passed, things were terrible. I won't lie to you. He got involved in some nasty stuff and did things... things we don't speak of anymore. He was in a dark place, but Maeve and I... we worked hard on him, and he got the help he needed. He changed and gave up the drugs. Whatever those guys were looking for, it's not drugs."

"Whatever they wanted, they looked hard for it. They couldn't get into Da's office; neither could I. The keys aren't on any of the keyrings Maeve left for me. Do you know where it might be? It's not a regular key. You would notice it right away."

"I don't have a clue," Cillian offered.

"You won't find it anywhere," Maeve interrupted the conversation. Finn stood up and approached her.

"Do you know where the key is?" Finn asked.

"He would never tell me," Maeve admitted. "He was the only one who ever went in there. It was his private space, and I respected that. I asked him a bunch of times what he was keeping in there because it worried me. Conor would just shrug it off and tell me it's nothing to worry about. He would slip in and out of there, but I never saw the key or where he kept it."

"I think whoever is trying to find that key may be involved in whatever happened to Da," Finn admitted. "Liam was right about having protection around you, Maeve. If those people were willing to break into the house, there's no telling what they might do to get what they want, especially if they think you might know where to find what they are seeking. Do you have anyone with you today?"

"Right now, just Preacher," Maeve nodded toward Cillian. "The others are all at work on job sites. I'm sure someone will be by later today, though."

"It might be good for you to just stay put here until then, for your own safety," Finn stated. "Do you know what site Liam is working on today?"

"He's down at the Sloatsburg site where the accident happened," Cillian replied. "Why?"

"I think it's time my brother and I had a little talk," Finn said firmly. "I think he may know more about all of this than he is letting on."

14

Siobhan found herself struggling to stay focused throughout the day. Between meetings, phone calls, emails, and new cases coming in, there was more than enough to keep her busy. Still, everything that came along kept getting interrupted by the thoughts of Finn. It was unlike her to get distracted from her work like this, and she fought her emotions all day long to help with her concentration. Lunch provided her with a quick respite to check her phone, but she had no further messages from Finn since that contact earlier in the morning. She felt conflicted, like a disappointed teenager who didn't hear from her crush, but at the same time worrying that Finn may be digging too deeply into what happened to his father and how the Cosantóir was involved, potentially leading him straight into danger himself.

Twice Siobhan typed out the message *You OK?* But she always deleted the message before it got sent. She was holding her phone in her hand, thinking of what, if anything, to text, when the cellphone rang and surprised her, causing her to drop it on the floor and have it careen under her desk.

"Shite!" she exclaimed as she found herself crawling on the floor. She stretched to reach the phone as it vibrated, moving slowly across the worn linoleum floor with each subsequent vibration. Siobhan finally clutched the phone and pulled it toward her. She blew the dust bunnies off the screen and pressed answer immediately before the caller could hang up.

"Hello?" she said quickly, anticipating Finn's voice on the other side of the call.

"Well, hello there," the voice answered. Disappointment crossed Siobhan's face when she realized it was Gavin.

"Oh, hello, Gavin," Siobhan said properly, standing up from the floor and brushing the dust off her pants with her free hand.

"Don't sound so excited to hear from me," Gavin said. Siobhan detected a tinge of anger in his voice. "I thought I would hear from you already today to set up our lunch date for the week. I guess we can put it off if you have better things to do."

"No!" Siobhan insisted. "I'm sorry; it's been a crazy day today, and I just haven't had time yet. What day would you like to meet?" Siobhan frantically pulled up her calendar on her computer.

"How's Wednesday at 12?" Gavin asked.

"Absolutely," Siobhan answered without checking closely to see if she had anything else scheduled. She knew getting the ball rolling on funding took precedence over everything else. "We can meet around here if you want, at the diner, or An Artistic Taste…"

"I'll set something up and have my assistant contact you later with the details," Gavin insisted. "It will be useful to get to talk about all of this. Did you enjoy your afternoon yesterday with Finn?"

Siobhan wasn't sure just what Gavin was getting at.

"What? What do you mean?"

"When I saw you two together at Rushing Duck, you looked rather cozy. Just like old times. The next time I looked over toward your table, you two were gone. I was just wondering how your day went."

"It was fine," Siobhan rushed. "Gavin, I really have to go. I have people waiting to see me. I'll be waiting to hear from your assistant, okay? Thanks for getting back to me. I appreciate it. You know it means a lot to the organization."

"Right… to the organization," Gavin said gruffly. "Talk to you later."

Gavin hung up abruptly.

Siobhan gazed at her phone, unsure of what to make of the interaction. She had intended to call Gavin. The contact was of urgent importance to A Safe Place if she wanted to keep moving forward. She had simply gotten lost in work and other thoughts. Now she worried she had upset Gavin and rocked the boat. Siobhan picked up her desk phone and connected directly to Tracy.

"Tracy, can you make sure my Wednesday stays clear? I'll be meeting with Gavin, and I'm determined to get the funding. I have to be laser-focused for this one."

"You got it, boss," Tracy answered. "You have one scheduled meeting in the morning that I can shuffle for you. I'll keep the whole day open for you."

Siobhan sat back in her desk chair and pulled a few dust bunny fragments from her hair before turning her attention back to her phone.

You Ok? I've been thinking of you all day. Can't wait to see you.

This time there was no hesitation before hitting send.

****

The ride to the job site from the hospital was just minutes. It gave Finn little time to think about the potential consequences of confronting his brother. Taking Liam on at any time was never a wise decision, but to do it at work, in front of his crew and members of the Cosantóir, added an extra element of danger for Finn. Liam didn't want to be shown up under any circumstances, and the odds of him being extra ornery in front of those who either looked up to him or feared him were immense.

Finn spied the job site as he drove north on the road. Even though it was set back a bit, the visible signs of many trees cut down made it evident. Large equipment necessary not just for clearing land but performing all the underground work dotted the landscape, waiting to do the heavy lifting. Finn pulled off onto the dirt road that led to the work area before stopping at the security gate. Finn worried about how he would gain access. However, once the security guard, a young man who seemed more interested in what was on his cell phone than security, eyed Finn's green bike, he assumed he was part of the Cosantóir and waved him through.

The dirt road wound through large swaths of ground that had been dug out of the earth. Machines worked loudly moving trees and land so that there would be space for whatever was planned as part of the area's growth. Finn noticed several of the Cosantóir bikes parked just outside the makeshift building on-site and drove to park there. He hadn't set foot on a sandhog site in ten years, and all the sights and smells flooded his senses, bringing back what it was like to work in the tunnels. The constant dampness, the smell of sweat, diesel, and machinery, the din of the site above and below ground all came flooding back as Finn made his way towards the house at the location.

House was always an ironic term to Finn. The hog house at the job site was far from home. It was usually a series of trailers with no windows and cramped quarters. Sandhogs used the location to store their items, rest between shifts, grab a shower or nap, or even do laundry. The house had its share of conveniences like a small commissary and kitchen tended by a retired sandhog. Finn pulled open the trailer door and was inundated by the smell of mildew, cigarettes, and cigars.

Finn's entrance caused a few heads to turn immediately towards him. He didn't recognize any of the faces he saw at the lockers or tables, though a couple of men had their heads down, resting on the table itself. The faces turned quickly from Finn and went towards the older gentleman behind the counter set up at the far end of the trailer. Realizing that this man was probably the hog house's keeper, Finn approached him first, hoping to find out where Liam might be. He stood before the man, who looked to be older than his father, and smiled.

"Good morning," Finn said politely. "I'm looking for…"

"If you're looking for work, son, I'm not sure anything is available on this shift," the man interrupted before he thrust a semi-clean coffee pot onto the Bunn machine to brew up another batch for the men inside.

"No, I'm not looking to get on the job," Finn told him. "I'm looking for Liam… Liam O'Farrell. I heard he might be working here today."

"Aye, he is," the gentleman remarked. "He's the walking boss on this job. Probably already down in the tunnels. If you need him, you'll have to wait until his shift is over."

"I just need to talk to him for a few minutes," Finn pleaded. "Can you radio down to him and ask him to come up? If not, I can go down there and find him. It's important."

"You sure as shit can't go down there, son," the man laughed, "and calling Liam out of a job… I may as well just ask him to shank me right here. Sit and wait or leave me a name, and I'll see if I can get it to him at the break in about 4 hours."

"I can go down," Finn insisted. "I've worked the tunnels before."

"You got your book?" the man asked, holding out his hand.

Finn hadn't even seen his book, which showed you were part of the union, in the ten years since he left home.

"I don't have it with me, no," Finn admitted.

"Then you're not going anywhere." The man turned back towards his stool behind the counter, sat, and looked up at the television playing without any sound on.

"They don't need any shapers today?" Finn asked, hoping there might be a need for an extra hand that would get him into the tunnels. The older gent was surprised Finn even knew some of the sandhog lingo.

"Don't think so," he answered. "Like I said, I think the shift is full."

"We are short one guy," a voice bellowed from behind. Finn spun around to see Darryl's imposing figure filling the space. "He's cool, Ian. He's Liam's brother. He's done the work before. Ronan didn't show today, so we need another mucker."

"It's on you, Demon, if something happens," Ian warned.

"I got it," Darryl assured Ian. "Let's go get you geared up," Demon indicated. He led Finn over to the lockers so he could store his belongings.

"I don't really need to work a shift," Finn stated. "I just need to talk to Liam."

"Dude, if you're coming down there with me, you're working," Darryl insisted. "Stow your stuff, and I'll get you a helmet, gloves, and pants. You'll need some boots, too. What are you, a ten?" Darryl asked, looking at Finn's feet.

"Yeah, I guess," Finn replied.

"We got extras that'll fit you," Darryl said as he began to go to the supply area. "You're lucky. I'm size sixteen… I always have to bring extras in case I need them."

Darryl retrieved gear for Finn and tossed it on the bench beside Finn.

"Let's go, man," Darryl said as he snapped his fingers. "You're eating into my shift."

Finn donned the all-too-familiar gear and plodded out behind Darryl to exit the trailer.

"What the fuck, Demon?" a harried man said to Darryl. "I asked about work on this shift two hours ago. This priss comes walking in, and you just bend over for him?"

Darryl grabbed the man by his shirt collar, lifted him off the ground, and pinned him to the wall of the trailer, shaking the whole place.

"Don't ever fucking question me if you want to be able to use those hands again," Darryl growled. "You won't even be able to make a fist to beat off into at night."

Darryl tossed the man aside, so he landed on the couch.

"I decide who works on my team. I've seen your work before, Riggins," Darryl barked. "You're all talk and no work. I need someone that is going to give me a good day of work. Finn here is booked; you're not. Deal with it."

Darryl guided Finn out of the trailer and towards the elevator shaft.

"When's the last time you did this?" Darryl asked as he pressed to call the elevator up.

"Ten years ago," Finn admitted.

"Well, you look like you're in good shape. Once your muscles start mucking again, they'll remember how it goes."

The elevator arrived up top, and Finn and Darryl stepped into the metal cage. Darryl took up most of the room himself, leaving Finn to feel more claustrophobic as the elevator began its steady descent. The heat of the August morning rapidly disappeared the further down they got. Finn was grateful for the heavier long sleeve shirt Darryl had insisted he change into by the time they reached the bottom, some two hundred feet or so below the surface.

Every time Finn set foot in one of the tunnels, he always imagined it was some other world. The caverns were immense and well-fortified. It was the kind of stuff he used to see in the movies when he was younger and took in one of those sci-fi films about slaves working hard underground for their Martian overlords.

Darryl led Finn over to where four other men were standing with their shovels and machinery.

"Shit, Demon, I was beginning to think you went back home for the day," a thin, muscular, dark-skinned man noted.

"Nah, not back home, Pick," Darryl noted. "I just wanted a quickie with your old lady. She says hello."

Pick scowled as the other men laughed at the joke.

"This is Finn," Demon said, introducing him to the others on the job. "He's working with us today."

"Not another Newbie, Demon," a pale older man said. "They can never keep up with us."

"Relax, Whitey," Demon told him. "Finn worked tunnels before. He's Conor's kid."

The men silently stared at Finn, looking him over.

"Really?" Whitey asked. "Conor never mentioned another son. Where you been hiding?" Whitey reached over and grabbed Finn's hands.

"No dirt under your nails and you look like you just came from a day at the spa with a manicure. These hands are too soft. You won't last two hours."

Whitey laughed as he let go of Finn's hands.

"I'll do just fine," Finn insisted. "I did two hours just fine with your wife last night."

Demon roared out a laugh, and the other men joined in. The remark even caused Whitey to crack a smile.

"Let's get to it," Demon yelled. He led the way to where the team would begin their work for the day.

It wasn't more than twenty minutes of mucking mud and dirt before Finn's muscles began to ache and burn. It was more rigorous than any workout he had done on his own or in the gym in many years. Darryl was right – his body began to adapt to the shoveling again just like it hadn't forgotten how to do it. It was not only the mud that had to be mucked but expelled concrete as well before it got the chance to harden. The first few hours Finn spent working were shoveling into muck bags for others to haul away. Hour after hour could be spent on the process, and the team might still only move about 100 feet for the day.

When Finn first began working, the others on the team rode him a bit, egging him on to work faster or move aside. Once they saw his determination and ability, he was becoming part of the group. Finally, after four hours of labor, there was a call for lunch. Finn wearily moved over to a lit area and sat himself down on a dry spot on the floor. Darryl came over and sat next to him, handing Finn a bottle of water.

Finn took two long gulps to soothe his parched throat. He grabbed a green bandana that Darryl had given him and wiped some of the soot and grime off his face.

"No lunch?" Whitey asked as he sat next to Finn. Finn heard Whitey's knee pop as the man flexed it several times after sitting.

"I didn't know I'd be working today," Finn told him. Whitey reached into his box, pulled out his sandwich, and tore it in half, handing it to Finn.

"Can't have you dying on us," Whitey said.

Finn tore into the corned beef sandwich with vigor, finishing off his half and his bottle of water in no time at all. He wiped his mouth on the bandana, streaking spicy mustard from the corner of his lips onto the cloth. Finn stood up and stretched a bit to loosen his tightening muscles.

"If you need a piss, the portable is about a hundred yards that way," Darryl said as he pointed down the tunnel. "You better hurry; the line's likely to be long, and we only have 15 more minutes."

Finn hustled off and found that just two people were waiting to use the toilet. Finn got in there and then quickly regretted his choice. The place was foul and fetid, with dozens of men using it all day long. He did his best to hold his breath and get out as fast as he could.

Finn strode back to the rest of his team and was greeted by Darryl.

"Come with me," Darryl said in his deep, commanding voice.

"What's up?" Finn asked as he worked to keep up with Darryl's pace.

"They asked for two of us to come up and help move one of the machines. You wanted to see Liam – this will be your chance."

Finn's stomach tightened as the floodlights filled this more recent area of the tunnel. He squinted, straining to see through the lights and the dust that thickly filled the air. It didn't take him long to spot Liam standing there, directing some of the sandhogs with what they should do next. Darryl came up to Liam first, with Finn just a few paces behind.

"I needed two of ya, Demon," Liam looked. "You bring a scrawny muppet with you instead?" Liam pointed at Finn, still unable to see clearly that it was his brother. It wasn't until Finn stepped forward into the light that Liam saw him clearly and then scowled.

"What the feck are you doing here?" Liam growled.

"He's working on my team today," Demon defended. "He's done a damn fine job all morning. He's more than capable of handling whatever you need, Liam."

"Bullshit," Liam spat. "Get your arse out of my tunnel now, brother, before I squash you."

"Liam, I have to talk to you about what's going on with Dad."

"Don't concern yourself about Da, the tunnels, or anything else around here. Crawl back to where you came from. Or go over to Ginger's box and see what she's got for you... unless she finally decided to have a real Irishman instead of you. I'd be happy to tumble with her and let you know how it goes." Liam shoved Finn, sending Finn to the ground before he cackled loudly.

Liam turned his back and moved toward where the workers were. Finn reacted quickly, launching himself at his brother and taking him down to the dirt. The two men skidded through a patch of mud as they wrestled, with Finn ending up on top of Liam and raining blows down on his brother. Finn felt several punches land on Liam's jaw and his right eye before Liam jerked a knee into the small of Finn's back and followed it up with a left hook into Finn's ribs.

The last blow rocked Finn off his brother and sent him tumbling to the turf.

"You've toughened up over the years," Liam smiled as he spat blood onto Finn's shoes. "It's about feckin' time."

Finn struggled to get to his feet and winced, and he felt the soreness in his ribs as he struggled to breathe. Before Finn could stand, Liam swept his left leg across Finn's, bringing him down to the ground with a thud. Pain shot through Finn again as he saw his brother closing in on him. Liam grasped Finn's overalls' bib and pulled him close so they were face to face. Liam cracked a punch across Finn's left eye. The moment Finn felt it, stars filled his eyelids, and he began to fall over, but Liam jerked him back up.

"No, no, little brother," Liam laughed. "I'm not done yet. You need to remember where you stand in the family. Maybe if you hadn't hidden behind Ma's apron for so long, you could handle it better. Glad she's not here to see ya like this."

Finn spotted Liam grinning through his rapidly swelling left eye and reacted. A guttural yell escaped Finn's lips as he blasted the left side of Liam's head with a right fist. Liam tumbled straight to the ground in a heap. As he fell, he released his grip on Finn and Finn crumpled to the ground, his head bouncing off the dirt floor.

15

There he was, at the bottom of the staircase again, feeling for the lump on the back of his head and the marks on his face. Only this time, his mother wasn't there to comfort him. Dark shadows loomed at the top of the stairs while Finn could hear raised voices echoing in the hallway. The faint sound of sobs and then coughs were heard as well. Finn struggled to his feet, feeling as wobbly as ever. He wasn't wearing his sandhog clothing anymore. He was in his favorite pair of jeans and gray wolf t-shirt he regularly wore as a preteen.

Following the sobs, Finn found himself at the door to his parents' room in his old house. He barely pushed on the door with his fingertips so that it creaked open. He saw his mother lying in bed, working through another coughing fit. Finn was not a preteen anymore but into his teens. A glance in the mirror above his mother's bureau let him see the long blond hair and ratty scruff of a teen beard in his reflection.

Finn went to his mother's side, pulling up the chair positioned next to the bed that he often sat in. He was careful not to bump the IV pole that was commonplace in the bedroom now and gently picked up his mother's hand and took it in his own. Her skin was paper-thin, and her hand was cold and darkly bruised from needles. Aoife's hand closed around his, entwining her thin fingers with his.

"Finn," she breathed out with incredible difficulty, "are you okay? I heard more fighting. Are you hurt?"

"I'm fine, Ma," Finn lied, as he often did about the fights he had with his father. "Do you need anything?"

"Just sit with me for a bit, please," she said. Aoife closed her eyes and began to lightly hum "the Gartan Mother's Lullaby," a song she often hummed to Finn while he was younger. Tears welled in Finn's eyes as he tried to comfort his mother.

"I know you'll do great things, Finn. Believe that you can the way I believe," his mother said softly, her eyes still shut.

"I still need you, Ma," Finn replied.

"You'll always have me here with you, you know that," Aoife whispered. Her eyes opened slightly, and she smiled at her son. "No tears for me, Finn. You can do this. There's more to this family than you know. Tá grá agam duit."

Aoife closed her eyes again, smiled, and began to hum. Finn rested his head down on the bed, face down, and sobbed. He felt his mother's hand run lightly through his hair as he wept.

Finn lifted his head from the pillow and saw Siobhan with her hand just moving back from Finn's scalp. It took a moment to gather his bearings before realizing he was in the ER at Good Samaritan. The bright lights around him caused him to squint and sent shooting pain through his head. Finn moved his head away from Siobhan's hand and rested back on the pillow.

"Hold on, Finn," Siobhan told him as she went outside the curtain that surrounded the bed he was in. Finn heard some commotion going on around him. All the beeping of devices just added to the dull ache he experienced inside his skull.

Cara appeared with Siobhan and stood next to Finn's bed. Cara checked Finn's vitals on the monitors and then gave a glance at the wounds he had.

"How you feel, tough guy?" Cara said as she looked at the swelling around Finn's eye.

"Remember that New Year's Eve party at Darren's where we drank his Dad's Napoleon brandy? I feel like that, except I also got dragged down the road by a snowplow."

"Ha!" Cara laughed. "All I remember is the next day Darren's dad coming home and telling Darren to go out and throw snow on the puke you left next to the front porch. You took a good beating from Liam, you know. I've seen his handiwork on others in here. You're lucky you aren't up in the ICU with your Da. I'll go get the doctor to look at you."

Cara left the cubicle so that Finn was alone with Siobhan. She stood at the foot of the bed with a confused look of relief and disbelief on her face.

"What the hell were you thinking, Finn? Going down there and picking a fight with Liam is a death wish. You know better. And what were you doing there working in the first place? You ran out of here and left me to get away from all that shite ten years ago, and here you are riding a club bike and working with sandhogs like nothing has changed."

Finn groaned as he sat up a bit in bed. He felt his rib cage and saw where they had wrapped him already.

"Two broken ribs, you gowl," Siobhan scolded.

"Bon, I know it doesn't seem like the best decision to make," Finn began. "Liam knows something about all this, though. I went there to talk to him, but things got out of hand before I even got the chance. You think I wanted to do any of this? Things are going on that don't add up."

"And every time you try to find out what that is, you end up getting smacked around," Siobhan added.

"Not my first choice of methods of discovery, I can assure you of that."

Finn winced once more as he tried to get comfortable on the bed. Siobhan walked over and placed another pillow behind Finn's back and then used the bed controls to sit him up more. Siobhan glided her fingertips from just under the bruise around his left eye to the welt showing on his stubbled jaw.

"I'm getting tired of having to pick you up after you get hurt this week," Siobhan said with a grin. She leaned in and gave Finn a soft kiss on his lips. Finn tried to extend the kiss, reaching out to hold her hip, but the pain in his ribs and on his cracked and swollen lips was more than he could take.

"Sorry," Finn answered quietly.

"Did you learn anything?" Siobhan asked.

"Yes, Mr. O'Farrell, did you learn anything?" a voice asked from beyond the curtain. A hand appeared and pulled the curtain back so that Detective Fremont could saunter in.

Finn fidgeted in the bed and took hold of Siobhan's hand.

"It's not often I get to see the same man assaulted twice in three days, and he's still able to sit up and talk to me," Fremont offered. "Just what is it you were trying to learn?"

"I have some longstanding unfinished business with my brother," Finn said coldly. "It goes back many years."

"I gathered that much," Fremont said. "Looking at the records of your brother, the Cosantóir, and your family is like a Who's Who of allegations and crimes over the years. Somehow, it's always managed to just go away. Even the abuse allegations against your father where you were involved."

Finn sat up and glared sternly at Fremont.

"Those records are sealed," Finn growled. "How did you…"

"You know, Mr. O'Farrell, as someone who deals with the law, that someone that has been around as long as I have can get information when they really want it. Why didn't you ever agree to testify against your father?"

Siobhan looked at Finn, awaiting an answer to the question.

"That's none of your business," Finn told the detective. "Do you have a reason for being here?"

"As I said," Fremont continued, "when I heard the call coming to the Sloatsburg site and that you and your brother were involved, I had a vested interest to see what it was about and if it's tied to your father somehow. Anything you want to add?"

"Nope," Finn replied.

"Will you be pressing charges against your brother? With his record, I can hold him without any trouble."

Finn turned to face Siobhan to see if she had any reaction. She stared back at him, her green eyes glistening as she gripped his hand tightly.

"I don't think so," Finn answered. "Family squabble… nothing more."

"You aren't making this easy for me," the detective said firmly.

"I didn't realize it was my job to do that for you," Finn told Fremont. "You can leave now."

"I intend to," Fremont told him, "right after I place Liam under arrest."

Finn sat up again.

"I just told you I wasn't pressing charges against him!" Finn yelled.

"I was coming to bring him in today anyway," Fremont offered. "Your charges would have been icing on the cake. We're arresting him on assault and attempted murder charges in your father's case."

"What evidence do you have?"

"Nothing that I need to share with you, Mr. O'Farrell," Fremont told him. "Feel better. I'm sure we'll be talking soon."

Finn attempted to get out of bed before Siobhan stopped him.

"Finn! Don't. You need to stay in bed." She placed her hands on his shoulders and guided him back down.

"Bon, I don't know what Liam has to do with all this yet, but there's no way he would have done something to our father. I have to do something."

"Right now, what you need to do is sit here and rest. You're in no condition to do any type of arguing."

Siobhan pulled the chair up as close to Finn's bed as she could. She laid her head on his arm, and Finn reached over with his left hand and stroked her hair.

"I'm just getting you back," Siobhan whispered. "Don't do something to leave me again."

Finn sat quietly, his fingers running through her red locks.

I'm trying not to, he thought to himself.

****

Siobhan stayed with Finn all day, making sure there were no problems when the police came in to talk to him, when doctors visited, or even when members of the sandhogs and the Cosantóir checked in to see what happened and how he was faring. She held his hand as much as she could, keeping him close, even when he drifted off to sleep and had the fitful dreams that made him cry out on occasion. When the hospital insisted that Finn be admitted for the night for observation, it took all the strength Siobhan had to convince Finn it was the right thing to do. When he finally acquiesced, Siobhan pulled strings with Cara to spend the night in the room with Finn.

Siobhan learned from Cara that Liam had indeed been arrested. While Finn had undoubtedly gotten his share of licks in on his brother, Liam's injuries were not deemed severe enough to prevent him from being taken into custody once the hospital was done with him. Cara let Siobhan know that Liam didn't go without a struggle, and it took several officers, handcuffs, and more to lead him out of the hospital.

Finn tossed and turned several times, almost yanking out the IV he had in, but Siobhan was able to calm him. After his last episode at about 2 AM, Siobhan took down the bed's side rail and slid in next to Finn. She put her head on his shoulder, held his right hand with her left, and rested her other hand on his chest over his hospital gown. His heart, which had been thumping wildly, calmed down almost immediately when Siobhan comforted him.

It was nearly 6 AM when Cara came in and gently woke Siobhan.

"Hey," Cara whispered, "you better get out of his bed before the next shift catches you."

Siobhan opened her eyes and crawled out of bed, pulling the blanket up to cover Finn.

"He was up and down all night," Siobhan told her friend. "It was the only thing that seemed to help him."

"His injuries were severe," Cara reminded her. "He's lucky there wasn't any internal bleeding or head trauma."

"It's more than the current injuries," Siobhan noted. "He's still dealing with the past, and it clearly hurts him."

"I don't think he's the only one in that boat, Vonnie," Cara said.

"What does that mean?" Siobhan said defensively.

"Vonnie, Finn's got a lot of baggage, including the way he left all of us. That doesn't just go away after a few days back home."

"He didn't leave all of us the same way he left ME, Cara," Siobhan replied. "I know he's dealing with a lot of shite past and present. And I know he came back home to deal with his past with his Da, but that gives us a chance to face everything too. I've had a feeling ever since he got home…"

"Not one of your feelings, Vonnie," Cara sighed. "I know how badly you want this to work out, but I don't want to see you get crushed again. What is going to happen once everything with his father is resolved? Do you think he's going to give up his luxury life in Saratoga to come and live with you in Harriman? You have to face reality. This isn't some romance novel where everything works out perfectly – it's real life. I love you, Vonnie. You're my sister, through and through, and I'll stand by you, but I don't want to see you torn apart like you were ten years ago."

"That's not going to happen," Siobhan asserted. "I know what I'm facing and what I'm… and we… are dealing with."

Finn began to stir in bed and opened his eyes, glimpsing Cara and Siobhan in the room.

"What are you two conspiring about?" Finn said hoarsely.

"Trying to figure out where they put your wallet so we can do some serious shopping," Cara added. "Just go back to sleep."

"Haha," Finn laughed, groaning as he felt his ribs ache again.

"You okay?" Siobhan asked worriedly.

"I'm alright," Finn told her.

"Vonnie, why don't you go get some coffee," Cara remarked. "I'll watch Superman here until you get back."

Siobhan left the room, and Cara approached Finn. She checked all his vitals and the dressing on his wounds.

"How you feeling, Tiger?" Cara asked.

"Better than yesterday," Finn replied.

"You look a bit better. The swelling has come down in some places. Those ribs are going to be a problem for you for a while."

"For how long?" Finn asked.

"Usually a month or two," Cara told him.

Finn groaned at hearing this.

"Are they going to let me out of here today?"

"I'd say chances are good, as long as you have no signs of a concussion. Two head injuries in a few days is not a good thing, Finn. Maybe you need to take it easy for a while," Cara advised.

"Easier said than done, Cara," Finn told his friend. "My plate is a bit full right now."

"Let me just remind you of one thing, Finn O'Farrell," Cara chided. "With all you are doing, don't you dare hurt Vonnie. If you break her heart again, I'm breaking the rest of your ribs, hear me?"

"I'm not trying to hurt her, Cara."

"Try really hard, Finnbar, or the beating your brother gave you will seem like a day at the sandbox."

"When did you get so tough?" Finn said with a smile.

"You've been gone too long, Finn," Cara answered. "I've always been this tough. Get better and be nice to our girl."

"I promise." Finn crossed his heart with his index finger.

16

It was late Monday evening before Finn got released from the hospital. Only then would the hospital allow it if Siobhan agreed to take him home and watch over him for a few days. It took work on Finn's part to convince Siobhan to bring him back to his father's home instead of going to her place.

"I can't leave Jameson by himself," Finn rationalized.

"Since when did you become a dog person?" Siobhan asked as she guided Finn gently into the passenger seat of her car.

"I don't know," Finn admitted. "I just feel a kinship with him, I guess. I'm sure he doesn't like being alone. Besides, there is more room at my father's place for…" Finn's voice trailed off as he smiled at Siobhan.

"For what, Mr. O'Farrell?" Siobhan replied with mock surprise.

"Well, the bed in the guest room is king-sized, so there's more space. Don't get me wrong, your place is nice, Bon. I just thought we would be more comfortable here."

"So, you just assume I'm going to spend the night with you? There are other beds in that house, you know. Besides, maybe you shouldn't be engaged in any activities with your injuries."

Siobhan drove along as Finn sat quietly, pondering what she had said to him. He couldn't tell if she was serious or not, something Siobhan relished. She glanced at him several times with a grin on her face. When they drove past the turn for the Hog House, Siobhan noticed some worry from Finn.

"What's wrong?" she asked him. "Did… did you want me to go there?"

Siobhan had never set foot in the Hog House but had heard all kinds of stories about what went on there. Of course, she had no idea if they were real or not, but based on the reputation of the Cosantóir, it was difficult to fathom that it was all made up.

"No," Finn insisted. "I wouldn't dream of bringing you there right now. I'm not in any shape to defend myself and you. I was just wondering what was going on with Liam."

"You can reach out to Cillian. I'm sure he will give you details if he has them. Or Maeve might know something."

"Good point," Finn said as he rested against the back of the seat.

Siobhan reached Conor's home and took great care in assisting Finn out of the vehicle. Before they had even got to the front porch, Jameson came bounding over to greet them.

"What are you doing out here?" Finn asked as he scratched the dog's head.

"There must be a dog door in the house somewhere," Siobhan surmised. "There's no way Cillian would have just let him run around all day."

"Unless someone has broken in again," Finn said quietly. Siobhan had a look of fear come across her face.

Finn turned the doorknob on the front door and felt that it was locked. He fished the key out of his pocket and used it, making sure to quietly open the door. With the door open, Jameson wasted no time and bounded in.

"If anyone's in there, he'll find them first," Finn told her. Siobhan had gripped Finn's hand as he led the way into the house and through the living room towards the kitchen.

Finn arrived in the darkened kitchen and flipped on the lights, brightening the room immediately. All that was present was Jameson sitting next to an empty dog dish, with his tail thumping on the floor.

Siobhan let out a sigh of relief as she let go of Finn's hand. She laughed as she opened the cabinet to locate the dog food and filled Jameson's bowl. He obediently sat there, waiting for her to signal it was okay for him to begin eating.

"He listens better than you do," Siobhan noted to Finn as she gave the 'okay' for Jameson to dive into his morsels.

"I don't remember you being this sarcastic," Finn retorted as he sat in one of the wooden kitchen chairs. He grimaced as he sat down.

"Is there anything I can get you?" Siobhan asked him. "Are you hungry? I know the hospital meals aren't the best."

"I'm not hungry for any food," Finn said wickedly.

"Jesus, Finn, you have a one-track mind," Siobhan said as she went to sit in the chair next to Finn.

"Only when you are around," he told her. Finn reached out and grabbed Siobhan, pulling her to his lap before she had a chance to sit in the chair. He curled the palm of his hand around her neck and drew her lips to his. When they broke the kiss, Siobhan felt breathless.

"Let's go to the bedroom," Finn said as he pointed in the direction of the master bedroom off the kitchen.

"In your father's room?" Siobhan said with surprise. "I can remember a time when you scoffed at me for suggesting such a thing."

"We were eighteen back then, Bon, and I never knew when my father would come walking through the door."

"I know, you were so cute then," Siobhan laughed as her hands rested on Finn's shoulders. "I tried my best to entice you, but you just wouldn't do it. Big scaredy-cat."

Finn's face went from playful to serious in seconds.

"That's not funny, Bon," Finn told her as he moved her hands off her shoulders.

"Finn, I'm sorry," Siobhan told him. "You know I didn't mean it that way. It was a joke."

Finn turned his head to the side, but Siobhan placed her hand on his cheek and guided his gaze back to her.

"I wouldn't joke about something like that, Finn. Especially not after the things I have seen in my line of work. What your Dad did to you was wrong, and it wasn't your fault. I never saw that side of him when I was around him."

"Yeah, Da was great at putting on his manners for guests," Finn offered. "Good Ol' Conor… cordial and inviting. He was the best functioning drunk I ever saw in front of other people. I would always hear about how nice a guy he was from everyone I met, especially on the job sites. No one had a bad thing to say about him. Of course, they didn't live with him either."

Siobhan brought Finn in for another kiss and then held his head against her chest.

"Let's go upstairs," she told him softly, taking him by the hand to lead him up and out of the chair.

Finn gingerly moved up each step with Siobhan's assistance until they reached the top of the staircase. He then guided Siobhan to the bedroom he was in. Finn flipped on the light and sat on the bed. He struggled a bit to reach down and take off the boots he had on until Siobhan knelt to assist him. She tugged one boot off, and then the other, and tossed them to the side. She then rose in front of Finn and placed her hands at his waist so she could lift his t-shirt over his head. She was gentle, taking care not to mess with the bandages around his rib cage. Siobhan ran her hands lightly over Finn's chest, feeling the muscles above and below his bandages. Finn watched as she touched him, noticing just a hint of her stomach peeking above the jeans she wore where the gap between her shirt and pants existed. He reached out with his hands to unbutton her jeans, but she stopped him.

"Uh uh," Siobhan smiled. "the doctor said you should take it easy."

She stepped back and lifted Finn's legs up onto the bed as Finn slid over so that he rested in the middle. Siobhan climbed on the bed, kneeling between his legs, and opened the button of his jeans. She slowly slid the zipper down, lingering as each tooth clicked on the zipper so that she could feel him grow and squirm with each movement. Once the zipper was down, Siobhan grasped the waist of Finn's jeans and tugged them down his legs to get them off his body so she could throw them on the floor.

Siobhan's hands worked up Finn's legs and paused at the bulge in his black boxer briefs. She offered a light squeeze, making the briefs feel even tighter to Finn. She tucked her fingers underneath him and squeezed again before sliding her fingers up and over his covered shaft. Siobhan pulled the briefs down and off Finn's body, and her hands immediately returned to their previous spots. She let her thumb glide over the glistening head of his cock, swirling in the liquid oozing from him. Finn's body shivered beneath her touch as she reveled in how she was making him feel.

Siobhan kneeled back and pulled her shirt up and over her head. She rapidly unhooked the lilac bra she wore and then slowly, steadily, moved her body up against Finn's. When her breasts reached his drooling cock, she let her cleavage envelop him, rubbing him between and against her body slowly. Finn did all he could to maintain himself as he groaned loudly.

"Dear God, Bon," Finn growled.

"Now you get religious on me?" she purred as she picked up the pace of rubbing against him.

After sliding back down him one more time, Siobhan knelt back again and then stood up on the bed. She giggled as she tried to balance herself so she could unzip and remove her jeans without falling off the bed or on Finn. She finally was before Finn clad in just her lilac bikini panties before she seductively peeled them off. She went back to her position, this time positioning herself so that Finn felt just how wet and aroused she was. She brushed against him, allowing him to experience her wetness while she got a jolt against her lips. Siobhan reached down to his cock and placed her fist just under its engorged head, holding it tightly as she rubbed it directly on her swollen clit.

"Bon, I can't take much more…" Finn said as he tried to sit up to reach her. Siobhan pushed him back down with her free left hand as she continued to rub for both of them, bringing them each close to the edge before stopping. Finn looked at her with frustration in his eyes. "What?" he said.

"Where are your condoms?" Siobhan panted.

"In my bag," he hinted as he nodded with his head.

Siobhan slid off the bed, and Finn watched as she bent over to his bag to remove the box. She turned back towards him with a big smile and placed the box on the nightstand before grabbing one of the foil packages.

"We'll keep them close by," she ordered.

Siobhan tore the package open with her teeth. She carefully placed the condom on Finn, desperately hoping that he wouldn't burst with just her touch. Within seconds, she was ready to have him inside her. She hovered above Finn for a moment, teasing him to the hilt, before slowly lowering herself onto him. Siobhan began to rock back and forth, building a steady rhythm. She kept her eyes open and focused on Finn the entire time, even though part of her wanted to close them and get swept up in the ecstasy occurring within her. She kept her left-hand flat on Finn's tight abs and brought his right hand up to her left breast, allowing him to knead and fondle her. It wasn't long after this that she felt overcome as she tightened around Finn, holding his cock tightly inside as she came just moments ahead of him.

Siobhan collapsed her body on Finn's. She pressed her head to his chest, and she could hear and feel his heart pounding rapidly in the afterglow. Finn's hands worked through her cascading hair gently before she lifted her body off his and moved to the side. Siobhan's left hand snaked down and deftly removed the condom, tickling the extremely sensitive underside of his cock with her index finger. Finn rolled to his side, squinting as he felt some pain in his ribs before he grabbed both her hands and held them in his.

"You're making me crazy," Finn told her.

"Then I did things right," Siobhan laughed before moving in to kiss his neck. She then cuddled up next to Finn, resting her head on his shoulder while carefully placing an arm beneath his bandaged chest.

****

Siobhan noticed Finn stirring several times throughout the night. Each time it happened, she wrapped her arms around him to hold him. The practice calmed him down quickly, and it comforted her to know that holding him made him feel better. The last time she was awakened, however, was not because of Finn. Something caused her to sit up in bed with a jolt. She scanned the room quickly and saw only Finn sleeping soundly and some dim light sneaking through the curtains. Siobhan went to lay back down, but she saw that Jameson was on high alert as well, lifting his head with his ears perked.

Siobhan crept out of bed and peered out the window that overlooked the backyard. She could see nothing through the blackness, but the feeling in the pit of her stomach would not go away. Without turning on the light, she found Finn's t-shirt on the floor and put it on and opened the bedroom door to slip out. Unfortunately, Jameson would have none of that and dashed out the door ahead of her. His paws scrabbled down the wooden steps, and he disappeared into the darkness of the rest of the house.

Siobhan didn't hear Jameson running or barking, so she was unsure of where he was or what else might be in the house. She stepped lightly on each stair, trying to move so the wood would not creak beneath her feet. She reached the bottom step and looked out the front window next to the door. No outside lights had been triggered, though this provided Siobhan with little comfort. She recalled what had happened to Finn in the house just days before and worried that whoever it was had come back to perform a more thorough search.

Reluctant to turn on the lights herself to alert anyone that might be outside, Siobhan moved to find her handbag that she had left on the couch. Once there, she pulled out her Glock G43 that she had recently begun carrying in her purse when she got her concealed carry permit. She held the gun at her side, hoping she wouldn't need it but preparing for the worst.

Siobhan slid into the kitchen and saw Jameson sitting outside the master bedroom door. She and Finn had closed the door before they came upstairs, and it remained that way. Once Jameson saw Siobhan, he moved to her side and then to the back door leading out to the patio. Siobhan was unsure if Jameson would dart if she just opened the back door. She grabbed his leash and put it on him before she unlocked and opened the door.

Jameson obediently walked at her side as she stepped onto the cold patio floor. Siobhan stayed underneath the patio's overhang, knowing that if she stepped out onto the lawn, she would trigger the motion lights, and she might not get the chance to react to any intruders. She spied across the expanse of the yard. There had clearly been a thunderstorm earlier in the evening as water slowly dripped from the overhang, and the air was cooler than it had been. Some lightning off in the distance illuminated the clouds over the lake and gave a bit of brightness in intervals to help her view.

Jameson let a slow, low growl out as he stared off to the left. Siobhan followed his gaze but saw nothing. The growl became a bit more intense as she stood in the darkness, and it was then she saw it. There was a shadow off in the far corner of the property near the lake's left side. A brief flash of lightning lit the area a bit more, and then there was no doubt in Siobhan's mind that not only was someone there, but they were staring at her. Jameson pulled on his leash and barked now, wanting to break free and face the intruder.

"Jameson! Stay!" Siobhan commanded. She unlocked her gun and lifted it to eye level, preparing to fire if needed.

A chill ran down her spine, and Siobhan felt a touch on her shoulder. She spun and gasped, pointing the gun. Finn ducked quickly and pulled Siobhan's arm down and to the side, so the gun was pointed away from both.

"Fuck, Bon!" Finn yelled. "What the hell are you doing?"

"I woke up with this feeling that someone was watching us," Siobhan said as she regained her composure and locked the weapon. "Jameson felt it too. I came down here and... there was someone out there, Finn. I saw the shadow. He looked right at me."

"Where was he?" Finn asked as he began to look for signs of anything.

"Off to the left, just by the lake."

Finn walked out onto the damp grass, and the floodlights lit up the backyard. There were no signs of anyone present. Finn began to stride further toward the water.

"Jameson, come!" Finn ordered. Jameson broke from his sitting position and darted to Finn, keeping pace with him while staring out into the woods.

Finn scanned back and forth but saw no one. He did hear rustling in the woods moving past trees or on leaves, but it could just as easily be deer moving about as it could be a person. He tread lightly on the grass until he got back to the patio where Siobhan still stood.

"Whoever or whatever it was..."

"It was a 'who' Finn," Siobhan insisted. "I saw him. He was clear as day."

"I thought you said you only saw a shadow?"

"I did, out here," Siobhan replied. "But... when I had that feeling, I saw him, and it woke me up."

"Bon, I know how you are, and with everything going on right now, it's easy to see why you might think that and dream about it..."

"This wasn't a feckin' dream, Finn," Siobhan retorted. "I saw him here," she said as she brought a finger to her head, "and then out here."

Finn put his arm around Siobhan and led her into the house so they could sit at the kitchen table. Siobhan placed the gun on the table as Finn grabbed bottles of water for each of them.

"When did you start carrying a gun?" Finn asked seriously.

"I got my license years ago," Siobhan told him. "My conceal carry permit just came a few weeks ago." "Why do you need that? I'm a defense lawyer, and I don't have a gun." "Because I deal with a lot of unhappy people, Finn. Husbands who beat their wives to a pulp and don't like that we protect them. Adults who abuse kids, kidnap kids, or worse. I've been threatened more than once." "Jesus," Finn said as he reached over and took Siobhan's hand. "I had no idea." "Yeah, well, I guess we're learning a lot about each other in a short time," Siobhan told him. She ran her index finger over Finn's knuckles. "Should we call the police?" "And tell them what? That you had a feeling someone was outside? I don't think that will help much. No, I'm going to pay Detective Fremont a visit tomorrow on his turf. I need to find out what they know about all this so we can learn more about who may be behind everything and why."

17

Siobhan was shaken after the incident and tried to avoid going back to sleep. Finn held her closely all night, staying awake to keep watch while she got a few hours of rest. When sunrise came, Finn gently woke her so that she could get up for work.

"I need to get back to my place to change," Siobhan spoke as she put on her clothing from yesterday. "You need to stop interrupting my days so much."

"Is that what we're calling it? Interrupting your day?" Finn mocked.

"You know what I mean, you dope," Siobhan scolded. "It seems like I have to keep showing up to pick you up off the floor lately. I thought that was what Darren was for."

"No offense to Darren, but I'd much rather see you than him," Finn added.

He walked up behind Siobhan and wrapped his arms around her waist. He planted light, soft kisses on her neck, causing her to moan slightly.

"Finn, I really need to go…" she said, her resolve wavering.

"Okay, okay," Finn relented. "I have stuff to take care of this morning anyway. I need to check on Dad, check on Liam, and find out more about what's going on at the other side of the lake. Sooner or later, this all has to start adding up."

"Promise me you'll be careful," Siobhan said as she turned to look Finn in the eyes. "No more hospital visits or injuries, okay? I can't take any more of it, and neither can your head."

Siobhan stood on her tiptoes so she could reach and kiss Finn's forehead.

"Let me know what you find out. I'll be at the office all day."

Finn followed Siobhan downstairs and out onto the front porch. Jameson obediently tagged along to say his goodbyes. He then sat next to Finn as they watched Siobhan get into her car and head up the driveway. Finn locked the front door and made his way to the kitchen to fetch some coffee.

It wasn't long after the pot was made that there was a knock on the door. Finn glanced at his watch and saw it was just about 6:30, and he couldn't figure who would be at the house that early. He looked around the kitchen and then the living room for anything he might use as a weapon if he needed to but found nothing. The sound of a key in the lock put him on high alert as he hid just inside the doorway to the kitchen. Jameson took a more aggressive approach and went right to the front door, barking fiercely. Finn figured once the barking started, whoever might be trying to enter would cease coming in, but the door flew open, and the barking stopped. Finn peered around the corner and saw Cillian there petting Jameson.

"Jesus, Cillian, I was getting ready to bash your head in. I thought it was another intruder."

"Glad to see your senses are good even after all the rows you've been in lately," Cillian joked.

"What are you doing here this early in the morning?" Finn asked.

"Bringing back your bike, for one," Cillian said as he tossed the keys to Finn. Finn snatched them mid-flight and winced while he did it.

"How are the ribs?" Cillian asked, pointing to Finn's ribcage as he slid past him and into the kitchen to get some coffee.

"They only hurt when I cough, laugh or breathe," Finn told him.

"Fighting Liam on his turf, in front of his people... I'm surprised you're standing today."

"Maybe it wasn't my smartest decision, but I had to do something," Finn stated. He sipped his coffee as he went to sit at the table. "Any word on him?"

"I know they are holding him at Orange Correctional right now, but he hasn't been charged with anything yet. After they patched him up at the hospital, they put him in cuffs, and off he went. I can't believe he had anything to do with your Da. It doesn't add up."

"How is Da doing?"

"Some slight improvements, I'm glad to say. He's still in the coma, but the swelling has come down, and he does respond by wiggling his toes a bit. Small steps, but it's an improvement. I'll be taking Maeve down there again this morning. You coming along?"

"I think I have some other things to take care of first before I can get there today," Finn told him. "We saw someone watching the house last night."

"We?" Cillian asked.

"Siobhan and I," Finn said casually as he took another sip.

"Oh," Cillian said with a smile as he sat back in his chair. The leather of his jacket squeaked against the wood. "I didn't realize you've had company here."

"Yes, a couple of times, if you must know."

"None of my business, Finn. I think it's nice that you have rekindled things. So," Cillian offered, changing the subject, "did you get a look at who it was last night?"

"No, I didn't," Finn lamented. "Bon said she saw someone, but she didn't get a close look. By the time I got down there, whoever it was had gone."

"You think it was the same guys who broke in?"

"There's no reason not to," Finn surmised. "I can't have made that many enemies in the few days I've been here. It must have something to do with Da. I'm going to poke around a bit more today and see what I can discover."

"If you need help, just let me know. I can have a couple of the boys tag along to help you. You're not exactly in the best shape to defend yourself well right now." Cillian finished off his coffee and put his mug down on the table.

"I best be off then," Cillian said. "Keep me posted on what you know. I'll say a prayer for you."

"Thanks, I guess," Finn said. "How are you getting where you need to go if you rode the bike here?"

"Whitey followed me over on his bike," Cillian told him. "He'll ride me to the Hog House, and then Maeve and I can leave from there. Be careful, Finn."

"That seems to be the mantra for the day so far," Finn said quietly.

****

Finn's first stop of the day needed to be with Detective Fremont, but when he phoned the number on his business card, the people at the station let him know he was out. Instead, he drove to Goshen so he could try to see what was going on with Liam. Finn wondered if Liam had been formally charged with anything or if they were just holding him there trying to get information. He couldn't imagine that tactic would be successful, knowing how stubborn his brother had always been in the past.

Finn arrived at the prison and asked about Liam. One of the initial officers he met there informed him that Liam was not in a cell at the moment. When the officer declined to give Finn any more information, Finn produced his identification and let them know he was Liam's attorney and demanded to see his client. It took a bit of insistence and some time to get through security. Still, Finn was finally brought to the area of interview rooms where Liam was now. Finn could enter after showing his credentials and found Liam sitting at a small table with Detective Fremont and another detective, a woman, sitting across from his brother. Liam looked up, surprised to see his brother standing there.

"Aye, I guess you survived," Liam laughed.

"Mr. O'Farrell," Detective Fremont said as he rose, "You can't be in here. We are involved in an interrogation."

"Mr. O'Farrell is my client," he announced. "I would like some time to consult with him before this interview continues."

"Is that right?" Detective Fremont said, spying the smile on Liam's face. "If he's not your attorney, he has to go."

Liam sat coolly for a moment before he nodded.

"He's my lawyer," Liam acquiesced. "Out with the lot of you."

Detective Fremont scowled at Finn and took the officer and the other detective with him.

"You don't have to go, cutie," Liam said to the female investigator as he watched her walk toward the door.

"I don't think you really want me in here alone with you, Mr. O'Farrell," the detective spat.

"Ohh, a feisty one!" Liam laughed. "What do you say, little brother? Think she can go a few rounds with me?"

"Liam, shut up," Finn ordered as the detectives left.

"Turn off any listening devices as well, please," Finn shouted as he stared at the glass lining the far wall.

Finn waited a moment before he looked at his brother. Liam still had a wide smile.

"Looks like you got roughed up a bit, boyo," Liam scoffed. "Sleep well last night?"

"Have they charged you with anything yet?" Finn asked properly.

"Not a thing," Liam admitted. "They told me you weren't pressing charges against me for assault, and they keep asking me about Da, but I haven't said nothin'."

"I'm not pressing charges," Finn stated. "Do you know anything about what happened to Dad?"

Liam's face turned serious.

"Look, 'brother,' why would I tell you, and why would you care? It all means nothing to you, right?"

"I wouldn't be sitting here right now if that were true," Finn admitted. "If you don't want my help, I can walk out the door and leave you here. My guess is they are getting ready to charge you with attempted murder, assault, and whatever other charges they can include to go along with Dad's injuries. If you're okay with that, stay here and rot. If you want to leave here today, be prepared to answer some questions. It's your call."

Finn leaned back in the chair, squeaking it through the current silence in the room as Liam stared at him.

"You really can get me out of here today?" Liam asked, leaning forward. Finn heard the shackles around Liam's wrists and ankles jangle as he moved.

"Yes, guaranteed," Finn assured him.

"Okay… you've got a deal," Liam answered. "I'd shake your hand, but they don't seem to trust me around here. Just let me tell you, little brother. You might not like what you're gonna hear."

Finn rose and went to the door of the interview room and knocked on it. An officer came back in to stand guard over Liam while Finn was led into the viewing room where Detective Fremont and others had gathered.

"So?" Detective Fremont stated.

"Have you charged him yet?" Finn asked.

"Charges should be in my hand at any minute. Attempted murder second-degree, assault first-degree… for now. I'm sure we can add other things once pieces are put together or your father dies. You're really going to defend this piece of garbage?"

"I haven't seen any evidence yet that shows why you think he did it or is involved," Finn added.

"It doesn't matter," the female detective added. "Once he's charged, he'll never make bail. He's got priors and is a flight risk."

"Are you a lawyer too, Detective?" Finn asked her. "He's only got a few misdemeanors on his record. He's never been convicted of any violent crimes. As for the flight risk, we'd agree to an ankle monitor so he could be free on bail."

"He's never been convicted because witnesses always back out of testifying against him and any of the other Cosantóir!" the detective shouted. "Do you know what your brother has been accused of in the past? Assault, intimidation, robbery, stalking, selling firearms... the list goes on."

"Accused, never convicted," Finn said confidently.

"You let him walk out of here, you're no better than he is," the detective responded.

"I'll see you at the arraignment," Finn said as he walked out of the room. Liam was being led past him as he exited.

"They are going to arraign you this afternoon," Finn told his brother as he kept pace. "I'll see you there. Don't say anything to anyone."

Liam smiled and nodded and then blew a kiss to Detective Fremont and the female as he went.

"That doesn't help," Finn scolded.

"I know, but it makes me feel good," Liam chortled as he was led away.

"Stay out of trouble for the next few hours!" Finn yelled.

"No promises, little brother," Liam yelled back.

With a few hours to kill before the arraignment, Finn hopped back on the motorcycle. He decided to pay a visit to Patty Wells, the realtor handling the lots on the lake's other side. He went back to his father's house to change clothes, slipping into the one suit he brought with him so that he could look his best for the realtor and for the court afterward. As he dressed, he heard his cellphone buzz with a text message.

I hope it's going well for you. My day has been nuts. Call me later.

Siobhan ended her message with a green heart emoji.

Always thinking Irish, Finn thought to himself with a grin.

Once he was dressed correctly, Finn made his way over to Patty Wells' office. There were only a couple of cars in the parking lot, and both were high-end BMWs. Someone was doing well selling real estate. Finn reflexively straightened the gray silk tie he had donned for the occasion before hopping off the motorcycle and went into the office. The air conditioning blew strongly throughout the room, and only one person's head popped up over the side of a cubicle like a meerkat to see about a potential customer. Finn went directly to the desk inside the door where the receptionist sat.

"Good morning!" the older blonde beamed at Finn. Finn watched as her eyes looked his suit up and down, and he knew she was trying to figure out if he had money or was just playing the part. "How can I help you?"

"I was looking for Patty Wells," Finn said politely. "Is she in?"

"Oh, I'm sorry," the woman said as her smile faded. "She's out with a client this morning. Did you have an appointment with her?"

"No, no, I didn't," Finn replied. He amped up his charm level as he reached into his jacket and pulled out one of his business cards.

"I'm Finn O'Farrell," he said as he handed her the card. "I'm down visiting family and thought I would look at some of the properties in the area. I'd like to have someplace to stay when I come down more often. I heard Patty was the one to talk to if I wanted to see property over around Shadowmere. I took a ride over there the other day and saw some nice spots around there, but there was a big fence up, so I couldn't go down the road. I was wondering if any of those are available."

"Gee, I don't know," the woman said. "Patty handles all the Shadowmere listings personally. You'd have to speak with her."

Finn glanced down and noticed the nameplate resting on the desk so he could pick up the woman's name. He also noted no signs of a wedding or engagement ring, and he turned up the charm.

"Say, Sandra, I know you're probably not supposed to do this, but if you could give me any info at all about that area, you would be doing me a big favor. Money isn't an object if that's what you're worried about; I'm ready to spend big bucks right away. I'm sure Patty wouldn't be upset about it."

Finn noticed how Sandra was looking into his eyes, and he flashed a smile that he hoped would seal the deal.

"You have to promise me you aren't going to tell anyone about this or that I gave you the information," Sandra said softly. She began to type rapidly into her computer and waited for a screen to pop up. Once it did, she waved Finn over to her side of the desk.

"These are Patty's files on the Shadowmere developments," she told him. "She keeps them password-protected, but it's the same password for her computer – Garfield. You know, like the cartoon cat. Anyway, it looks like most of them are already sold to the same LLC that bought the lots behind the fence."

"What's the LLC name?" Finn said, trying not to appear too anxious.

"What good will that do? They already own the land," Sandra asked him.

"Well, I'm a lawyer. I know a lot of people all over New York. It could be someone I have worked with before. Just peek, please?"

Sandra highlighted the lot and pressed enter.

"Tangled Webb, LLC," Sandra told him. "That's a pretty weird name."

"Sure is," Finn agreed. "Thank you so much for your help, Sandra."

Finn patted her hand softly as he moved to the other side of the desk again.

"Do you want me to set up an appointment for you with Patty? I can add you to her calendar. She's free tomorrow morning, and I am sure she'd love to show you some properties."

"I have to run out to meet a client," Finn told her as he looked at his watch. "I'll give your office a call tomorrow so we can set something up. Thanks!"

Finn quickly escaped the office and made his way to his bike to get on the road and back to Goshen. He thought about the LLC and knew that he could get more information about it with just a phone call. Since New York had changed the laws regarding the anonymity LLC was often used for, it was much easier to track the owners than before. Knowing who owned the land might give him some better insight into what was going on.

Finn waited around the courthouse for a bit for Liam to be brought in for his arraignment. The time allowed him to check in with Susannah, his assistant at the law firm, and ask her if she could have one of the associates investigate Tangled Webb for him.

"Sure, I can do that," she answered. "Does this have something to do with one of the cases you are working on?"

"Not really," Finn admitted. "It's more of a family thing."

"Finn," Susannah said in a hushed tone, "Is everything okay? It's not like you to be like this. I haven't heard from you in days. Is your father doing better? Bob Morris keeps asking me if I have heard from you and when you might be coming back. You have appearances and meetings next week that are planned."

"I'm sorry, Susannah," Finn told her. "There are a lot of things still up in the air. Honestly, I don't know when I can get back. My father is still in a coma. There are problems with my brother, and... well, a bunch of other personal things I didn't plan on. I'll give you answers as soon as I have them, I promise."

"Don't leave me hanging here, Finn," Susannah told him. "You know I only stay at this firm to keep working for you."

"I'll do my best, I promise."

"I know all about you and your promises," she chided.

"I think I am getting better about that, too," Finn admitted. "Get me the information about the LLC as fast as you can."

Finn spied the officers bringing Liam into the courtroom.

"I have to go. Get me answers! Bye."

Finn hung up and hustled into the courtroom. A few other people in handcuffs dotted the room, and either had attorneys, family, or no one at all there for them. Finn took a seat behind Liam. Liam turned and smiled at his brother.

"I thought for sure you wouldn't show up," Liam said. "I have to say, I'm impressed, little brother."

"Don't be impressed yet," Finn replied. "Let's see if we can get you out of here."

Liam's case was called before Judge Amy Garrett. Liam was brought to the defense desk, and Finn followed him. After the bailiff read the case, Liam was asked to enter a plea.

"Not guilty, your honor," Liam attested.

"I assume this is your attorney, Mr. O' Farrell?" Judge Garrett asked.

"Aye, it is," Liam answered.

"Finn O'Farrell, your honor. I am representing the defendant," Finn stated.

"A relative of yours?" the judge asked Liam.

"My younger brother, Judge," Liam smiled.

Judge Garrett shook her head as she looked at the docket and then turned to the District Attorney's table.

"Mr. Moford, do you have any bail requests?"

"We ask the defendant to be held without bail, your honor," Mr. Moford said. Finn looked over at the ADA. Moford was trying to make a name for himself, Finn assumed, based on how he appealed to the court. "The defendant is violent, part of a known gang, and is a flight risk."

"Your honor," Finn spoke, "Mr. O'Farrell has never been convicted of any violent crimes. He has a few misdemeanors on his record, and that is it. As for being part of a gang, that's ludicrous. He is part of a motorcycle club that rides together, made up of people he works with. He is gainfully employed and a respected leader in his union. We ask for his release."

"Nice try, counselor," Judge Garrett said with a smirk. "While there are no violent convictions on his record, your brother has a somewhat checkered past, at best."

"Judge, the prosecutor has no evidence to tie my client to the crime mentioned. He has an alibi for the timeframe of the accident…"

"Accident, Ha!" Moford scoffed. "Your Honor, Conor O'Farrell, the defendant's father, nearly had his head taken off by a piece of machinery dropped down the shaft he was inspecting. The defendant's prints are on the device."

"Along with a dozen other men who work that job site and others," Finn shot back.

"As for his supposed alibi, all the people that will vouch for him are members of his gang, and each has criminal histories of their own."

"Your Honor, I object to the constant reference of the motorcycle club as a gang. My father, the injured party in this case, started the club over thirty years ago. They are all Sandhogs."

"They are what?" the judge asked.

"Sandhogs, your Honor," Finn answered. "That's the term for the people working in the tunnels. The union dates back over 170 years."

"The so-called 'club' has a long history of illegal activity, judge," Moford interjected. "If you look at my brief, you will see that the Cosantóir has been linked to a bevy of criminal activity over the years."

"I've read the brief, Mr. Moford," Judge Garrett replied, placing the folder down. "I have to agree with Mr. O'Farrell; the case seems a bit light on evidence."

"We believe we can unearth people who will come forward, your Honor," Moford stated. "However, if Mr. O'Farrell is roaming free, we worry about witness intimidation and threats. If your Honor sees fit to impose bail, we ask it to be set at one million dollars."

Liam let out a loud belly laugh.

"Keep your client quiet, Mr. O'Farrell," Judge Garrett scolded Finn. Finn shot Liam a glance, and Liam just grinned it away.

"A million dollars is highly excessive, Judge," Finn replied.

"I agree," Judge Garrett nodded. "Bail will be set at $200,000, cash or bond. If Mr. O'Farrell can make bail, he is ordered to wear an ankle monitor so we can keep track of his whereabouts."

"Hey!" Liam shouted. "I can't work in the tunnels with one of those damn things on!"

Finn grabbed hold of Liam's arm to shut him up.

"Your Honor," Finn said calmly, "my client works hundreds of feet below the surface and in different locations. Having a monitor will be a hardship."

"Then I guess he'll be staying home or in jail. Your choice, Mr. O'Farrell," Judge Garrett added as she pounded the gavel and got ready for the next case.

The bailiffs came over to gather Liam and take him back to holding before going over to the prison.

"I thought you were getting me out, you eejit!" Liam snarled.

"Relax," Finn said. "You are getting out."

"I can't get a hold of 200 grand," Liam said. "I'm fucked."

"I'll put up the bond," Finn said, walking with his brother. "You'll be out in a few hours."

"You? Why would you do that? To soothe your guilt or to flash that you have a lot of money?"

"Neither," Finn snapped. "Because I need you out so we can figure out what happened to Da. Keep your mouth shut for a few more hours, and you'll be free. I have to take care of the paperwork."

Finn spent some time making Liam's bail arrangements and got everything posted in a few hours. It wasn't money he had expected to lay out for anything, and his hope had to be that Liam wouldn't screw up. He waited outside the jail and called Siobhan to let her know he took care of Liam at least.

"That was an amazing thing you did," Siobhan told him sincerely.

"Not really," Finn said as he played it down. "It's for selfish reasons. If he's tied up in any of this, I need to find out. His ego is big enough where he won't be able to resist telling me. I can't wait for this day to be over."

"Me too," Siobhan said with a sigh. "It's been crazy here today, even more than a usual Monday."

"How about you meet me at Millie's when you're done? We can blow off some steam and hang out with Darren for a bit. Unless you have other things you might like to do," Finn said slyly.

"Oh, and what other things might there be, Mr. O' Farrell?" Siobhan answered. Finn imagined Siobhan was grinning and blushing at the same time.

"Do you want me to say it? Because I will. I'm standing outside a prison right now, Bon. Inhibitions aren't exactly running rampant here. I'd be glad to slowly start to unbutton your shirt and…"

"Okay, I get the picture," Siobhan said in a hushed tone. "Just be glad you weren't on speakerphone. Perhaps you do need some time out in public to control yourself. I'll give Cara a call and see if she is free. Meet you at Millie's at around 6?"

"Perfect. See you then," Finn said and hung up just as Liam was walking out of the building.

"Wow, I thought for sure you would just leave me in there," Liam spoke. "If it were you in there, I sure as hell wouldn't be standing here."

The two started walking toward the parking lot when Finn noticed several of the Cosantóir gathered around where he had parked the bike. He groaned internally and knew he was in for more trouble.

"Hey!" a large, bearded man yelled. Finn recognized Danny, one of the club members he had scuffled with days before. "Did you ride this bike here? This is one of Conor's."

"Yeah, I rode it here," Finn admitted.

"Not smart, brother," Liam told him. "You should know better. You can't ride one of ours if you're not one of us."

"How's about I finish off what I wanted to a few days ago before Maeve stopped me?" Danny asked as he strode up in front of Finn to block him from the bike. Finn turned to look at Liam and saw he couldn't get any support from his brother when Liam just shrugged. Another fight was the last thing he needed right now.

Demon stepped up and stood next to Finn.

"Back off, gimp," Demon told Danny and gave him a shove. "He just bailed Liam out of jail, and he worked his ass off with me and the other Hogs down in the tunnels, which is a damn sight more than you have done in years, Danny."

"I got hurt on the job," Danny griped. "You know that."

"You mean you milked the system to get disability," Demon spat back.

"Doesn't excuse him riding one of our bikes," Danny said, now in front of Demon. Demon towered over everyone and had more than a few inches on Danny. "I think he has lessons to learn."

"You don't want to go there, brother," Demon said through gritted teeth. "He's Conor's son and has Liam's back. That's all I need to know to stand by him."

"Liam, are you okay with this?" Danny asked, turning to their defacto leader. "Say the word, and I'll take them both down a peg." Danny reached into his back pocket and pulled out brass knuckles, slipping them onto his right hand.

Finn looked at Liam once more. He knew the club members were turning to Liam for leadership now with Conor laid up. He figured his brother would do what would make him appear the best and most formidable. Finn began to shift his feet, bracing himself to throw a punch and get ready to dodge anything else.

"Stand down, Danny," Liam replied. Liam moved over and stood between Danny and Demon.

"What? Are you fucking kidding me?" Danny said in shock.

"No, I'm not," Liam said sternly. "You want to start a fight fifty feet away from the jail? We'll all end up in there, and I'll get the worst of it. Use your head, you eejit."

"This is your Get Out of Jail Free card, brother," Liam said through his teeth as he turned to Finn. "You don't get a second one."

Finn nodded in agreement.

"You can ride the bike," Liam offered. "Ceannaire stopped riding it years ago anyway."

Ceannaire was a word Finn hadn't heard used in many years. Gaelic for 'leader,' everyone called his father that when he was growing up. Whether he met men Conor worked with or rode with, they all looked up to his father as their commander.

"This is complete shite, Liam," Danny barked. "You going soft on the kid because he's your brother? Did somebody bend you over while you were in the jail cell today?"

Liam grabbed Danny by the jacket collar and tossed him to the ground like a rag doll.

"Say one more thing like that to me, Danny, and you'll wish it were someone in a jail cell looking to fuck you instead of the beating you'll get from me. Now, who's giving me their bike to ride so I can get home and have a drink?"

Liam stared down at Danny and held out his hand to lift him off the ground. He pulled Danny to his feet and snatched Danny's bike keys from his hand.

"Thanks, Danny," Liam smiled. "I'm sure one of the brothers can let you ride bitch."

The Cosantóir began to disperse, and Finn breathed a sigh of relief. He looked to Demon, who still stood in front of him until he watched the others walk away.

"Thanks, Darryl," Finn offered.

"No problem," Demon replied. "Brothers watch out for each other, right?"

"Sometimes they do," Finn said.

"Hey, what you did was a stand-up thing," Demon told Finn. "Not many people in your shoes do that. That gets points with me. Liam can be a dick sometimes…"

"Sometimes?" Finn interrupted.

Demon chuckled. "Yeah, well, that's who Liam is. But the truth is I know he'd go to war with me at work, at home, with the club, wherever. Even if it doesn't look like it now, he respects you for bailing him out. He'd still be sitting inside if it weren't for you."

Demon climbed onto his Harley and sat back as he watched Finn get on his bike.

"Darryl, no offense, but how the hell did you find a bike to fit your…"

Darryl let out a big laugh.

"My physique? It wasn't easy, dude. A lot of customization and a lot of time learning to do things myself. This baby cost me a fortune, but it's a sweet, comfortable ride. You coming back to Hog House?"

Now it was Finn's turn to laugh.

"No way," Finn said as he grabbed his helmet. "I'm running out of lives to use. I think I'll let things cool down a bit before I talk to Liam. Thanks again, Darryl."

****

By the time Finn arrived at Millie's, it was nearly six. Finn walked in to see a sparse crowd. A few older gents gathered at the end of the bar around Paddy, talking politics, soccer, and which whiskey is best. Finn nodded as he walked past the men.

"Conor O'Farrell's boy," Paddy said to the men as he pointed at Finn. The three others around him all nodded at the revelation as Finn made his way down to his reserved seat at the bar. Darren wasn't behind the bar yet, so Maggie came down to wait on him.

"You know that seat is reserved," Maggie smiled. "That's Millie's seat. Darren always leaves it open."

"Oh, I'm sorry," Finn told her as he stood up. "He let me sit here the other day, so…"

"You must be Finnbar," Maggie said, offering her hand while trying to keep a straight face.

"It's Finn, actually," he corrected.

"I know," Maggie laughed. "Darren said he'd give me ten bucks if I saw you come in and said that to you. I'm Maggie."

"Thanks, Maggie," Finn replied. "Is he around?"

"He's just round back in his office. He'll be out in a minute. You can sit in Millie's seat; I was just teasing you. You are like the prodigal son come home, you know. Can I get you a Guinness?"

"Please," Finn answered. "And buy a round of whiskey for the gents, on me."

"Oh boy, you are really looking to butter them up, aren't you? You know they are like stray cats that bunch. You feed them, and they won't leave you alone, and there will be more of them tomorrow looking for you."

"It's okay," Finn laughed.

Maggie began to pour Finn's drink and then gave shots to the octogenarians at the other end of the bar.

"Courtesy of Mr. O'Farrell, gents," Maggie said.

She strode back down, finished pouring Finn's Guinness, and placed it in front of him.

Finn held up his glass to the men.

"Slainte," he offered as they all picked up their beverages and drank.

"Boy, you just fit right in now," Darren said as he came around the corner and got behind the bar. "They're going to expect that now, you know."

"I've been warned," Finn told him.

"Sure, you'll just go back home to Saratoga, and I'll be left here to deal with them. Unless, of course, you end up staying around for a while."

"Why would you say that?" Finn asked as he sipped his beer.

"I don't know. Maybe a certain redhead that has caught your attention again."

"Darren…"

"Look, I know it's only been a few days back here," Darren started, "but you can't deny what's happening. You've spent every day with her; you're clearly into each other. You can't just walk away from that."

"Darren, it's more complicated than that," Finn admitted. "I have a career, a home, a life in Saratoga that I have spent a long time building. The time I have spent with Siobhan has been incredible, but there's still a lot of bad memories and bad blood here for me. I don't know what I am going to do."

Cara and Siobhan came walking into the bar, and all the old men stood up as they walked past, greeting the ladies sweetly.

"Great," Darren said as Siobhan came over and sat next to Finn. "Now they know you know the pretty Irish girls too. They will never want you to go. See? You have to stay."

Darren went to pour a Guinness for Siobhan and make a rum and Coke for Cara as Siobhan looked to Finn.

"What did he mean, you have to stay?" Siobhan said, worry on her face.

"Nothing," Finn told her. "He's just a pain in the ass. Let's not talk about any of that stuff right now. It's been a long couple of days. How about the four of us blow off some steam?"

"Sounds good to me," Cara answered.

"Let's go grab some dinner and then go back to my Dad's place to hang out. Like the old days," Finn said as he took Siobhan's hand.

"I can't just leave," Darren said, waving his arms around the bar.

"Oh, for feck's sake, Darren," Cara said. "It's a weeknight. Who the hell is coming in here? You've already got the old soldiers here. You know it won't be more than them."

"I think I can handle closing up tonight, Darren," Maggie told him. "Go hang out with your friends."

Darren nodded and smiled.

"Fair enough," Darren said. "Let me just grab my things, and we can head out."

Finn sipped on his Guinness while Siobhan looked at him.

"You okay?" she asked, wrapping her arm in his.

"Yeah, just tired," Finn told her.

"We don't have to go out tonight if you don't want to," Siobhan replied. "We can go home and... rest," she smiled.

"Oh no, Vonnie," Cara interrupted. "You've had him all to yourself for days. He can spend some time with the rest of us. Besides, I want to see his Da's house."

"It's okay, Bon," Finn answered. "I could use a night out with friends."

It was only after Finn said this that he realized he never had a night out with "friends." The people he called friends back home were either clients or colleagues, not anyone he could call a friend. He had isolated himself from the world for the last several years, and for the first time in a long time, it felt good to be around people that he knew cared about him and had his back.

The four friends walked out to the parking lot and stood in front of the entrance to Millie's.

"So, who's driving?" Darren asked. "No sense in us all taking four different cars."

"I've got the bike," Finn said, pointing to the motorcycle.

"You're riding?" Siobhan said with surprise.

"Yeah, it felt nice to get on one again."

"Well, I think the gents should chauffeur us around tonight, Vonnie," Cara said. She hooked Darren's arm and pulled him toward his car. "You can ride with Finn," she smiled. "We'll follow you."

Before Siobhan could reply at all, Cara and Darren were off to his car. Siobhan turned to Finn and gave a nervous smile.

"If you're afraid to ride on the bike with me, it's okay. You can drive," Finn told her.

"Afraid?" Siobhan answered. "The only thing I'm afraid of, Finn O'Farrell, is that you don't remember how to ride one of these things. Let's go."

Finn got out the spare helmet and passed it to Siobhan. She climbed onto the back of the bike and wrapped her hands around Finn's waist as he started the motorcycle up. Finn felt her squeeze tightly when the engine roared, and once they were on the road, she seemed to relax a bit. Finn drove through Monroe and down 17M to the Empire Diner. The diner was always a frequent spot for the friends in their younger days, and Finn felt like it would be fun to stop in there again.

He pulled the Harley into a parking spot and shut off the engine. Siobhan hopped off quickly and handed the helmet to Finn.

"Not bad," Siobhan smiled.

Darren pulled his car into the spot next to Finn.

"Really?" Cara said as she climbed out of the car. "The diner? I thought you would take us out somewhere fancy."

"What's wrong with the diner?" Finn asked.

"Nothing, I love it," Cara remarked. "But I can go here any time. I wanted to spend some of your money."

"I'll tell you what," Finn offered. "You can get whatever you want on the menu."

"Careful, Finn," Darren warned as he held the glass door entrance to the diner open for the ladies, "she can pack it away when she wants to."

"Quiet, you," Cara answered, punching Darren in the stomach as she went inside.

The four sat at a booth, laughing and reminiscing. At the same time, they went through plates of appetizers before having burgers, something they all always ordered when together. They talked about the trouble they would get into as kids, and the fun times they had with each other.

"Ugh," Cara said. "Remember when they would drag us down to Shea Stadium, Vonnie?"

"How can I forget," Siobhan laughed as she dipped a fry into ketchup. "The two of them would sit there riveted to the game while we wandered around the stadium. I'll never forget the one where you somehow got us into the visitor's clubhouse so you could steal a hat."

"What?" Finn said with shock. "I don't remember that."

"We probably never told you," Cara laughed. "I went down and flirted with this young, naïve clubhouse boy and convinced him to let us slide in just for a minute. I grabbed a Pirates hat and ran out. It only cost me a kiss and a peek down my shirt. Totally worth it."

"I remember that!" Darren remarked. "Finn, that was the game that the first baseman for the Pirates hit two homers to beat us. We just missed snagging the first one."

"Right, that eight-year-old kid outwrestled you for the ball," Finn added.

"Little bugger," Darren grumbled. "It should have been mine."

"In your defense," Finn said, "she was a tough girl."

The waitress came around to clear the table and ask about dessert.

"I'm kind of full," Finn told her.

"Forget it, Finn," Cara said as she slammed her hand on the table. "This is where I get you. We'll take one of everything."

The waitress laughed until she realized Cara was completely serious in her statement.

"You really want me to bring one of everything? We have about 15 items in the case right now."

Cara looked at Finn and grinned.

"Go ahead," Finn acquiesced.

Plate after plate was brought to the table with slices of cake, cheesecake, pie, pastries, and pudding.

"What, no, tapioca?" Cara said as she dove into a piece of blue velvet cake.

"Sorry, we don't have it," the waitress apologized.

"I think you have enough of everything else that you won't miss it," Darren told her.

The quartet made as big of a dent as they could in the desserts before boxing up what was left to bring home. Finn paid the bill, spending nearly $200, as Cara walked out with bags of containers. Finn led the way back to his father's home in Harriman, with Siobhan holding him while driving the bike through the darker, windy roads.

The floodlights lit up as the motorcycle and Darren's car pulled in front of the house.

"Shite, man," Darren said as he got out of his car. "This is your Da's house?"

"I don't believe it either," Finn said. He walked to the front porch was greeted by Jameson running from the backside of the house. Jameson stopped short when he saw new visitors.

"Is he okay?" Darren asked as he halted.

"If you don't make any sudden moves, sure," Finn said sarcastically.

"No, seriously," Darren asked. "He looks like he could take an arm off."

"He's a marshmallow," Siobhan laughed. "Jameson! Come!"

Jameson bounded down the steps to greet Siobhan and wagged his tail happily at her as she squished his face in the palms of her hands.

Finn led everyone into the house, and Cara and Darren were in awe of each room. Finn corralled Darren to help him out in the garage so they could grab a cooler and fill it with some beer to bring out to the back.

"Damn, Finn," Darren said as he looked at the spacious garage. "No offense, but where was your Da hiding all this stuff when we were kids?"

"You got me," Finn replied. "I know he makes good money being a Hog for so long, but something tells me there was more to it than that. I just have a bad feeling about all this. Maybe he finally pissed off the wrong person or extorted someone, and the accident was payback."

"You haven't found anything in the house?"

"No, and his office is locked. No one seems to know anything about what's in there or where the key might be. I'm fairly sure whoever broke in here the other night knows what's in there," Finn told him.

"Come on, you tools," Cara yelled from inside. "We're waiting on the beer!"

"You better hurry before her Highness has an aneurysm," Darren said.

The two carried the cooler with ice and beer through the kitchen and onto the back patio. The friends sat around for hours, lighting the fire pit, listening to music, and talking. Finn and Siobhan cuddled up together in an oversized Papasan chair.

When it had reached about midnight, Cara tossed the throw blanket she had on to the side.

"I want to go for a swim," Cara said.

"Right now?" Finn asked.

"Yes, right now," she commanded. "And you all are coming with me."

Cara pulled Darren up from his position on the ground until he was standing.

"Let's go, lovebirds," Cara chided. "You guys as well."

"Cara, come on," Siobhan said, hoping to talk her out of it. Cara had already taken her shirt off and was stripping out of her jeans.

"Come on, nothing," Cara yelled. "I'm not letting this beautiful lake go to waste. We always wanted to sneak in to swim these lakes. Now we don't have to!"

Cara grabbed Darren's hand and dragged him along with her. Finn watched as Darren tried to kick off his sneakers and jeans before they reached the dock.

"We better go and make sure they don't kill themselves," Finn said to Siobhan.

Finn and Siobhan got to the end of the dock just as Darren was jumping in. He splashed both as they watched Cara floating out in the water.

"Get in here, you two!" Cara ordered.

Finn started taking off his clothes until he was down to his boxer briefs. He looked over at Siobhan.

"I didn't bring my suit," she said coyly.

"Neither did I!" Cara yelled. "Get in here in your skivvies, Vonnie. It's nothing we haven't seen before. Some of us have seen even more."

"Nice," Siobhan scolded.

"Do you need some help?" Finn asked as he approached Siobhan. He positioned his hands at the hem of her shirt and lifted the shirt over her head. Before he could help her with her jeans, Siobhan slapped his fingers away.

"I think I can do the rest," she said playfully.

In seconds both Finn and Siobhan leaped into the water together. Even though the water soaked through the bandages Finn wore around his ribs, he didn't care.

"This water is freezing," Siobhan said as she trod water.

"Here," Finn offered, swimming over to her and taking her in his arms. He pressed his body to hers and gave her a kiss under the watchful eyes of Cara and Darren.

"That's what I'm talking about," Cara said. "Now it's just like old times."

She snuck up behind Darren and dunked him under the water before she swam away. Darren chased after her, trying to keep up as she swam off towards the shore to the left.

"Are you feeling better?" Siobhan asked as she clung to Finn.

He watched as the water glistened on her face. Between the lights in the yard and the moonlight, he had never seen Siobhan look so beautiful.

"Better than ever," Finn replied.

18

Finn rolled to his left and tried to put his arm around Siobhan, but he felt nothing but rumpled blankets and pillows. He opened his left eye to spy Siobhan, wrapped in just a towel, perched on the edge of the bed.

"I'm sorry I missed out on the shower," Finn yawned.

"I'm sorry, I didn't mean to wake you," Siobhan said as she sorted through her bag and pulled out clothes. "I have to get dressed for work."

"Come on, Bon," Finn pleaded as he sat up. "Call in sick. Take the day and spend it with me."

"Finn, I can't do that. There's just too much going on right now that needs my attention."

Siobhan let the towel drop to the floor as she began to dress. Finn stared as he watched Siobhan slide into her underthings, enjoying the movements and curves of her body until he couldn't take it anymore. Finn tossed the blanket aside, scooted to the bottom of the bed, and wrapped his hands around Siobhan's waist, pulling her back onto the bed with him. Siobhan let out a faint scream and laugh before Finn started to kiss her, silencing her giggles as they turned into gentle sighs.

"Finn, I have to…" Siobhan began as she felt Finn's lips on her neck. He knew just which spots always got to her as her eyes closed, and she relished in his soft touch.

"You don't have to do anything," Finn offered as his hands worked down from Siobhan's shoulders to her breasts.

"I can't," she said more forcefully as she summoned the energy to push on Finn before his hands could reach her nipples.

Finn sat up with disappointment.

"Okay, how about this," Finn countered. "Just take the morning to be with me. We'll grab some breakfast, and I want to take you someplace. I promise to have you back at your office in the afternoon. You can work, and then I can see my Dad and Liam and see where things stand. Sound fair?"

Siobhan contemplated the offer from Finn.

"I don't know, Finn..." Siobhan said as she went back to looking for clothes to wear to the office.

"It's not even 7 AM yet," Finn told her. He sat behind her on the bed, spreading light kisses on her shoulder as he eased down her bra strap. "Just a few hours, I swear. I... I want time with you."

Siobhan's resistance waned as the soft kisses hit their target.

"When was the last time you took a day off, or even a morning off?" Finn asked. He pulled her body close to his, enveloping her in his arms. Finn's fingertips began to graze Siobhan's bare thighs, sending goosebumps up and down her body.

"It's been a long time... Ohhh..." Siobhan moaned as the kisses started up on the nape of her neck again while Finn's fingers moved to the front of the thin navy cotton bikini panties she wore.

In no time at all, Finn had worn down Siobhan. His touch, his kisses, and more had her squirming on the edge of the bed, pushing herself against his hands while his fingers worked their magic on her. She felt his hardness pressing firmly against her back as he touched her. Finn's hands were everywhere that she wanted them to be before his seduction had succeeded. Siobhan spun around and kissed Finn hard while she grasped his left hand and held it firmly against her warm, wet panties. Finn kept up his motion, circling around her clit with his index finger outside her panties before diving in. Siobhan panted loudly at the initial touch.

Finn took hold of Siobhan and tossed her back onto the bed, so her head hit the pillows. His fingers hungrily tore down her panties, and he quickly reached for the condoms on the nightstand, tore the package open with his teeth, and hurriedly put the condom on so he could slide inside her. Both groaned at the motion when Finn entered her, and Siobhan wrapped her legs around Finn's waist so she could draw him deep into her and keep him there. Movement occurred at a furious pace before Siobhan tightened around Finn, lifting her back off the bed as she clenched and came, with Finn following her ecstasy with his own orgasm.

Siobhan worked to get control of her breathing again as Finn moved to her right.

"I could wake up like this every morning," Finn laughed.

"Be careful what you are saying, counselor," Siobhan replied. "I might hold you to that. I hope this isn't how you persuade everyone to go along with you."

"Well, not everyone," Finn grinned. "Does that mean you'll take the day?"

"I'll take the morning," Siobhan insisted. "But you must get me to the office today, Finn. I mean it."

"Scout's honor," Finn said as he crossed his heart with his fingers.

"You were never a Boy Scout," Siobhan chided as she reached back for her bag to seek out a clean pair of panties.

"Okay, as a lawyer, I swear…"

"Don't even go there," Siobhan interrupted. "Being a lawyer doesn't make you more trustworthy, you know. If anything, you're more devious now," she said with a smile.

"That's fair," Finn said, "But it worked." Finn stood his naked body in front of Siobhan and bent down to kiss her.

"I'll take a quick shower, and then we can go," Finn told her. "Want to join me?"

"If I join you, we are never getting anywhere but this bedroom today," Siobhan replied.

"That's not such a bad thing," Finn growled as his right hand reached for Siobhan. Siobhan pulled back, slid to her right, and stood up.

"Go take your shower!" she scolded. Her right hand slapped Finn's bare backside to shoo him along.

Finn scurried into the bathroom and showered rapidly, leaving the growing stubble on his face. He had been clean-shaven for years and liked the way this new-found look changed his face. When he appeared back in the bedroom, he saw Siobhan standing before the mirror over the dresser. She was wearing a pair of white denim capris and was busy tying a light blue collared shirt into a knot so that the knot rested below her breasts and revealed her midriff.

"Is that one of my shirts?" Finn asked as he watched.

"It is," she admitted. "I didn't think you would mind sharing, and then I can change into my work clothes when I get to the office."

"I don't mind at all," Finn said in awe. "It looks a thousand times better on you."

"I don't know," Siobhan said as she tied her hair into a ponytail. "I'll bet you're pretty sexy in one of those expensive suits," she said, nodding at the suit hanging on the back of the door.

"I'll be glad to model one for you later if you agree to just wear that shirt."

"You have a deal!" Siobhan laughed. She gathered up her bag and sat on the bed as it was her turn to watch Finn dress for the day. She marveled at it all, from the black boxer briefs that clung to his toned body to the fitted black t-shirt and blue jeans he put on. Finn sat in the chair opposite the bed as he put his boots on and grabbed his wallet, phone, and keys.

"Grab your bag," Finn stated. "I hope you have a jacket too."

"Why?" Siobhan asked as she followed Finn down the stairs to the kitchen, where Jameson sat patiently, waiting for his breakfast.

"We're taking the bike today," Finn told her as he poured dry dog food into Jameson's bowl. "That's okay, isn't it?"

"Sure," Siobhan said hesitatingly. "I didn't realize you were getting back into that so much."

"I've never really stopped riding, Bon," Finn remarked. "I have a bike in Saratoga; I just don't use it much. It just feels... different... being back here. It feels right."

"It's fine," Siobhan told him. "I'm just surprised you took to it again so quickly, especially after rehashing the past."

"I think it will be okay," Finn reassured her. "It will be like old times."

Finn donned his leather jacket as Siobhan put on a windbreaker Finn found in the hall closet. He took Siobhan's hand and led her out to the bike, giving her a helmet to wear as he loaded her bag in one of the saddlebags. Finn strapped on his helmet and got on the bike, with Siobhan following and wrapping her arms around his waist.

"All set?" Finn asked.

"I'm all yours," Siobhan answered.

Finn started up the bike and slowly took off down the driveway and out onto the road. He drove through Monroe, heading to the Dunkin' Donuts in town without much of a thought. He parked out front, and the couple walked into the store and up to the front counter. Finn turned to the counter and saw Annie standing in front of him.

"Hey there," Finn said nervously.

"Hi," Annie said abruptly. "I was wondering if you were going to bother to stop in after leaving me stranded on the dance floor at Millie's." Annie peered around Finn and saw Siobhan standing behind him.

"Is that who you ditched me for, or have you moved on from that one too?"

Finn sighed.

"Annie, I'm sorry, I really am," Finn told her. "I saw Siobhan," he said as he turned back to her before swiveling around to Annie, "and I needed to talk to her. I didn't mean to leave you like that."

"No problem," Annie said with a smile. "I just wanted to make you sweat and squirm a bit. We barely know each other, and trust me... I had plenty of dance partners after you left. I do have to say, it was a first for me, though. Guys don't leave me standing there, especially in the outfit I wore that night. You must be someone special," she added, looking at Siobhan.

Embarrassed, Finn fumbled through ordering coffee and breakfast sandwiches. He waited patiently at the side counter for the order as Siobhan slid into a booth and waited. Annie finished waiting on a very tall young man and handed him a tray of iced coffee and iced tea before bringing Finn's items over to him.

"She's pretty," Annie remarked.

"Yes, she is," Finn answered as he grabbed the coffees.

"I hope I didn't fuck it up for you," Annie told him. "You deserved it, though."

"It will be alright," Finn assured her. "She'll give me a hard time about it."

Finn paced over to the booth and placed the coffee and sandwiches on the table before sliding into the chair opposite Siobhan.

"That's the girl you were with at Millie's that first night," Siobhan stated. "Do all your interactions with women go that well?"

"To be honest, that one was better than most," Finn said. "There are usually a lot more curse words involved, and I'm not nearly as nice or responsive."

Finn looked up and saw Siobhan nodding at staring at her coffee. He reached across the table and took her hand.

"Hey, Bon, you don't have to worry about her. We were just flirting that night, is all. I'm…"

"Before you finish that sentence, Finn, you need to think about what you are going to say," Siobhan said solemnly. "Don't make promises to me that you are not going to keep. I'm not doing that again." She picked up her coffee and sipped, and she stared at Finn.

Finn looked directly into her emerald eyes.

"Bon, I don't know what's happening day to day while I'm here. There are a lot of balls juggling in the air right now. I am sure that the time I spend with you here is what I look forward to the most."

"Let's leave it at that for now," Siobhan said with a smile. She unwrapped her sandwich and took a bite, wiping crumbs from the croissant from her mouth. "So where are we off to this morning?"

"It's a surprise," Finn insisted as he sat back and sipped his coffee. "You'll know when we are on our way there. Eat your breakfast."

Once the sandwiches and coffee were finished, Finn and Siobhan went back out to the bike to begin their adventure for the morning. Finn started the motorcycle and was off down Route 17M and headed out towards Route 6. Siobhan nervously clung to Finn as they went up the steep roadway. The wind rippled her windbreaker, and she pressed her body close to Finn's.

Siobhan experienced the motorcycle's vibrations throughout her body. They descended Route 6 and made their way towards the Palisades Parkway Circle. When Siobhan saw Finn skirt past the Palisades' exit, she knew just where they were headed.

The turnoff for Bear Mountain Park arrived quickly. Finn maneuvered the bike to the parking area and found a spot that provided some shade for the bike so it wouldn't be scorching hot from the August sun. He dismounted and helped Siobhan off the motorcycle, taking her helmet from her.

"I haven't been up here in years," Siobhan smiled.

"Me either," Finn added. "Come on." He took Siobhan's hand and led her towards the pavilion. They entered the building and were hit with the loud music emanating from the carousel before them. The lights and carved animals spun around with just a few people on board.

"Want to?" Finn asked Siobhan.

"Of course!" she said excitedly. She dashed towards the ticket stand like a gleeful child and waited patiently for Finn to stride over. He paid for tickets, and Siobhan stood anxiously by for the current ride to stop so she could get on and choose the horse she always selected when she rode the carousel in her younger days. She immediately hopped onto the white horse with a pink and blue saddle, edging out a young girl who was clearly eyeing up the same ride. Finn walked onto the platform and got onto the horse next to Siobhan's.

"I think that little girl was mad at you," Finn said quietly.

"This was ALWAYS my ride," Siobhan insisted as she laughed. The ride began to spin slowly as the horses moved up and down in time with the recorded

music. Siobhan gripped the pole and watched as the faces
of the crowd outside the carousel looked on. She glanced
over at Finn, who reached his hand out to take hers as
the ride continued for the blissful three minutes before it
began to slow down. Once the ride stopped, Finn went
over and lifted Siobhan off her horse, placing her on the
platform. She gave her wooden ride a quick pat on the
nose.

"Thanks, old friend," she said to the horse as
Finn led her outside.

"That was so much fun!" Siobhan said, elated.
She spun around in the grass as they began their walk
away from the pavilion and towards the trails. They
walked the path along Hessian Lake, seeing a few families
already staking out picnic tables for the day, so they had
a view of the lake. A few areas already had their portable
grills going for a day of feasting and fun.

"I should have brought fishing poles," Finn said
as they continued along the lake trail.

"Gah, Finn, you never fished," Siobhan mocked.
"Cara and I did the fishing. You and Darren were too
busy getting into trouble."

"I can fish," Finn insisted as they walked.

"You got squeamish with worms and grubs,"
Siobhan laughed. "You couldn't bait a hook, never mind
take a fish off one."

"Next time, I'm bringing fishing rods," Finn said
authoritatively.

"Next time," Siobhan replied with quiet
hopefulness.

The couple strolled along the trail, passing the
pool, and moving towards the Trailside Museums and
Zoo. They passed under the distinct wood sign at the
entrance and followed along the path through the woods
to view some of the zoo's different animals. They paused
to see beaver frolicking in the water before coming upon

the area where the bears and coyotes were housed. The sparse crowd in the morning looked on as two black bears sat on the rock formations staring back at the people. The coyotes were not very active either, preparing themselves for the heat that was expected later in the afternoon.

Finn and Siobhan continued along the trail, reaching the butterfly garden. Siobhan walked through the area and had two magnificent butterflies alight on her. One landed on her shoulder while the other, a bright speckled blue, perched itself on her left hand. Finn picked up his phone and snapped a photo of Siobhan in awe of the butterflies flitting around her.

Once they left the trailside zoo, they made their way back toward Hessian Lake and then to the Appalachian Trail's stone steps that led to the Bear Mountain Summit. They traversed the 800 steps carefully as hikers made their way down from the summit.

"I don't remember this hike being grueling," Finn huffed.

"You were a lot younger and hadn't spent years behind a desk," Siobhan said as she stepped past Finn and went ahead of him.

"I work out every day," Finn told her. "I'm in better shape than you."

"We'll see about that!" Siobhan squealed as she took off up the steps. Finn watched her move away from him as he picked up his pace, reaching the top moments after Siobhan got there.

With scarcely a cloud in the sky, the view from the summit was spectacular. The view overlooked the local mountains' lush greenery and offered a peek at the New York City skyline in the distance.

"I forgot how beautiful it is here," Finn said as he took in the view.

"I'm sure there are beautiful spots in Saratoga as well," Siobhan said as she put her arm around Finn's waist.

"Oh, there are. I just never see them," Finn answered. "You know, the whole trapped behind a desk thing."

"You just need to make time to enjoy it, Finn," Siobhan said. "You always used to do that. We went all over the place, whether we were supposed to or not. You can get back there."

"I'm not sure I can," Finn told her. "There's a lot back there I'm not happy about… or that I regret," Finn told her as he stared at Siobhan.

"Ná bí aiféala ort," Siobhan said to Finn.

"You know I have no idea what that means anymore," Finn told her.

"It means don't regret it," Siobhan answered. "My Grandma used to say it all the time. Don't regret what you've done, Finn. I know now that you did it for a reason. I just wish you had shared that with me, is all. Maybe things would have been different for us. But that's in the past now; we can't change it, but we can grow from it."

"Yeah, it's the growth thing I have always had a problem with," Finn said.

"Well, it's a good thing I'm here to help you then," she smiled.

"Oh, you're helping me plenty," Finn told her as he took her in his arms and swung her around. Siobhan squealed as she moved, drawing the attention of the few other people at the summit. Finn stopped spinning and put Siobhan down before he looked off to the left.

"Come on," Finn said as he grabbed Siobhan's hand. He walked her a short way down the path before pulling her off the trail and through some overgrown brush.

"Finn, where are we going?" Siobhan asked as she held his fingers with one hand while trying to avoid brambles with the other.

Within a few yards, they had reached a secluded clearing. Finn tossed the small backpack he had with them onto the ground and pulled out a plaid blanket that he spread. He sat down and patted the blanket next to him, beckoning Siobhan over to him.

Siobhan sat down, and Finn put his arms around her.

"You don't remember?" Finn asked.

"Remember what?"

"This spot," Finn remarked. "This is where we were when I first kissed you. We had come up here on July 4th to watch the fireworks. We left Cara and Darren at the summit and snuck off here. You stared up at the sky, watching the display, and I couldn't take my eyes off you. You took my breath away. Finally, I couldn't wait anymore, and I leaned over and kissed you."

"I remember," Siobhan said with a sigh. "All I kept thinking was 'he finally did it!' If you didn't do it that night, I was giving up on you, you know."

"Hey, I was a shy guy, and we had been friends for years. It took some courage for me to do that."

"So what about now, Mr. O'Farrell? Still need some courage?"

Finn turned to his side and cradled Siobhan's face in his hands. His lips met hers, and what began as a soft kiss steadily turned to one with more passion and fire. The two kissed over and over until Finn had guided Siobhan to where she lay on the blanket. His right hand deftly worked its way up to the knot in her shirt so he could undo it, opening the shirt up to reveal her bra. His hands grazed across her breasts before he took the fullness of them in his hands, eliciting a moan from Siobhan's lips. Finn hungrily brought his mouth down from Siobhan's throat to the tops of her breasts, kissing and caressing each in turn before he unhooked the front of the bra.

Siobhan held Finn's head at her breasts, guiding his lips and tongue to her sensitive, aching nipples. It wasn't long before Finn's hand wandered down across her belly to the button of her capris. He unbuttoned and unzipped them quickly, giving his hand access to more of her body. Finn slipped two fingers down the front of her panties and slid inside Siobhan as she let out a groan from deep within her.

Finn used his left hand to reach his jeans pocket before letting out an exclamation.

"Fuck," he panted.

"What's wrong?" Siobhan rasped.

"I forgot... I mean, I didn't think to bring any protection." Finn breathed heavily as he knelt between Siobhan's legs.

"Finn, it's okay... I want to... you can..." she gasped as she felt Finn wiggle his finger slowly inside her.

"No, we shouldn't... I want to, believe me," he huffed. Finn turned back and look at the surroundings and then smiled as he glanced at Siobhan.

"That doesn't mean we can't do anything else."

Before Siobhan could say anything or react, Finn had leaned forward and begun to ease her panties down her legs. After tossing them aside, he returned between her legs and began to kiss and lick her inner thighs, all the while continuing his movement with his fingers. Siobhan gasped loudly when she felt Finn's tongue on her and then in her as he tasted Siobhan.

"So beautiful," Finn whispered as his tongue circled her clit, getting closer and closer each time until Siobhan felt the very tip of his tongue graze across her. She moaned again and gripped the blanket beneath her into her fists. Siobhan arched her back off the blanket to bring herself even closer to Finn's mouth, allowing him to go deeper.

In moments Siobhan's body began to shudder as she cried out, reaching down to take some of Finn's hair within the grasp of her left hand.

Finn peered at Siobhan and watched as her bare chest rose and fell rapidly. He could see a blush covering her cheeks and chest, and her eyes were closed tightly as she worked to regain her composure. When her eyes peered at him, she let out a soft sigh and smiled widely. Siobhan sat up and faced Finn, kissing him deeply.

"Well, let's see if I can't just return the favor," she purred.

Siobhan pushed Finn down on the blanket and sat between his legs. Her right palm rested on the zipper to his jeans as she gave a light squeeze to feel the strength of his cock through his pants. Finn groaned at the touch as Siobhan's hand went to work on unzipping the pants. Once down, she tugged at his waist to pull down his jeans. Finn's hands moved up to Siobhan's chest, kneading her breasts as she fumbled with his briefs to get them down.

It was then that Siobhan suddenly stopped moving. Finn glanced up at her and saw her staring straight ahead.

"What's wrong?" Finn panted. "You aren't teasing me again, are you? I don't think I can take it right now, Bon..."

"Finn," Siobhan whispered, her eyes glancing down at him. "Someone is watching us."

"Where?"

Finn went to move, but Siobhan placed her left hand on his chest to keep him in place.

"He's looking right at me now. Straight ahead. He's further back. I don't think he's just some perv getting off."

"Enough of this," Finn snarled. He rolled Siobhan to his left so she was beneath him and he could get a look. He saw a dark figure set back in the woods in front of him, and in a flash, Finn stood, zipped his jeans, and took off. The figure began to move as soon as it spotted Finn and had a good head start. Finn struggled to get through the brush and traverse the rocks through the woods, and by the time he reached the initial spot where he saw the figure, it was gone, and there were no indications which way it went.

Finn made his way back to Siobhan, who had dressed and sat nervously on the blanket.

"He was gone before I could get a good look," Finn told her. He took Siobhan's hand and helped her to her feet before gathering up the blanket.

"What is going on?" Siobhan said with concern. "He... he was staring right at me, Finn. Watching me move."

"It could have been some teenager," Finn replied as he tried to dismiss the incident. In his head, he knew it was the unlikely answer. "Let's go."

Finn took Siobhan by the hand and led her back to the trail so they could descend the steps. Siobhan stared at everyone they saw and passed, attempting to determine if someone they saw was whoever gawked at her.

"Bon, don't worry," Finn assured her. "I'm sure it was nothing. Some kid who has a story to tell his friends."

"You don't really believe that do you?" Siobhan said as they walked back through the zoo to get to the entrance.

"Why would someone follow us here? How would they even know we were coming here? I planned it but didn't tell anyone. Hell, even you didn't know, and you could have turned me down."

"The same reason someone broke into your father's house, have watched the house, and did something to your Da," Siobhan insisted.

"I have to go confront Liam and learn what he knows," Finn resolved. "This has to end. I'll drop you at your office and head over to the Hog House."

"Finn, you're walking into a hornet's nest if you go there," Siobhan said as they reached the motorcycle. She came over and touched his cheek. "I don't know if that's a good idea. You've had enough injuries in the last few days."

"Bon, the only way I'm going to get anywhere is to go to that house. I have to figure it out, and Liam is the one to get me there. Besides, it looks like it's already past lunchtime, and I promised I would have you at the office by then."

Finn handed Siobhan her helmet before he got on the motorcycle. She assumed her position behind him as they left the park. Siobhan kept looking around, still hopeful she might recognize someone or see them following behind the bike. Even then, she didn't notice anything that caught her eye.

They reached the parking lot of A Safe Place, and Finn pulled the bike up to the front door. Siobhan dismounted and took her helmet off before she grabbed her bag from the saddlebag.

"Thank you for a mostly lovely morning," Siobhan smiled. She tapped on Finn's helmet to get him to take it off before she leaned in to give him a kiss.

"I'm sorry it wasn't perfect," Finn lamented.

"It's not your fault." Siobhan embraced Finn, feeling the leather of the jacket he wore and the stubble on his face. "Just be careful at the House, okay? I want to be able to pick things up where we left off later," Siobhan grinned and tossed her red hair back before tying it into a quick ponytail. "Pick me up at 5?"

"Yes, Ma'am," Finn agreed. He watched as she ascended the front steps of the building, rang the buzzer, and looked into the camera. When the front door swung open, Siobhan gave Finn a wink and walked inside. Finn pulled his helmet back on and began the short ride over to Hog House.

Siobhan smiled as she went inside and said a gleeful good morning to Benny at his usual perch by the front door. She noticed that Tracy was not at her desk, so Siobhan made her way directly towards the office to make a quick change before anybody got a look at her. She bypassed a couple of staff members engaged with women. She saw more than the usual crowd dining for lunch, both indications of a busy day. Siobhan momentarily felt guilty about taking the morning off unexpectedly. Still, she was glad she got to spend extra time with Finn. There was still no telling how long just all that would last.

Siobhan walked into her office and shut the door rapidly. She stripped out of her capris and slid into a black skirt. She began to undo the knot on the shirt, thinking she could smooth it out and wear it with her skirt before there was a frantic knock on her office door.

"Vonnie?" Tracy said anxiously. "You in there?"

"Come on in, Tracy," Siobhan replied.

Tracy entered and shut the door behind her immediately.

"Where the hell have you been? I've been trying to reach you for hours," Tracy panicked.

"I'm sorry, I just needed a mental health moment. Finn and I went…" Siobhan noticed Tracy staring at her opened shirt and the brambles stuck in her hair. Siobhan quickly pulled them from her strands and tossed them aside before going into her bag and grabbing a white linen tank top to put on.

"Vonnie, did you forget about Gavin Elliott?" Tracy remarked.

Siobhan pulled down the hem of her shirt and then froze.

"Shite!" she exclaimed. "Lunch today!"

"Yes, lunch today," Tracy insisted. "He called all morning trying to reach you. He said he tried your cell, but you never answered it. Then I tried your cell. Finally, at noon, he just showed up here looking for you. He was pretty upset that you stood him up."

Siobhan dove into her bag and pulled out her cellphone. She saw five missed calls from Gavin, several texts from him asking where she was, and calls and texts from Tracy as well. She noticed her phone was on silent, something she never did because she always wanted to be available. Finn must have done it with the hopes of having her full attention.

"I can fix this," Siobhan said as she sat down at her desk and took a deep breath. She hit redial on Gavin's number and dialed his office.

"Gavin Elliott, please," she said in her most professional voice when his admin answered the phone. "It's Siobhan McCarthy."

"I'm sorry, Ms. McCarthy," the admin said sweetly. "Mr. Elliott isn't taking any calls right now. Would you like to leave him a message?"

"Please ask him to call me as soon as he can," she told the woman before hanging up.

Siobhan scanned her phone and found Gavin's personal cell number. The call went directly to his voicemail.

"Gavin, it's Siobhan," she began. "I am so sorry about today. I got caught up in some other business outside the office and lost track of time. Please call me back so we can reschedule. I'll be glad to come out to your office any time, even today, so we can talk. Thanks."

Siobhan hung up and looked at Tracy, who still seemed in a bit of shock.

"He's either busy or not taking my calls," Siobhan said. Siobhan watched as Tracy slumped into the chair opposite her own.

"Now what?" Tracy asked.

"I don't know. I hope I haven't fecked this all up," Siobhan said nervously.

19

Finn pulled up the dirt road, the bike kicking up gravel and dirt as he accelerated over the hill to the front of the Hog House. Even though it was a weekday afternoon, there were plenty of bikes parked out front, and a couple of the Cosantóir were out on the front porch having a beer when he came to a stop. Both bikers rose from their chairs and looked closely to see who was riding a bike with their colors and logo on it. Finn removed his helmet and sighed. He started flexing his fingers before he took two steps towards the porch, preparing to defend himself as best as he could with the injuries he had suffered the last few days. One good punch to the ribs would take him down fast.

"Can't say I recognize you, buddy," the one dark-haired man said to Finn. "But you're riding one of our bikes. I don't think you belong here. What do you think, Brody?" He turned to his younger-looking, drinking pal and waited for a response.

"I think you're right, Deck," Brody said as he swigged the rest of his beer and tossed the bottle aside. He hopped off the porch, landing right in front of Finn before he could descend the stairs.

"Just once, I'd like to come here without having to hit someone," Finn said as he shook his head at Brody, who looked to be no more than 21.

"Don't worry, my friend," Brody said with a smile. "You won't even get the chance to hit me."

Brody swung his right hand wildly at Finn, who simply stepped back and let Brody lose his balance. When the young man stumbled, Finn hit him just below the rib cage with a left hand that left Brody gasping. He grabbed Brody by the back of his jeans and tossed him aside.

Finn moved up the steps as Deck took a few menacing steps toward him. Cillian opened the screen door, letting it come between Deck and Finn before punches could be thrown.

"Easy, Declan," Preacher said sternly as he held the door to separate the two. "this is Conor's boy."

"You didn't see what he did to Brody," Declan insisted.

"I saw enough from the window. We don't need to threaten everyone that comes here before we find out why they are here, do we?" Preacher asked.

"Just looking out for our own," Declan said as he strode past Finn to help Brody get to his feet. "He came up on one of our bikes, and I didn't recognize him. Liam said to watch out for anyone out of place."

"I hear ya," Preacher nodded. "But I'm telling ya Finn here is fine. Come on inside," Preacher waved Finn in so he could close the screen door before Brody got his wind back.

"Thanks... again," Finn told Cillian. "You seem to have a knack for showing up just in time."

"Part of my charm," Cillian said with a smile. "Let's have a pint."

"I need to talk to Liam," Finn said as Cillian led him to the bar. Eyes were on Finn as he made his way across the floor to the back of the room where the bar was.

"You may want to give him a few minutes," Preacher said as he held up two fingers to the bartender. "He just got some company up in his room."

"Cillian, Liam knows something," Finn said in a hushed tone. "I don't think he was directly involved in what happened to Da, but I'm sure he knows the reasons behind it. I have to get to the bottom of this before someone else gets hurt."

"Did something else happen?" Cillian asked seriously.

"I have had people spying on Siobhan and me for the last two days," Finn told him. "It's just a matter of time before they get closer and try something. They know there is something in Da's house, and I need to know what that is."

"All I know for sure is that your Da was under a lot of pressure with this new job. He was always getting phone calls and getting into arguments on and off-site. I wish I knew more I could tell you."

"Ever hear of Tangled Webb, LLC?" Finn asked.

"Doesn't ring a bell to me," Cillian admitted.

The bartender placed the Guinness in front of Preacher and Finn. Preacher held up his glass to Finn's.

"Slainte," Finn offered.

"And to your Da," Preacher said as he held his glass up. "To Conor!" He yelled loudly, and all the drinks in the room went up with a cheer.

Finn took a long sip of stout and looked down at the bar.

"He's improved a bit more," Cillian said as he leaned next to Finn. "Doctors say the swelling is going down, and his breathing is getting better. They are hoping he'll be ready to come out of the coma soon."

"Thanks," Finn replied. "I know I need to get down there to see him again. It's... it's complicated."

"I know how it is, Finn," Cillian told him. "I've been your Da's friend for over forty years. I know what he was like. I had many conversations with him about it and with your mother. It has taken a lot for you to be here. It's an important step for both of you. Maeve is with him, and a couple of the boys stay with her for as long as she is there. I'd let you know if things turned dark."

Finn took another draw of his Guinness when a loud thud was heard coming from the floor above. Many of the people looked up at the ceiling, laughed, and toasted with their drinks again.

"Sounds like Liam is done," one biker chortled.

Finn placed his glass on the bar.

"I'm going up there now," Finn insisted and marched across the room to the staircase before Cillian could stop him. Finn noticed a couple of the Cosantóir make moves to get up and go toward him until Cillian waved them off.

Finn marched up the stairs, unsure of just which room Liam's was. There were more bedrooms than he remembered when he last came here, but he figured Liam, with his ego, would want the largest room. Finn hooked left at the top of the stairs and made his way down the wooden hall, his feet creaking the floorboards with each heavy step he took. Finn built his determination with each move and reached the door at the end of the hall that looked to be over the main entertainment room downstairs. Finn considered knocking, but all manners and politeness went out of the window as he remembered who he was dealing with.

The door wasn't locked, and Finn turned the knob and entered. Liam was sprawled out on his king-size bed, with a young woman sitting topless in the recliner next to the bed.

"Well, come on in, little brother," Liam said with a snort. "I'm afraid you missed the show, but if you want to hang out for a bit, I'm sure I can get going again. Or maybe you want to take a tumble with her yourself? I'm sure she don't mind, do you darlin'?"

Finn glanced over at the blonde in the chair and saw she was looking him over.

"He's kind of cute," she laughed. "I never did brothers on the same day. Sure, why not?"

"Thanks, but I'll pass," Finn offered. "Liam, we need to talk now," Finn added an edge to his voice so that Liam might appreciate the seriousness.

"Ah, it seems my brother put his serious hat on, Darlin'," Liam said. "You'll have to go."

"Shit, Liam, you told me I could take a nap up here," the woman whined as she reached for her black tank top on the floor. "Every fucking time something comes up, and you toss me out."

"I'll make it up to you," Liam told her as he gave her buttocks a smack when she walked over to him. Liam pointed at his lips, and the woman obediently leaned down and gave him a kiss. She sneered at Finn as she brushed past him and left the room.

"This better be good, brother," Liam said as he sat up on the edge of the bed. Finn watched as Liam's large frame bent over, picked his red boxer briefs, and slid them up his legs. "Lana is one of the best I get around here. Kicking her out of my bed is a setback, if you know what I mean."

"Yeah, I get it," Finn replied. "We need to go over things now. I've been beaten up, followed, and spied on since the moment I got to town, and I want to know why."

"Maybe your reputation proceeds you," Liam laughed. "How the feck should I know why people are after you?" Liam reached over to his nightstand and grabbed the vape pen that was there, lighting it up. The familiar odor Finn knew since his childhood began to fill the room as Liam inhaled. He then held the pen out to Finn.

"No, I don't," Finn said as he waved off his brother.

"Really? Who knew you were such a prude? Does Ginger have something to do with that? Pussy-whipped again already?"

"I don't have time for this shit, Liam. Can we get down to some answers? You promised me if I got you out of jail, you'd cooperate."

Liam nodded as he leaned back against the headboard and took a hit off his vape pen.

"Aye, and thanks for that. They fitted me for my new bracelet this morning," Liam answered as he lifted up his left leg so Finn could see the ankle monitor he wore. "Pain in the ass."

"It's better than sitting in a cell waiting on attempted murder charges," Finn answered.

"I suppose it is," Liam agreed. "And now you're here to collect."

"Yes," Finn insisted. "What do you know about what happened to Da?"

"Not a damn thing," Liam replied. "It happened at 3 AM. I sure as hell ain't at a job site that early unless they are paying shift differential. I was here fast asleep when Maeve got the call about him."

"Well, somebody's lying here," Finn told him. "The police aren't going to arrest and charge you unless they have something to go on."

Liam reached over to the nightstand and opened the top drawer. He pulled out a bottle of Powers Irish Whiskey and pointed behind Finn.

"Grab a couple of glasses off the shelf there, brother," Liam asked. Finn got up and collected the old-fashioned crystal glasses and handed them to Liam. The latter immediately poured two fingers of whiskey into each glass and passed one to Finn, who sat and stared at the glass.

"Surely you're allowed to have a drink," Liam bemoaned. "Does she have your balls in her purse? Christ, man, you've only been back for a few days."

Finn took the glass firmly.

"Slainte," Liam said as he raised the glass and downed the whiskey in one gulp.

"So?" Finn asked as he sipped his whiskey.

"So, what? I just told you I was here."

"The police must have some evidence if they are willing to point at you."

"Yeah," Liam grunted. "They gave me some shite about fingerprints on the equipment that fell and an argument I had with Da earlier in the day. A dozen guys touch that equipment during the day. I'm sure I can't be the only prints on there."

"And what about the argument?"

"It was nothing," Liam dismissed. "We have arguments on-site all the time. Da wanted to hold back going down to the tunnel because he said the shaft was reinforced with shoddy materials. He was worried about a cave-in by the elevators. I told him he was being stubborn and costing us work. We got into, and then it was over."

"So, you didn't say anything that people might misunderstand?"

Liam sat quietly for a moment and puffed on his vape again.

"I told him he's just getting in the way on the job, and we'd be better off without him there. I'm sure a lot of the guys on the crew heard me yell it. It doesn't mean I wanted to do something to him."

"Yeah, but it gives them enough to make your life uncomfortable with the prints. Why would you say that?"

"Because I was pissed off. Da and I say shite to each other all the time. We have an understanding that way," Liam added.

"An understanding," Finn huffed. "I must have missed the day where he was handing those out."

"Jesus, man," Liam raged. "Are you still on all that? You need to get over it."

"Get over it?" Finn barked as he stood up and approached his brother. "He beat the shite out of me whenever he felt like it. I guess your 'understanding' exempts you from getting hit with belts and thrown down the stairs. That last time left me getting stitches in my head."

"Yeah, Da was a mean drunk and abuser; I get it. And you had it rough; we all did."

"I don't remember him doing any of that to you. You never went down the stairs."

Liam rose from the bed and looked down at his brother.

"I had more than my share before, during, and after you were around," Liam growled. "He wasn't exclusively a prick to you, you know. As for the stairs, that last time you went down them wasn't because of Da. You seem to forget parts of that. I was the one who pushed you down the stairs."

"What? That's not right. I remember Da swinging at me," Finn said with confusion.

"He swung at you, alright," Liam answered. "I pushed you out of the way before he hit you. He would have broken your jaw. You went tumblin', he missed, and I shoved him against the wall. By the time I looked back, Ma was already with you at the bottom of the steps."

"Why... why did you do that?"

"Who the fuck do you think looked out for you? You were seven years younger and a lot smaller than me. I had lived through Da's stuff for years already. I knew what was coming, especially once he knew you were afraid of him. So, I stepped in sometimes and took it. That is until..."

"Until what?"

"Until Ma got sick, and I saw how coddled you were and how much attention you were getting because she knew what Da was doing to you and couldn't do

anything about it. I got tired of it, taking it all for you…
the golden child. I left you to fend for yourself."

"Thanks for that," Finn spat back.

"It seems to have worked out for you," Liam said.
"You got your fancy job and apartment, plenty of money,
women everywhere. And it toughened you up. You sure
as hell wouldn't be standing in front of me right now if
you were how you used to be. You even took a beating
from me. Not many can stand a few days later and say
that."

"If you're waiting for a thank you for that, you're
out of your fecking mind," Finn responded.

"Say what you want, brother," Liam said as he sat
down on the bed. "The truth, whether you like it or not,
is what I just said. You are who you are because of your
past, good or bad. You got opportunities I was never
going to get. I could see it when you were a kid. You
didn't want a life like… this," Liam said as he waved his
hands around the room. "Me? I love it. I wouldn't have
it any other way, and that's fine. I can spend the next
twenty years working tunnels and riding."

"So," Finn began as he sat in the chair. "Then
why… why have we hated each other for all these years?"

Liam sighed.

"For me, I just couldn't do it anymore. Years
standing up for you and protecting Ma. Once Ma was
gone, I knew it would be worse, and it was for a long
while. I couldn't take it for all three of us anymore, and I
was so much bigger than Da at that point I knew he
couldn't hurt me, particularly when he was drunk. I
would laugh him off, and I think… well, that's when he
would go off on you. I heard it… more than once. The
last fight you had with him before you left, I held myself
back from coming out in the hall and throttling him so
you could just go. When I saw that you were handling
yourself, after you left and Da was raging on the front

lawn as you pulled away, I dragged him back into the house and to his room and told him that was it. He had no one left to give shite to. He was horrible after that, which is why I came up to see you at Maureen's to try to get you to come back. I didn't know what else to do. You said no, and Maeve intervened to help me out. She saved him, and probably me too. As for hate… hell yes, I hated you. You were Ma's favorite, smarter than me. You were going places. I wasn't."

The brothers sat in silence for a few minutes as Finn sipped his whiskey and Liam poured himself another.

"He is different now," Liam told his brother. "No drugs, no drinking. He's a leader in every way."

"Not in every way," Finn shot back. "He never acted like a father. He was not the leader of the family."

"He never got the chance to," Liam told Finn. "By the time he cleaned himself up, Ma was gone, and so were you."

Finn sat back in the chair and finished off his whiskey and shook his head.

"That's a lot to digest," Finn stated. "Outside of all that, I'm no closer to finding out what is going on now. Whatever people are stalking me for must be in that office. Do you know how to get in there?"

"No clue," Liam said. "I never saw him open the door. I've been in there a few times to talk to him, but the door was always locked and closed if he wasn't in there. Maybe there's a secret passage or something," Liam scoffed. "Besides, what could he have in there?"

"Something that other people are willing to hurt or maybe kill for," Finn told him as he rose from the chair. He placed the empty glass down on the nightstand and looked at his brother.

"I have to get back to the house before I go to pick up…" Finn interrupted himself.

"Aye, yes. Ginger has you wrapped up tight again, doesn't she?" Liam laughed.

"Think what you want," Finn said with a slight smile. He began to walk toward the bedroom door and turned to face Liam before he opened it.

"Liam… I just want to say… well, I didn't know you…"

"Stop right there, little brother," Liam said, holding up his hand. "If you're going to get all sappy and sentimental, take it to your girlfriend; I'm not interested. Our relationship has been fine for years. Let's not muck it all up with the mushy stuff."

"Fair enough," Finn smiled.

"Finn!" Liam shouted as his brother opened the door. Finn turned to look at him.

"Find out what's going on," Liam said solemnly, "and make sure you let me know. No one messes with family… or the Cosantóir."

Finn nodded and made his way down the hallway and the stairs before going right out the front door to his bike. He was watched the entire way closely by members of the Cosantóir to see what he was going to do. Finn took off on the motorcycle and went directly to his father's house.

He stormed inside, determined to find a way into the office. He looked at the intricate lock on the door with its odd-shaped design and keyhole. He checked the hinges on the door to see if it would be easier to remove them, but even the hinges looked as though they were sealed and reinforced.

"Who the feck makes it this tough to get into an office?" Finn said out loud. He sat down in the hallway outside the door and put his head in his hands. Moments later, Jameson marched over and sat in front of him and licked his hands.

"There you are," Finn said, surprised Jameson had not greeted him immediately when he entered the house. "Where were you?"

Finn glanced down the hall and saw that the door to his father's bedroom was open. He walked over quietly and flipped on the light, illuminating the ceiling fan. Finn looked around the room, hoping he would spot something, anything that might give him help or a clue, but he saw nothing. It was then he spied something on the far wall near the bottom of the dresser. Finn looked and then saw Jameson march through the square and into the adjoining room, his father's office.

Finn dove down to the floor to look at the square. He could open the flap, but there was no way his body or anyone over the age of five might fit through the opening. He used his smartphone as a flashlight to look around the darkened room but only saw the bottoms of chairs and a desk. He scanned the light across the room and was startled when he lit upon Jameson, who sat happily next to another dog door, the one that clearly led to the outside of the house.

"Well, that's one mystery solved," Finn said out loud before standing up. He walked back out to examine the lock some more but saw it wasn't going to get him anywhere. He trudged to the kitchen and grabbed a bottle of water from the fridge before slumping down in a chair.

Jameson padded into the kitchen and sat next to his empty dog dish. Finn got up and poured some hard food into Jameson's bowl, accidentally spilling some all over the floor.

"Damn it!" Finn exclaimed.

He searched for the broom and dustpan before finally locating them in the hall closet. By the time he returned, Jameson had wolfed down the food in his bowl and worked on the extras on the floor.

"Better than the broom anyway, buddy. Enjoy."

Once Jameson had vacuumed up the extras, he sat next to Finn and rapidly wagged his tail, so it thumped on the floor. Finn had no choice but to turn his attentions back to the dog.

"You looking for some attention today?" Finn asked. "I know I've been leaving you alone a lot. There's just been so much going on." Finn rubbed and patted Jameson's head before stroking his ears and working down to the dog's neck and under his collar. It was then that Finn noticed it.

He stopped petting Jameson and got down on the floor to sit next to the dog. Finn took hold of the dog collar and examined it closely. It had some of the typical tags on it. Still, it also had a more oversized silver medallion with a shamrock in the center. It might have all seemed perfectly ordinary to most people, but Finn noticed the curve of the stem of the shamrock and the odd shape it took. He ran his thumbs over the shamrock and felt it was slightly raised from the surface of the medallion, enough where he could get his fingernails under the edges. In seconds, Finn had popped the shamrock off and was holding it up to the light.

"No fecking way," he whispered as he saw the noticeable key notches in the stem.

"No one wonder he's the only one who could get in there," Finn said to Jameson. "No one else could get close to you for the key."

Excited, Finn walked to the office door and placed the key in the lock. A simple twist to the right and Finn heard the lock click. He pushed down on the door handle, and the door swung open.

Finn reached to his left and found a light switch on the wall and flicked it on. Bright light from the overhead fixture filled the room. The office was not what Finn expected. A large oak desk sat in the center of the room with the window behind it. Solid bookcases lined the far wall, a leather couch, and two leather chairs took space, along with a small file cabinet and what Finn knew was a gun safe.

Finn moved to the desk and sat down. There were a couple of folders on the desk that held no pertinent information. He turned on the laptop on the desk, hoping to get into it, but he had no idea what his father's password might be. He opened the center drawer of the desk and found nothing but office supplies. The top side drawer had some folders and information, all to do with the Cosantóir club. Finn saw nothing incriminating that might help him out. It was the bottom drawer that caught Finn's attention.

The bottom drawer contained an old wooden box, one that Finn remembered seeing on his mother's dresser for many years. He placed the box, which had a painted scene of an Irish cottage on it, in the desk's center. He carefully opened the top to examine what was inside.

There were some things to be expected in there, like pins and commendations from the union and the Sandhogs. Finn came across pictures as well. Several were of his father and mother, and some just of his mother alone. There was a wedding picture of the two of them, and underneath was a photo of the family – all four of them – standing and smiling at what looked to be a Fourth of July celebration in Harriman. Finn didn't recall ever seeing this picture or that there was one where all four of them smiled. His father even had his hands around both boys. There was also a set of keys in the box, and the Indian keyring let him know that this was for his father's special bike.

Finn placed the photo down on the desk and kept looking. He found two flash drives, neither of which were labeled. He also discovered a blank index card underneath the drives that stated: "in case." Beneath that was a folded piece of paper. Finn pulled the paper out to examine it. All it showed was a list of six names, all female.

Finn didn't recognize any of the names that appeared. He wasn't sure who they might be or how they connected to his father or the Cosantóir, but he began to get a sick feeling in his stomach.

Finn chose the first name on the list – Paula Thomas – and typed the name into a Google search on his smartphone. After getting millions of replies, he narrowed the search and included 'Harriman' in the search box.

A news story appeared on top from over a year ago, detailing Paula Thomas's disappearance. The article noted that her live-in boyfriend was also found beaten in their apartment and had nothing to tell police regarding what may have happened. It did not seem anything unique or unusual that might tie either person to his father, but Finn had concerns.

He hesitated before trying a search on the next name – Amanda Reed. Finn typed the words in, and, sure enough, an article came back from nine months ago about how she had gone missing. Her husband reported her missing and the last piece, dated three months ago, still showed no evidence of her whereabouts.

A chill ran up and down Finn's spine. He spent time researching the other names on the list, and all came back with similar stories of the women that were nowhere to be found with no leads or clues. Police often assumed the women just decided to leave for one reason or another.

Finn looked at his watch and saw hours had passed, and it was time for him to go get Siobhan from A Safe Place. Finn packed up the box but kept the list, the flash drives, the keys, and the family photo and put them all in his pocket. He made sure to close the office door and lock it if someone decided to come back, and he took the shamrock key with him.

"Watch the house, Jameson," Finn said as he walked to the living room where the dog had taken up residence on his bed.

Finn had just a short ride to A Safe Place, leaving him little time to sort through the information. He hoped that with Siobhan's help that they might be able to sort things out.

20

Siobhan spent the next several hours in the office trying to put out fires while fretting over her screw-up regarding Gavin. In a perfect world, with a rational human being, the situation could be resolved. However, Siobhan knew Gavin was one of those people who gets what he wants when he wants and pouts about it when things don't go his way. She sent him texts and called his cell several times throughout the afternoon, but she never heard anything back.

Siobhan had been called down to one of the counselor's offices to sit in on a conference with a woman going through a rough time with her husband and had numerous ER visits for herself and her child. Siobhan held the woman's hand while the counselor explained all they could do to help her immediately and down the road. The woman seemed more at ease the more they talked, and Siobhan was pleased that it looked like they could help. Then, there was a rapid knock on the office door, and the door flew open.

All three women in the room leaped in surprise as the door swung wide, and Gavin Elliott stood there. Tracy came up behind him.

"I told you that you couldn't come back here!" Tracy yelled. Benny was not far behind her, ready to take control of the situation.

"You owe me a conversation," Gavin stated pompously to Siobhan. Benny was right behind Gavin now, ready to escort him out of the building with just a nod from Siobhan.

"It's fine, Benny," Siobhan responded as she rose. "I am so sorry about all of this," she said quietly to the frightened woman.

"Follow me," she said through gritted teeth to Gavin. She brushed past him and trod down to her office, her heels clacking loudly on the floor. Benny moved close behind and stopped at Siobhan's office door. Siobhan pointed inside so Gavin would enter.

"I'll be right out here if you need me, Ms. McCarthy," Benny proclaimed. Crossing his arms and leaning against the wall.

Siobhan shut the door loudly and stood in front of Gavin, who had parked himself in one of the office chairs.

"What the hell do you think you're doing? We run a safe, confidential organization here, and you go and do that? That woman has been through a harrowing experience that you made worse by doing what you did."

"Then I guess you shouldn't have blown me off today," Gavin said snidely.

"Are you serious with this, Gavin?" Siobhan replied, astounded. "I missed our lunch meeting, and you go off like this? How many meetings have you 'forgotten' about with me?"

"When I miss meetings, it's for a good reason, not to go off with somebody," Gavin answered. "Obviously, running this organization isn't a primary concern of yours right now."

"Don't ever question my dedication to this job," Siobhan yelled. "And how did you know I was off with somebody this morning? I never told anyone what I was doing."

Gavin shifted in his chair a bit.

"I assumed you were out with Mr. Wonderful since you two have been so chummy," Gavin said.

"Bullshit," Siobhan said. "Were you following us?"

"Don't be ridiculous," Gavin scoffed. "I have better things to do than follow you two all around the

mountains. Are you getting paranoid now, Siobhan?
That's another step in the demise of this place, you know.
I'm sure the board of directors would be extremely
interested to know how you passed on a meeting with
one of their largest donors and supporters. I can't
imagine they would put up with it."

"Are you threatening me now, Gavin?"

"Not so much of a threat, sweetheart as it is…
blackmail," Gavin said with a chuckle. "I realized when I
saw you and Finn together at Rushing Duck that it meant
the end of us…"

"Us?" Siobhan asked, bewildered. "When was
there ever an 'us'? We were never a couple, Gavin."

"Really? All the fancy dinners, the concerts,
helping you meet people at fundraisers? The way you
would wrap your arm around mine? Come off it,
Siobhan," Gavin railed.

"It's called doing my job," Siobhan insisted. "I'm
trying to raise money. You were a means to an end,
nothing more."

"I see," Gavin nodded. "Well, then I guess this is
as good a time as any to tell you that I won't be donating
anything else or putting you in contact. When the board
sees your donations dry up, I don't believe they will think
twice about letting you go. Then I can move forward with
things."

"Move forward with what things?"

"This property, for one," Gavin told her. "This is
going to be a prime spot along the road towards the hotel
and casino. I can think of more than a few places that will
fit nicely here. The board will be glad to sell me the land
when they see how unusable this dump is and when they
need the cash because they have no donations."

Siobhan stood in stunned silence for a moment
before reacting.

"I'll never let that happen," Siobhan said. "The board won't believe you."

"I thought about that," Gavin said as he rose and stood in front of Siobhan. "You do have the goody-goody reputation, or at least you did until now."

Gavin pulled out his smartphone and showed pictures to Siobhan. They were pictures of her and Finn at Bear Mountain, walking the trails and such. There were also pictures of them together in the clearing, with Siobhan topless on top of Finn.

"Where… you said you didn't follow us," Siobhan whispered in disbelief.

"I didn't," Gavin said as he snapped his phone back into his pocket. "I was honest. I didn't follow you and have better things to do. That doesn't mean I didn't hire someone to do it for me. A few well-placed pictures on the Internet and emails sent to the board should be enough to get what I want. Unless, of course, you want to work with me."

"Work with you?" Siobhan said.

"Sure," Gavin said. "You can leave this job, resign quietly for whatever reason you want. Once you're out, the board will sell to me. I'd be happy to give you a job on my staff so you can work under me," Gavin said with a lascivious grin.

Siobhan was stunned. She took a moment to gather herself and reached over to Gavin, putting her arms over his shoulders.

"What a flattering offer, Gavin," Siobhan said, looking him right in the eyes. Her hands slid down his chest over his suit jacket and came to rest on the blue power tie he wore. She moved her hands up to the Windsor knot, perfectly tied, and began to tighten the tie even more. The movement caught Gavin off guard as he felt the tie constrict his throat.

"I'd rather clean bathrooms for a living than work for you," she hissed. "Do what you have to do, you son of a bitch. Benny!"

The office door swept open, and Benny watched as Gavin's face started looking purple.

"Yes, Ma'am?" Benny asked Siobhan.

"Show Mr. Elliott out, please," Siobhan said as she shuffled Gavin over to Benny before releasing her grip. Gavin gasped loudly as he worked to get his breath.

"And make sure you note that he is forbidden from entering the building again," she said forcefully.

"I'll take care of it," Benny said as he took Gavin by the arm and led him down the hall.

"You'll regret this!" Gavin shouted as he left.

"I doubt it," Siobhan yelled back. She walked back into her office and slumped into her desk chair. "What else can happen today?" she aloud.

****

Siobhan spent the next several hours working between taking care of the business at hand and worrying about just what Gavin might do. She tried to develop plans that would allow her to explain things to the board and what Gavin was doing. Still, she was unsure that even her standing with the board would be enough to overcome the pictures and whatever Gavin might lie about to get his way.

Siobhan's headache coursed through her body, and she reached for the bottle of Tylenol in her desk when her phone buzzed.

"Ms. McCarthy?" Benny's familiar voice echoed on the speakerphone.

"What's up, Benny?"

"There's a man here to see you," Benny answered. "I've never seen him before, but he says he is here to meet you and pick you up. Finn O'Farrell."

Siobhan sighed.

"He's fine, Benny. Let him in, please, and point him toward my office?"

It was moments before Finn opened the office door and stepped inside. Siobhan rushed from around the desk and threw herself into Finn's arms, hugging him tightly.

"God, I'm glad to see you," she told him as she held her body tightly against his. "This day has been too much. Let me tell you…"

"Before you get started," Finn interrupted, "I have to tell you something. I got into my father's office."

Siobhan stared at Finn.

"You did? Did you find anything?" she asked.

"More than I expected to," Finn said solemnly. "He had some flash drives tucked away in there. I'm not sure what is on them yet. I thought maybe we could look at them and find out."

"Sure," Siobhan agreed.

"There's something else, too," Finn offered as he took the list out of his pocket. "I found this in his desk as well."

Siobhan examined the paper and the names on it.

"What is it?" she asked.

"I wasn't sure at first," Finn responded. "So I looked up the names online. Bon, these are all women who have disappeared over the last two years. They just up and vanished, no trace. That doesn't just happen. I think Da and the Cosantóir, or somebody else, worked together and made these women disappear."

"That's… that's a big accusation, Finn," Siobhan said as she sat down. "Do you know for sure?"

"Not 100%, no," Finn admitted. "But I've been working within the law long enough to know how people think and do things. This fits in every way."

"What are you going to do?" Siobhan asked.

"Do? It's obvious, Bon," Finn began. "I have to call Detective Fremont and let him know what I found. I have to tell him that my father might be some kind of serial murderer, or at least involved in some way."

Finn took out his cellphone and began to look for Detective Fremont's number. When he found it in his recent calls, he pressed the call button.

"Detective Fremont, please," Finn said into the phone.

"Finn, wait," Siobhan said as she got up from her chair.

"What?" Finn said as he held the phone.

"I don't think you want to do this," Siobhan said to him.

"What are you talking about? I knew he was a monster when I was a kid. Everyone tried to convince me he had changed, but he's still the same evil he was back then."

"Finn, stop!" Siobhan yelled. She grabbed the phone from his hand and disconnected the call.

"Bon, what the hell are you doing?" Finn asked in disbelief.

"Your father didn't kill those women. He had practically nothing to do with them disappearing."

"What? Then who did?"

"I did," Siobhan admitted. "I made those women disappear."

21

Siobhan stood in front of Finn and waited for a response. Her fingernails dug into the edge of her desk, and she tried to get any hint from the look on his face to what he was thinking.

"You? But why? And how?" Finn said confusedly.

"The why is the easy part," Siobhan admitted. "Finn, these are all women that were in danger, either from ex-husbands, boyfriends, family members, or stalkers. They had exhausted options looking for help from the police and the courts. Most had been beaten badly at one point or another. It's my job to make sure they are protected, so I found a way to make them disappear."

Finn sat down in the chair as Siobhan continued.

"I knew it wouldn't be an easy thing to do, and I needed help with it. I needed someone who could help me get around the laws, get paperwork for me quickly, and provide protection for these women and their children. I looked at all my options, and none were great. That's when I thought of your Da."

"Of course, if you need something done under the table, he's your man," Finn said sarcastically.

"That's not what I mean, Finn," Siobhan told him. "Your Da... he's different. Changed. He wants to help people and look out for them. I don't know if he was just trying to atone for past sins or what, but he has changed. I had heard from a few other charities that he had helped them out with donations, toy deliveries at Christmas, funding barbecues for seniors, all kinds of stuff. I also knew what I required was going to ask more of him than any other organization and that it would have to be kept quiet. I approached him about it, and he didn't even blink an eye and said yes. I know it sounds ridiculous... your Da, with his history with you, looking out for battered women and families... but he was a bigger help to me than anyone else could possibly be. He helped me get new identities, set families up in apartments away from here, give money to get them started, and provided transportation and protection for all of them when the time came to flee. The Cosantóir rode alongside the women as they relocated to keep them safe."

Finn sat back, rubbing the stubble on his chin, as he tried to absorb all that Siobhan had just told him. He broke the silence and looked over at her as she nervously chewed her thumbnail.

"I know what you did... and what you do... is important, Bon. Still, don't you think you should have told me sooner? That this might have something to do with the reason someone is going after him? A jealous husband or boyfriend, or someone desperate to find one of these women that found out he was involved in this?"

"It never even crossed my mind, Finn," Siobhan replied. "Who would take on your Da and the Cosantóir like that? I guess if they thought he might give up information on their whereabouts, but he wouldn't do that. It would make more sense for them to come after me."

"And you think they aren't doing that?" Finn told her. "We have guys stalking us for days everywhere we go that might be looking to hurt you. Is that why you started carrying the gun?"

"Yes," Siobhan admitted. "It's licensed, and I am registered for concealed carry. It's all legal, Finn. And as for the stalking, well, I think I know part of the answer to that, too. Seems Gavin Elliott has been the one keeping close tabs on us... or at least me. He showed up here today after I blew him off for lunch. He's trying to blackmail me, Finn, so he can get this property. He has pictures of me... of us... at the park."

"Jesus, is there anything else you're going to drop on me?" Finn said with exasperation. "What else haven't you told me?"

"Nothing," Siobhan said forcefully. "I'm sorry if my life and career are interfering with how you go about things. This is more than just about you, Finn. I wasn't trying to hide anything from you."

"Are you sure? Because it doesn't seem that way right now."

"Me? You're the one who hid everything that happened with your father from me and then ran away for ten years to hide some more. Don't preach to me about explaining things and doing things the right way," Siobhan yelled.

Finn stood in front of Siobhan and looked down into her eyes.

"I've got to go," Finn huffed. "I need to figure this all out."

"That's going to be your answer?" Siobhan said incredulously. "You're going to run away again? Go, Finn. At least it's something you're good at."

Finn stormed out of Siobhan's office and dashed down the hall, exiting the building as quickly as possible. He hopped on the motorcycle, revved the engine high, and spun the back tire as he left the gravel parking lot.

Siobhan sat stunned in her office by what occurred. She had planned to tell Finn about her connection to his father, but none of it ever linked up for her the way it did so quickly for Finn.

What if it is my fault Conor is hurt? She thought to herself.

Siobhan gripped the gold crucifix she wore around her neck and said a silent prayer for forgiveness.

When she opened her eyes, she was startled by Tracy's appearance in front of her.

"I didn't want to interrupt you," Tracy said to her.

"It's okay," Siobhan sighed. "The nice thing about talking to Him is that I can do it any time I want."

"I saw Finn leave in a hurry," Tracy stated. "Everything okay?"

"Maybe... I don't really know right now," Siobhan admitted. "Just add it to the pile of things to take care of today, I guess. Even worse, he was my ride home tonight."

"I can give you a lift," Tracy said. "It's no trouble."

"No, Tracy, but thanks," Siobhan smiled. "You go home. I'm going to work late and try to climb this mountain. I can get a ride from someone or call an Uber."

"Okay, but if you need me, just give me a call. Good night," Tracy said as she left Siobhan's office.

"I don't know what I need right now," Siobhan said as she tossed her pen on her desk.

****

Finn headed for 17M and picked up speed. Suddenly, he had much more to process than he thought he would when he got to Siobhan's office. Knowing what she and his father had been involved in created all kinds of potential scenarios for trouble. Should he tell Fremont and the police about it so they could investigate it further? Revealing it all to the law would undoubtedly create problems for Siobhan, perhaps even at the cost of her job.

Finn slowed the bike down as he got close to the turn for the Hog House. He considered going back to see if anyone else was aware of the connection. At the very least, he could also try to get into the flash drives to see what information was contained on them. However, Finn had no idea just who was trustworthy at this point.

Instead, Finn accelerated the bike and moved down 17M toward Suffern and the hospital.

Unsure of just what he would get out of a visit with his father, Finn was determined to go anyway. He had already had confrontations for the day, so what was more? He rationalized. He parked his bike and made his way to the ICU unit quickly. Before he reached his father's room, he was met by an excited Maeve in the hallway.

"Oh, Finn!" Maeve exclaimed as she gave him a big hug. "He's awake! Conor is awake!"

"When did that happen?" Finn asked.

"About an hour ago," Maeve told him as they walked toward Conor's room. "I was in there reading parts of the newspaper to him. When I got to the baseball scores and started telling him about how the Mets were doing, he opened his eyes wide and looked right at me. He's been up since then."

"Has he said anything?" Finn said anxiously.

"No, no hon, he can't talk," Maeve lamented. "He's still on the ventilator right now. The doctors are watching him closely and doing tests to see when they might be able to take him off. They also said they can put a speaking tube in when he's ready to try talking. This is such blessed news! You have to excuse me. I'm going to call Preacher so he can spread the word to the boys."

Maeve gripped her cellphone and walked towards the elevators so she could go outside and make calls. Finn stood at the door to his father's room for a moment and then pushed it open to move inside. He put on the obligatory gown and other PPE before he went in. He saw his father lying in bed, eyes wide open, as he stared at the ceiling. Finn paced over near the bed and looked down at his father. He saw his Da's eyes get wide with fear, unsure of who it was in the room with him. Conor's head thrashed a bit from side to side, and he grunted.

"Da! Da! Take it easy!" Finn implored him. "It's me. It's Finn."

Finn ripped off the cap and mask he had on so that his father could see his face. Conor's eyes worked to focus on Finn.

"So it takes someone dropping machinery on you to get us in the same room together, huh?" Finn said with a nervous laugh.

"Aunt Maureen is worried about ya. She's been calling me every day to get your status. She's... she's the one who told me what happened. Do you remember anything about what occurred?"

Conor shook his head no and then wriggled around more on the bed. He was clearly frustrated that he couldn't talk or move around.

"Da, easy," Finn said as he reached over and put his hand on his father's forearm. "You don't want to pull anything out. You've been in a coma from the head injuries. You can't talk right now on the vent. Try to relax."

Finn kept his hand on his father's forearm. After a minute, he noticed that the fingers on his father's hand were twitching. Conor was looking down at his hand while his fingers moved.

"Are you doing that?" Finn asked. Conor nodded in assent as he kept trying to move his fingers. Finn moved his hand down to help bend Conor's fingers back and forth to get some movement. Conor winced when Finn first helped but soon was able to flex a few fingers at a time. Finn smiled at the accomplishment, and it was then that Conor entwined his fingers with Finn's, holding his son's hand.

Finn looked over at his father's face, and it looked like he was trying to smile and say something. Finn stared back, unable to determine what his father wanted.

"Who are you?" Finn asked him. "You're not the man I remember. The Da I know didn't think twice about drinking too much, partying, and then coming home to take things out on his sick wife and kids. You fecked me up good, Da. Part of me was glad when I saw you lying there, motionless. I thought it was karma, you know? But now… everything seems different now. You're sober, working hard, loyal… hell, you're even helping abused women get out of town. Yeah, I know about it. Siobhan and I have been together since I got to town. My question is – why did it take you so fucking long to change? You couldn't do any of this when I was here as a kid who needed a Da? For ten years, I've been keeping all this shite bottled up inside me. Now I have you as a captive audience, you can't talk back or hit me or anything, and the truth is… the truth is I want to forgive you, but I don't know if I can."

Finn looked into Conor's eyes and saw tears welling up in them. Conor grunted and moved his head as he desperately tried to communicate. Still, nothing came out and made him more frustrated. A nurse walked in and saw what was going on.

"You need to step back, sir," she said to Finn as she separated his hand from Conor's.

"What's wrong?" Finn asked.

"It's typical when you come out of a coma like that. Probably some delirium from being out and the pain medication. It can be frightening when you can't move around or talk. I'll give him a sedative to help him calm down."

The nurse injected Conor's tube with something, and in moments the thrashing had ended. Conor lay back peacefully, closing his eyes.

"When will he be off the ventilator or be able to talk?" Finn inquired.

"Hard to say," the nurse said honestly. "His chart says they are hoping to try tomorrow to see how it goes. He'll probably need a speaking valve and will only be able to talk for a few minutes. He's going to be out for a while now, but you're welcome to stay with him."

"Thanks," Finn said as Maeve walked into the room.

"Oh, I'm sorry, Finn," Maeve said. "I didn't know you were still here. How's he doing? Did he respond to you?"

"He did, sort of," Finn answered. "He used his eyes and... well, he wiggled his fingers a bit and held mine."

"That's fantastic!" Maeve raved as she hugged Finn.

"That's a good thing, right?" Maeve asked the nurse.

"It sure is," she replied.

"I should get going," Finn said to Maeve.

"No, stay if you want," Maeve offered. "I'm sure it will be fine if we are both in here, right?" Maeve asked the nurse.

"I think it will be okay," the nurse replied. "He's going to sleep for a while, though."

"Well, just in case he wakes up, I want to make sure he sees a face he'll recognize," Maeve smiled.

"Maeve," Finn began, "you stay with him. I still have a couple of other things to take care of. I'm trying to piece together this whole mess."

"I heard," Maeve told him. She took Finn's hands in hers. "I know what you did for your brother. That was a good deed, Finn. You didn't have to help him like that and get him out. Hell, you didn't have to be here at all. It shows me... us... that family is important to you. Thank you."

Finn simply nodded and moved forward to give
Maeve a kiss on the cheek.

"Let me know if anything changes," Finn told her
as he left the room.

Finn let out an enormous exhale when he got out
of the room. He saw his fingers trembling as he went to
press the button to call the elevator. Even though his
father had not said a word to him during the entire
exchange, Finn still experienced the emotion of it. The
reality was that it may have been the most intimate and
meaningful moment of their relationship.

Finn reached into the pocket of his leather jacket
and gripped the two flash drives still tucked inside. He
decided his best course of action was to go back to Hog
House, look at the drives, and see if anything might give
them some clues about what was going on.

****

By the time Finn arrived at Hog House, the place
was in full celebration mode over the news about Conor.
The Cosantóir and guests were all crammed around the
bar in the entertainment room with shots and beer glasses
and bottles in plentiful supply. Finn reached near the bar
and saw Cillian sitting at the end talking to Darryl. Cillian
greeted Finn with a large smile.

"Have you heard the news?" Cillian said as he
raised his pint glass. He pointed at the bartender, held up
his index finger, and then pointed at Finn.

"I did," Finn answered as he walked up next to
where Cillian and Darryl sat. "I saw him down at the
hospital."

"It's a beautiful thing," Cillian replied. "Having
you back here to see your Da and him getting better. God
is certainly good."

"Amen," Darryl added as he drank.

"Cillian," Finn said as he grabbed his freshly
poured pint, "is there somewhere we can go and talk?"

"Sure," Cillian said as he drained his Guinness.

Cillian led Finn to one of the back bedrooms. He opened the door and guided Finn inside. The room was sparsely decorated and furnished, with nothing more than a bed, a dresser, a desk, and a couple of chairs.

Finn looked around, amazed at how little was there.

"Aye, I don't need much in life," Cillian said as he admired his space. "Reminds me of my days in the monasteries and rectories. It's peaceful and calming, Finn. You should try it."

"The rectory?" Finn scoffed. "That ship sailed a long time ago, Cillian."

"No, not that," Cillian laughed. "I was talking more about fewer possessions. It's very freeing. You'd be surprised how unburdened you can feel without all that stuff cluttering up your mind and your life. Anyway, I'm guessing you didn't come here for philosophical or religious conversation."

"No," Finn said, glad to have Cillian back on track. "I got into Da's office and found some things, including these."

Finn held up the flash drives to Cillian.

"Have you looked at them yet?" Cillian asked.

"Not yet," Finn answered. "I just found them before I went to the hospital. I was hoping I could look at them now."

"Sure," Cillian said as he pulled out his laptop from its case on his desk. "I need the computer," Cillian chuckled. "No TV in here, and the boys don't always want to watch what I like out there."

Cillian started up his laptop. Once it was running, Finn handed one of the drives over so Cillian could plug it in and access it. Once they got into the drive, they saw just one folder in there. Finn clicked it open, and pictures and video files popped up. A brief look at the pictures showed many of them were from job sites around the area that Conor had worked at or inspected. Further down the list were scanned images of documents, emails, and texts. Upon closer inspection, Finn saw that there were several from Tangled Webb, LLC to his father. Each one was imploring him to work with the company to get these jobs done faster and under budget. The last two files were both videos taken just two days before Conor's accident.

Finn opened the video and saw a picture of the elevator descending a shaft to a job site. Conor stopped the elevator at one point to take a closer video of the walls around him.

"See this?" Conor said in his raspy Irish brogue. It was the first time Finn had heard his father's voice in over ten years and sent chills through his body.

"This shaft is just waiting to collapse. It's not a matter of if; it's when. There's no quality reinforcement here and puts all the men at risk."

Once Conor reached the bottom, he sauntered through the job site, pointing out every safety issue he found along the way. There were risks involved in using outdated or faulty equipment, areas not up to proper codes, and more. When he reached the end of the tunnel where digging was still occurring, Conor pointed out that they were dangerously using explosives to cut down on the use and rental of expensive machinery.

"This whole job site is a clusterfuck," Conor said as he turned the camera on himself. Finn could see the concern on his father's face. "This needs to be shut down."

That video ended, and Finn began the next one. The only picture that could be seen was what looked like the inside of a pocket. However, the audio was clear as day. Conor was making his case to other people in the room with him.

"This can't go forward. I won't allow it," Conor insisted. "I'm reporting it to the union and the state. I won't have my men down there."

"That will set us back weeks or more," said a woman in the room. Her voice became shrill the more she berated Conor.

"Easy, easy," a third voice intervened, a male. "Conor, to be honest, we don't want the union on this job. I can get the work done cheaper by having my own laborers come in and do it, and I have to deal with the union whining to me every day."

"Is that what you've been doing when my guys haven't been on-site?"

"I would never admit to that," the male offered. "That would leave me open to fines and suits. As far as I know, all the work done down there is from Sandhog work. If something goes wrong, it's on you."

"That's shite, and you know it," Conor barked.

"If you had just taken the money we offered you at the start, we would all be much happier," the woman complained.

"You're not buying me at the expense of safety," Conor retorted. "I've seen enough brothers maimed or killed on jobs to know how important it is that this work is done right. If you can't abide by that, then perhaps you need to be in another line of work."

The camera began to move as Conor did, and a door was heard slamming behind him before he started walking down the hall.

"Conor, wait!" the male voice yelled. Conor stopped moving as the voice approached him.

"We have to be able to fix this," he begged. "There are millions of dollars riding on this project, future construction, more jobs... more jobs for you and your men. You're going to throw that away over a silly misunderstanding? Come on, let's go have a drink and talk about it."

"I don't drink," Conor said sternly. "And there's nothing to talk about. What you're doing is illegal, and it ends here. You went too far this time, Elliott."

Conor walked away again, and the phone was seen jostling about in his pocket once more. A car door was heard opening, and then Conor's face was before the camera again.

"I hope you got all that," Conor said into the lens before the video stopped.

He said Elliott, Finn thought to himself. Gavin Elliott. The voice fit what Finn knew.

"Your Da did get that site shut down for the day before he got hurt," Cillian remarked. "A bunch of us showed up for work that morning and were locked out of the site by the union. That's when Conor and Liam had their big fight."

"What happened to Da was no accident, but Liam had nothing to do with it," Finn added. "It's Gavin Elliott who's behind all this. This might be the evidence we need to bring all this to an end."

****

Siobhan sat at her desk for hours, trying to catch up on paperwork she had let slide lately. She paid invoices, answered emails, and more until she looked up from her computer and heard nothing but silence around her. She rose from her desk and opened her office door to look up and down the halls. Siobhan saw that all the other offices and cubicles were dark and quiet.

Siobhan went back to her desk and turned to her computer. Her mind wandered around to what Gavin had threatened and what was going to happen. Siobhan opened a Word document and began typing until she realized she had a letter of resignation in front of her on her screen. All she would have to do is send it out to the board members, and it would be done. Gavin would get what he wanted in the end. Still, the organization would spare itself from a scandal, and Siobhan could move on to something else. It gnawed at her that she would be giving up what she loved because of someone else's greed, but she saw no other way.

Siobhan saved the document in her files but decided not to send it out just yet. She looked back at her phone to see if there was anything from Finn, but nothing appeared. She tapped out a text to make the first contact after their argument.

Hey – we need to talk about everything. Call me or text me back, please.

She hit send quickly before she changed her mind.

Her desk phone let out a loud ring that echoed through the quiet and jolted Siobhan upright. She took a breath and looked at her phone and saw it was the after-hours line. The calls only came to Siobhan's phone if the other lines were busy already, so Siobhan took a deep breath and picked up the line.

"A Safe Place. This is Siobhan," she said in her calmest voice.

At first, there was nothing but silence on the other end.

"Hello?" Siobhan asked again. "Is anyone there? If it's not safe for you to talk, just tap once on the phone for yes, twice for no. We can work out getting help to you."

"I'm here," a voice said to her softly. Siobhan knew the woman had been crying.

"Is it safe for you to talk to me?" Siobhan asked.

"Yes, I think so... I mean, I'm alone right now, so, yes," the woman said.

"Okay. My name is Siobhan. What can I do for you...? I'm sorry, I didn't get your name."

"My name... my name is Sandra. My husband... he's been out of control... and I'm afraid. I need to do something," the woman said, her voice cracking.

"Okay, Sandra. Are you safe right now, or do you need me to send the police?"

"No, no!" Sandra said emphatically. "No police! I can't... I can't handle that right now. I just need to get out of here before he comes back. Please help me."

"It's fine, Sandra," Siobhan said in a soothing voice. "Is it just you, or are their children involved?"

"It's just me," Sandra said with a tremble.

"Do you have a car or a ride, or do you want me to send someone for you?"

"I have my car," Sandra answered.

"Do you know where our building is in Harriman?" Siobhan asked. "You can come right to us, and we can help you. We'll give you a place to stay and help you figure things out."

"I know... I know where you are," Sandra answered. "I can be there in five minutes."

"Great," Siobhan said. "When you get here, just come up to the front door. I'm going up to give your name to the security guard so he will know to let you in."

"No, please don't hang up on me!" Sandra pleaded. "Can you... just stay on the phone with me until I get there? I'm in Monroe, and I'll be there soon, but I'm afraid."

"I'll stay with you, Sandra," Siobhan assured.

Siobhan picked up her purse and began to walk towards the front door. She tried to make small talk with Sandra to hopefully calm her, but she seemed to be having little luck. She neared the front desk area where J.J. was now on shift, checking the monitors when Siobhan walked in.

"Evening, Ms. McCarthy," J.J. smiled. "Heading out?"

"Not just yet," Siobhan said, covering the speaker of the phone. "I'm on the phone with someone coming in here. Her name is Sandra."

J.J. nodded and glanced at the monitor with a camera in the parking lot when a long white car pulled in.

"Someone just pulled into the lot," J.J. indicated, pointing at the screen as the car pulled out of the view of the camera.

"Sandra, are you here?" Siobhan asked into the phone.

"Yes, I'm here," she said. "I'm afraid to get out. What if he's out there watching me?"

"Don't worry, Sandra," Siobhan assured her. "I'll come out to you, and we can walk in together."

Siobhan nodded to J.J., and he buzzed the front door open so Siobhan could go out. She looked to the far right and saw the car parked out at the end nearest the entrance to the lot. Siobhan scuffled her way over to the passenger side of the vehicle and knocked on the window. The window glided down, and Siobhan got a look inside. Sandra looked to be middle-aged, her makeup was smeared from crying, and there was a clear slap mark not only on her left cheek, but her left eye was also black and blue and swelling.

"Sandra, come on out and let's get you inside," Siobhan said softly. "You look like you might need some medical attention. I can have a doctor here to help."

"I... I don't know... I don't know if I'm ready..." Sandra said, acting like she was going to start the car up again.

"Sandra, wait!" Siobhan insisted. She tried to open the passenger door, but it was locked. "Can you let me in? Just so we can talk for a few minutes. No pressure. We can talk, and you can do what you want."

"Fine," Sandra answered. Siobhan heard the click of the lock and was able to open the door. She scooted onto the bench seat of the car and shut the door.

"Are you alright?" Siobhan asked with concern.

"I'm okay," she sniffled. "But… I'm sorry. I'm so sorry," Sandra cried as tears flowed.

"Sorry about what?" Siobhan asked. "You have nothing to be sorry for. This isn't your fault."

"Yes, it is," Sandra said as she seemed to look past Siobhan and out the passenger window. Siobhan turned around just as a man got in the car next to her and pushed her over. Before the door closed, the light illuminated the man's face, and it was Gavin.

"What are you doing?" Siobhan said as she pushed back against Gavin, scratching his cheek deeply with her fingernails.

"Fuck!" Gavin yelled. "Will you take care of this?"

"Gladly," a voice said from the backseat as Gavin grabbed Siobhan's arms and held them in place. Before Siobhan could turn around, a cloth was covering her face tightly. She struggled against it, gasping for air until she felt her head grow dark and foggy as she passed out.

22

Finn spent time going over the videos and all the documents, pictures, and messages he found on the flash drive. From what he could put together, it looked like Tangled Webb was deeply tied into all the construction projects going on around the area and wanted to try to cut as many corners as they could. It wasn't long after he began his search that his cellphone rang and he saw it was his assistant Susannah.

"Hey, Sue, what's up?" Finn said as he kept reading.

"I got that information you wanted on Tangled Webb. Sorry it took me so long to get back to you. Some of us are working up here, you know."

"What have you got?"

"Well, the primary owner of the LLC seems to be a Patty Wells. She's down in that area. It looks like they own a lot of property that is under development there. There are some partners listed as well, but it looks like they are smaller investors," Susannah told him.

"Would one of the names happen to be Gavin Elliott?" Finn asked.

"Yep, he's on here," Susannah confirmed. "Friend of yours?"

"Far from it," Finn added. "Can you email me what you have, Sue?"

"Already sent to you," she said proudly. "You should have it in your inbox."

"You're the best," Finn crowed.

"Finn, I hate to ask this with all going on with you right now," Susannah began, "but I have to know... is everything okay? If you're in some trouble, I'm sure I can get..."

"Thanks, Sue, but I'm not in trouble," Finn insisted. "I'm just trying to help out my family."

"Okay, I'm just checking on you," Susannah assured. "Stay safe and hurry up and get back here before they start asking me to do work for Bart Johnson and his team. That guy must have never seen a bottle of mouthwash."

Finn chuckled before answering.

"I'm working on it. I... I don't quite know what's going to happen yet. I'll keep you posted."

"You better," Susannah warned.

Finn hung up on the call and checked his email to see the LLC information Susannah had sent. Patty Wells was listed as the primary of the business. It made sense as to why she was so keen to sell all those properties at the top price. Having Gavin involved was just icing on the cake.

Finn closed the laptop and grabbed the flash drives and stuffed them into his jeans pocket. He glanced at his watch to see it was nearly 9 PM. He considered calling or texting Siobhan to see how she was and if she was still angry with him but thought that she might need some space between them for now. Finn went out to the bar area, where things were more raucous than before since Liam had wandered down from his room and joined the party. As soon as Liam spotted Finn, he grinned and came over to him.

"Aye, little brother! I didn't know you came back. I guess you heard the news about Da."

"I did," Finn nodded. "It's grand, for sure."

"Now that he's awake, hopefully he'll be able to let the police know I wasn't involved in any of this so I can get this contraption off my leg," Liam said as he lifted his leg to display the monitor.

"I wouldn't get my hopes up too fast," Finn cautioned. "He just woke up, and he's still on the vent.

He may not be able to say anything for a bit yet or even remember anything. It's a head injury, you know."

"Do you always have to be such the sound, rational voice of reason in the room? Jesus, brother, lighten up a little bit. Have a shot with me."

Liam thundered his fist on the bar and put his arm around Finn.

"Shots of Jameson for my little brother and me!" Liam shouted. "Feck, a shot for everyone on me!"

The crowd let up a thunderous roar of approval as everyone moved toward the bar to get a shot of Irish whiskey. Liam grasped the two shot glasses and passed one to Finn.

"Teaghlach," Liam said as he looked at his brother.

It was one of the few Gaelic words that Finn recognized since his mother used it when he was younger.

"To family," Finn replied.

"You can use Gaelic, you know," Liam said after downing the shot. "I know you haven't forgotten all of it."

"No, I haven't," Finn admitted after feeling the warm whiskey go down his throat. "It just doesn't bring up the best memories all the time."

"It's not a time for mopin', little brother," Liam insisted. "This is celebrating. Someone turn the music up!" he roared.

Traditional Irish music came blasting through the speakers, loud enough to drown out the din that had already filled the room. Liam led Finn around the room, stopping to chat with people here and there. With Liam at his side, no one dared to give him a second glance. After lots of talking and even some laughs and smiles, Finn began to loosen up and feel more comfortable. Preacher and Darryl joined Liam and Finn at a table out on the front porch. Cillian regaled them with Sandhog's stories with Conor years ago when Liam was little, and Finn hadn't even been born yet.

Finn's phone buzzed in his pocket. He hadn't even realized the phone was on silent the whole time. He looked and saw that he not only had missed calls from Siobhan, but he had missed texts as well and that she was the one phoning him now. Finn rose from the table to take the call.

"Bon, I'm sorry I missed your calls and texts. I was down at the hospital with Da. He's awake now, and they're hoping he'll be able to talk soon. I wanted to apologize for the argument. We do need to go to the police with what I have found. It turns out Gavin is involved with this realtor, Patty Wells, and there's some shady stuff going on. I know I shouldn't have…" Finn got his speech out before he was interrupted.

"So, Conor is awake?" a male voice said to Finn. "And from what you just said, I guess you found the evidence I've been looking for all week. Both things create problems for us, Finn."

Finn stood quietly for a moment before he realized it was Gavin on the phone.

"Where's Siobhan?" Finn yelled. "You better not have done anything to her, you gimp, or I swear…"

"I love it when you guys get all worked up and switch to your Irish slang," Gavin laughed. "Siobhan always does the same thing."

"Where the feck is she, Gavin?" Finn barked.

"Relax, Finn. She's… safe with me, for now. Of course, if you don't follow my directions… well, I guess that could change. I would never want to hurt her, but I can't guarantee that my other associates feel the same way. Here's what you are going to do. You are going to take whatever you found in Daddy's office, put it together, and bring it to me. When I have it, I'll make sure you get Siobhan in your hands."

"I don't have anything to give you," Finn said, hoping Gavin might buy into it.

"Somehow, I doubt that," Gavin replied. "I've had people watching your father's house before you even got here, and then watching you after. I know where you have been going, including the job site, the lake, and the realtor's office. It would have been so much easier if you had never shown up. Actually, it would have been easier if your father were six inches more to the left and the machinery took him out, but that's for another day. Now enough of this. Just bring me what you have."

"Where and when?" Finn asked.

"Let's make it dramatic. Meet me at 11 PM at the Bear Mountain Carousel."

"It's closed up there. I'll never get in," Finn told him.

"Finn, you underestimate my power in the area," Gavin gloated. "I know enough people to get things done. You won't have any problem getting there, I promise. Come by yourself. I don't want any unexpected or unwanted company. Though I am sure Siobhan is darling as an entertainer and would take care of everyone for me. I know she puts on quite a show for you, at least. Those pictures and video... wow. Good stuff."

"I can't wait to see you," Finn said through gritted teeth.

"Good!" Gavin laughed before hanging up.

Finn stared down at his phone as he tried to comprehend all that was going on and what he had to do.

"Everything alright with Ginger?" Liam said sarcastically. "Does she need you to come home and wash the dishes?"

"Not funny, Liam," Finn said seriously.

"What's wrong, boy?" Cillian asked.

"Siobhan… Gavin Elliott has her. He's holding her hostage until I bring him the stuff I found in Da's office."

"Gavin Elliott?" Liam asked. "That little snit that was younger than you? He's the arse who has the construction for most of the projects up here. I always knew that twat was no good. Shifty look and greasy smile, always tryin' to be everyone's friend while he gets ready to stab you in the back. He's been looking to screw the Hogs for years. Let's go take care of him," Liam said as he stood up.

"It's not that easy, Liam," Finn said. "He wants me to come alone to get her at Bear Mountain."

"Of course he does," Liam chortled. "Then he can snuff both of you and have nothing to worry about. Don't be a fool, brother. Darryl and I will go with you."

"Any time, brother," Darryl added as he rose from the table.

"No, I need to do this. Liam, you can't go anywhere. They are tracking you with that monitor. As soon as you leave the perimeter, the cops will know about it. Just stay put," Finn insisted.

"I can still go with you," Darryl stated.

"No, Darryl," Finn told him. "They want me alone. I know it's a risk, but I can't get others involved in it."

Finn turned back to Liam.

"Liam, if something happens to me… just make sure to tell Da… tell him…"

"Shut-up, eejit," Liam said as he clasped his brother's firm handshake. "Tell him yourself when you see him next. I'm not your messenger boy."

Liam cracked a smile.

"Watch yourself up there, little brother. You tend to lead too much with your left. If I can telegraph it, anyone can."

"I'll keep that in mind. Thanks," Finn answered.

Finn made his way down the steps and to his bike. He thought about heading to the police or even going straight to Bear Mountain and staking out a spot so he could perhaps surprise Gavin, but neither solution felt right to him. Instead, he rode back to his father's house.

Finn entered the house and quickly went to the door to his father's office. He pulled the clover key from his pocket and unlocked the door. Jameson promptly came to his side and followed him inside, wagging his tail the entire time.

Finn looked around the room and walked over to the gun safe. It featured a keypad for the electronic lock, and Finn had no idea what the passcode might be. He walked over to the desk and pulled out the box that had the keys in it. He sorted through but never saw anything until he noticed the corner of a piece of paper protruding from the lining of the inside top cover. Finn gingerly tugged on the corner and saw there was a slit in the fabric that he could guide the paper through. All that was printed on the paper was 121678.

"It's worth a try," Finn sighed as he walked over to the safe and punched in the digits and saw the keypad light turn green. He opened the safe and thought about the number he just used for a moment before realizing that it was the day of his parent's first date.

"You sentimental dog," Finn muttered as the safe opened.

Finn was far from an expert when it came to guns. He did know how to shoot, something Conor had insisted upon as he grew up despite his mother's pleas against it. They would routinely go out hunting, to the gun range, or an open field, and practice with rifles and handguns, but it had been a long time since Finn did any shooting at all.

Finn passed on any of the rifles and picked up two of the handguns and clips for them. He stuffed one into the pocket of his leather jacket and the other into the back of his jeans before closing and locking the gun safe again.

Finn made sure he had the flash drives with him and his phone as he got ready to go back out. When he left his father's office and re-locked the door, he turned and saw Jameson sitting by the garage door entrance. Finn stopped and considered for a moment before feeling the keyring in his pocket. He then walked into the garage, pressed the automatic door opener, and walked over, and took the tarp off the Indian Blackhawk Chief motorcycle.

"If I'm going out for you, Da, I'm taking your bike," Finn said aloud as he sat on the motorcycle. Jameson came over and sat next to Finn and whined.

"He takes you out on this, doesn't he?" Finn said as he looked at Jameson, who had lifted his right paw to ask for an invitation.

"Sure, why not?" Finn said as he patted the sidecar. Jameson dashed around in glee and jumped into the sidecar, sitting properly with his tongue already out in excitement. Finn looked into the sidecar and saw a harness for Jameson, and he helped the dog get safe and secure. He also saw a pair of goggles and held them up.

"These too?" Finn asked Jameson. Jameson thumped his tail back and forth on the sidecar's interior as Finn put the goggles in place around his companion's eyes. It looked like Jameson grinned widely now that he was ready to go.

Finn started up the bike and got it in motion. It rode nothing like the modern bike Finn had been accustomed to. It took a bit of work for him to understand the engine and driving with the extra weight of the sidecar as he made his way through town and toward Route 6.

Finn took the ride to Bear Mountain to develop a strategy for what to do once he was there. There was a large white car parked at the far end of the darkened parking lot. Finn crept close to it before turning his motorcycle off and taking off his helmet. He dismounted and warily walked up to the car before looking inside. There was no sign of anywhere there.

Jameson's whine got Finn's attention as he turned back toward the bike. Finn went over and unhooked the harness from the seat and took off Jameson's goggles so he was free to bounce out of the vehicle.

"Stick close, buddy," Finn said as he patted Jameson. "You're the only friend I've got right now."

Crickets and frogs chirped to a deafening din as Finn crept closer to the Carousel building. Even with being as alert as possible, Finn was wary of an ambush. This week, he had been injured enough where he was far from his best if he got into a fistfight. Any use of weapons put him at a severe disadvantage. Even with the guns he held, he was no expert marksman. The best he hoped for is to get out of there with Siobhan and worry about everything else afterward.

Finn reached the entrance doors to the Carousel building. He tugged on the heavy door, pulling it open enough where he and Jameson could slip through and close the door without raising a lot of noise. He peered into the darkened rotunda and saw nothing but the shadows of the carousel cast from the moonlight streaming through the far window.

"You need to stay here, buddy. In case I need you. Stay," Finn commanded. Jameson obediently sat to wait until he received further orders as Finn worked to the interior room where the carousel was.

He had taken just a few steps across the floor when the lights on the carousel burst out. The organ music shrieked and echoed in the room, and Finn instinctively knelt to see if he could get a better look and avoid any threats. The carousel moved past him slowly, and he saw the form of Siobhan, hands tied to the pole of her favorite carousel horse ride, gag in her mouth. He then watched as Gavin appeared from behind the carousel, stepped across the moving ride, and out onto the floor in front of Finn.

"Glad you made it," Gavin said with a smile.

"Get her off there," Finn ordered.

"Easy, Finn," Gavin held his hand up in a stop motion. "She's fine. A little groggy, probably, but she was coming around. She's a feisty one for sure, isn't she? It took a lot more to knock her out than I thought it would."

"I hope she was the one who took that chunk out of your cheek," Finn spat back.

Gavin's hand went up to his cheek and touched the tender flesh of the gouge marks that Siobhan's nails had left on him.

"Hmmm, yes, that. I owe her one for that one. Maybe later, when she's awake a bit more, and will move around some. I love to watch her move, don't you?"

Gavin grinned lasciviously at Finn.

"Let's get this over with," Finn boomed. He reached into his pocket, felt past the gun to make sure it was still there, and grabbed the flash drives. "This is what you wanted."

"Ah, wonderful," Gavin said as he took a step toward Finn. Finn pulled his hand back.

"Get her off the ride first," Finn insisted.

"Fine," Gavin sighed. "Bring her down, please," Gavin commanded.

Finn heard rustling in the back as he saw the ride come to a slow stop. Seconds later, he saw Siobhan being led toward him, hands still tied. She was led by a couple of men that Finn recognized once they got closer to him. Gavin stopped the two before they reached Finn.

"Hold on," Gavin spoke. "Toss the drives to me."

Finn tossed the two drives to Gavin, who caught them in what Finn noticed were leather-gloved hands. Gloves meant not wanting to leave fingerprints, and Finn knew all too well where this was going.

Gavin examined the flash drives and then nodded to the men who brought Siobhan to him. He took her in his arms and could see that while she was awake, she was far from coherent. Her green eyes had a faraway, glassy look to them. Finn also looked at the two men and recognized them as Cosantóir when he first went to Hog House – Danny and Ronan. He noticed that Ronan had a massive bandage on his forearm.

"I'm glad to see the dog got a good piece of you when you jumped me," Finn smiled.

"Fucking mutt," Ronan grumbled. "I can barely close my hand thanks to him."

"I guess you'll have to start using your left hand instead," Finn quipped. "Or have Danny Boy here give you a handjob."

Danny reflexively launched a punch toward Finn, who gracefully ducked out of the way and laid Siobhan on the floor before clocking Danny with an uppercut right that had him flailing backward toward Gavin.

"Enough, for now, Danny," Gavin ordered. "You'll have plenty of time to do what you want."

"Using Cosantóir against each other, Gavin?"

"It was working well until you came along," Gavin said. "We use them to do the muscle work we needed to be done and to sow some discord with the Sandhogs and the Cosantóir. The plan was to do away with your father and have it pinned on Liam so we could get rid of them both in one swoop, and then Danny here could take over the club and the worksites. See, he's a bit more amenable to the way I do business than your father. He's willing to look the other way or let me have non-union guys on jobs. Who knew your father had become such an upstanding citizen?"

"Bad news for you, though, is he's awake now," Finn replied. "Once he starts talking, you're finished."

"Not a problem," Gavin answered. "See, Danny here can get in for a visit. Conor expects him there. When he does... well, people get sick and die in hospitals all the time. If we time it right, we can still get it blamed on Liam."

"And what about Siobhan and me?"

"You didn't really think I was going to let the two of you just walk out of here, did you? No, Finn, I'm sorry. I believe this is where your second chance romance comes to an end. Turns out the two of you came up here for a late-night rendezvous and had an accident. A tragedy, really. In the end, it works out well for me anyway. I had hoped to have Siobhan on my side. I tried to win her over so that eventually, she would love me and leave that job and let me take care of her. Then I could get the land, tear down that dump, and have what the investors want and still have her. It's a shame it didn't work out that way."

"Maybe because you're a slimy scumbag," Siobhan's voice rasped.

Finn turned to look at Siobhan, who was now sitting up on the floor and coughing. He knelt next to her immediately.

"Are you alright?" Finn asked her. He looked into her eyes and saw clarity now as she smiled at him.

"Better, now," she told him.

"Very touching," Gavin said with a slow, sarcastic clap of his hands. "Let's get on with this. I have breakfast plans in the morning with investors." Gavin nodded to Danny and Ronan, and both men removed pistols from their pockets and pointed them at Finn and Siobhan. Siobhan gripped her hands around Finn's waist.

"I'm sorry," Finn said softly. "I..."

Siobhan interrupted Finn.

"Me too," she said with a smile and a tear.

Danny and Finn raised their pistols, but a loud voice echoed from the back of the hall.

"Jameson go!" the voice yelled.

In an instant, Jameson had growled and was leaping through the air, savagely attacking the hand that held the gun Ronan pointed.

"No!! Fuck!!" Ronan yelled as he was knocked to the ground.

Danny stood stunned, watching the attack. He tried to point his gun toward the dog but could not get a clear shot.

"Danny, shoot 'em, please!" Ronan yelled.

Danny fired one shot and missed. It found its mark in Ronan's right leg instead.

"Ahhhh!" the injured man screamed.

Before Danny could get off another shot, there was a push on his right shoulder and a left hand crunching down on the side of his face that dropped him to the floor.

"See, little brother," Liam said with a smile. "That is how you lead with a left."

Liam looked down and saw Danny scrabbling on the floor near where two of his bloodstained teeth lay.

"Oh, Danny. That must hurt like hell," Liam said before planting the toe of his boot deep into Danny's ribs to elicit a groan.

Danny struggled to get to his feet and pulled a knife from the top of his boot. As he readied to lunge toward Liam, Demon came from the darkness and bull-rushed into Danny, driving him through the gate around the carousel. Danny's head rattled against the metal as he slumped over and had the knife skittering across the cement.

"Where did they come from?" Gavin said as he stepped back, realizing he had no protection now.

"For fuck's sake, Gavin, can't the idiots you hired do anything?" a female voice said as she appeared from the dark.

Patty Wells appeared from the shadows, pointing a pistol of her own.

"I'll do this," she said as she pointed and got off two shots toward Finn and Siobhan.

Finn cradled Siobhan and closed his eyes with no time to react, fully expecting to feel the bullets hit him through his jacket. To his surprise, he opened his eyes and was struck by nothing. There was a weight on top of him that pressed him down, and he saw that Darryl had draped his body over him and Siobhan. Darryl opened his eyes and smiled down at Finn.

"Lay still, pretend you were hit," Darryl whispered as he winked at them.

Finn and Siobhan lay still, but they heard Liam react.

"You fuckin' shot me, you bitch!" Liam roared. Finn turned his head to see if he could look at his brother. He saw blood trickling down Liam's right arm as he walked toward Patty and Gavin. Before she could point and get another round off, Liam smacked the gun from her hand with his left and swiftly connecting with a head butt directly to Patty's nose. Liam struck with immense force, tearing the bone and cartilage of her nose, and sending her crumpled to the floor.

Liam cackled and then turned to look at Gavin.

"Now, what about you, you piece of shite?" Liam said.

Gavin didn't stay around long enough to answer and ran toward the far door and outside.

In the ruckus, Ronan had managed to free his hand from Jameson and limped out the front door of the building. Finn rose from the floor to go to Liam while Darryl helped Siobhan sit up.

"I'm Darryl… friends call me Demon," Darryl grinned to Siobhan.

"Thank you, Darryl," Siobhan said as she hugged his large frame.

"Liam, where are you hit?" Finn said.

"She got me on the shoulder. The other whizzed by and nicked off a part of my ear. Nothing bad that hasn't been done before. You want to go after that SOB?"

"I'll get him," Finn said hurriedly. "Why... why did you come? You know, you'll go to jail for this," he said as he looked at Liam's ankle bracelet lit like a Christmas tree.

"Yeah, probably. Glad I know a lawyer to get me out. As for why... well, I'm always protecting you, it seems. Go."

Liam ushered Finn out the back door so he could find Gavin. He walked over and first poked Patty with his boot, and she didn't respond at all. He then went to Danny's body. When he kicked him lightly, Danny groaned.

"Where's the other maggot, Demon?" Liam asked.

"Crawled out the front door," Darryl told him as he and Siobhan stood up. "I'll go get him." Darryl began to walk out the front as Liam turned to Siobhan.

"You okay, Ginger?" Liam asked.

"Yes, just... scared is all. Will Finn be okay?"

"He'll be fine with that rich snot, don't worry. If Finn can cause me some hurt, he knows how to handle himself," Liam told her.

"I'm glad you came," Siobhan replied. "If you didn't show up, we would have..."

"Hey..." Liam said to her solemnly. "Teaghlach."

"Teaghlach," Siobhan repeated, nodding.

Siobhan heard screaming coming from out front and raced out there to see what was going on. She stood by the doorway as she watched Darryl looming over Ronan, with Jameson rigidly attached to his hand.

"Get him off, Demon, please," Ronan pled. "He's killing me."

"He won't listen to me, man," Darryl said. "Jameson is particular about who he takes orders from. You should know that. Looks like you're a goner, dude. Probably better that the dog tears you apart anyway once word gets around that you sold out the Cosantóir and the Hogs."

Siobhan came running over to where the men were. She saw blood flying everywhere and decided what to do.

"Jameson! Come!" She yelled.

Jameson looked up from his task and dropped Ronan's arm. He took his post next to Siobhan and sat regally, licking the blood and saliva from his lips.

"Ahh, thank you, thank you," Ronan said frantically. "Please, get me to a hospital. Maybe they can save me."

Siobhan looked at the stump that was now Ronan's left hand and turned to Darryl.

"It's bad, Darryl," she whispered. "We need to help him."

"Cops will be here in a few minutes," Darryl said. "I'm having some fun until then."

"I think you're a lost cause, Ronan," Darryl told him. "You're one arm was bad from the first one, but this... forget it. You're fucked. You're better off crawling off into the woods to die. Or maybe go to the bears and just let them have at you. That seems like a fitting end. I can drag you there."

"No!" Ronan yelled with panic in his eyes. "Demon, please. It... it was all Danny's idea. He thought we could make a lot of money and then take over the Cosantóir, run things differently, make some under the table cash. It was a lot of money, Demon. How could I say no?"

"You just say it and put your brothers ahead of greed, man," Darryl told him. "You're a sorry excuse of a Cosantóir, a Hog, and hell, a human."

"Fuck you, Demon," Ronan spat blood in his direction. "And what are you? A black Irish clown who don't belong here anyway."

Darryl took two steps forward and, with his left foot, put the weight of his 315-pound frame down on Ronan's bleeding stump.

Ronan's scream was bloodcurdling and caused Siobhan to cover her ears. Darryl looked back and saw the fear on Siobhan's face. He eased off Ronan's arm, now covered with dirt, grass, and gravel mixed with broken bone and bloody sinew.

Darryl bent down to whisper into Ronan's ear.

"If the lady weren't here," Darryl whispered, "You'd be Zoo Chow right now." Darryl kicked hard across Ronan's chin, knocking the bleeding biker unconscious.

"Let's get you inside and see if Liam needs help," Darryl said as he took off his enormous leather jacket and placed it around Siobhan. She swam in the coat but clutched it around her shoulders, and she and Jameson followed Darryl back to the carousel.

****

Finn pushed open the back door just in time to see Gavin dashing halfway across the field between the carousel and the parking lot. He knew Gavin would try to get to his car and get away with all the evidence. Finn had the guns, but he was nowhere near a good enough shot to hit Gavin from the range he was at. Instead, Finn took off running.

Even with his injured ribs, his conditioning let him close ground on Gavin faster than he thought he would, especially after Gavin turned and looked to see Finn coming and stumbled. Gavin reached the white car and fumbled through his pocket for the keys so he could click the doors open. He pulled the ring from his pocket as Finn lowered his shoulder and slammed Gavin into the car, shattering the driver-side window. Air pushed out of Gavin's body as he fell to the ground, losing his grip on the keys as they slid underneath the car. Gavin looked up at Finn as he gasped for each breath.

"It's done, Gavin," Finn huffed. "You're finished."

"It doesn't have to be," Gavin said as he groaned and tried to stand up. "I can make you extraordinarily rich. Just name your price, and you can take care of Siobhan like a princess."

"I don't give a shite about your money," Finn said. "I do alright on my own."

"I can get you that partnership you want," Gavin said. "I know Bob Morris well. One call from me, and you have it. Or I can set you up at some other firm. Whatever you want."

"You don't get it, do you?" Finn said with a laugh. "You can't buy your way out of this one. Too many people know. You've got three people up at that carousel who worked with you who will turn on you without a problem to get the best deal they can. You're looking at a laundry list of fraud and extortion charges to go along with attempted murder."

"I guess there's nothing left for me to do," Gavin said as he bent at his knees and coughed. He lifted his head up and grinned at Finn before lunging toward him and tackling Finn. Gavin got on top of Finn, and Finn saw the glisten of the knife in Gavin's right hand before he felt it plunge into his side. Blood pooled on Finn's shirt as he groaned, and Gavin prepared to stab him again.

"Sorry, Finn," Gavin said as he looked at the blood on the blade. "That must hurt like a bitch. I might have hit an organ, I don't know. I'm not much for fights. Looks like you came home for nothing."

Gavin gripped the knife in his fist and swung it hard towards the existing wound on Finn. Finn yelled and rolled hard to his left, flipping Gavin over and striking his combatant's head hard on the ground. The jolt caused the knife to fly from Gavin's hand. Finn pulled his knees up to pin Gavin's hands down to the ground. Blood spilled down Finn's shirt onto Gavin's before Finn reached into his pocket and pulled out the handgun. He released the safety and loaded a round into the chamber before pointing it to the middle of Gavin's forehead.

Gavin froze.

One action. That's all it takes to take down your prey, Finn thought in his father's voice. Conor used to tell his son whether they were hunting, wrestling at home, or at the end of one of his drunken tirades.

"Oh, please," Gavin pled.

"One action will do it," Finn whispered with a gun steadily in his hand.

"Finn!" the voice yelled to grab Finn from his trance. He saw Siobhan running toward him. She came to a stop just short of where Finn sat on Gavin with the gun.

"Don't do it, Finn," Siobhan implored.

"He's not worth it, man," Darryl said as he walked toward Finn. "Give me the gun, Finn. I got him. He ain't going nowhere."

Finn leaned to his left, his eyes closing, as he collapsed into Siobhan's arms. Siobhan's hand went to Finn's side and immediately was drenched in blood. Somewhere through the fog, Finn could hear Siobhan yelling for help.

24

Finn batted his eyes several times as he worked to clear his vision. When he focused, he could see the stairway at his parents' old house. A quick look to his right and Finn saw his mother, kneeling beside him and holding his right hand.

"Finn, don't worry. You're going to be okay," his mother said in her soothing voice.

"Ma… please, just stay with me for a little…" Finn said softly. It was his younger body , but his adult voice speaking to his mother.

Aoife smiled at her son widely.

Finn glanced up the stairs, and he could see himself standing in front of his father. His father was slapping him with his backhand, over and over, as he held Finn precariously by the scruff of his t-shirt. Finn noticed that after the last backhand, his father pulled the hand back and turned it to a fist, getting ready to land a punch on Finn. A shadow stepped from behind Finn and shoved him, and Finn watched his younger self tumble down the stairs to the position on the floor he occupied now. Conor's punch missed utterly, and he hit the wall opposite the stairs, leaving a hole. Finn stared on as Liam, younger, leaner, but just as big, pinned his father against the wall, holding Conor's arm in a chicken-wing hold and pressuring his shoulder. Finn saw Liam whisper something into Conor's ear and then toss him away from the steps and down the hall toward the spare room where his father often slept off whatever it was that riled him up that day. Liam looked down the stairs at Finn's body and then marched off down the hall in the opposite direction toward his room.

Finn turned back toward his mother and saw she was no longer dressed in her everyday clothes around the house. She was clad in the beautiful green dress that Maureen had chosen for her on her funeral day. She was also standing by the front door, the door open, and the wind blowing her hair lightly across her face.

"Ma, don't go," Finn cried. "I need you here."

His mother approached him, bent down, and placed her white-gloved hand on Finn's cheek.

"You don't need me here anymore, darlin'," his mother beamed. "You need me here," as he pointed toward Finn's heart. "And I'm always there for you. You have others around you who are there for you. You just never saw them before. Teaghlach, Finn."

Finn's mother took his hand once more, and Finn brought the gloved hand to his lips to kiss it.

When he opened his eyes, Finn gripped Siobhan's hand tightly in his. He saw it was at his lips, and Siobhan excitedly smiled at Finn.

"Go get a nurse!" Siobhan yelled to whoever else was in the room.

"Finn? Can you hear me?" Siobhan said, looking into his groggy eyes.

Finn nodded, and a slight gurgle filled his mouth. His throat was intensely parched, and coughing began. A nurse appeared to Finn's left and checked his vitals. It was moments before he recognized it was Cara looking him over. Darren's concerned face popped over her shoulder seconds later.

"Hey there, Finnbar," Darren joked. "Welcome back to the land of the living."

Cara reached back and slapped Darren.

"Are you daft? Don't go saying that to someone when they just woke up?"

"Why it's true, isn't it?" Darren stated. "It is true," Darren said as Cara looked at Finn's eyes. "They lost you for a bit on the table but brought you back. Feisty bastard you are."

Finn coughed and felt pain in his ribs and his side. His hand went to his right side, where he was covered in bandages.

He turned back to Siobhan.

"The knife wound got your gallbladder and part of your liver," Siobhan said as she held Finn's hand tight. "You lost a lot of blood, and, yes, they did lose you for a bit on the operating table but praise God they brought you back."

"You want to sit up a little, Finn?" Cara asked him. "It might be more comfortable, especially for when you cough."

Cara moved Finn into more of a sitting position, and Finn moved his head around to focus on the room. His gaze moved from left to right before it settled on Siobhan.

"How… how long have I been here?" Finn said in a throaty voice.

"The ambulance brought you right from Bear Mountain to here," Siobhan began. "They did the emergency surgery, and then you were touch and go for a bit until you stabilized. It all started four days ago."

"What happened? How's Liam?" Finn asked.

"The police showed up after you collapsed," Siobhan spoke. "They took Gavin, Patty Wells, and Danny into custody. Ronan got airlifted to Westchester, but they couldn't save his hand or the other part of his arm. He's being held at the hospital."

"As for your brother," Cara added, "We were going to open up the O'Farrell wing here at the hospital. With you, Liam, and your father down here, it's more than the nurses want to handle."

Finn looked at Cara for more information.

"Liam had superficial injuries. Took a piece of an ear, and the other bullet went through clean. He'll be fine."

"And Da?" Finn asked.

"We moved him out of the ICU a couple of days ago," Cara told him. "He's as ornery as you might expect and wants to go home."

"Good," Finn said as he rested his head back into the pillow.

"How long will I have to be here?"

"Probably a couple of more days just so we can make sure there are no infections or anything. Then you can hobble on home. You'll be taking it easy for a bit," Cara told him.

Finn looked back at Siobhan and saw her smiling at him as she held his hand.

"Hey, barkeep, come with me and buy me a candy bar. I'm hungry," Cara said as she slapped Darren's shoulder.

"What am I? Your ATM machine? You drink free at my place, and I still have to buy candy?"

"You don't have to buy me candy," Cara told him. "You GET to buy me candy."

Cara led Darren out of the room, so Siobhan and Finn were alone.

"I'm... I'm sorry," Finn blurted out before Siobhan could say anything.

"Sorry for what?" Siobhan asked. "Getting stabbed while you tried to rescue me? Getting hurt for days protecting me from one thing or another? Making me happy? Which one is it, Finn?" she mocked.

"I'm sorry for what I've put you through for the last ten years," Finn said. "I was a fool, Bon. Yes, there are many issues with my Da still to be worked out, but I let ten years slip away that I could have had with you because I thought being alone was the best way for me to

deal with things. I needed more than that. I still need
more than that."

"What does that mean, though, Finn?" Siobhan
asked. "I can't ask you to just toss away the life you made
in Saratoga any more than you can ask me to leave here.
I know it isn't fair to throw this on your plate right now,
with the way things are, but it's the reality of the
situation."

A nurse knocked on the door and peered her
head in.

"I'm sorry to bother you," she said sweetly. "I just
wanted to see if you were up for a visitor."

The nurse disappeared again before a wheelchair
appeared from around the corner and was guided into the
room. There sat Conor, looking at Finn. Conor had
smaller bandages around his head now, and gray stubble
had grown into a semblance of a beard.

Siobhan smiled as she took the chair from the
nurse and brought it around to the right side of Finn's
bed.

"I can leave you two," Siobhan said as she
gathered her things, but Finn grabbed her hand and
gripped it tightly.

"No, no, Vonnie," Conor said, his voice not quite
as strong as Finn remembered it being. "You can stay for
this. You're a part of it."

"How are you?" Conor asked Finn politely.

"I guess I'm getting better," Finn answered
cordially. "What about you?"

"Ack, I am ready to be out of this place. The food
is god awful, the staff can't get anything right, and when
they took that feckin' catheter out, I think I saw Mary
herself. Another day or two, and Maeve can take me
home."

Finn nodded, and there was an awkward silence
in the room for the longest minute on record.

"Finn," Conor said, clearing his throat, "I know… I know I did a lot of terrible things to plenty of people, especially you. I can't change what I was like back then and how you remember it, and I'm sorry I've saddled you with those memories. I can give you all the excuses in the book – drinking, drugs, your Ma's passing – but none of it makes it right. All I can tell you is I wish that man never existed, and I'll spend the rest of my life trying to make up for that. That's why when Siobhan asked me for help with those women, I was more than willing to do it. If a little bit of effort and muscle on my part can help some family avoid what… well, what ours was like… then I'm all in. I don't expect you to let it go just like that; You shouldn't. I hope, though, over time, that we can talk about it and maybe someday make things better than they have been for most of your life. That's it."

Finn stared at Conor, unsure of how to react. All the rage Finn had felt when he first arrived back in Harriman had dissipated more than he thought was possible already. Finn looked to Siobhan, who squeezed Finn's hand to let him know she supported whatever he decided to do or say.

"Da… I'm willing… I'm willing to work at it, to listen, and to talk if you are. I can forgive you, but it will take time."

"That's all I'm asking for, son," Conor added. He slowly lifted his right hand and placed it on Finn's left arm, giving it a squeeze. "Now get better. We've got some celebrating to do once we are all out of here. Can someone get me out of here so I can go take a piss?"

The nurse came back in and looked at Conor scornfully as she wheeled him from the room.

"I'm proud of you," Siobhan said as she rested her head on Finn's right shoulder. "That wasn't easy to do."

"I know I couldn't have done it without you," Finn told her as he kissed Siobhan's forehead. Siobhan reached over and held Finn's head in place so she could place a soft kiss on his lips.

"No, you couldn't have," Siobhan gloated. "It took you this long to realize you need to have me around? It's a good thing you have your looks going for you, or you would be lost in the world."

"I would be," Finn added.

****

After four more days in the hospital, Finn was finally released. His father and brother had both left the hospital before him so that they were heading back home when Siobhan came to the hospital to pick Finn up. Siobhan filled in the events as she knew them regarding Gavin and Patty Wells.

"Patty Wells was the brains behind it all," Siobhan recalled. "She's the one who reached out to Gavin first and set the whole thing in motion. They both made a ton of money doing cash deals, buying and selling. She double dipped and got commissions and profits from sales, and they both were rolling in it with all the commercial properties sold. It wasn't until she started insisting on cheaper costs for building out water and sewer tunnels that they ran into problems with Conor. He wouldn't give them what they wanted and wouldn't go for bribes or threats. Patty pushed the issue with Gavin, and he convinced Danny to follow your Da to the worksite and arrange the accident. They didn't count on him surviving or you showing up."

"And now?" Finn asked.

"They're all trying to blame everything on each other. It's a comedy of errors, Finn. My guess is when it finally all comes to trial that they'll all be doing some time. Gavin will get to see what life is like without a silver spoon."

Siobhan drove them both from the hospital past the Hog House and back into Harriman. She pulled into the lot at Millie's, where more than a few cars and motorcycles were present.

"What are we doing here?" Finn asked. "I thought we would go back to your place and relax."

"Hmmm, I don't know if your idea of relaxing is conducive for healing, Mr. O'Farrell," Siobhan said with a smile.

"It's a celebration," Siobhan said as she got out of the car and went around to help Finn climb out of the vehicle.

The couple walked into Millie's, and applause and cheers surrounded them. Friends and family and Cosantóir were all together in one place. Cara came up and gave Finn a kiss on the cheek before she led the couple over to their reserved spots at the end of the bar. Darren had two Guinness expertly poured waiting for them to sit down.

Liam rapped his knuckles on the bar to get everyone's attention.

"Alright, all of ya'. My Da's got a few words to say before the drinking can start. Go ahead, Da."

Liam ceded the floor to Conor, who shakily rose from the wheelchair he still needed to use.

"Here's to Finn," Conor said as he held his glass. "We're glad he's home safe and part of our family. Slainte Teaghlach!"

The crowd shouted 'Slainte Teaghlach' in response as everyone took a drink.

Darren had set up a buffet opposite the bar, and people began to help themselves to lunch while Siobhan and Finn sat at the bar.

A tap on Finn's shoulder caused him to spin around to where he saw Annie standing and smiling at him.

"Annie?" Finn said with surprise. "What are you doing here?"

"I volunteered donuts and coffee when I heard they were throwing you a little party, and I didn't want to miss seeing you," she beamed.

Darryl came walking over to where Finn sat.

"You should go get some lunch. The food is great," Darryl said as he took a forkful of corned beef into his mouth.

"Okay, Dad," Annie said as she patted Finn's shoulder and walked toward the buffet.

"Annie's your daughter?" Finn said with eyes wide open.

"Yeah, she can be a handful," Darryl said. "Raised her myself after her mother left when she was twelve. She's a good girl. I just wish she would meet a nice guy."

"I'm sure she will at some point," Finn rushed, hoping to move on from the subject.

"Come with me for a minute," Finn said over the noise to Siobhan. He took her hand and led her toward the entrance so they could go out to the parking lot.

The sun shone directly down on them, so Finn moved underneath a large pine tree near the far end of the lot for shade.

"Is everything okay?" Siobhan asked. "Do you feel alright?"

"I feel great," Finn said, "and the party is wonderful. I just wanted some alone time with you to talk about… things."

Siobhan stiffened a bit when she heard this.

"Okay," she said with resignation. She had expectations in her mind about what Finn would say.

"I know everything is kind of jumbled right now, personally and professionally for you," Finn began.

"I'll figure it out," Siobhan answered confidently. "The pictures… they are what they are. If they ever get out. The police confiscated the phones, so I doubt they will see the light of day. All the money Gavin brought to us, though, is another matter. I don't know how we'll keep going."

"That's what I've been thinking about," Finn said. Finn heard a text message beep on his phone and checked it and smiled. He then saw a silver Subaru Forester pull into the lot and park. Susannah came running out, holding papers for Finn. She sprinted over to him and gave him a gentle hug.

"Bon, this is Susannah," Finn said. "She's my admin at the law office."

"Nice to finally meet you," Susannah said. "Finn has mentioned you often over the years."

"Really?" Siobhan said with surprise. "A lot, huh?"

"Oh, yes," she answered. She handed a stack of papers to Finn. "This is what you wanted."

"Thanks."

Finn turned toward Siobhan and opened the folder on top of the pile. He pulled a document out and handed it to Siobhan. Siobhan stared at the paper and looked at Finn.

"Finn, this is a check for $250,000," Siobhan said.

"Yes, made out to A Safe Place. It's my first donation. I know it doesn't cover everything you need, but it should help give you a start until I can sell my condo in Saratoga. I can get you more after that."

"Sell your condo? Why are you selling your house?" Siobhan asked in disbelief.

"Because it's too far for me to commute from here to Saratoga every day. I'm lazy and like my five-minute drive to work."

"What are you talking about, Finn?" Siobhan said with exasperation.

"I made some choices," Finn said, "while I was in the hospital. I'm taking some leave from the law firm. As far as they know, I need time to heal. That will give me time to get myself set up here. I decided it's time to come home. I'm going to open my own practice here. I think there's plenty of need for a good defense attorney here."

"Second folder, boss," Susannah said as she tapped the pile Finn held.

Finn opened the folder and read over the following document.

"I've already secured office space over at Triangle Plaza. It's not the Ritz, but it's a start. Susannah will be working with me."

"Why… why are you doing this?" Siobhan asked. "You're giving up everything you know."

"No, I'm not," Finn insisted. "I'm getting back to what I knew, what I missed. As tough as it was for me growing up here, Bon, the time I spent with you… was the best time of my life. I was never as happy as I was when I was with you. Coming back here and connecting with you again and has made me realize all that, and I want it back – that is, if you'll have me back."

Siobhan stared at Finn as she took in all he had said. She then got a serious look on her face.

"And just where do you think you'll be living, Mr. O'Farrell? There sure isn't room at my place."

"My Da is going to put me up for a bit at his place until I can get my own spot," Finn smiled. "Maybe I'll look for a nice place around the lake."

Siobhan pressed herself into Finn's arms and hugged him tightly.

"Is tú mo ghrá," Finn whispered into her ear.

"I love you too," Siobhan whispered back.

"I'm happy you two are together," Susannah interjected, "but I had a long drive down from Saratoga. Can I get a drink and something to eat?"

Finn laughed, and he took Siobhan's hand as they led the way back inside Millie's.

The crowd let up a cheer when all saw the couple together.

"Word is you're going to be staying around for a while," Cillian said as he came up to Finn.

"Who told?" Finn asked.

"Ah, your Da was never any good at keeping stuff like that to himself."

Finn leered at his father, who just shrugged his shoulders.

"I'm old and forgetful," Conor added. "I have to tell people things before I forget them."

"Thanks, Da," Finn replied.

"You know, if you're going to be around here," Darryl began, "you probably are going to want to join the Cosantóir."

"I don't know about that," Finn said reluctantly.

"I don't think your lovely lady will have any objections," Darryl remarked. "If anything, she's the one who knows the good side of us more than anyone."

"You don't just join the Cosantóir," Liam interrupted. "It's a process, a probation period, and there's a matter of tats involved. And you are supposed to be a Hog. No way you're ready for any of this after living up in the boonies. I don't think you can hack it."

"I can get the Cosantoir tat," Finn added, "but my tunnel days are done."

"I'm sure we can give him a pass as a legacy," Conor added as the leader. "Still need the tats, though. You must get a Gaelic tat before the Cosantóir emblem. Them's the rules."

"I know what to get," Finn said. "It will be a Holy Trinity knot. In the circle will be síocháin, teaghlach, grá."

"Peace, Family, Love," Siobhan said softly. "I love it."

Acknowledgments

This book was a labor of love that allowed me to go back into the family heritage and where I grew up and still live today. There are many people to thank for all the effort that went into writing.

First and always, thank you to Scarlet Lantern Publishing for giving me a chance to write from my heart and create something to be proud of.

Thank you to Christina Hauser and Liz Harrison for being fierce readers as I wrote to keep me on the straight narrow with the story as it developed.

Thank you to Dawn Barclay for assisting me with some real estate research and insight and the rest of the Hudson Valley Romance Writers of America, a fantastic group of writers supporting and helping me along the way.

All my family and friends who turn up with messages and support all the time and, whether they know it or not, have helped craft the characters and events of this and all my books.

To Allison Geraghty for her fantastic artwork and design to create a look and logo for the Cosantóir.

To Sean Geraghty for being by my side day and night through the pandemic and the craziness of writing through all this.

And to Michelle – without you, none of this is ever possible. The constant love and support you provide go beyond what mere mortals can offer.

Made in the USA
Columbia, SC
01 June 2021

38824290R00180